KIT'S LAW

A NOVEL BY
DONNA MORRISSEY

VIKING

Published by Viking

Penguin Books Canada Ltd, 10 Alcorn Avenue, Toronto, Ontario,
Canada M4V 3B2
Penguin Books Ltd, 27 Wrights Lane, London w8 5TZ, England
Penguin Putnam Inc., 375 Hudson Street, New York, New York 10014, U.S.A.
Penguin Books Australia Ltd, Ringwood, Victoria, Australia
Penguin Books (NZ) Ltd, cnr Rosedale and Airborne Roads, Albany,
Auckland 1310, New Zealand

Penguin Books Ltd, Registered Offices: Harmondsworth, Middlesex, England

First published 1999

1   3   5   7   9   10   8   6   4   2

Printed and bound in Canada on acid-free paper ∞

CANADIAN CATALOGUING IN PUBLICATION DATA

Morrissey, Donna
Kit's Law

ISBN 0-000000
I. Title.
00000   1999A
00000 00000

Visit Penguin Canada's Website at **www.penguin.ca**

Contents

KIT'S LAW

A NOVEL BY
DONNA MORRISSEY

PROLOGUE

IF YOU WERE TO PERCH ON A TREETOP and look down on
Fox Cove, you would see a gully, about twenty feet across
and with a brook gurgling down its spine to the seashore
below and flanked on either side by a sea of rippling grass,
cresting with Queen Anne's lace, and scented with a brew of
burning birch, wet ground and kelp.

To the right of the gully, and about a hundred yards down
from a dirt road, is a grey, weather-beaten house, its windows
opened to the sea, and its walls slanted back, as if beaten into
the hillside by the easterly winds gusting off the Atlantic and
whistling up the gully's channel. And if you were to hop onto
a windowsill and look inside that house, you would see three
women. The eldest sits in a rocker by a fire-blistering wood
stove, her iron-grey hair hanging down around her fat-
padded shoulders, and a pinched look on her wrinkled old
face as she sucks on something sharp. Standing behind her,
drawing a comb through the grey tresses, is another, younger,
with flaming red hair, a furrow deepening her brow, and her
tongue nipped betwixt her teeth as she clumsily attempts to
gather the old woman's hair into a bun and fit it into a hairnet that she dangles from one finger. Sprawled across the
daybed and watching the two is me, the youngest, with fine
yellow hair falling away from my forehead, and a smile, I
imagine, rounding the curve of my cheek as I watch.

CHAPTER ONE

THROUGH THE COLOURED GLASS

THE WALLS INSIDE THE CHURCH IN Haire's Hollow were sparkling clean up to the point where the A-shaped ceiling began. There they were coated grey by the smoke sifting out through the cast-iron, pot-bellied stove, and out of reach of the women who came with their scrubbing buckets once every month. Sometimes, when the sun shafted through the windows, I would watch the black specks of coal dust swirl through the air along with the silver glints of dust motes and lose sight of the rows of hat-coiffed heads and slicked-back brush cuts lining the pews in front of me. And sometimes I could almost shut out the tinny shrill of the Reverend Ropson's voice as he flapped his black-clothed arms, shrieking God's word down to us from the altar.

I snapped to attention as the reverend suddenly swooped around to the front of the pulpit and grabbed hold of the wooden coffin resting before it, sending the dust motes swirling madly.

"God's law orders that there *be* order," he rasped, his

hoarse whispers snaking with the vengeance of a rattler's hiss through the ears of everyone listening. "In all things—man, nature and animals! And when we cut short the life of another, as was done to Rube Gale, the man lying in this box before us today, we have broken this law! And we pay! Perhaps not today. Or tomorrow. But, hell burns forever, my brethren! And no sinner escapes!"

He paused, his eyes raking over the congregation and his tongue flicking over dry, bloodless lips. And what with his balding head crouched back in his shoulders as if he was about to spring on the first person that twitched and brought attention to himself, I felt that my grandmother Lizzy (known to me as Nan) was right when she leaned her hefty size across me and my mother, Josie, and muttered into Aunt Drucie's dozing ear, "He might sound like the lily, but be the Jesus, God forgive me for cursin' in church," she hastily crossed herself, "he got the smell of a swampin' bog hole to me."

The Reverend Ropson's eyes bore down on Nan, the flush in his clean-shaven cheeks breaking up to the roots of his thinning grey hair.

"And neither is it ours to judge the soul of the man who put him there!" he snapped, leaping back up to the pulpit. "It's our own souls that God orders us to judge, orders us to look deep inside and witness. Else we become like the brute beasts and wallow in the stench of our own body's desire for sin."

"Heh, he'd be the one to know," Nan muttered again, this time loud enough for those around us to hear. "If puttin' yourself above others was against the commandments, then be Jesus his soul's as crusted as a shit-covered rock in a gull's roost."

The reverend's eyes flashed to our pew.

"Sinners!" he hissed, pointing his finger seemingly to Josie. "All of us! Sinners!"

With a yelp Josie rose out of her seat, long red hair flicking around her face, and before Nan could grab hold of her, she was scrabbling out of the pew and running towards the door. Necks twitched to turn, but the reverend's finger, now moving across the room like the barrel of a British loader, kept everyone staring straight ahead. Except for Margaret Eveleigh's haloed head of red ringlets. The second the reverend's finger struck out, she was swivelling around, along with those of her ribbon-bedecked best friends, all staring after Josie's back as she bolted through the door. Giggling into their white-gloved hands, they cowered beneath their parents' chastising looks and whipped their heads back to Rube Gale's coffin. The Reverend Ropson gave a small bow as the door slammed behind Josie, and with a look akin to satisfaction, made the motions of the cross in the name of our Father, and signalled for the pallbearers to lift Rube's box and lead the march to the graveyard.

"Where's you goin', Lizzy?" Aunt Drucie whispered in surprise as Nan scurried out of the pew, dragging me behind her before the pallbearers had a chance to lay a hand on Rube's box. Tightening her coat around her thin, stooped shoulders, Aunt Drucie hurried to catch up as Nan blazed through the church doors and heaved herself out into the chilly November air, taking the church steps two at a time, her feet splayed out like a duck's as she shifted her weight first to one spike-heeled foot, then to the other.

"What about the buryin'?" Aunt Drucie gasped, catching up as Nan unhooked the church gate and swung through it.

"I've had all the preachin' me stomach can take for one mornin'," Nan said. "You go on and I'll see you at the card game, tonight."

"My, my, is something come over you, Lizzy? And how come Josie keeps runnin' off like that?"

"Christ, Drucie, you'd sleep through your own funeral if you had a chance to sit through it," Nan thundered, taking the turn around the corner of the church. She brought up short as Doctor Hodgins appeared before us, a deep frown between his dark, brooding eyes, and his tufts of white hair more tousled than usual as he drearily shook his head.

"Keep a berth, Lizzy," he said, holding out an arm to warn us back. "There's more to this day than the reverend's Amen."

Nan's cross look was replaced by one of fright as she brushed aside Doctor Hodgins's arm and stepped around him, me and Aunt Drucie crowding besides her. There, calm as anything, whittling on a slab of wood as he slouched against a limb-bared poplar tree outside of the cemetery, was Shine, the moonshine runner who had appeared on the shores of Haire's Hollow some four years before. He, along with his drinking buddy, Rube Gale, had plagued the outporters ever since, with their stills and drunken rampages— till Rube was found dead a few days before, strangled and lying in dog's shit besides Shine's still, his face half chewed-off by human teeth. Shine's teeth, the outporters argued.

"Will ye look at that!" Nan half whispered, as Shine, a brown worsted cap pulled down over his large, grizzled head, with the tips of his dirtied brown hair as greased as the sweat sliding down the slope of his nose, started whistling through his rot-rutted front teeth as he kicked at a mound of dirt piled high besides a fresh dug hole besides him.

"My God, that looks like a grave he got dug!" Aunt Drucie half whispered.

"His threat to anyone with thoughts of going to the Mounties," said Doctor Hodgins.

"And I s'pose that's their headstone he's whittlin' on," snorted Nan. "Be the Jesus, he got the nerve, takin' over the Almighty's callin'."

"And he's a mean enough bastard to go through with it," said Doctor Hodgins. "In all my years, I never seen anything as vile as Rube Gale's corpse."

"Why'd Shine do it?" asked Aunt Drucie. "They was buddies."

"Buddies!" scorned Nan. "The likes of Rube Gale and Shine don't have buddies, they haves Satan grovelin' through their liquor-poisoned veins. And once they gets plastered, they'd carve their own youngsters into stewin' meat, then go callin' out for 'em the next day they sobers up."

Aunt Drucie shivered.

"And Jimmy Randall's ear!" she moaned. "My God, Doctor, did you ever see such a sight, the lobe chewed right off."

"It was a sight," said Doctor Hodgins, patting Aunt Drucie's shoulder and nodding towards Nan. "I'll see you girls, and you, too, Kit," he added briskly, relaxing his puckered brow with a smile upon seeing me. "I got a baby waiting to be born."

"Maisie, agin, no doubt," said Nan as Doctor Hodgins tugged on a strand of my hair, making ready to leave. "Born to breed, that one was. Tell her to keep her legs crossed next time!" she hollered as Doctor Hodgins disappeared around the corner of the church. "Unless she's thinkin' on outfittin' her own sealin' boat some day. C'mon, Kit." Nudging me alongside of her, Nan strolled boldly towards Shine.

"My God, careful you don't get too close to that lunatic, Lizzy," Aunt Drucie warned, reaching after Nan to pull her back.

"He'll be some crazed before he ruffs up a hair on my

head," said Nan, marching steadily forward. "Stand back!" she suddenly hollered, swinging out her arm to shield me and Aunt Drucie as Shine's runt of a skinny white crackie dog come running and yapping out from behind the pile of dirt alongside the hole. Ignoring the spike of one of Nan's heels, the dog scampered over, sniffing its cold nose around my legs.

"You like dogs?" Shine asked nasally, his mulish eyes creeping over my face.

"Merciful Father," Nan whispered, crossing herself as Shine weasled his eyes onto hers. She looked up as the Reverend Ropson came around the corner of the church into the cemetery, leading the pallbearers, the few weeping mourners and most everyone else from Haire's Hollow to Rube's grave site. They stopped at the sight of Shine, and a rippling of gasps shot through them as they took in the grave-like hole he had just dug, and at what appeared to be a headstone he was now whittling.

Aiming her spike heel towards the dog's face, Nan jabbed at the dog as it abandoned my leg for hers, and giving Shine the look of the dead, bawled out in a voice loud enough to be heard by those resting under the sod as well as those standing above it, "If you was to dig it bigger and put a few others includin' yourself in it, I'd be glad to pitch the dirt in over ye." With a fiery look at the reverend, and leaving Aunt Drucie gaping after her in wonder, she latched onto my arm and marched down the road, keeping me tight by her side as if I was the exclamation mark to everything she just hollered.

The dirt road through Haire's Hollow lay bare before us, the loudly coloured houses dotting its landside, heavily curtained against the wind blowing off the wide-open harbour. Hugging the bank to its waterside was a clutter of weatherbeaten sheds, stage heads and outhouses. Shafting through this clutterment was a long, planked wharf that cut out over the water amongst a fleet of painted punts and motorboats that were scattered across the lopping waters of the harbour like a handful of slung jellybeans. And squat to the side of the wharf near the road, wearing oilskin coveralls hitched up over his shoulders with elastic suspenders, and with a peaked cap pointing back over his matted grey hair, was Old Joe, slitting a knife across the belly of a codfish. Pulled up on the beach besides him and turned upside down to the sun was his motor boat, glistening from a fresh coat of kelp-green paint. His brows quirked upwards by way of greeting as Nan and me drew alongside.

"Name a God, where'd you get that colour paint?" Nan asked with some wonder, leaning heavily on one hip as she caught sight of the boat.

"Well, maid, I had a bit of blue and a bit of yellow and I mixed it up with a bit of tar, and that's the colour I come out with," said Old Joe, giving me a wink as he ripped out the fish guts and slung them to the gulls that were still flapping and squabbling over the last bloodied mess he had tossed their way.

"Well, brother, you won't have to worry about catchin' any more fish," snorted Nan, "'cuz they'll be divin' for the bottom when they sees that cuttin' through the water."

"Hah, Lizzy, wait till you sees her floatin'," said Old Joe, with a toothless grin. "She'll be lookin' good then, with her arse half outta the water. Have they buried Rube, yet?"

"I allows the weeds are already takin' root," said Nan. "'Cuz for sure there won't be many lilies sproutin' outta the likes of Rube Gale's liquor-rotted corpse."

"Hard to scrounge up tears for a moonshiner," agreed Old Joe.

"It's not their killin' each other that gets me goin'," Nan

went on, "but the terrorizin' and tarmentin' they brings on everyone else when they crawls outta the woods with their drunken nonsense—not that I'd give two cents for Jimmy Randall's ear, mind you, for his heart is as black as any shinerunner that crawled outta the woods."

"Now, now, Lizzy," said Old Joe.

"It's their cowardliness that gets me goin'," argued Nan. "If the Mounties can't pin Shine for murderin' Rube, then why don't we all gang together and put him in a boat and send him back down the bay where he come from?"

"Aye, but Shine got a way of gettin' back at them that goes after him," said Old Joe, waving a bloodied hand to Aunt Drucie as she come huffing up behind us.

"Merciful Father, he's fixin' on killin', agin," she cried, rapidly patting her chest as if to hold back a racing heart. "Did you see him, Joe? He got the hole dug outside the cemetery, just like the grave, waitin' to kill the first one who reports him to the Mounties!"

"Hah, he won't have to worry about liftin' his shovel any more this day—or the morrow!" said Nan, taking up her stride and starting back down the road. "'Cuz the coward-liest souls in all of Newfoundland cowers in this God-forsaken bay."

"Hold on, Lizzy, here, take a fish for your suppers," Old Joe called out, scrounging around in his bucket and coming up with two gutted codfish.

"They looks a bit soft," said Aunt Drucie, peering more closely at the fish.

"Aye! Shore fish. I don't like goin' too far out this time of the year," said Old Joe, slapping the fish inside a cardboard box besides him, and tucking in the flaps. "The bloody squid is a mile thick. I allows if you fell overboard, they'd have the skin sucked off your bones before your clothes got wet."

"Pooh! You're one for fishin', you are, afraid of a squid," Nan called back from the side of the road.

"Just bury me on the land, Lizzy," sung out Old Joe, passing the cardboard box to Aunt Drucie. "'Tis the watery grave that plays on me mind, not squid. Here you go, Kit." He scrounged back down into his bucket and come up with an orange-speckled starfish. "Heh, your very own star. Dry it out and nail it to your room door so's you can make wishes every night 'fore you goes to sleep."

"Mind now, she don't get her hands dirty," said Nan, as I squirmed back from Old Joe's gift with an apologetic smile. "My son, the young are too proud these days to be seen walkin' with a fish, they rather a canned turnip from May Eveleigh's store."

"How old you be, Kitty?" asked Old Joe, leaning forward, the sun glistening merrily in his rheumy old eyes.

"Twelve, almost thirteen," said I.

"Thirteen!" exclaims Old Joe, his brows bushing together in mock shock. "Sure, 'twas only yesterday you was born! Tell you what, Kitty Kittens, how's about if Old Joe dries your star and brings it out to you?"

I smiled and, waving goodbye, ran to catch up with Nan and Aunt Drucie who were dodging on down the road.

"Good day to ye," he called out.

"Good day to ye," Nan called back without breaking stride. "Be the Jesus, if you can expect something good from a day that starts off with the dead!"

"Heh, Lizzy, 'tisn't Rube Gale that got you goin' this mornin', for sure," said Aunt Drucie.

"I'll tell you what got me goin' this mornin'!" Nan said, coming to a stop and glaring down into Aunt Drucie's pointy, wrinkled face. "The reverend and his bleedin' pointin' finger is what got me goin'. Be the Lord Jesus, they

knows who to pick on. If they had the guts to go after murderin' lunatics the way they goes after helpless babies, they
wouldn't be all holed up in their houses now, too scared to
go out for fear of gettin' their faces chewed off."

"Name a God, did you see Rube's face afore they shut
the coffin?" Aunt Drucie asked, keeping after Nan as she
swung around and started off down the road, again. "No different than if the dogs got at him. And you can still see the
tooth marks on Jimmy's ear. Shine's a dog, a bleedin' bloody
dog . . . "

"And there's the blessin' of it," Nan cut in. "Lunatics like
Shine don't take much to figure, not like some others we
know," she added as her sights fell on the Reverend Ropson's
wife unlatching her gate. "Good day to you, Missus," she
called out, marching straightaways towards Mrs. Ropson.

Mrs. Ropson dropped the latch at the sound of Nan's
voice, her short, fat arms flapping off from her sides like a pair
of seal's flippers. And what with the little pockets of fat jiggling
around the corners of her mouth as she turned to face us, she
reminded me of an old harp seal floundering on thin ice.

"Good day, Lizzy," she returned in the same tones one
might say goodbye.

"The sight of Shine drive you outta the graveyard, too?"
Nan asked, chatty enough, leaning on one of the fence
pickets.

"I caught sight of him as I passed by," Mrs. Ropson
replied with a small smile, reaching for the latch again. "Sidney's asthma gets bad this time of the year. I thought it best
to come straight home after the service."

A sudden whooped cough from Nan cut short the splurt
of sympathies setting forth from Aunt Drucie. Then, cranking her brow and lifting her chin a tad higher, she firked a
strand of hair from across my cheek to fit behind my ear.

Mrs. Ropson followed the gesture, her eyes barely grazing mine before dropping the latch properly into place and turning back to Nan.

"So, how's Kit?" she finally asked in the silence that followed.

"Healthier than the cure, maid," Nan promptly replied, patting my cheek. "And almost as smart as your Sidney, they says. All hundreds, isn't that what you gets, Kittens?"

I nodded, eyes to the ground.

"That's nice. Well—good day, then," Mrs. Ropson said, turning up her garden path.

"Make sure to bar your door," Aunt Drucie called after her. "What with Shine still on the loose and diggin' graves, nobody's safe."

"Ha!" Nan snorted. "I been barrin' my door since long before Shine come up the bay. Tell the reverend it was a nice sermon," she said to Mrs. Ropson's back. "I s'pose even the likes of Rube Gale deserves some respect; pity you got to be dead to get it.

"The bloody ones from away," Nan charged, widening her stride to take Fox Point, the hill leading out of Haire's Hollow, me and Aunt Drucie half running to keep up. "You'd think be the Jesus, God forgive me for cursin', that they was born in God's pocket, they sits so Lord Jesus straight. The way they walked into my house that day, brother—turned me stomach. And the likes of May Eveleigh!" Here, Nan spat as if she had potato rot in her mouth. "You'd swear be the Jesus, she was from away herself, the way she sucks up to the reverend and his wife. The same with Jimmy Randall! As if their own wouldn't good enough for 'em. If you asked me, brother, they makes Shine look like a pussy-footed angel whenever they gets crossed, and they got crossed by me then. And the next time you gets a hundred in school, Kit, you make sure you brings that test home to me, and I plasters it betwixt the eyes of every face in Haire's Hollow that thinks I'm not fit to raise a youngster."

"My, my, you keeps as clean a house as any, Lizzy," Aunt Drucie answered, struggling to keep back a yawn and keep up with Nan at the same time. "You knows we all knows that."

"And I'd have the same as everyone else, too," Nan snapped, "if poor old Ubert could've took to the sea. They put him in his grave; every year others gettin' picked over him for the jobs on shore."

"Poor old Ubert, he was no fisher, but he was a good man. And the only brother I had to do anything for me," said Aunt Drucie.

"And he was as good a father to Jose as most others would've made."

"I dare say he was," Aunt Drucie agreed. "'Tis not every man who'd put up with Josie and her ways."

"And he kept her youngster, same as if it were his own."

"And that he did, my dear."

"And he was one for work, never mind everyone thinkin' he was a hangashore."

"The sea's not for everyone, for sure," said Aunt Drucie. "I gets sick meself just looking at it some mornin's." She came to a stop halfways up the hill, bent over, hand to her side. "Wait up, Lizzy, maid, I catches me breath."

Nan stopped, breathing heavily, and looked back over the stovepipes of Haire's Hollow, puffing grey, woodsmoked clouds into the air. The parishioners had left the graveyard by now, and were standing around in smaller groups, some in front of May Eveleigh's store, and others, mostly the men, trailing across the road to the wharf to talk with Old Joe, or to check on their boats bobbing alongside on the water. The youngsters were darting everywhere, and climbing over woodpiles, woodhouses and boats, and screeching louder than the seagulls fighting over Old Joe's fish guts. Margaret Eveleigh and her best friends, I saw, were gathering around a mountain of cut spruce trees, piled high on the beach a little ways down from the wharf.

"How come they're havin' a bonfire, tonight?" asked Aunt Drucie. "Guy Fawkes Night is not till November, ain't it?"

"They'll probably have five more bonfires before Guy Fawkes Night," said Nan. "Sure, the young can't wait for nothin' these days."

"My, my," tisked Aunt Drucie. "Like goin' to church on Thursday, sure. Is you goin' to the fire, Kit?"

"No," I said, shaking my head.

"Yes you is goin'," said Nan, starting back up Fox Point. "S'posin' I got to drag you there. She's a bit like meself, is Kit," she added to Aunt Drucie. "Won't go nowhere."

"Sure, it'll be fun for you, maid," Aunt Drucie puffed, patting my arm. "The fun we use to have on bonfire nights, hey, Lizzy?"

"We use to have the fun then, for sure," said Nan, breathing hard. They stopped talking, saving their strength for the last part of the hill. Finally we were at the top of Fox Point, out of sight of Haire's Hollow, and with thick evergreens lining both sides of the road. A muddied, leaf-strewn path led off the road to Aunt Drucie's small, two-roomed house, wedged amongst an entangled growth of lichen-flowing spruce trees.

"I swear to God, it gets harder and harder to get home every day," groaned Aunt Drucie, giving way to a yawn and trudging wearily onto her path. "See you at the card game, tonight, maid."

"What about me fish?" asked Nan.

"Your fish! My, my, I forgot I was luggin' it," said Aunt Drucie, unflapping the box and hooking her finger through the gill of a cod. "Here," she said, hoisting out the fish for herself and passing the box over to me. "You carry it for your grandmother."

"Here, give me, she'll get it on her good dress," Nan said, nudging me to one side and taking the box from Aunt Drucie and tucking it under her arm.

"Sure, she's goin' on thirteen and you still treats her like a youngster," Aunt Drucie grumbled.

"I s'pose, maid," said Nan. "That's probably 'cuz Jose never ever grow'd up, and I keeps thinkin' the same of Kit as I do of her, don't I, me darlin'?" she asked, chucking me under the chin.

I grinned, and started down the road besides Nan.

"See you at the card game," Nan called after Aunt Drucie.

"Aye, see ye in a bit," called back Aunt Drucie.

Another hundred yards and me and Nan come clear of the trees, the wind hitting us bold in the face, looking down over the sea, a mile wide and forty miles long, flanked high on each side by hills of green forested wood, patched red and yellow by the fall air. A short distance ahead was the turn-around, where the road come to an end in a wide circle, and down over its edge, on the seaward side, was our grey, weathered house, shining silver in the sun, and squat against the side of the hill. The mouth of a gully, just off from our front door, was steeped in shadow, and disappeared down the sharp incline of the bank onto the beach below.

Nan and I walked in silence, her brewing over May Eveleigh's and Jimmy Randall's proud ways, and me stewing over having to go back to Haire's Hollow and stand around a bonfire all evening, listening to Margaret Eveleigh and her best friends squeal and laugh foolishly over the slightest thing. Perhaps, I could talk Nan over. I liked it when I could stay home, and have the house to myself, and sit quietly in the rocking chair next to the stove, listening, as my own fire crackled its way up the chimney.

Josie come bounding up over the gully to greet us, hair streaming onto the wind, and squelching any thoughts of a quiet evening alone, even if I were allowed to stay. Usually when there was something taking place, like garden parties or Guy Fawkes Night, she would be gone with her men friends by now, no matter how hard Nan fought to keep her home. Seeing my cat, Pirate, shoot out from beneath the house and scoot down the gully past Josie, I made to run after him.

"Where you goin', hey? Where you goin'?" Josie demanded in her rough, bark-like tone, grabbing hold of my arm as I darted past her.

"Get away," I yelled, hitting at her hand and scrabbling to get away.

"Get away, you get away," she barked, yanking on my arm.

"Stop it, stop it!" Nan ordered, slicing her hand between the hold Josie had on my arm. "And for the love of the Lord, Jose, go comb out that maggoty head of hair, and you, Miss Martle," said Nan, jabbing a finger at me as Josie ran off around the house, leaving me rubbing my arm and glaring after her, "you can wipe that look off your face, 'cuz she's your mother, retarded or no, and is as good as anybody else in Haire's Hollow to ask you an important question about where you're goin' without gettin' her eyes clawed out. Here, where you goin'?" Nan bawled out as I started running away.

"To get Pirate," I said, skidding down over the lip of the gully. Coming to the brook that gushed down the gully's

cleft, I started running with it, leaping rocks that bubbled
out of its waters, jolting to quick halts when nothing
appeared to catch my foot, and springing to the gully's side,
slipping and sliding down its muddied slopes, then back onto
the rocks again, leap leap leaping till finally I was racing full
tilt down onto the beach, with the wind washing my hair
back off my face and streaming the water out of my eyes.
Tipping my face to the sun, I dashed along the frothing edge
of the waves thundering upon the shore, licking the salt off
my lips, and feeling my feet scrunching down through the
pebbled grey beach rocks to the black wet sand below.

The sun glinted on something yellow and I stopped running. It was a piece of yellow glass, a big piece as wide as my
hand. I marvelled at its clearness and, holding it over my
eyes, smiled as the warm golden colour shrouded everything
with Midas gold. Surely a worthy piece for our treasure, heh
Pirate, I thought, spotting the tom as he appeared through
the trees and skirted along the woods' edge, as far up from
the water as he could get. For a pirate, he certainly didn't like
water.

Slipping the piece of glass into my pocket, I sauntered
along to Crooked Feeder, a noisy river that spliced down
through the woods some ways ahead, and splayed out over
the beach, cutting it in half, and pouring into the sea. It use
to be a favourite game of mine, when I was smaller and
Pirate first wandered out of the woods looking for a home,
to scavenge the beach, looking for pieces of coloured glass.
Jewels, I called them, for my growing treasure. And Pirate
would become a pirate—henceforth his name—who would
try to waylay me, claiming the jewels for his own looted
treasure. And when I became tired of battling down Pirate
and his fleet of thieves lurking in the woods, I would lie on
my back, looking up through the pieces of coloured glass,

and imagine myself living in such coloured worlds as the Midas world, where everything I touched turned to gold.

Only I wouldn't want to stay in such a world, I thought, coming up to Crooked Feeder. It would be a hard thing to see nothing but yellow all day long. Despite the cold, it was warm to snuggle amongst the boulders along the river's edge and have them break the wind and let the sun shine full on your face. It didn't matter what colour anything was when the wind was broken and the sun was shining. Simply close your eyes to the burst of red the sun made burning onto your eyelids, and listen to the gulls crying out to one another, and to the waves rolling up on the shore and suckling their way back out, and soon enough even the most horrid day turned quiet inside of you. And that, I imagined, on days like today, with the reverend pointing the finger of shame at Josie again, and Nan threatening to bury the half of Haire's Hollow in one grave, and Margaret and her best friends hooting and giggling behind their gloved hands, was what everyone must want the most—to feel quiet.

"What you doin', hey? What you doin'?"

Startled, I opened my eyes. Josie was kneeling on top of one of the boulders, staring down at me, her browny green eyes squinting in the sun, her windblown hair tangling around her face. Scrambling to my feet, I glowered at her and started walking back up the beach towards the gully. She barrelled past me as she most always did, even when I was a youngster, bawling to catch up with her. I bided my pace, even though it was getting late and Nan would be having a fit, wondering where I was.

"Take off them boots, take off them boots," Nan bawled out as Josie bolted in through the door ahead of me, tracking water and mud across the clean, canvased floor. "My God, you're like the squall of wind."

"I's not a squall of wind! You's a squall of wind!" snapped Josie.

"The Lords have mercy, what I got to put up with!" cried Nan.

"What you got to put up with! What you got to put up with?"

"What I got to put up with? The likes of you talkin' back, is what I got to put up with! And me head's splittin' from that Serpent's hissin' still swarmin' through me ears. Be the Jesus, Jose, if you ever gets up and runs outta church again because a him and his finger-pointin', I'll rake the hair off your head, haulin' you back. Now for God's sake go and make sure you got enough wood cleaved for the night." Nan flopped down in her rocking chair by the stove, her face red from all of the walking and talking she was after doing this day.

"And where you been, my girl?" she asked as her eyes lit on me. "Fry up that bit of fish I got cleaned for supper, and you can take that scowl off your face because if the wind changes, you won't be a pretty sight, and you're goin' to that bonfire, pretty or no pretty."

I scowled harder and, snatching the knife off the bread-box, hacked the head off the fish lying across the cutting board. The wind never changed, yet the scowl stayed and grew deeper as we finished supper and the sun began to drop behind the hills. Belching loudly, Nan went into her room to take off her church dress and to wash up. Coming back out, she hauled on her coat, bawled out to Josie, who was napping on the daybed, to chop some wood for the night and pointed me out the door before her.

CHAPTER TWO

GUTTIN' FISH

IT WAS DUSK BY THE TIME WE got back to Haire's Hollow. Shoving open the door to May Eveleigh's store, Nan stepped inside and squinted through the bright white light thrown off from the two lanterns that started swinging on their ceiling hooks from the sudden gust of air. The store was empty except for May Eveleigh, tall and thinner than a reed, weighing out flour on a set of scales that sat on one end of the counter. She squared back her shoulders as Nan slammed the door shut, sending the shadows from the swinging lanterns ricocheting wildly across the shelves of canned food behind her.

"How you doin', maid?" Nan asked, as she trod across the floor, wheezing loudly, and leaned across the counter in front of May.

"I'm fine, Lizzy," said May, turning back to the bag of flour she was weighing and rolling down its flap.

"Take your time, take your time," said Nan, sticking her hand into the glass candy jar sitting on the counter and pulling out a handful of hard green candies. She popped one into her mouth and one into mine as May Eveleigh marked a price on the bag and laid it on the shelf behind her.

"Now, then, what can I get you this evenin'?" May asked, brushing flour dust off the front of her dress.

"A cut of cheese, for sure, maid. Kit, here, can't do her homework unless she's nibbling on a bit of cheese. Heh, I tells her she'd be mistook for a mouse if she weren't so pretty and doing so smart in school."

May gave me a tight smile, her eyes sticking to the spit glistening on my bottom lip from where the hard green candy had set my mouth to watering. Her hair was pulled back in a bun at her nape, showing up the brown spots dotting her temples and the hollows of her sunken, narrow cheeks. "Widow's spots!" Nan had whispered to me once after May had grumbled about Nan's store bill not getting paid on account of her government money getting lost in the mail. "Grows on the face of them that don't got a lick of charity in their bones."

"Will that be all, Lizzy?"

"My, my, I can't think," Nan grumbled. "Kitty Kat, do you remember anything else I needs?"

"A reel of white sewin' cotton, bit of salt pork and a bag of marshmallows."

"My, my, the mind on that one, twelve years old." Nan preened as May started gathering up the order. "And I only muttered the words under me breath this mornin'." She leaned forward to say something more as May shoved the order into a bag, but was interrupted by the door swinging open behind us, and the ringlet-haloed Margaret, May's girl, come prancing in, the lanterns swaying overhead. "Well now, isn't she the one!" Nan breathed. "And that red hair— sure, just like my Josie's. Landsakes, they could be blood."

Margaret halted in her tracks, her eyes widening in horror.

"It's not red!" she gritted.

"It's auburn," May said, throwing Nan a frightful look of her own as she started flicking through the stack of credit books sitting on the counter, looking for Nan's.

"All the same to these old eyes, maid," Nan said, holding out a hard green candy to Margaret. "Here, my dear, want one? Sure, you're in the same grade as Kittens, ain't you?"

Margaret looked scornfully at the candy and, glaring at me, screwed up her nose.

"Well!" Nan sucked in her breath, scandalized.

"Something wrong?" May asked, pulling out Nan's book.

"Your girl just mocked me."

"I don't look like no Jose Pitman," Margaret sung out.

"Margaret!" May scolded. "Here." She took a bag of marshmallows off the shelf and tossed them on the counter to Margaret. "Now, go on down to the fire."

"First I wants a bag of candies," Margaret demanded of her mother.

"Mercy," Nan said under her breath.

"Lizzy just offered you a candy; you didn't want it. Now, go on. Right now!" May said, her voice rising threateningly.

"I wants my own candies," Margaret yelled, a sideways glare at Nan. "You said I could."

"Margaret . . . !"

"You said!" Margaret insisted.

May give a fitful laugh.

"So I did," she said, ignoring a sniff from Nan. Reaching inside the jar, she took out a handful of the hard green candies and, rolling them inside a small brown paper bag, tossed them along the counter to Margaret. "Now, get on. And mind you don't get sick on marshmallows."

Smiling brightly, Margaret sallied past me and Nan and ran for the door, muttering something under her breath.

"What'd you say?" Nan roared, shoving herself off from the counter and turning to face Margaret.

"Noth-*theeng*!" said Margaret grandly, taking care to stress the "th" sound the way the ones from away did. Screwing up her nose at me again, she flounced out the door, then slammed it.

"Well, sir!" Nan half whispered, turning back to May as the lanterns swung wildly.

"Must've been a fight she and Kit had at school," May said. "Is there anything else you need, Lizzy?"

"Humph! If there was, it's gone outta me mind, now," Nan said crossly. "Can't says I remembers a time when one of mine mocked me; still for all, Jose is only half there. But it's like they says, now," she said, leaning across the counter towards May and dropping her voice as if she was parting with a mighty secret, "you never believes of your own what you believes of others. C'mon, Kittens, afore you makes me eat my words." Wrapping an arm around her grocery bag, she pushed away from the counter and tramped heavily towards the door. "See you at the card game, May, maid," she hollered, as I skitted through the door ahead of her.

"Spotty-faced old bag," she sputtered, slamming the door as Margaret had done, and setting off down the road in the growing dark. "Be the Jesus, you don't have to look far down that one's gullet to see what's in it. Nothin'! Soul as parched as a sun-dried sponge! Here's your marshmallows, Kit," she said, digging into the bag. "After you's finished with the fire, come on over to the church basement and we walks home, together."

"Can't I just go home from the fire?"

"Why? So's you can sneak off home the second me back

is turned? You's goin' to that fire, girl, and say no more. C'mon, I goes with you."

"No, Nan, I'll go," I said quickly.

"And I'm goin' to make sure you do," she huffed. "C'mon, c'mon, the card game's startin'."

Orange-flamed smoke tunnelled along the beach from the bonfire, and every youngster in Haire's Hollow was shrieking and running through it. Excepting for Margaret Eveleigh and her best friends. They were all crowding around the far side, roasting marshmallows on skinned alder sticks, and looking snootily at the younger ones running around. One of the older boys, big, blond-haired Josh Jenkins, showing off the way he always did around Margaret, grabbed the stumped end of a chopped spruce from the pile of boughs nearby and rolled it onto the fire, nearly smothering it. Thick white smoke poured up through the branches, and Josh started bouncing the spruce, so's to fan the flames beneath.

Suddenly, Shine's white crackie dog appeared out of the smoke, yapping crazily at the fire. Looming behind him was Shine, his whiskered face as black as the night, and his eyes flickering red in the firelight. The youngsters stopped their running and stared in surprise. Then Shine grabbed a young boy by the ankles, and whilst everyone watched in stunned horror, he held him upside down and started swinging him towards the smoking boughs. A shriek sounded from the boy, and with that, the rest of the youngsters started back to life and began running and shrieking up over the bank onto the road, Margaret and her friends amongst them.

"Mother of the Blessed Virgin, he's gone mad this time," Nan cried out, shoving the bag of groceries into my arms and lunging towards Shine. Grabbing hold of the back of his shirt, she started shaking him. "Put him down, put him down," she hollered as Shine held the struggling youngster even closer to the fire. A flame shot up through the boughs, frighteningly close to the boy's fear-stricken eyes, and he screamed louder.

"I said put him down! Put him down!" roared Nan, yanking harder on Shine's shirt. The crackie come yapping and snapping at her ankles, and letting go of Shine, she lifted her foot and planked it in the dog's belly, sending it tumbling backwards, howling. Dropping the youngster at Nan's feet, Shine raised his hand in mock salute to the elders, who were by now running down over the bank with their youngsters half-hiding behind them.

"It's the bitch he is," Nan shouted, flailing her fist in Shine's face. And he, grinning like the lunatic, backed his way into the tunnel of flaming white smoke after his dog.

Then everyone was crowding around Nan, and the youngster stopped crying as his mother swooped her arms around him, and the father, Jimmy Randall with the chewed-off ear, started shaking his fist and cursing Shine's cowardly soul to hell. And then everyone was arguing and talking at the same time over how you couldn't even let the youngsters go to a bonfire any more without worrying about them being killed, and how the Mounties was too God-damn scared to go after the likes of a murdering lunatic like Shine, and how it was left to women to save the youngsters, and God bless Lizzy Pitman's heart for taking no heed of her own keeping, and saving young Teddy Randall from being roasted alive like a dried squid.

Then the smaller youngsters were ordered home for the night, while the bigger ones were allowed to stay out for a while longer with the fire, as long as they kept their eyes open and come yelling if Shine poked his black heart back amongst them. And then the men and women started back to their card game in one of the rooms in the three-room schoolhouse, and Nan, lifting the grocery bag out of my arms, clamped a tight grip onto my hand and brought me along with her.

"For sure the higher-ups might be comin' after me tomorrow if I leaves her outside with Shine on the loose," Nan said, taking her seat across from her partner, Old Joe, at one of the card tables, and dragging my chair in closer. "Still for all, their own is out gallivantin',", she added a bit loud, glancing around at the other outporters taking their seats across from their partners at the half-dozen or so other tables scattered around the schoolroom.

"Heh, Lizzy, it's a thing of the past. Kit's too grow'd up now to be sent to some orphanage," Old Joe replied, lifting off his cap and smoothing back his mat of curly grey hair, before tossing a deck of cards on the table.

"Thing of the past, me arse. If I was one to let others walk over me, they'd be out to me house in the morning with their fancy white gloves on . . . and that Jimmy, hah! Too bad Shine never chewed his bald face off!" Nan said, hauling in her chair and popping a hard green candy into my mouth. "Who we up against, first?"

"The reverend's wife and May Eveleigh," said Old Joe. "Now, Lizzy, don't go gettin' heated up," he cautioned. "It's not May and Mrs. Ropson who's out terrorizin'."

"Heh, not so's anybody could understand it," Nan said, rolling up her sleeves and grabbing up the card deck as their two opponents started walking skittishly towards them. "Have a seat, May, Missus," she invited, dealing out a round, and scooping up her hand.

"Your bid, May," said Old Joe as May and Mrs. Ropson sat down and pensively picked up their cards.

"I'll pass," said May, folding her hand and sitting poker-back straight on the edge of her chair. "Praise the Lord, if the Mounties hears about tonight, they might come out and haul Shine off."

"If they can't pin him for murder, they won't pin him for foolin' around with a youngster at a bonfire," said Old Joe. "Pass me, too, Lizzy. You got a bid, Mrs. Ropson?"

"They can't put a man in jail for murder without witnesses," said Mrs. Ropson, carefully scrutinizing the faces around her before folding her cards. "I pass."

"Twenty-five," shouted Nan, tossing two cards to the wayside and leaning her face close up to Mrs. Ropson's. "Shine wouldn't be on the loose to murder anybody," she shot out, "if others hadn't been too cowardly to tell the Mounties about him chewin' off ear lobes."

"I thought it was only Mope that seen him chew off Jimmy's ear," said May.

"That's right, it was only Mope," said Old Joe. "And Mope's always too drunk to remember anything the next day, we all knows that. What's your trump, Lizzy?"

"Clubs," said Nan. "Funny thing, sir," she went on, dealing out fresh cards as everyone ditched their non-trumps, "how everyone knows how Shine was growlin' and snarkin' like a mangy dog when he was chewin' Jimmy's ear off, yet nobody was there to see it. How come we all knows he was snarkin' and growlin' if nobody was there and seen it? Here, Kittens." Nan leaned forward and popped another candy into my mouth, getting herself a good view of Mrs. Ropson's cards and the five of clubs that was sure to down her and Old Joe.

"Because Mope seen it and told before he blacked out," May explained, frowning deeper with each card she picked up. "It was when he woke up the next mornin' that he had it all forgot. What's trump? Did you call trump, Lizzy?"

"Spades," said Nan. "And Jimmy never see nothin'!" she

added with a snort. "Someone chewed his ear off and he never seen nothin'. Well sir, that's a strange thing."

"It was his birthday," said May, laying down the queen of spades. She looked around apologetically. "I expect everyone's entitled to a drop on their birthday."

"More than a drop; gets your ear chewed off and don't remember nothin'," countered Nan. "Be the Lord Jesus, he wouldn't crawlin' up the reverend's arse that night, and you needn't concern yourself with that one, Missus," she added, turning to Mrs. Ropson. "It got nothin' to do with you and the reverend."

"Trumpin' right off?" Old Joe asked May, lifting his cap to scratch the side of his head.

"Wait a minute, take back that queen," said Mrs. Ropson, the fat on her cheeks jiggling as she reached out her flipper-like hand and flicked the card back to her partner. "You said clubs was trump, Lizzy."

"No, sir, I never," said Nan. "I said spades."

"You said clubs. I remembers because I got the five."

"Well, my dear, I'm not goin' to bid twenty-five on clubs with you sittin' there with the five of trump, and me sittin' here with the five of spades. Unless you thinks I'm cheatin'!" Here, Nan threw her cards down on the table and scraped back her chair, looking wild-eyed from May to Mrs. Ropson.

"Now, now, Lizzy, pick up your cards. You're foolin' up the game," pleaded Old Joe. "She said spades," he said to Mrs. Ropson, trumping his king on May's queen. "Now, Missus, lay your ace on that—if you got it."

"I can renege," said Mrs. Ropson, clutching her cards tighter to her bosom as Nan pulled her chair back in.

"No you can't!" hollered Nan, planking both elbows back on the table. "Not when there's a trump laid, you can't renege! Not unless you got another trump!"

Looking like she was going to bawl, Mrs. Ropson threw her ace on Old Joe's king and snatched back her hand as Nan's sailed through the air, slamming her five of trump on the ill-fated ace.

"And you can thank your partner for that one," said Nan, gleefully hauling in the trick. "Never lead off with a trump unless it's for your partner, heh, heh."

"Who we up agin, next?" she asked Old Joe after three more rounds had gone by and they had whumped their way to victory.

"Jimmy Randall and poor old Rube Gale's mother," said Old Joe with a wink at me as May and Mrs. Ropson limped away from the table. "And, Lizzy, this time will you let 'em get a bit warmed up afore you starts beatin' the crap outta 'em?"

"Uummph, like poor old Ubert use to say now," Nan said, rolling her sleeves back up as she spotted Jimmy Randall, fingering his chewed-off ear, slowly making his way towards her. "There's plenty of ways to gut a fish, and I allows there'll be one more afore this night is out, heh, Kitty Kat?"

By the time we got home from the card game, Nan was all tuckered out. Stoking up the fire, she eased herself into her rocker and coaxed Josie into taking down her hair from her hairnet and combing out her long, thick plaits. Aside from splitting wood, it was the only thing she trusted Josie to do, declaring me too short and light-fingered to maul at her head the way she liked it.

I sprawled on my back across the daybed, my eyes taking in all four corners of the small room. The wick was low in the lamp, creating the dim yellow light I liked best, and flickering shadows around the cups on the open-shelved cupboards, the legs of the wooden kitchen table, and the splits, stacked high behind the crackling, black-topped stove.

"Go to bed, me darlin'," Nan murmured as my eyelids began to drop.

Shoving myself to my feet, I trudged down the hallway towards my room. Taking a quick look over my shoulder, I saw Nan with her eyes closed, and Josie with her brow knitted as she concentrated on combing out Nan's braids. Inching away from my room door, I ducked into the small half-room that served as a closet at the end of the hall. It was shelved on both sides, and stacked with sheets, quilts and woollen blankets. Climbing onto the third shelf on the right-hand side, I crawled beneath the bedding and breathed deeply, savouring the musty smell of the mothballs Nan had poked amongst everything to keep it smelling fresh.

I dozed sleepily. Soon after, Josie thumped off to bed. My eyes sprang open. I listened as Nan got up from her rocker *squeak squeak*, then walked to the sink for her glass of water *creak creak*, then hobbled down the hall *creak creak creak*, her room door opening *squeak* and shutting. And all was quiet. And I held my breath. Silence. Then *squeak*, and I tensed, waiting, my lungs bursting and the blankets near smothering me. Then a shriek from hell as Nan rammed her hands in under the blankets, jabbing at my ribs, my eyes, my belly, till I fell screaming out of the shelf, begging for mercy and running off to bed with her swatting at my behind.

"How can you tell?" I asked.

"Blankets don't breathe."

"I was holdin' my breath."

"That's what I heard: you holdin' your breath."

"But that don't sound like nothin'."

"Nut-*theeng*, nut-*theeng*, not *nuthin'*," bawled out Nan, taking on Margaret Eveleigh's proud-sounding talk. "Be the Jesus, if May Eveleigh's crowd can say nut-*theeng*, nut-*theeng*, then so can we. Now get to bed, you're like the savage."

CHAPTER THREE

LIZZY'S PROPHECY

THE SAVAGE WAS MARGARET EVELEIGH the next day in school when she hurtled a folded piece of paper on top of my desk with "GULLY TRAMP'S GIRL—I'M GOING TO KILL YOU" scratched across it. Turning around in his seat, Willard Gale, second cousin to Rube Gale, with clusters of sores crowding his raw, reddened nostrils and his dirt-grimed hair smelling as rancid as stale fat, snatched the note out of my hands and stuffed it in his pocket.

"Willard!" snapped the teacher, Mr. Haynes. Grabbing the leather strap off the wall with large, chalky hands, he stomped down the aisle, his chunky legs hitting against the sides of everyone's desks as he come. Willard cringed back in his seat, his chin bowed to his chest, and I quickly ducked my head into a book.

"What did you put in your pocket?" asked Mr. Haynes.

Willard said nothing.

"Hold out your hand!"

Willard crouched deeper and... Crack! The leather belt smacked across the top of his desk.

"I said hold—out—your—hand!" Mr. Haynes ground out, and I knew without looking that his longish black hair had fallen over his forehead by now, and that the red bulb of his nose had changed into a livid purple.

Swish! The belt whistled through the air and thudded dully across padded flesh. Willard cried out, and he must've pulled his hand back because all I heard for the next savaged minute was the swishing of the belt smacking across the top of his desk, over and over and over, until Willard started bawling, more from the fright I allows, than of having the belt hit him. Then Mr. Haynes stomped back to the front of the room and, picking up a piece of chalk, scrawled across the board "I will not tell tales out of school" and ordered all of us to write the sentence one hundred times in our scribblers. Then, while we were writing as fast as our arms would let us, he marched up and down the aisle, ripping the pages out of our scribblers as we filled them up, and scrunching them into little balls, fired them into the coal bucket along the side of the stove at the back of the classroom.

The bell rung for recess, saving us from more writing, and flexing my fingers to get the cramp out of my hand, I ran out of the schoolhouse into the yard, savouring the fresh-smelling air. I had hardly filled my lungs when Margaret grabbed me by the collar and shoved me up against the picket fence.

"Your mother's a tramp and your grandmother's a loud-mouth pig and you tell her I don't look like no tramp of hers—you hear me, Gully Tramp's Girl?"

I stood still as anything as Mr. Haynes, his hair smoothed back over his forehead and his nose still flecked with purple, come up behind Margaret.

"What's the matter, Margaret?"

Margaret dropped her hands by her side and give Mr. Haynes a pouty look.

"Kit called me a tramp."

I gaped at Margaret like a guppy fish and tried to keep my face straight as Mr. Haynes bent over, boring heavily squinted eyes into mine. I stiffened as he laid a heavy hand on my shoulder and gave me a little shake.

"Apologize to Margaret," he said quietly.

"I'm sorry," I half whispered.

"Say it agin!"

"I'm sorry."

"Say—I'm—sorry—Margaret!" he stated slowly, lips peeling back over gritted teeth.

"I'm s-sorry, Margaret."

He kept staring at me, his fingers digging into my shoulder, and my eyes wavered, not able to go far, as his face was a scant inch from mine, mostly to the bulb of his nose, and I saw that it wasn't that his nose was purple, but that it looked purple from the dozens of tiny reddish veins meshing it.

"Is that all right, Margaret?" he asked, his eyes still searching out mine.

"Thank you, Mr. Haynes," said Margaret, smiling sweetly. Then she ran off, leaving me struggling between the meshed, red veins and the boring, squinting eyes.

"Do you remember what I told you about reform school, girl?" he asked, his voice dropping lower, still.

I nodded.

"That's good," he half whispered. "You keep remembering, you hear me?" He gripped his fingers deeper into my shoulder, giving me another little shake, then stood back up and walked across the yard into the school. I watched, surprised that he had left me standing by the fence with no further threat of punishment, and churning through the things he had told me about reform school. For sure, he'd told me enough times. From the very first day when I started school and cried to go back to the gully with Nan, he took time to tell me about the reform school. It was a place near the orphanage where bad orphan youngsters were sent, where awful things happened to them, like having their heads shaved and dunked in kerosene for getting head lice, and being stripped naked and thrown into tubs of ice-cold water for daydreaming when you was suppose to be listening, and being strapped for getting a sum wrong, even if you'd never seen that kind of sum before. Now, here I was in grade six and never cried for Nan no more, never got a sum wrong, never got head lice, never yawned or daydreamed or not listened, and here he was, still threatening to send me to reform school.

I trailed back inside the school after recess and paid strict attention to working out long-division sums, careful not to come under Mr. Haynes's attention. But, while I was readying to leave my seat after the bell rung for the end of the day, he ordered me to stay behind and write "I will not say bad words" one hundred times in my scribbler. I scribbled as fast as I could, knowing Nan was outside, waiting to walk me home from school. She always came to get me these days, what with Shine chewing up people and whittling out tombstones. By the time I got my one hundred lines wrote and met her at the school gate, she was after learning from some of the youngsters as to why I was kept in.

"What in hell's flames bad words was you usin'?" she bawled out the second she seen me coming through the school door.

"None," I mumbled.

"None? He kept you in for sayin' None? That's a bejesus

bad word to be sayin'—None! Out with it, my girl; what bad word was you sayin'?"

"I never said one. Honest!"

"Then what did he keep you in for?" Nan's eyes flew open, and she tore off towards the school door. "Be the Lord Jesus, if he starts pickin' on you, agin . . . "

"No, wait—it was an accident," I cried out, running after her and grabbing hold of her hand.

She stopped and swung around.

"What do you mean—an accident?"

"Me and Margaret and Melissa were callin' out words and a bad one popped out."

"Outta whose mouth?"

"Outta mine."

"How come it popped out outta yours and not one of theirs?"

"It popped outta theirs, too."

"Then how come alcohie Haynes never kept them back?"

"H-he never heard theirs."

"Uummph, but he heard yours? Be the Jesus, if I thought for one second he punished you and let the rest of 'em off with it, I'd fix his features around to the back of his head."

"He just never heard them, that's all. C'mon, Nan."

I managed to get her out of the schoolyard and walking down the road.

"I'd have liked for him to been standin' there when that precious red-headed Margaret Eveleigh mocked me last night," she grumbled. "I dare say she's the picture when the teachers and doctors and reverends and every other uppity-up from away is lookin' at her. Miss Hollywood Star! What bad word did she say?"

"I . . . dunno."

"You dunno?" Nan stopped walking. "How come you dunno when you was there?"

"I forgets."

"Forgets? I thought you was smart? Is you keepin' something back?"

"No. It was a bad word. I can't say it."

"Well, I'm tellin' you to say it."

"She said Jesus."

"'Jesus!' The likes a that little snot saying Jesus. Well sir, if I had to say curse words like that and my mother found out, I wouldn't be pitched yet and she been dead for thirty years. What word popped outta your mouth?"

"Ah . . . damn."

"Damn? Sure, that's not a bad word."

"Look!" I pointed to a bunch of people gathering on the wharf as Old Joe cut across the harbour towards them in his kelp-green motorboat, waving his cap in his hand excitedly.

"Name a God, what's goin' on now?" Nan asked, lurching forward and heading for the wharf. I followed after, glancing back at the schoolhouse door with a sigh of relief.

"It was as good as anything I ever seen, sir," Old Joe was saying, balancing his spindly legs on the bow of his boat while tossing up the painter to his brother. "See, it's like this. The Mounties figure on gettin' Shine for buildin' stills and runnin' shine, seein' how they can't get him for murderin' Rube. So . . ."

"So's what's the good of that?" Maisie Pynn sung out, coming up behind me and Nan, jiggling a squirming youngster on one hip. "If they did put him in jail for chewin' off Jimmy's ear, he'd only be out again afore winter's out, shootin' up the place."

"Well, yes, if he gets back out," said Old Joe, swinging himself onto the wharf and excitedly turning to face everyone.

"But that's not what they're figurin' on. See, it's like this: if they can get Shine behind bars, then anybody that seen him killin' Rube might get the courage to come forward and testify. Then, they can keep Shine in jail for good."

"Well, if ye hadda come forward about him chewin' off Jimmy's ear, he'd already be in jail," said Nan.

"Heh, Lizzy, there was more talk come outta that than good, for sure," said Old Joe, "but it don't matter about any of it no more 'quz Shine's gone."

"Shine's gone?!" muttered one of the fishers.

"Where'd he go?" asked Maisie.

"Hell's blazes, for all I know," exclaimed Old Joe. "He's gone—that's the main thing. The Mounties was out from Deer Lake last night and asked me if I knowed if Shine was makin' moonshine somewheres around here. I ain't never seen his camp, so I took 'em down to Mope's shack to get Mope to tell 'em, because for sure Mope knows; Shine's been keepin' him drunk the past month to keep him quiet about seein' him chewin' off Jimmy's ear. Anyway," Old Joe give a gummy grin, winking at me as he seen me standing next to Nan, and went on with his story. "See, Mope's just as scared of the Mounties as he is of Shine, and when he seen them comin' through the woods, well, sir, he starts quiverin' and shakin' all over, with his eyes bulgin' out of his scrawny little head and then, one of the Mounties says, 'Mope, if you'll tell us who makes the moonshine, we won't put you in jail.' And Mope goes runnin' off down through the woods and out on the beach and everything was black as pitch with the moon shinin' on the water, and Mope points up to the moon and says, 'Up there, sir, is your man; it's God that makes the moon shine.'"

Everybody burst out laughing, Old Joe the loudest.

"Was he drunk?" a fisher asked.

"Drunk?" Old Joe managed to get out between guffaws. "Sir, there was a stink a spirits comin' off him that could've addled the heads of a cackle of saints."

Another burst of laughing and Nan fair stomped her foot.

"Be the Jesus, ye'll be laughin' tomorrow when Shine gets drunk and takes his gun to shootin' up the place, agin."

"He won't—I told ye, he's gone," sung out Old Joe. "When we left Mope on the beach and walked back up through the woods, we happened across Shine's still. The Mounties blowed it up. And this morning when Sim and Jir went by checkin' their snares, they heard Shine roarin' through the woods like a cut bear. And now, he's gone. I just went by his camp; nothin' left but dog shit."

"Nothin' wrong with that, sir," Old Joe's brother said, standing his wiry self alongside Old Joe. "As long as he's gone."

"Aye. Gone to torture some other poor martles," Nan said, gripping me by the arm and marching back off the wharf. "He'll be back, mark my words," she called out over her shoulder. "And it'll be someone else that'll pay for your cowardice."

"Now, now, Lizzy," Old Joe called cajolingly after Nan, but the rest of his words were lost as Maisie and everyone else took up in agreement or disagreement of Nan's prophecy, and Nan kept walking straight ahead down the road to the gully, me tight by her side, and sputtering crossly about the lily-livered souls of timid men.

CHAPTER FOUR

PARTRIDGEBERRY PATCH

T HE NEXT MORNING NAN WAS up banging a wooden split on the side of the stove, yelling for us to get up; the frost was light on the ground and the time was right for picking the partridgeberries on her secret partridgeberry patch.

"Not goin'," mumbled Josie from beneath her feather pillow.

"You's goin', whether you wants to or not," Nan hollered, clanging the split louder. "Now haul your lazy arse outta bed and get dressed. Get up, Kit, get up; I got the porridge made."

I groaned, my feet hitting the cold canvas floor, and quickly skimmed on a pair of tights and a pair of slacks. There was no arguing with Nan when it come time to pick the partridgeberries, and even Josie, despite the arguing coming through her room door, stomped around, hauling on socks and sweaters.

"Hurry on and eat," Nan ordered as we walked sleepily into the kitchen and sat before the two bowls of porridge she had laid, steaming, on the table. "We wants to get goin' afore anyone comes nosin' around. Be the Jesus, they'd be hidin' in the trees for a chance to get at my patch. Jose, how many more spoons of sugar you goin' to put in them oats? Mother of Mary, you could sweeten a bucket of black tea with the sugar you got in them oats."

"I don't like black tea, you go get black tea," Josie said loudly, glaring at Nan as she dumped another spoonful of sugar into her bowl.

"I said put that sugar down," Nan all but roared, lifting the rifle off its hook on the wall and slinging its strap over her shoulder. Where'd I put them bullets, Kit? I'd like to get a couple of partridges today, but I allows if anybody hears me shootin', they'll make it a fine excuse to follow the shots and come lookin' with the guise of worryin' about me. Be the Jesus, you can't fart around here without them crawlin' up your hole to have a look. Where's them bullets? Anybody see them bullets? Hurry up, hurry up, we're losin' the day."

The sun crept up over the eastside hills, its rays scarcely touching the quilted leaves that were still fixed to the trees as we bundled out the door, weighed down with buckets, backpacks and the loaded rifle. Nan sniffed at the frost in the air to figure its temperature, while her eyes scanned the road from Haire's Hollow, then swept down over the gully and the wind-driven sea, checking for snoopers.

"Follow ahead, Jose," she called out, "and don't ramble too far in front. I don't wanna have to go searchin' for you, this day."

"Don't wanna go berrypickin', don't wanna go berry-pickin'," Josie kept muttering, cutting up to the mouth of the gully and heading across the meadow. I followed behind, the heat from the Thermos of tea inside my backpack like a hot sun burning through my skin. The Queen Anne's lace, knee-high with the grass, were wheat-brown beds of fluff, stilled beneath the thin sliver of frost that veiled them.

"You sure it's the right frost?" I called over my shoulder to Nan.

"You can tell by the way it creeps up the window in the mornin'," said Nan. "When it's clear like ice and ribbed on the bottom—that's the killin' frost. Your berries are dead. Good for moose and caribou pickin's. Now, there's them that picks 'em anyway, and that's why their jam is as tart as a whore's arse. It's when the frost is still white, more snow-like than ice, that's when you picks 'em, that's when they're the plumpest from their summer juices. Now, too, there's them that picks 'em too early, and their jam is just as tart because the worm is still inside the berry and gets cooked into their jam."

"Margaret Eveleigh said there's no worms in berries."

"Bah, Margaret Eveleigh!" Nan snorted, her bucket clanging against a tree trunk as we left the meadow and fought our way through the woods. "What would that little snot know about pickin' berries? For sure her mother's jam is the worst I ever put in me mouth. Pig's mash! And that's why none of 'em got any berry patches left any more and schemes to find mine; becuz they cooks the berry before the worm gets a chance to get out and plant their next year's pickin's."

"Margaret said worms don't have mouths to carry seeds."

"Oh, and is that what Miss Hollywood Star says," Nan said, panting heavily and dropping the bucket at her feet. "Well you tell her that the worm is the bleedin' seed, and when it crawls into the ground, it plants itself, and there you got next year's berry. And if her mother and everybody else caught on to that, I wouldn't be the only one left with a berry patch, and them nosyin' up me hole to find it."

Nan kicked the bucket to one side and sat down on a rock, resting her back against a white birch. "Sit for a spell, I catches me breath," she said. "Sit down, Jose, we might see a partridge. Jose! Jose!" she bellowed as Josie kept charging through the woods. "Sit down, we looks for a partridge." Nan watched till Josie kicked the leaves off a rock and squatted down, before hoisting the gun off her shoulder and resting the butt betwixt her breasts. "Margaret Eveleigh, bah!" she went on, quietening her voice and aiming the barrel towards the bush in front of us. "It's the timin', Kittens. You got to wait for the right timin', and it ain't always as easy as lookin' at the frost on the window. Look at your poor mother over there. She haven't got the sense God give a nit, but, be the Jesus, she knows when to lit out a door when she's tryin' to get her own way with something. And she knows how to back down from a fight, even when she's the one that started it. And that's what the likes of Margaret Eveleigh won't ever know, when to keep her trap shut, and when to keep it open. Shhh . . . " Nan grabbed a tighter hold of the gun and squinted hard into the bush. She looked over to make sure Josie was still sitting there, and cocked the trigger. A twig snapped and something brown and furry appeared through the leaves.

An ear-splitting crack sounded through the air as Nan pulled the trigger.

"Aagghh!" she bawled out as the gun jumped and the barrel slammed against her collarbone.

"Aagghh!" I screamed as Pirate leaped out of the woods, meowing like a fire-singed demon, and tore back across the path we had just come.

"That's Pirate!" Josie barked, coming to her feet and pointing to where Pirate disappeared through the underbrush.

"Hell's tarnation, what's the cat doin' out in the middle

of the woods!" Nan roared, hauling me back down as I made to run after Pirate.

"That's Pirate! That's Pirate!" Josie kept yelling, stomping back towards Nan, still pointing after the cat.

"I knows it's Pirate, Jose," Nan cried out, slinging the gun back over her shoulder and shoving herself back up on her feet. "I can tell a cat from a bleedin' partridge, now get on ahead, else there'll be no time to pick berries on this day. My gawd," she muttered, picking up her bucket as Josie started back through the woods again, with me following, looking over my shoulder after Pirate. "You'd think I killed him, the way you's are all gettin' on. What in hell's flames is a cat doin' out here, anyway?"

"He follows me," I said.

"Heh, he won't be followin' you much after this," Nan said. "It's like I said now; timin's everything, but sometimes, 'tis only the hand of God that can save ye."

Another half-hour walk and we broke onto the barrens, a rolling land that began with the edge of the cliffs looking out over the bay and rolled inland as far as the eye could see. Bereft of trees from a fire near on twenty years ago, it was wide open to the wind and fog, and a hunter's nightmare on snow-drifted days or fog-blanketed evenings, with not even a stump to mark a path or point to the edge of the cliffs. And there were stories aplenty about berrypickers getting lost or near falling over the cliffs on bright, sun-lit days from being hunched over, picking berries and not watching where they were wandering. Nan's partridgeberry patch was another half-hour's walk over the barrens, along the cliff, and spreading down over a grade that dipped about halfways down to the sea. With a bit of skill and a good pair of boots, it was possible to climb the rest of the way down the cliff and come out onto the beach.

"Your grandfather and me use to climb down to the beach and build a fire for our cup of tea, years ago when he was alive, God bless him," Nan said after we had picked the firm, red berries for a while and was taking a rest, leaning our backs against a matted mound of rocks. "We use to bring her with us," Nan murmured, gazing after Josie as she wandered around the back of a knoll, her hair as red as the moss that capped it. "Like the goat, she was, climbin' over them cliffs." Nan turned her face to the wind, listening as the gulls screamed out over the surf. I watched as she closed her eyes and her jaw slackened. It was what she liked doing best, she'd often say, sitting on the sun-splotched barrens with the moss crusty beneath her feet and wild with purple, reds and browns. And on sunny days like today, she once said, up here on the cliffs and with no trees breaking the sight, the air was so blue that it felt like she was living amongst sky.

"Nan," I said after she had dozed for a bit and was snorting herself awake again, "do you think they'll try and put me in the orphanage, agin?"

Nan sat up straight.

"Be the Jesus, Kit, is they startin' on you in school, agin?"

"No, Nan."

"Tell me, now . . . "

"Noo, Nan."

"Is you worryin'?"

I shrugged and plucked a handful of berries from a bush nearby.

"Now, you listen to me, Kittens," Nan said, resting her hands on her knees and leaning sideways to see into my face. "As long as I walks the face of this earth, no one got the guts to come after you, agin. I met 'em at the door, I did. And it wouldn't everyone, just May Eveleigh and Jimmy

Randall, and the reverend and his wife. I bade 'em to come in, I did, and pointed out to 'em where to sit. They sat. And when they was finished tellin' me what they come for, I went into the room and come out with you wrapped in a blanket in one arm, and the rifle loaded and cocked in the other. Be the Jesus, they never had much to say after that. One be one, they rose up and walked out, the reverend first, then his Missus, and May, and Jimmy Randall last. And if it wouldn't for throwin' a fright into you, I believe I would've put a bullet in Jimmy Randall's leg that day, 'cuz the ones from away, they got no sense of how things are around here. But, when your own kind turns on you, that's what turned my stomach that day, and been turnin' me stomach every bleedin' day since, and they knows that me finger itches to pull a trigger every time I walks past their judgin', shameless faces."

I fingered the berries that were resting on the palm of my hand, hearing Nan's breathing over the sound of the wind and the surf.

"Heh, me darlin'," she said so low that it might have been the wind whispering. "I'm not one for pretty words, but it was a blessed evenin' the day that you were born, 'cuz the shack's been warmed ever since—even though I knows the cold you feels sometimes."

The berries rolled onto the ground and I turned my face from Nan's as I tried to pick them back up.

"Do you want your tea?" I asked.

"There's a girl," Nan said, sitting back on her rear, and splaying her black-stockinged legs out in front of her like two rounded stovepipes. "You got me maudlin, you have. Now, go stand on them rocks and see where Jose is. Heh, I dare say she's tucked into a sod, havin' a nap by now. Be the Jesus, she's not one for work, heh?"

Josie was nowhere to be seen. I scampered around several more mounds, calling out her name and searching over the barrens. Nothing. I heard Nan bawling out something and I turned back. Climbing on top of the knoll where I had last seen Josie, I saw Nan standing on the edge of the cliff, her fists raised and flailing through the air, the wind breaking her screams and tossing them thither. I stood for a minute, a sickness creeping through my stomach. Then Nan started running back to where we had left our backpacks. Only it wasn't a backpack that she was reaching for, but the rifle. Turning, she ran towards the edge of the cliff again, her body loping from side to side as she thrust her heavy frame forward. Then I was running, too.

"Get the hell's flames back, Kit!" Nan hollered as I come up behind her on the edge of the cliff. Roaring out Josie's name, she pointed the gun down to the beach and fired. I shoved myself in front of her and stared in horror as Josie, cuddling up to Shine on a log besides a bonfire, dropped the liquor jug that she was holding to her mouth and, scrabbling to her feet, started running up the beach. Shine come to his feet behind her, a stream of blood running down his face from where Nan's bullet had winged him, and railed his fists up towards Nan.

Bang! Another shot fired out from besides me and Shine leaped backwards as the bullet slammed into the rocks beneath his feet. Then he was running down the opposite end of the beach from Josie.

"Run, you bastard!" Nan screamed, firing off another shot, this time at a punt that was pulled up alongside and must have been Shine's. It jumped as the bullet rammed into its side, and Shine come running back into sight, swinging his fist up at Nan, and trying to push his boat off from shore. Another bang, and a piece of the rudder splintered beneath

Shine's hand, and Shine, his roars broken on the wind, cursed Nan to hell before scrabbling out of sight down the beach again, blood dripping from his face and fingers.

"Get everything together, Kit," Nan sung out, swinging herself back to the backpacks. "There's no tellin' what that bastard'll do next."

"What about Josie?" I asked, hurrying after her.

"She'll make her way home along the beach," Nan said. "There'll be no catchin' her on this day."

"S'pose the tide comes in."

"Then she'll have to swim alongside the cliffs, and it'll be one bleedin', bloody lesson she won't forget for a song."

Tossing a backpack on my back, and picking up the buckets with their bottoms scarcely covered with berries, I chased through the woods after Nan.

CHAPTER FIVE

JOSIE'S BATH

IT WAS AROUND TWO IN THE AFTERNOON when we got home. There was no sign of Josie. Nan paced back and forth, back and forth across the kitchen, stopping every so often to rest her elbows on the windowsill and look through the window down over the gully. Then she'd sit back in the rocking chair and rock, her arms folded across her breasts, and a deep scowl etched across her brow.

I picked the few berries clean that we had brought back, and stewed them in a dipper on the stove, checking out the window myself at the slightest sound made by the wind or by Pirate.

"We'll give her another twenty minutes," Nan finally said, coming to her feet and crossing over to look through the window, again. "If she's not back by then, you'll have to run for Old Joe, Kit, and tell 'em to come over in his boat, I wants him. And you don't tell nobody what it is we wants with him," Nan ordered, pointing a warning finger my way. "They got enough dirt on us to wag their tongues about, they don't need more. Especially the shootin'," she added, walking back to the rocking chair and sitting back down. "That's just what the Reverend Ropson needs, be Jesus, a reason to bring the law on us. Then it won't be just you and your mother he'll be tryin' to poke away somewheres, but me too. And that's where I'd shoot him dead, swear to God."

The door suddenly thrust open and Josie was standing there, her hair a wind-tangled heap around her muddied face, and her clothes soaked from the waist down. Nan come to her feet, but before she had chance to open her mouth, Josie was stomping past her, down the hallway to her room.

I shut the door behind her, wrinkling my nose. There was always a smell that come off her, like the smell of rotting dogberries after they had dropped and laid fermenting over time. And it was always strongest when she came back from being with her men friends. Today, mixed with the smell of moonshine and saltwater, it smelled worse.

"What're you wrinklin' your nose, at?" Nan demanded.

"She stinks," I muttered, going over to the stove, not thinking to take a look at Nan before speaking. A blast of air swiped across my face as Nan reared her face before mine and let go with the spite she had been saving for Josie.

"Stinks! Oh, she stinks do she, Miss High and Mighty Sweet Smellin' Kit Pitman!"

"That's what May Eveleigh says," I whimpered, backing away.

"May Eveleigh says?! Who says May Eveleigh says?"

"Margaret said she says."

"Haa! Back to Margaret, agin, is we? That brazen little bitch!"

Then Nan went into a fit as ever I'd seen. Snatching the poker from behind the stove, she stoked up the fire, cursing and swearing, and then dragged the wooden wash tub out

from the back room and kicked it up the hall to the middle
of the kitchen floor. Emptying the kettle of hot water into it,
and dipping out what was left in the hot-water tank on the
side of the stove, she stalked, still cursing and swearing, to
the hallway and bawled out Josie's name. Josie yanked open
her room door, still wearing her wet clothes, and stood glaring down the hallway at Nan.

"Come here!" Nan roared.

"I won't come here, you come here," Josie roared back,
stomping up the hall into the kitchen. Then all hell broke
loose.

"You'll come here like I tells you," Nan bawled out,
catching Josie by the arm and dragging her, kicking and
barking, towards the tub of steaming hot water. "Be the
Jesus, it's a God-given right to be clean, but He left it for we
to do some of the work," Nan ranted, ripping open the front
of Josie's blouse and sending the buttons spinning through
the air like ice pellets.

"Who's clean? You's clean! Stop, stop!" Josie yelled.

"I'll stop when I's finished," Nan yelled back, hauling the
blouse off Josie's back, and raking the straps of her slip down
over her arms. Gripping her by the bare shoulders, she
shoved her to her knees by the side of the tub and I was
reminded of Mary Magdalene at the Altar of Benediction,
weeping over Jesus' feet and then wiping them dry with her
hair. Only there were no humbling tears on Josie's face as
Nan snatched up handfuls of her thick, matted strands and
shoved Josie's head into the soapy water—just bubbles, bur-
bling up to mix with the rest of the suds. Pulling her head
back up, Nan slouzed the cloth across her face and down the
broad of her back and beyond, scrubbing with the same
vigour she used on dirty socks, lathered in lye and splayed
across the front of the scrub board.

Gripping onto the edge of the tub, Josie screwed up her face and cried like a baby. Still Nan kept scrubbing. When finally she was done, Josie got to her feet and tandered down the hall to her room, her body redder than a cooked beet.

"You'll be next, young martle, if you goes puttin' on airs around here," Nan threatened, pointing the dripping wet rag at me as I inched my way after Josie. "She might be a tramp, but she's better than them that made her so, for it's a damn sight easier to clean the rot off a crotch than the shame off a dirtied soul. Think about that before you starts hangin' your head before the likes of Margaret Eveleigh." She took a threatening step my way, and without losing a precious second I tore off to my room and slammed the door.

The next morning I got up, but Nan didn't. Inching open her room door, I peered inside and turned to stone. She was lying with the back of her head on her pillow, her eyes rolled back in her head, and her mouth dropped open like she was about to sing out to one of us when God took her. I slumped against the wall and crouched down to the floor. I couldn't see her face from here, only the bottoms of her feet sticking out from beneath the blanket—greyish white, the creases caked white with dried dead skin, and her toenails, thick and yellowed, curling back over the pads of her toes. Josie come thumping down the hall, and catching sight of Nan's face through the doorway, she poked her head inside for a closer look. Then she walked over to the bed. Staring hard at Nan's face, she reached out and slapped her.

"You wake up!" She slapped, again. "Wake up!"

"She's dead!" I said weakly, the words sounding as though they were coming from someone else's mouth.

"Who's dead? She's not dead. Wake up!"

Leaping to my feet, I grabbed hold of her arm as she went to hit Nan again.

"She's dead!" I half yelled. "See her eyes? You don't sleep with your eyes open."

She stared at Nan's eyes, then pushed me back and poked at them with her fingers.

"Stop it!" I shrieked.

"You stop it! You stop it! What'd you do?"

"I didn't do nothin'!"

"You did! Yes you did! Stop it! Stop it!" She fought against me as I tried to hold onto her hands. Then she drew back and struck me a stunning blow to the face. When my head cleared, she was gone. I ran to the door, then stopped and dropped onto the stoop. There would be no catching her on this day. And what would I be wanting her for anyway?

I don't know how long I sat there. Seagulls cried. The wind gusted. But I only saw dead! Nan, dead! The gully, dead! Nan, dead! The first snow fluttered around my feet like ripped lace. And still I sat, thinking nothing, feeling nothing. Doctor Hodgins pulled up by the side of the road in his car with Josie sitting besides him. She slammed out of the car and tore down over the bank and inside the house. Doctor Hodgins came hurrying behind her, the wind tugging his tufts of hair, and Josie's frenzy quickening his step. He paused besides me, my frozen state mirroring that of Nan's, and laying a hand gently on my head, he hastened inside at the sound of Josie slapping Nan.

"You can't wake her, Josie," I heard him say. There was a shuffling as he tried to hold her back. Then she was barking and shrieking, followed by a thump as he must've got her up against a wall. Then she was charging out through the door, her hand jamming my head against the side of the door jamb as she climbed past me and ran down the gully. She didn't go far, just to the other side. Then she squatted down and stared back at me as I stayed sitting on the stoop.

Slowly, her body began to rock—back and forth, back and forth—and a hard moaning started coming from her. Her hair slipped further and further forward as she rocked, till her face was screened by a curtain of red. Still she rocked. It felt like every inch of her soul was thrown into that moaning and rocking, and as I watched, I felt my head nodding too. And then the snow was swirling around her, and the rocks, and the brook, till it seemed like the whole gully was rocking and moaning alongside of her and alongside of me. Tears swelled in my eyes and I felt Doctor Hodgins sit down besides me as great wrenching sobs heaved out of my chest. And if it weren't for his hands holding onto my shoulders, I believe I would've sobbed my soul into heaven that day, leaving behind a sack of skin and bones as dry as the skin coating Nan's feet.

CHAPTER SIX

MRS. ROPSON'S DUTY

DOCTOR HODGINS LAID NAN OUT in the church to keep Josie from slapping at her face. He wanted to take us into his home, but his wife, sick with tuberculosis for all these years, was worsening. So he had Aunt Drucie come stay with us until after the funeral. What with her never having youngsters, and her husband sinking through a bog hole and drowning ten years ago, she had no one to stay home for. Plus, she was the closest to us, her house being halfway between the gully and Haire's Hollow.

I didn't mind her coming too much. She'd had the sleeping sickness for some years now and spent most of her time napping on the daybed, or slouched back in Nan's rocker, dozing. Josie wasn't home long enough to notice who was staying with us. Since the day of Nan's passing she hardly spoke to me, except to yell and then run off down the gully.

On the day of the burial, Doctor Hodgins went looking for her. I sat at the table, wearing my new red shift that Nan had brought from May Eveleigh's store and had hid away in her room for me for Christmas. Aunt Drucie sat across from me, her green veiled hat pinned a little crookedly on her head, and her eyes and nose red from bawling.

"I don't know what's goin' to happen to ye, Kit," she sniffled. "You and your poor mother. The reverend's all for sendin' you off to the orphanage in St. John's, but Doc Hodgins won't stand for it and is figurin' on askin' me to come servin' for you. You knows I'd do it; she was my best friend, Lizzy was." Aunt Drucie broke down sobbing again, wiping her nose with a scrap of white, wrinkled cotton she had hemmed around for a handkerchief. "And too, we're family, no different than if I raised ye, meself." Blowing her nose, she reached across the table and patted my hand. "Would you want that, Kit—Aunt Drucie to come look after ye?"

I nodded, as I did to everything asked of me the past days, my heart too laden to do much of anything else.

Aunt Drucie paused in her tears, her eyes beseeching mine as she mouthed a silent sigh for the gift of charity I had just bestowed upon her, no different than if Nan herself had been sitting alongside of me, handing me to her.

"I'll do me best for ye, Kit, I pray to God, I'll do me best," she quavered, sitting back in her chair and dabbing at her eyes. "How old be you, now? Twelve? Soon thirteen? Sure, another year and you won't be needin' nobody to care for you; wouldn't young Suze Gale only thirteen when she was pregnant and married?"

I nodded and Aunt Drucie leaned forward, dropping her voice to a fierce whisper.

"And it's a good thing for the reverend and the higher-ups that I'll be takin' care of ye, 'cuz I allows Lizzy would come back and haunt the bejesus out of every livin' soul in Haire's Hollow if they was to have their way and send you to an orphanage somewhere—after all they put her through when you was born. Although 'tis a sin Doctor Hodgins's wife's so sick," she added tearily. "'Cuz for sure he would've took you and your poor mother in. My, I remembers when all the talk was goin' on about his wife wantin' a baby, and was wantin' to adopt you, but he wouldn't let her. They says it's been eatin' at him ever since. They says that's when she started gettin' a bit low minded, after Doctor Hodgins put a stop to her adoptin' you. Course now, Lizzy had a say about that, too. She always said the doc's wife looked so sickly and blue with the cold that if she had a youngster, they'd have to wrap hot-water bottles around her tits to warm up a bit of milk."

A knock sounded and Aunt Drucie half stood as Old Joe inched open the door and stood inside, his curly grey hair wetted neatly back off his forehead, and his cap in his hand.

"Oh, 'tis you, Joe," Aunt Drucie said, her voice becoming all teary again. "Come on in then, and take a seat," she offered, sitting back down and pulling out a chair alongside of her.

"I'll be goin', agin," Old Joe mumbled, shifting uncomfortably as he stood besides me. "I-I just wanted to see Kit for a bit before ... before ... " His voice broke and he fumbled around in the pocket of his pressed Sunday pants and brought out the orange starfish he had offered me the day of Rube Gale's funeral. "I dried it for you, like I said," he whispered, dropping to one knee and holding it before me. "Might be I brung it too late ... but, there'll be other wishes, Kittens ... "

His voice choked off and I looked into his seeping, wind-wrought eyes.

"You just remember the verse," he whispered hoarsely. "Starfish, star bright. Then you closes your eyes and thinks the rest."

He placed the fish onto my outstretched palm and wrapped his hands around mine.

"You nail it to your room door," he urged gently, rising to his feet. "Your very own star. And if it don't bring you what you wishes for, you come to Old Joe, and he'll get it for you."

Then he was backing out the door and Aunt Drucie was weeping brokenheartedly.

"Poor J-Joe," she sobbed, "what's he goin' to do now without his ole card partner. My, they were a p-pair, they were."

The door opened again, and this time Doctor Hodgins walked in, smoothing back his tufts of hair, with Josie besides him.

"My oh m-my, she looks froze to death," Aunt Drucie moaned as Josie, scowling at me, kicked the mud and snow off her boots, and stomped down the hall to her room.

"Why don't you go help her get dressed," Doctor Hodgins said to Aunt Drucie.

Aunt Drucie got up, still dabbing at her eyes, and followed after Josie. Surprisingly, Josie let her into her room without any fuss. Doctor Hodgins sat down besides me, the cool fall air wafting from his clothes, like mint against my face. He fingered the starfish I held in my lap, then took it and laid it on the table. Taking hold of my hand, he held it in his and studied my palm.

"I can't take your pain away this time," he said finally, his voice gruff with gentleness. "I expect no one can, but the grace of God. Do you believe in God, Kit?"

I nodded, my mouth as empty of words as my eyes were of tears.

"Do you believe your grandmother is in a nice place?" he asked softly.

I nodded again.

"She won't ever leave you completely, Kit. There'll always be a part of her right here with you. Believe that." He paused, then, "I talked to Josie about angels. I don't think Lizzy was big on angels."

"She—didn't like feathers."

"Apparently. So, I talked to her about spirits instead, and how they are soft and warm, and not easily seen, and how Lizzy is a spirit now, and even though we can't see her, she's listening and watching us all the time, and lying down with us at night to help keep us warm while we sleep." He tightened his grip on my hand. "I don't know how much of it she understood. Perhaps you might want to reassure her of that sometimes."

I nodded.

"Kit, you can come live with Elsie and me."

"I want to stay here," I said, my eyes widening in alarm.

"Shh, you don't have to leave if you don't want to. I'm asking Drucie if she'll oversee things, here cook, clean Sleep over, if that's what you want. She'll be good company for you, help with things." He paused, then, "I understand how Josie wouldn't take well to moving. But, it's different with you, Kit. You're growing up fast, and there's things you'll need. I know Elsie's not that well, but you might be good for each other..."

"I won't leave," I said, my voice rising.

He smiled and little crinkles ran off from the corners of his eyes like ripples on a quiet pond.

"Don't worry, Kittens. I promised Lizzy a long time ago that I would see to you, and that you would never have to leave your home. And you won't. You have my word."

Something of my doubts must've been written in my eyes, for he tightened his grip on my hand again, and added gruffly,

"You're going to be fine. Anything you need, I'll see to it that you get. You just come to me. Will you promise me that?"

I nodded and he stroked the back of my hand with the pad of his thumb, the same as Nan when she was stroking the down off a turr's breast—all careful and tender like, so's to not rip the skin and sap the oil from its meat.

"Perhaps you should go see how Josie's making out with Drucie," he said, laying my hand back on my lap and giving it a little pat. "Lizzy won't like it if I'm late getting her girls to her funeral."

I walked down the hall to Josie's room, thinking Nan wouldn't be liking any of it if she was here, most specifically being laid out in church and with the Reverend Ropson looking over her corpse. And it was a dirty deed the reverend done her, when halfway through the service he went into his sermon on sin with such a vengeance that I could feel Nan's toenails uncurling as she lay there, muted in her coffin. And once, when the reverend pointed his finger somewheres in Josie's direction while calling the congregation sinners, I thought the coffin shifted. Shrinking closer to Doctor Hodgins, I half expected the lid to pop open any second and Nan along with it, pointing a finger of blasphemy at the reverend and blasting his hypocritic soul to hell.

Just what the reverend's hypocrisies were, except trying to take me away from Nan and sending me off to an orphanage the day I was born, I didn't know. Yet, aside from the scant few who took tea with him, everyone else in Haire's Hollow felt the same as Nan, although they were all equally pressed to say why. For the most part, the reverend walked amongst everyone and talked their talk, and was always taking their fight to St. John's when the fishers was getting a low cut on a quintal of fish, or the loggers being gypped on a cord of wood.

"It's in the way he goes about it," Old Joe said to Nan, once. "He's worse than Lucy Gale; gives you a piece of boiled cake just so's she can show off her new plate, then begrudges you every crumb that goes into your mouth."

"Be the Jesus, it ain't the cake he's begrudging ye," Nan had replied. "For he loves to flick his arse off to St. John's every chance he can get. It's havin' to talk with ye in the first place to find out what the matter is that dirties up his pretty platter."

And it was a dirty job he done Nan during her burial service. Fixing his eyes on Josie and me, sitting in the front pew alongside of Doctor Hodgins, he left off on his sermon on sin and went into another on the folly of foolish pride with such hissing and spite that most of the congregation hung their heads in shame for the way he was taking the final say in the bad blood between him and Nan and the bad blood that, in a way wasn't quite clear to anyone in Haire's Hollow, that had silently grown between him and Doctor Hodgins. And by the way Doctor Hodgins laid his hands protectively around mine and Josie's shoulders as he stared down the reverend during his preaching, and by the way the reverend's words lost some of their spite whenever he tripped over Doctor Hodgins's brooding look, it became clear that the battle was far from over simply because the general lay dead in a box at the reverend's feet.

It was the day after the funeral that they came—in much the same way Nan said they came all those years ago when they first tried to take me away from the gully. Excepting for the reverend and Jimmy Randall. They didn't come on this day. Just May Eveleigh and Mrs. Ropson. And it wasn't Nan who stood to greet them. It was me and Doctor Hodgins.

Nodding politely at Doctor Hodgins, May sat down straight as a ruler on the edge of the daybed and looked expectantly to the reverend's wife who was easing herself a little uneasily into Nan's rocker. I could tell by the way Mrs. Ropson kept looking to a spot besides the door where Doctor Hodgins was now standing that that was where the reverend must've stood as they faced down Nan, who must've been sitting on the far end of the daybed, away from May Eveleigh, where I was now sitting. After greeting them by name, Doctor Hodgins smoothed back his tufts and pleasantly asked, "Would you like a cup of tea, ladies?"

"I wouldn't put you to the trouble, Doctor," Mrs. Ropson said, wiping her cold, red nose with a small crumpled hankie, her voice a trifle too pleasing.

"No trouble at all," Doctor Hodgins replied. "Kit?"

I rose and went to the bin, taking down the teacups.

"A little cold water in mine," May Eveleigh said. Then she tut-tutted shockingly, "Some cold for October, Doctor. I allows we'll never see the sun again."

"It's always colder out here by the gully," Mrs. Ropson said with a little bivver. "No trees to buff the wind."

"Some of us like a good breeze, Mrs. Ropson," Doctor Hodgins replied merrily. "Need any help, Kit?"

I walked slowly towards Mrs. Ropson, carefully holding out the cup and saucer so's not to flop the tea over the sides. The tip of a cold fingernail grazed my knuckle as she accepted the cup and my hand shook a little as I went back to the bin for May Eveleigh's. Everyone served, I glanced with relief at Doctor Hodgins and sat back down, stealing a look at May Eveleigh as she copied sipping her tea as smartly as Mrs. Ropson. Aside from slurping a little too loud, she appeared to be doing it just right. Doctor Hodgins watched, too.

"It's a good cup a tea," May finally said, lowering her cup. "Thank you, Kit."

"Yes, thank you," Mrs. Ropson said, smiling up at Doctor

Hodgins. "Well, well, it's a good turn you're doing the family, Doctor, helping out like this. The reverend's disappointed he couldn't come with us today, but he's got a wedding down in Pollard's Point and a baptism in Purpy's Cove. And then he's off to St. John's. But, he feels blessed he was here to bury Lizzy."

"I'm sure Lizzy feels blessed as well," Doctor Hodgins replied solemnly. Mrs. Ropson gave a curt nod and tracked May Eveleigh's eyes around the place. There wasn't much— the room we were sitting in served as a kitchen and sitting room, with three small bedrooms leading off from a narrow hallway, and the small room at the back that served as Nan's closet. Everything was clean—the wooden bin, criss-crossed with a thousand cuts from a thousand diced carrots and potatoes, and the wood bleached from a thousand scrubbings; a sanded plank nailed across the wall over the bin served as a shelf for the dishes; the cupboards below, hidden behind a curtain of red cotton that Nan hemmed and hung to keep out the dirt.

The tops of the stove were polished black, and its white enamel sides were gleaming, except where pieces of the enamel was chipped, showing the black underneath. We didn't have curtains in the kitchen, didn't need them. Nobody came around our place, and Nan liked looking down over the gully onto the sea from her rocker. The blue-and-pink flowery canvas covering the floor was scuffed bare where Nan always stood by the bin, and in front of her rocker, and the spot in front of the doorway leading down the hall. Time enough to get new, Nan always said, when the tar gluing it down starts gluing your socks down as well.

The way the house leaned to one side bothered her. You couldn't drop a ball of yarn around your ankles without it rolling out of sight, she'd say. And she always complained, with a wink to Aunt Drucie, about how she got a stitch in her side sometimes, just by walking up the hall from the closet.

Still, her crocheted angel with the red halo hanging on the wall over the daybed was pretty. And her wandering Jew lit up the window by the door. Too, I liked the multicoloured throw that she had knitted out of a hundred different pieces of leftover wool, and laid across the daybed that me and May Eveleigh was now sitting on. I fingered a corner of the soft wool as May cleared her throat, readying to speak.

"Drucie's sleepin' sickness," she said, snapping everyone's attention onto her, "it seems to be catchin' up with her a lot, these days. There's some of us that's not convinced that she can handle the mother properly, even if she was able to stay awake, most times. We're concerned about the girl."

"Thank you, May," Doctor Hodgins said, rubbing at his chin and sounding deeply touched. "But you, more than anyone, know the outporters take care of their own. Kit and her mother will be fine."

"Drucie doesn't seem all that fit herself, these days," Mrs. Ropson spoke up, the little pockets of fat on the side of her mouth jiggling as she leaned forward and laid her cup on the corner of the table. "Certainly the mother will need a stronger hand than hers." She forced a chirpy little laugh and sat back. "Course it's hard for me to say anything, seeing's how hard Lizzy judged me the last time I tried to do my Christian duty by her. But it's the girl's—ah, Kit's—interest that concerns me and the reverend. That's why he wanted me to come out here today, even though my knee is swelled with arthritis again, to make sure Drucie can handle what we've put on her."

"Duty is a fine thing and I'm sure the good Lord sees straight through to your souls," Doctor Hodgins said much too quickly. "However, Drucie has been a friend of Lizzy's all her life and has a way with Josie. I don't anticipate any trouble."

There was a studied silence. Then Mrs. Ropson cleared her throat.

"It's not always easy putting the well-being of the congregation over your own, Doctor," she said with a touch of scorn. "Duty to one side, there are concerns here that affect others in the community as well." She flicked her glance to May, like one passing over the reins of a horse.

"Well, yes," May said, shifting further to the edge of the daybed. "About Josie and . . . her ways. Well, now that Lizzy's gone, things might get out of hand . . . and be a bad influence on Kit."

"We can trust to Lizzy's upbringing that Kit is well aware of her mother's *ways*," Doctor Hodgins replied sharply. "And that she's well adapted to dealing with those *ways*." He turned to Mrs. Ropson ruefully. "There are other things of greater concern here. Perhaps, that's where your worries lie?"

Doctor Hodgins and Mrs. Ropson eyed each other like two dogs that just nosed onto the other's territory, leaving May Eveleigh staring after them with a sudden scent of another intrigue. Sensing her neighbour's perked ears, Mrs. Ropson dropped her eyes from Doctor Hodgins and turned to May with an apologetic smile.

"Our good doctor is well aware of the worries I have to put up with—Sidney's asthma attacks and my arthritis. It's hard taking on the concerns of others when you can't get out of bed most days, although nobody can say the reverend or I have fallen slack in our duties."

"Tut-tut my dear, no one can say you don't carry out the church's work," May said, her voice expressing shock at the thought. "Is that what's being said, Doctor?"

"No, no," Doctor Hodgins shook his head and smiled at the two women. "I've heard nothing but good about the charitable nature of the reverend and his wife. And about you as well, May. That's why I have no concerns about Kit and her mother's well-being. What the good Lord don't provide, I'm sure you ladies will. Hah," he exclaimed, glancing out the window looking up to the road, "here comes Drucie. Why don't Kit and I leave you to talk privately with her and rest your worries?"

I sprang to my feet and headed for the door.

"Where is Josie?" May asked, a strong look at Mrs. Ropson as she made a final attempt to hold Doctor Hodgins back and keep the meeting going.

"Out scouting Lizzy's partridgeberry patch," Doctor Hodgins replied.

"Berry patch! Well, well," May said, her interest suddenly snagged in another direction. "I'll be glad to help pick Lizzy's partridgeberries, if I knew where her patch was. Goodness, no one's ever been able to find that patch."

"And cursed will be the ones who do search it out," Doctor Hodgins said, jarring the door. "I guess it's for Kit to decide what's to be done with the patch."

May Eveleigh watched as I pulled on a heavy wool sweater that Nan knitted, and moved to stand besides Doctor Hodgins.

"Well, if you needs help, Kit," she said, trying to keep her voice soft, like one not quite knowing how to talk to a baby.

"A bit late for picking berries, isn't it?" Mrs. Ropson asked.

"Hah, the later the sweeter," Doctor Hodgins replied. "Right up to the second and third snowfall, isn't that what Lizzy claims, Kit?"

I nodded and, toeing the door open, squirmed outside

just as Aunt Drucie come puffing up to the stoop, her skinny, wrinkled face a brownish pink from walking in the chilly air.

"How you doin', Kit?" she asked breathlessly, unknotting her bandanna from beneath her chin and shoving past me to get inside out of the cold. "My, my, it's not fit, the wind's not fit."

"Good day, Drucie," Doctor Hodgins said heartily, standing to one side to give her room. "You've got some visitors. You be sure and have a nice chat, now," he said, patting her shoulder as she suddenly went quiet upon seeing the upper-ups that had come to visit. Quickly closing the door behind him, Doctor Hodgins laid an arm around my shoulders and we walked down the gully. Josie was squat behind a rock, keeping watch on who was coming and going.

"There you are, Jose," Doctor Hodgins called out. "How come you didn't come in to greet your guest? Follow along now, there's things we have to talk about."

There were a lot of things Doctor Hodgins talked about as we strolled down the gully and onto the beach, mostly warning Josie about running off with her men friends and risking having me sent away, and her left alone to fend for herself. And make sure you keep the house clean, he went on, and that you, Kit, go to school every single morning. You don't want to give them any reason to come snooping around, and if they do, you want a clean house to greet them and a clean hand to shake theirs.

For the most part Josie listened. Then, as Doctor Hodgins neared the end of his talk, and I slipped on a wet rock, she gave me a shove, toppling me sideways, and ran off towards Crooked Feeder.

"Hey, Josie," Doctor Hodgins called after her.

"She thinks I killed Nan," I said, taking hold of Doctor Hodgins's arm to steady myself.

"It's not going to be easy, Kit," he sighed, watching as she bounded sure-footed over the slush-covered rocks. He turned to me and, laying his hands on my shoulders, bent down and shook me, gently. "You've got your own grieving to do, along with fending off Josie's. But you'll do it. There's a lot of Lizzy in you, probably more than what's good for you." He smiled the saddest smile and, pulling my head against the breast of his jacket, continued speaking in his quiet, gruff way. "I wish I could make it easier for you, Kit. You can come live with me and Elsie any time, you know that, don't you?"

I nodded, his wool jacket scratching against my face.

"Are you sure you don't want to?"

"I'm sure," I muffled into his coat. He patted the back of my head.

"I know. I know. This is your home, why would you want to leave it?" He pulled back and looked at me, his eyes grey slits beneath their bushy brow. "Just remember what I told you—come to me if you need anything. Anything! You promise?"

I nodded.

"Promise me!" he repeated.

"I promise."

He stroked my cheek with the pad of his thumb and I was back to thinking on Nan buffing turrs again, and being careful not to break the skin and sap the oil. And then he was squinting his eyes into the salty wind as we started walking up the beach after Josie. His hand gripped my shoulder as our feet scrunched over the beach rocks and the loneliest seagull in the world cried out above us, drawing a single tear down the side of Doctor Hodgins's coarsened cheek.

CHAPTER SEVEN

GRIEVING NAN

DESPITE EVERYONE'S WORRIES ABOUT me and Josie, it was a good year that passed. Shine never came back. Doctor Hodgins came faithfully twice, sometimes three times, a week, and had supper with us. Old Joe and his brother kept bringing out truckloads of birch, and there was always someone dropping off a fresh fish, a bottle of beets or a chunk of moose meat. Aunt Drucie dodged over every morning, sometimes after I had already left for school, and she went home again right after supper each evening. Her sleeping sickness kept her occupied most of the time that she was with us. Feeling all tuckered out from her walk over, she liked to take a nap in the rocker to get her breath back, giving me time on the weekends to get the dishes washed, beds made and floors mopped. By the time she woke up, she'd forgotten that she'd seen an unmade bed and was telling everybody in Haire's Hollow how clean me and Josie was, and how we were the nicest girls in the world to work for because we never whined, mouthed back or asked for anything.

I took to watching how she cooked, and before the year was up, I could make a pot of pease soup, scrape and fry up a salmon, or throw together a pot of moose stew as quick as Nan; anything to get Aunt Drucie out of the house early. Not that I minded her so much, but I could best hear Nan when I had the place to myself, and when I could best find comfort. Sitting in her rocking chair, with the fire crackling in the stove and the wind hurtling the snow against the window, I could forget that she had passed on and feel her humming all around me, and see and hear everything she ever did and said, like looking at a picture, only I saw it in sounds: the creaking of the floor beneath the weight of her step, her ongoing argu-ing, the twittering in her throat as she sucked on the hard green candies and the rumbling in her belly while she filled up with gas. And it's like there's a smell that comes with the picture—a mixed-up smell of powder and skin and oily hair. And sometimes, when I just happened to be sitting there doing my homework or listening to the fire crackling, some-thing—like the whistling of the kettle or a whiff of dried salt from the starfish nailed to the inside of my room door— would trigger the picture and bring a feeling over me, like something soft, and nice, and big—so big that it felt like I was going to see something, like when you have a dream some-times and you wake up and you can't remember it, but the feeling is so strong that it's almost as if the feeling is the dream itself. And then, when I get that feeling, I get another one that hurts all over—like a big ache. And no matter how well everything was going with Aunt Drucie and school, that's what I felt like every single solitary minute since the day Nan passed on—like a big ache that hurt all over.

One night I woke up to the sounds of the rocker creak-ing. It was one of them nights where it felt as if Nan had lain with me and I felt warm no matter how cold the canvased floor. Hopping out of bed I crept down the hall and looked into the kitchen, half expecting to see her sitting there. It was Josie. A thin shaft of moonlight shone through the window, outlining her bulky form in the rocker next to the cold stove. She was still mad at me for Nan's passing, and I thought to go back to bed. But she looked cold, and Nan wouldn't have wanted her feeling cold. I took a step towards her and yelped as she suddenly reached out and grabbed me and pulled me into her arms. Still yelping, I scrabbled to get away, but she pinned me to her chest and started rocking. Hearing her sob, I went still. I noticed that the smell of fermenting dogberries wasn't so strong. And I noticed that she had laid her chin on the crown of my head, like Nan used to do when I was little. Despite feeling a pain in my side from where her fingers were digging into me, and despite my being too big to fit even a small bit comfortably on her lap, that aching feeling came in my throat and I stayed still for a long time with her rocking me like that—rocking and weeping, rocking and weeping. It was almost dawn when her arms slackened and I nearly slipped to the floor. Creeping back to bed, I listened as she soon got up from the rocker and went down the hall to her room.

The next morning she stomped past me in the hall and started cranking splits into the stove and lighting the fire like she always did before Nan's passing. And I made her tea and toast like I always did since Nan's passing. Yet despite her getting over her anger towards me, she hardly did any of the things she used to do while Nan was alive, like bounding up and down the gully, racing noisily across the house with muddied feet, barking out that crazy laugh at just about any-thing or shoving her face up to mine and sticking out her tongue. Mostly, she just sat in the rocking chair, or trudged off down the gully somewhere for hours on end. I couldn't think what she did with her time. Doctor Hodgins said she was seeking solitude to grieve Nan's leaving and it was best to leave her be. So, I left her be. One small blessing that came with her not doing any of the things that she used to do was that she never went off with the men when they came blowing their horns up on the road any more. And the smell of rotting dogberries slowly disappeared from her body.

One evening in late September, just a year since Nan's passing, I was coming down over the bank from the road, just home from the store, when I caught sight of Josie treading across the meadow towards the secret path leading to Nan's partridgeberry patch. I always remember the way she looked walking off across the meadow that day with the grass up to her waist, and the sun, a bloody red, going down behind the hill, touching on her hair and making it look like a flame that burned smaller and smaller the further she went. I told her that when she came home for supper. We were eating baked beans and Aunt Drucie was dozing in the rocking chair.

"Who looks like a flame? You looks like a flame!" She slapped her hand on the table and stared at me. I stared back. She had freckles that had faded and were now blended into her skin so's you couldn't see the spots any more, you just saw that she used to have freckles. Her teeth were jumbled in front and her eyes were a greenish brown with queer yellow flecks spotting them. Sometimes she had a way of staring at you till it felt like the flecks were small beams of yellow light shining straight through your head, lighting up your very thought. Then, most times she'd just walk away, leaving you wondering if she knew what you had been thinking, or if it just felt that way.

"What do you look like?" she demanded, slapping the table harder.

"Like Nan," I said, eyeing her carefully as I placed a forkful of beans into my mouth. She went silent at the mentioning of Nan's name, and sullenly picked at her bread. I thought to ask her then, who my father was. But I remembered Nan once saying to Aunt Drucie that that would be like asking which bean in the can made her fart.

My father! From the first day I entered the schoolyard I was told by Margaret Eveleigh, and everybody else around me, that I didn't have a father. Then, when Josh Jenkins figured out everybody got to have a father, him and Margaret pinned me in the corner, sizing up my features and trying to figure out whose father I looked like.

"You don't look like nobody," Margaret had said accusingly, and I ran off home to Nan, crying that I had a father and that I didn't look like nobody.

"Aye, it's not just the youngsters sizin' up your features," Nan had said. "For sure they're all frightened to death that you're goin' to start lookin' like one of theirs someday."

I suddenly lost my appetite for the plate of beans before me and left Josie sitting at the table forking around hers. Shoving another junk of birch in the stove, I smiled at Aunt Drucie as she sputtered awake and, pulling on my coat and boots, wandered outside looking for Pirate. I liked to think I entered the gully the same way as he—just appeared one day, with an offering in his mouth. Only, I wouldn't wish it was a half-dead robin. Aside from his not wanting anyone to touch him, it was the one thing I didn't like about Pirate—his killing instinct.

After I had pried the robin free from his jaws, I had put it in a box and kept it in my room, feeding it a little water and a couple of small worms, cut up like sausages. It never ate the worms, but it beaked back the water. When it got stronger, I'd chase Pirate out of the house and put the bird on my finger, lifting it gently up and down, up and down, till the air stirred its wings and soon, they were flapping a little more each time. After a week, it was flying off my finger to the table or the top of the chair. One day Pirate was waiting just outside the window, and when the robin flew off my finger to the windowsill, he lunged and caught it in his mouth. This time the little bird wasn't so lucky. I ran outside screaming, but Pirate was gone. The only thing left was a few feathers resting on the windowsill. I put the feathers in the special box where I kept my pieces of broken coloured glass.

Not finding Pirate spooking through the timothy wheat edging the meadow, and not particularly interested in walking far in the dull, grey evening, I wandered back inside the house. Josie had gone off somewhere, and Aunt Drucie was gone home for the day, leaving me to wash the supper dishes. She was sleeping more and more this winter, and cooking and cleaning less. Because we lived outside of Haire's Hollow, no one actually knew how much time Aunt Drucie was spending at our house or hers—which worked out fine with me. I'd taken over most of the chores by now and was only too happy to be sending her home more and more. Doctor Hodgins's wife had worsened considerably this winter and his visits were kept down to one, sometimes two, a week. And when he did come, he couldn't stay for long. And what with my mother taking off down the gully all the time, I was mostly alone. And that's when I liked it best—when I was alone, feeling Nan's humming all around me as I sat quietly by the crackling stove doing my homework and reading.

The one problem that kept upsetting things was when Josie forgot to split the firewood. She didn't usually. Cleaving wood was her one chore since she was a gaffer, and one she was always intent on doing. And during that first year after Nan's passing, she most always kept the woodbox filled and splits ready for the morning's fire. But, it appeared as if she became more and more despondent over time, and chopping wood became another one of those things that she didn't care about, any more. And try as I might, I just couldn't get that damn axe to slice through a junk of wood, getting it caught instead on a knot, or jammed at such an angle that no amount of prying could get it freed. On those evenings during the second winter without Nan, after Aunt Drucie had gone home and there wasn't enough wood to keep the fire going, and the wind was whistling in through every crack in the house, it was Pirate that kept me warm. Stretched across the foot of my bed, his was a quiet presence that brought comfort to a cold night. Crawling beneath my bedclothes and shoving my feet down beneath the spot where he was lying, it felt like Nan had already been here, leaving behind a tea plate, heated and wrapped in a towel for me to put my feet on like she always done in the winter time. On nights like this I stared at the orange speckled starfish shining dully through the dark, and wished that Pirate was a cat that could be touched.

It was after such a night that Doctor Hodgins came to visit. Buffing his hands from the cold, he stood in the middle of the kitchen, his breath spurting out in puffs of white.

"Good Lord, why's the fire out?" he asked, glancing at the empty woodbox behind the stove.

"I was up studyin' half the night and burned all the wood," I say.

"How you going to get to school on time with no fire lit and kettle not boiled?"

"It's Saturday."

"Heh, so it is." He scratched his head, looking a little confused. "Perhaps I should have come over and split you a cord."

"You knows she likes to do it," I said, nodding towards Josie's room door. He stood quietly for a minute, rocking back and forth on his heels, and I noticed that his hair was tangled, and his shirt was unbuttoned at the top, and wrinkled. "Is something wrong?" I asked.

He started buffing again, pacing the room.

"Nothing you can help with, I'm afraid. It's Elsie." His eyes darkened and his voice lowered as he turned to me. "She's took a turn for the worse. I'm taking her home to St. John's. There's a good hospital there. Plus her sister." He shrugged. "We'll just have to hope for the best."

"Will you come back?" I asked, suddenly terrified.

"Of course I'll be back," he said, trying hard to sound convincing. "Just as soon as she's well, again."

"Will that take long?"

"Maybe." His voice deepened further. "Maybe not." A look of unbearable sadness passed over his face and he moved quickly around the room, buffing his hands all the harder. "You make sure Josie keeps the woodbox filled, and that Drucie don't go to sleep while she's stirring the gravy." He jammed his hands in his pocket and looked at me with a forced grin. "I'll be back as soon as I can."

I forced a smile.

"We'll be fine," I said, not feeling fine at all. "You just take care of Elsie."

He smiled at me then, a sad little smile that did little to lighten the look of gloom around him. Trying hard to think of something to say, something that might make him feel better, as he had with me so many times, I ushered him out the door, making small of his worries about the unlit stove.

"You go on now, and don't go worryin' about us. It's nothing for Josie to split a load of wood. And Aunt Drucie will be here any minute, rousin' her out of bed."

"Mind you don't catch cold," he said, nudging me back inside from the winter's wind. Giving me a pinched look, he pulled the door shut behind him, sending an icy draught around my bare feet and legs. I shivered, huddling my arms around myself for warmth as I watched him through the iced window, trudging up over the snow-beaten path. More so than anyone, his was a presence that was deeply felt in the gully, in this house and in me—like the fire that had always burned steadily in the stove when Nan was alive. It was only after she had passed on did I feel the canvas cold beneath my feet. Even when I was the first one up in the mornings and the coals in the stove had gone out during the night, I had never felt the canvas cold beneath my feet. And now, watching Doctor Hodgins walk away from the gully to some distant city that I had only read about in books, I felt another coldness, one that touched me deep inside, drawing a small shiver of fear down my spine and leaving me feeling as cold as Nan's brow as she had lain in her coffin.

CHAPTER EIGHT

GULLY TRAMP'S GIRL

DOCTOR HODGINS WAS GONE BUT a week when Aunt
Drucie came down with the flu. Stamping the snow off
my boots as I came in through the door from school, I
started in fright to see her sleeping in the rocking chair, her
head lolled to one side, and her half-opened mouth drooling
onto her shoulder as the pan full of bologna smoked black on
the stove. Dashing across the kitchen, I snatched the pan by
the handle and dragged it back on the damper.

"Goodness... mercy ah... ahh... " She come to her feet
and let go with a fit of coughing and sneezing that sprayed
the pan of bologna and sizzled across the top of the stove.

"You go on home," I pressed her. "I can take care of
things till you gets better."

Nodding appreciatively, her throat too sore to do much
talking, she let me help her with her coat and bandanna and
trudged weakly out the door. I watched her walking up over
the bank to the road, her shoulders hunched beneath her
long, winter's coat, and a scarf wrapped around her face,

wondering if I shouldn't be walking home with her, and helping to put her to bed. But a chill was creeping around my own bones, and I went back to the stove, stogging it full with birch. The next morning I woke with my throat sore and swollen, and my nostrils as clogged as a weed-choked brook. Dragging myself through the freezing cold house, Josie not having chopped enough wood to bank the stove again, and not finding much of anything to eat that didn't need a fire, I put off going to school and took myself back to bed. Around lunchtime I roused Josie who was still comfortably rolled up in her blankets, and whined at her for not chopping enough wood, then ordered her to get ready and walk with me to Haire's Hollow to bring back some groceries.

The second we entered the store, May Eveleigh left off her conversation with Mrs. Haynes, the teacher's wife, and turned frowning eyes upon us.

I offered a bit of a smile towards Mrs. Haynes as she absently fastened and unfastened the top button of her fashionable coat, remembering how she'd told me, once, when I was coming out of church with Nan, how pretty I was. But there were no nice words to spare me this morning as May leaned over the counter towards us, nostrils flaring like a bird dog sniffing out its prey.

"How come you're not in school, today?" she asked.

"I'm sick," I said.

"Then how come Drucie let you out on a cold day as this?"

"I-I'm better."

"Who's better?" Josie demanded, peeling her eyes off the jar of hard green candies sitting on the counter to scowl at me. "You's better? You's not better."

"Then if you're better, how come you're not in school?" May asked, ignoring Josie.

I stared helplessly at what appeared to be a fading bruise on Mrs. Haynes's cheek. She gave me the sympathetic smile of one too busy being preyed upon herself to offer much to anyone else, and went back to fidgeting with her coat button.

"Because—I might get sick again," I said, turning back to May.

"She's sick agin!" Josie barked. "Sick!"

Whatever other questions May might've wanted to ask, she forgot them as the queer yellow lights from Josie's eyes suddenly blazed into hers. Then quick as anything, she rammed her hand inside the candy jar and, pulling out a fistful of the hard green candies, shoved two into her mouth and stood back with her lips reamed shut, as if expecting May to reach out and pry the candies from her gob as Nan would've done if she had been standing there.

Not sure if I should be acting sick on account of my not being in school, or acting better on account of not wanting to make Aunt Drucie look like she wasn't taking good care of me, I quickly took advantage of the sudden shift in focus and asked for a can of milk and a pack of biscuits. Snatching up the brown paper bag, after May tucked the groceries inside, I nudged Josie with my foot and scurried out the door.

The next morning, with every muscle bruised and my stomach a little queasy, I forced myself out of bed and stoked the fire. Hearing a steady hacking cough coming from Josie's room, I groaned and made her a cup of tea and some toast. Groaning harder still, I slung my school bag over my shoulder, and dragged myself out the door.

It was a grey, windy day, the air damp with unshed rain. Wet snow slushed around my rubber boots, and the ice beneath made it slippery for walking. Not seeing any smoke coming out of Aunt Drucie's chimney as I walked by, I ran down the path to her door and checked inside. She was in bed, bundled beneath a mountain of blankets, hacking and sneezing, and the house colder than the outdoors.

"You stay where you are, now," I called out as comfortingly as I could, ripping up some birch rind and shoving some splits in the stove. "It's a bad flu, you just needs to rest. Me and Josie'll be fine for a few days, you just stay in bed. There!" I said, putting a lit match to the birch rind, and then stogging the stove with split, dried wood. "A nice fire to keep you warm and boil the kettle."

"You're a good girl, Kit," Aunt Drucie croaked.

"Shhoosh now," I said, buttering up some crackers and mixing her a glass of cold raspberry syrup. "Here!" I laid the platter with the crackers and syrup on her bed and backed out the door. "I gotta go now, I'll be late for school. Make some tea when the kettle's boiled, and don't forget to put a bit of peppermint in it."

"Lizzy'd be proud of you, Kit."

"I expect so. Bye now," I said and hauled the door shut. I ran, slipping and sliding, down over Fox Point to Haire's Hollow. It was eerily quiet walking along the road through the outport, and I knew with a sinking heart that school had already started. The water lopped a dirty grey along the shore and I raised a listless hand to Old Joe as he called out a greeting from the wharf, while puttering about his endless tasks.

There were three rooms in the school—grades primer to six in one, seven to nine in another, and ten and eleven in the other. I was in grade nine, the same room as whose windows looked out at me as I hurried across the schoolyard. Edging open the classroom door, I kept my eyes down and walked as quietly and quickly as I could to my desk. Mr. Haynes had stopped talking as I stepped inside, and he now watched as I took out my geography book and flipped it open to somewhere in the middle. He started teaching again, and while I never took my eyes off the book for the rest of the morning, I knew he was flicking looks my way every chance he got—waiting, just waiting. And whatever it was he was waiting for, I knew with a foreboding certainty, he was going to make it happen.

Unpredictably, it was Josie that happened. It was just minutes before lunchtime when all of a sudden everyone was whispering and shuffling in their seats, and then busting into muffled giggles and outright laughing and groaning. Shifting my eyes sideways to see what was causing the commotion, I caught sight of her as she walked past the school windows, shoulders hunched forward into the wind and retching as she walked, the vomit blowing back into her face and sticking to the strands of her windblown hair as it flapped around her face.

Margaret Eveleigh grabbed me by the arm and pointed to the window, while most everyone else, their hands clapped to their mouths to keep back their groans, whipped around to see if I was seeing my mother walking down the road and puking into her hair. Ordering everybody to be quiet, Mr. Haynes snatched the strap off his shoulder and cracked it across his desk. It was as if my mother heard the smack, because at that second she looked up, and seeing everyone looking out the window and laughing at her, she stopped retching and smiled back, wiping at her mouth with the back of her hand. Then, upon seeing Mr. Haynes looking out as well, she waved. Everyone busted their gut and Mr. Haynes walked savagely down the aisles, welting his belt across whichever desk was nearest to him. Blissfully, the bell rang for lunchtime. There was a stampede as everyone tried to be first one out the door, bursting to let go with their jeering and hooting. For me, it was a choice of hanging back with

Mr. Haynes and his strap, or heading for the door with everyone else. I headed for the door.

Surprisingly, it was big, blond-haired Josh Jenkins that come out of it the worst. Gaming for Margaret's attentions, he stuck his finger down his throat and let go with a stomach-curdling urge that succeeded nicely in getting the attention of Margaret's best friends. But not Margaret! She was too intent on swooping down on me, a look of utter disgust marking her pretty pink cheeks, to notice Josh Jenkins. Only, I was spared on this day. Gaining more and more courage from the giggles of Margaret's best friends and getting carried away with the spirit of the moment, Josh ran up behind her and, grabbing hold of her ringlets, buried another gut-retching gag into the flaming red coils. All around, everyone hooted with laughter, and the younger ones, who had yet to suffer from Margaret's personal persecutions, started circling around her, bravely chanting "Josie, Josie."

Clawing back her ringlets from Josh's fanned fingers, Margaret spun around as if she had been whipped. Raising her fist to his quickly sobering face, she screeched loud enough for all of Haire's Hollow to hear, "You ever touch me again, pus-faced Jenkins, and I'll have you jailed—you and your slouch of a father for all the credit he got in our store and can't pay for." Her face burning brighter than the look of fervour dying in Josh's eyes, she caught sight of me trying to sneak off around the school, and swooped before me, a fury of red.

"Your mother's a dirty, rotten tramp!" she screamed, both fists flailing. "She's not fit to walk the roads. Do you hear me, Gully Tramp's Girl?"

Escaping to the back of the school, I huddled down on a small, flat-topped rock and rested my back against the wall. It was where I sat most days during lunchtime and recess.

No one else came back here, and it was warm, out of the wind and with the sun burning red on my eyelids. Only I felt cold this day, as cold as the morning Doctor Hodgins walked up the gully, on his way to St. John's. I was surprised that I felt cold. Not even when I was racing down the gully, with my feet slipping over the ice-covered rocks and the wind licking over my face with the breath of a thousand icebergs, did I ever feel the cold, outdoors. But it must've been a real cold day. Shivering, I pulled open my lunch bag and took out the slice of partridgeberry bread. That was when I first noticed Sid.

He was in grade ten, a different classroom from mine, and didn't hang around the schoolyard. He was the reverend's son and was born and raised in Haire's Hollow. But his mother saw to it that he never spent much time running around with the outport boys, keeping him home to help her on account of her being crippled all the time with arthritis, and sending him away to St. John's in the summers with her cousin's boys. He was nicknamed Mommy Suck. And when he did come out and about in the outport, he looked a sight with his puffed-up shoulders and poker-back walk. And the way he talked was more grand than the outporters, what with his mother, who was born and raised in St. John's, making him pronounce his "th" sounds and saying "catch" not "ketch," and "goodbye" not "see ya"—all which made for more name-calling at school, with "Dead Sid" being the most popular some days, and "Sid the Kid" on others. And what with the black pressed jacket and white shirts he always wore, and the small, hardcover books that looked like prayer books that he always carried around in his pockets, he looked more like a preacher going off to church than a young fellow going off to school.

On this day, when he came around the corner of the

school to where I was sitting, he was pale as anything, with fleshy red lips, squinty eyes that looked like blue dots behind his black-framed glasses, and his skin whiter than flour. His hair was yellow, the colour of mine, and he was looking at me the way he looked at everybody—his mouth partly opened and his lips working as if he was wanting to protest about something, but hadn't yet figured out what that something was.

I didn't want Mister Sidney Kidney staring at me, so I closed my eyes and pretended he wasn't there. When I looked up, he was gone. Along with everyone else in the schoolyard.

I began to breathe more easily in the silence. When I first started coming to school, it used to hurt my ears with everyone seemingly talking at once. Sid was to say later that it was because I had spent so much time alone in the gully, that I had gotten too used to the quiet. Funny, but I'd never thought of the gully as being quiet, what with the wind scratching the trees, and the water pounding upon the rocks, and Josie barking, and Pirate meowling, and Nan bawling out. And in the evenings when the seagulls all fought for roosting space in the tucamores around the shore, they made more noise than a thousand schools at recess time. Yet it all seemed to go together, somehow—the wind and the sea and the birds and Nan. Sitting there on the rock behind the school, I heard nothing but the occasional raised voice of some youngster tardying on his way home, and the joints in the schoolhouse squeaking from the frost. An empty, churning feeling weakened my stomach, in much the same way as it did on that first day of school when Nan left me alone at the schoolyard gate. Shucking my slice of bread to the crows, I got up and walked home.

CHAPTER NINE

THE REVEREND'S PLEDGE

JOSIE WAS IN BED WHEN I GOT HOME. Burning the last of the split wood to boil the kettle, I made us a pot of tea. The smell of vomit greeted me as I entered her room. I stood for a moment, staring down at her stiffened red strands splayed out on her pillow, and the glazed look in her eyes as she stared back at me.

"Doctor Hodgins," she said hoarsely.

"He's still in St. John's," I said.

She winced, swallowing against the rawness of her sore throat, then turned her cheek onto her dirtied hair. I thought of Nan, pointing the dripping rag towards me and hollering how it was a God-given right to be clean, but how He left it for us to do some of the work, and how she might be a tramp, but she was better than them that made her so. But the chanting of Margaret and the others in the schoolyard sounded over the rest of what Nan had said, and laying her cup on the small, wooden table besides her bed, I backed out of the room. She watched me, a glimmer of yellow igniting in her eyes. Turning my back, I left her room and wandered into my own. Climbing into bed I stared dismally at Old Joe's orange speckled starfish nailed to my door, and spent the rest of the day with my head buried beneath my pillow.

The next morning I knew I should've went to school. But, I never. Instead, I tackled the axe and the birchwood Old Joe had dropped off the day before. And with waddles of birch rind and bark, and a few splits of wood, I got a fire going long enough to fry up some potatoes and eggs. Josie was still sleeping, so I laid her plate next to the cold cup of tea she hadn't touched from the day before, and went back to my room. Pulling on one of Nan's old, flannelette night-dresses that hung around me like a tent and had a ragged edge around its tail from where Nan had ripped off a piece to make a good cleaning rag, I crawled back into bed—my throat sore, my bones aching and my feet knobs of ice from standing on the freezing canvased floor. Hoping Aunt Dru-cie wouldn't show up, I shoved my feet down to the warm spot beneath where Pirate was snoozing, and after eating the eggs and potatoes, pulled out the box of coloured glass from beneath the bed. Sorting the little robin's feathers to one corner, I picked out the bigger pieces of glass and idly lined them up against the window to catch the light.

It was a bright, sunny day, and cold clear up to the sun. And the sea was blue-black against the white of the snow. Closing one eye, I peered down over the gully through the largest piece of yellow. It tinted golden the wings of the seagulls gliding over the sea, but for the first time that I could remember, I took no heart from my childish game, and flicked the pieces of glass back into the box.

Around lunchtime, I heard Josie get out of bed, her step slow, heavy, its quickness buried along with Nan. Worried that she might go into Haire's Hollow again, I jumped out of bed and ran to the kitchen window. She was ploughing her way through the snow down into the gully. I watched her for a minute, her body heaving from side to side like a wearied old woman whose thoughts were so burdened that likely the snow was hardening and turning to ice beneath her feet. Pulling my coat on over Nan's nightdress and shoving my feet into a pair of rubber boots, I followed her.

It had snowed heavily during the night, and the drifts were up to my waist. Flapping my arms to keep warm, I followed in her footsteps down the centre of the gully, the brook long since frozen and buried. It was easier walking along the beach, the sea having kept it clear of snow. Yet the wind was strongest, cutting tears out of my eyes as I walked along, heading for Crooked Feeder. I climbed on top of a snowbank just before I got to the brook, and stopped. She was hunched down by the half-frozen water, rocking back and forth, back and forth, the way that she had on the day of Nan's passing. An easterly gust swept over me, its stinging coldness jarring a picture in my mind of her sitting in the rocking chair and rocking me all through the night. I thought to go over to where she was sitting. I shivered, and turning instead, I walked back up the beach.

I didn't see the car parked by the side of the road on account of the snow being piled so high. Climbing over the edge of the gully, I walked back to the house and shuffled in through the door. There, my eyes widened in fright. Standing by the stove was the Reverend Ropson. He was dressed in black as he always was, with a flush of pink staining his hairless face, and his paltry blue eyes as cold as the stove he leaned against. In one fluid movement he was across the kitchen and standing in front of me, the coiled thrusting of his serpent's head striking to within a hair's width of mine.

"Where's Drucie?" he half snarled, his whispering tone ricocheting round the house like a fiery wind.

I pressed back against the wall, fear rooting my feet to the floor.

"S-she's sick."

"And your mother?"

"Crooked Feeder."

"What's she doing down there?"

"N-nothin'."

He stared me over, his nose wrinkling as if the sight of me was more than his stomach could take. Then something of a satisfied smile caught at his lips as he took in my unbuttoned coat, and oversized nightdress ripped up around the tail and wet from dragging in the snow, and my fingers red from the cold, and the snot oozing out of my nose.

"Your teacher is concerned," he whispered severely, a thin smile marring his face. "He saw your mother sick yesterday, and now today you aren't in school. I thought we'd have a little meeting to see what can be done. Come with me, and I'll see to it that you're taken care of."

The knowing of just how the reverend meant to take care of me, and remembering that this time there was no Doctor Hodgins to stop him, jarred my rooted feet into action. I darted around him, heading for the hallway, but he clamped a hand onto my arm and yanked me back.

"No!" I screamed, kicking at his legs as he dragged me to the door. "It's just a cold! It's just a cold!"

"Quiet!" he snapped, dragging me kicking and screaming out of the house, and paying no more heed to my desperate cries than one would a vixen youngster. Grappling an arm around my waist, he half dragged, half carried me up over the snow-trenched path and onto the road by his car. Shoving me inside, he slammed the door shut against my flailing arms and legs and, scrambling round to the other side, quickly climbed in while I grasped desperately at the locked door handle.

"Sit back," he ordered, clamping both hands on my shoulders and shoving me back against the seat. I kicked and screamed harder. Then the palm of his hand smashed against the side of my face with the force of Mr. Haynes's belt, startling me into stunned silence. Revving up the motor, he speeded down the road, the car slipping and sliding, and sending me into another round of terror as I realized there was no escaping the moving car.

Twisting around, I flung my arms up over the back of the seat and scuffed my way up over. His fingers dug into my shoulders as he clawed me back down, but not before I saw Josie's flaming red head poke up over the snowbank by the road. Screaming and kicking with another burst of vigour, I fought back the reverend's arm holding me down, then gasped for breath as he hit the brakes, throwing me forward and slamming my head against the dash. The reverend cursed as we skidded out of control, and what with the smack to my head, and the car skidding from side to side, the queasy feelings that had been sitting in my stomach for the past two days erupted into a sour bile in my mouth and spewed out over the reverend's feet and onto the fine yellow strands of my hair.

Queer enough, it wasn't Josie's walking past the school windows and vomiting into her hair that shot through my mind as I hung upside down in the car, puking, but Josh Jenkins and the flush of red riding up over his ears when Margaret Eveleigh shot off her mouth about his father's unpaid store bill. And when the reverend slowed to a stop and got out of the car, cursing like no reverend man is supposed to curse, and climbed back in, dumping handfuls of

snow into my face, I was already sitting back up and wel-
comed the sweet relief of the clean-smelling snow. And when
we finally pulled up in front of the reverend's house, and Sid
opened the door to greet us, I was calm.

Sid stepped to one side as the reverend hurried inside,
pulling me behind him. It was a real kitchen, with cupboards
all around, not a cup in sight, and a chrome table gleaming
to one side. Voices chattered through an open doorway that
led into the sitting room, and to its right was a smouldering
wood stove. And to the right of the wood stove was a darkened hallway with a curling bannister leading upstairs.

"Did you get everyone?" the reverend asked as Sidney
Kidney brushed past us to take a stand in front of the darkened hallway.

"Yes, sir," said Sid.

"Landsakes, Reverend, where've you been; everyone's
waiting," Mrs. Ropson said worriedly, hurrying into the
kitchen from the sitting room. Her mouth dropped when
she seen me, her eyes quickly scanning my stained, ripped
nightdress, swollen eyes and wet, limp hair. "Goodness,
mercy, why'd you bring her here . . . "

Her words trailed off as May Eveleigh appeared in the
doorway behind her, then Mr. Haynes and his wife, and
Jimmy Randall with the chewed-off ear—all wearing their
Sunday clothes, and crowding in through the kitchen, their
eyes brailling over me, and their mouths opening and closing in speechless wonder as they took in the sight that I was.

"Found her wandering in the snow," the reverend said,
looking me over as if I was some rare duck.

"Where was Drucie?" gasped May.

"Nowhere to be seen, neither was the mother," said the
reverend.

"Landsakes, keep her on the mat," Mrs. Ropson cried

out, coming towards me holding out her hands, more to keep me at bay than to touch me. "Sidney, go on to your room, what with your bad cold. Quick—first get her a chair, mercy on this day." She bobbed her head from the reverend to Sid as Sid dragged a padded chrome chair over from the table to where I was standing, and what with her arms flapping and the little sacs of fat jiggling around her mouth, I was back to thinking on the old harp seal, again.

"It's a sorry situation," Jimmy Randall said, pumping himself up and down on tiptoe as he noted the reverend doing the same.

"Sorry, indeed. I apologize for being late," the reverend said, turning to everyone and ushering them back towards the sitting room. "But it's a good thing I did decide to go out there and investigate before starting the meeting. Is there tea?" he asked, pausing as Mrs. Ropson prepared to follow behind him.

"Goodness mercy, I forgot to make tea," Mrs. Ropson said, twisting around and hurrying towards the cupboards. "Sidney, come help me make tea, although it's in bed you should be with that flu," she said, swinging open the cupboard doors and rattling the teacups in their saucers as she lifted them down.

"You'll stay with the girl till after the meeting," the reverend said to Sid as he moved to help his mother at the sink. Sid stopped with a half-nod, then turned to me as the reverend shut the door, and motioned for me to sit in the chair he had drawn over from the table. I sat and glued my eyes to the floor as he brought the kettle over to the sink and poured the tea while Mrs. Ropson made quick steps back and forth, back and forth from the pantry to the bin.

"Take a little drop of peppermint in your tea, Sidney," said Mrs. Ropson. "Landsakes, your father knows how bad your asthma gets, he shouldn't have sent you running around, gathering everyone together."

Tea sloshed into a cup, and a spoon clinked against its sides.

"Pour another cup, Mum," Sid urged quietly. There was a silence from Mrs. Ropson, and then more tea sloshing. Then Sid was standing before me, holding a cup of tea in front of my face, its cool, minty steam seeping up through my stuffed nostrils. I accepted, looking no further than the cup, my hands shaking from a cold no fire could warm.

"Here," Mrs. Ropson spoke at last, putting a piece of cake onto a plate and laying it on the chrome table for Sid. "Mind you eats it by yourself. I got to cut up what's left over and you knows it won't last long, for no sooner is a body in another's house than he's wanting something to eat, as if bread taste like tarts coming from someone else's pantry."

She lifted the tea tray off the bin, and whatever crossed her mind when she looked over at me holding onto the cup of tea never got said, for Sid was opening the sitting-room door for her, and with a last fretting look at him, she went inside.

Closing the door behind his mother, Sid looked at me and grinned. Then pressing his lips together as if he had finally found something to protest against, he sauntered straight-backed to the table and cut his piece of boiled cake in half. Placing the second piece on another plate, he brought it before me.

I shook my head.

"If you're worried about it being the last—don't," he said. "She always has more hidden in the pantry."

I accepted the plate.

"Are you afraid they're going to send you to the orphanage?" he asked, dragging another chair from the table over to the stove. He sat down and faced me, his plate balanced on one knee and his cup of tea on the other.

"You look scared," he said, after it become clear I wasn't going to speak.

I kept silent.

"Everybody's afraid of something," he went on, conversationally. "Most times, whatever they're afraid of never happens." He flicked a quick glance over the tail of my dirtied nightdress. "Do you think it might be better if they did send you to someplace else?"

It was a thought I couldn't even think on.

"My place is just fine," I burst out, close to tears.

He shrugged, eating his cake in silence as I fingered the crumbs around on my plate. The murmur of voices coming from the sitting room grew louder. Laying my cup on the plate with the half-eaten cake, I handed it to Sid with a small nod.

"Guess you're not hungry, heh?" he said, and was taking the dishes to the bin when a loud rap sounded on the door and Doctor Hodgins, wearing a tweed winter's coat and a derby, shouldered his way inside, bringing the cold of the evening in with him—and Josie. She was wearing a dark blue coat that his wife used to wear to church, and her hair was tucked neatly beneath a black scarf. Spinning around in the centre of the kitchen, her eyes blazed with yellow as they fell on me.

I leaped to my feet with a cry at the sight of them, and shrank from the shocked look on Doctor Hodgins's face as he took in my dirtied state.

"Go home!" barked Josie, grasping at my arm and trying to hustle me past Doctor Hodgins towards the door.

"Just a minute, Josie," said Doctor Hodgins, raising a hand to stop her. He dropped to one knee to better examine me, and my mouth started to quiver at his show of kindness.

"Hush now," he said, laying a hand on my shoulder. "Tell me what's happened."

"Nothin'," I managed to say, biting back the choked tears on account of Dead Sid watching on. "I got the flu. And I'd gone down the gully to check on ... on her." I cast a miserable look at Josie, then back to Doctor Hodgins. "Then, the reverend came."

"Don't you worry," Doctor Hodgins said. "I'm back now, and everything's going to be fine." He cleansed the scowl off his face and mustered up a smile as the sitting-room door popped opened and Mrs. Ropson peered into the kitchen.

"Good evening, Flossie," he nodded politely, lifting his hat off his head. Mrs. Ropson turned to stone at the sight of Doctor Hodgins and Josie and then, clasping her hand to her mouth, bristled into the kitchen.

"Goodness, Doctor, you startled me, you did. When was it that you got back, then?"

"Just in time, apparently," Doctor Hodgins said, with another nod of acknowledgement as the reverend appeared in the doorway, a grim look on his face. "Josie was nearly froze to death, walking into Haire's Hollow to find Kit." He stopped and drew a concerned look over my bedraggled appearance. "Who isn't exactly dressed for visiting. May I ask what's going on?"

At this point May Eveleigh, Mr. and Mrs. Haynes and Jimmy Randall were all crowding back into the kitchen, and Doctor Hodgins, his dark eyes graven beneath his furrowed brow, nodded in turn to each of them.

"First, may I enquire after Elsie's health?" asked the reverend sombrely as everyone fell silent upon entering the room, and found places to stand alongside the wall.

Doctor Hodgins, still holding his derby, clasped his hands behind him and bowed his head.

"Elsie . . . has passed away."

"God bless her," said Mrs. Ropson woodenly in the silence that fell. Then grew a mingle of murmurs and everyone stood awkwardly between reaching out and touching Doctor Hodgins sympathetically and keeping to their spots.

"It was an easy passing," Doctor Hodgins added slowly. "She's resting in St. John's, next to her mother and father, where she wanted to be. She sends back a fond farewell to all of her friends here." He sent a solemn look around the room that ended with a gentle smile at me, and never in my life had the sight of someone looked so dear.

The reverend gave a little cough and spoke equally as solemnly.

"Her suffering was long. Pray she finds release in God's hands. This Sunday, we'll have a memorial service so's her many friends here can say their final farewell."

"If there's anything we can do . . . " May Eveleigh murmured.

"Pray give the reverend your coat and go sit in the sitting room, I makes you a cup of tea," said Mrs. Ropson, taking another cup down from the cupboard. "Indeed, it's a sad time for all of us; she was a dear, gentle woman."

"A good woman indeed, sir," Jimmy Randall said deeply, nodding to Mr. and Mrs. Haynes as if it was to them that he was making the declaration. They murmured back in agreement and everyone looked towards Doctor Hodgins and fell silent again.

"Your kindness has long been felt," Doctor Hodgins said, accepting a cup of tea from Mrs. Ropson and raising it in salute. "However, it's Kit and Josie who need your kindness right now. What say we finish up this business that has brought everyone together this afternoon."

"Indeed we shall," the reverend said hastily, motioning

everyone back into the sitting room. Mrs. Ropson followed, asking after everyone's tea and offering to bring in some sweet biscuits, if anybody wanted some, and the reverend followed behind her. Doctor Hodgins gave a last, reassuring look towards Josie and me before the reverend closed the door behind them.

Sid and I stood looking at each other, then at Josie, who had fallen quiet upon everyone's presence in the room and was now staring curiously around the kitchen. With her gloved hands resting on the edges of her pockets and her head tilted just so against the brown, curly fur on the collar of her new coat, she looked as if she could have been anybody.

"Take a seat, Josie," Sid said, holding out the chair he had been sitting on.

She sat down, eyeing Sid with the same intrigue she had just given his mother's shiny chrome table as he crossed the kitchen in two swift strides, then was back, offering her a piece of boiled cake on a plate. She accepted his offer, then watched as he beckoned me to follow him down the darkened hallway. I hesitated for a second, then looking at Josie with a finger to my lips for quiet, followed after Sid. The voices from the sitting room grew louder as we come before a French glass door, its windows covered with a white sheer curtain. I crept closer and peered through. The men were all standing around the women, who were sitting on a divan, except for Mrs. Ropson, who was sitting in a plump, overstuffed armchair with a crocheted shawl covering its back. She pulled the shawl down around her shoulders as we watched, her eyes fastened on the reverend, who was busy talking to the room at large, his gesticulating hands expanding on his thin, whispery voice.

"It wasn't a healthy picture I saw when I went out there,

Doctor, despite all you've done for the family. There was no fire lit, and the girl was outdoors in her pyjamas, loaded down with the flu. She looked as if she was half-frozen."

"Landsakes, the state of her when the reverend brought her in," Mrs. Ropson joined in, her lips quivering excitedly as she looked from one to the other. "Throwing up in the car, and her lips blue with cold. It's scandalous. It was good of you to try and help, Doctor, but we all had our concerns about Drucie taking on such a load. And now it's come to this."

The reverend give a sharp cough and brought everyone's attention back to him.

"My wife and I aren't the only ones with concerns for the girl," he said, looking at Mr. Haynes expectantly.

Mr. Haynes cleared his throat and strolled to the front of the room, his hands deep in his pockets, and his nose a pinkish hue.

"I do have concerns," he said, looking from Doctor Hodgins to the reverend. "Kit's been missing a fair bit of school. Plus her clothes don't look cleaned most days, and her hair is never combed. And there are other things." He tipped back on his heels and glanced around at the others the way he often did in school when he was about to start up a lesson. "She don't get along well with others. Sits by herself all the time." He shrugged. "Of course, the others make fun of her, especially when the mother is . . . about."

"Well," May said in the silence that followed, "I don't know about everything else, but I knows there's not much flour and yeast being bought. I wonder what they're eatin' without bread. And there's a bill growing . . . "

"Drucie never was that tractable," Jimmy Randall spoke up, fingering his chewed-off ear. "And even if she was, I can't imagine anyone, not even Josie Pitman, wantin' to eat her bread, what with her droolin' into it the way she does." He ended off with a satisfied look at the reverend, and shifted uncomfortably with the quiet that greeted his say. Then all hands turned to Mrs. Haynes, who had yet to speak. She raised her eyes from studying the rings on her fingers and shrank back a little from the encountered stares. Swallowing with great difficulty, she looked to Mr. Haynes and spoke quietly.

"The girl shouldn't have to suffer."

"There you have it, Doctor," the reverend spoke, as if all of what had been said was purely for Doctor Hodgins's benefit. "Short of being taken in, there's not much else can be done for Kit and Josie, and I can't imagine who, as kind as the people are in Haire's Hollow, would be willing to take in a full-grown woman and her girl; especially with the problems the mother herself presents. And, as was made clear when the girl was first born, it's not proper to separate the two, especially now as they've been together for this long. I feel there's but one proper alternative that would be suiting to them both, and that's the Sisters of All Mercy in St. John's. I have a friend there, the Reverend Saunders, that would pay special attention to their care." The Reverend Ropson paused, looking more grimly at Doctor Hodgins. "As attached as you are to the family, Doctor, it wouldn't be fair to keep them in their dire circumstances any longer."

Doctor Hodgins listened quietly while they spoke, a sad little smile turning up the corners of his mouth, one that appeared to be more for them, rather than for the sad picture they were painting of me and Josie.

"How's Kit's grades?" he asked, turning to Mr. Haynes.

"She's always managed to maintain good grades, Doctor," said Mr. Haynes.

"How good?" asked Doctor Hodgins.

Mr. Haynes shrugged.

"Very good."

"An A student?" persisted Doctor Hodgins.

Mr. Haynes nodded.

"She could go far if she had the chance," he added.

"Any disciplinary problems these days?"

"Not... disorderly, certainly."

"Must make it easier for you, not having to reach for the strap as often," Doctor Hodgins said evenly.

Mr. Haynes shoved his hands back in his pocket and looked over to May Eveleigh, seemingly anxious to escape Doctor Hodgins's attention.

"It's a long ways she has to walk to school. I don't suppose the wind might have something to do with her unkempt appearance?" Doctor Hodgins asked of no one in particular while circling around to where May Eveleigh was perched on the edge of the divan. Laying a hand on her shoulder, and in a suddenly softened tone that alarmed me by its trembling, he went on to say, "It's good of you to allow for the bill, May. There would be many pots without a pudding if not for your charity over at the store. I think everyone here would agree with that."

May nodded primly.

"I do's my best, although it's not always easy, especially now in the wintertime with no fish being sold and everything on credit."

"And there's those that never pays," Jimmy Randall burst out with a surly shake of his head. "You be an angel to keep 'em on, May."

"It's God's work, for sure," Mrs. Ropson said, throwing back the shawl and rising from her seat. "Would you like some more tea, May? How about you, Jimmy?"

"As I was saying," the reverend said, rubbing his clasped hands together as if they were cold. "It'll be a relief for the girl to have her mother taken care of. I've arranged it so's they can both stay in the same room."

"Did you ask her if she was cold?" Doctor Hodgins asked, smiling his thank-you as Mrs. Ropson refilled his cup.

The reverend raised his brow.

"Pardon me?"

"Your concern is that Kit was freezing to death," Doctor Hodgins said. "She's going on fourteen; they're as young as that bearing babies along the shore. Don't you think Kit's old enough to figure out if she's cold or not, and to put on extra clothes if she was?"

The reverend sighed.

"You saw her out there, Doctor. She was outdoors in a ragged nightdress."

"Her grandmother's flannelette nightdress, what Kit always wears when she's missing Lizzy. Is there none of us here who don't understand the peculiarities of grief?" Doctor Hodgins tiredly circled the room. "Perhaps things did get a little out of hand the past couple of days, what with Drucie, Kit and her mother all coming down with the flu, the same flu that's knocked out most of Haire's Hollow, so's I've been told. And isn't what's happening here today a just enough reason as to why Kit wouldn't approach any of you for help with chopping a little firewood?" He ended his say with his eyes on May, who hung her head the way Josie did once, when Nan caught her stealing the hard green candies out of her apron pocket.

"Mercy, Doctor," Mrs. Ropson said, laying down the tea pot none too gently. "You can see for yourself the condition of the girl."

"It—it's her mother's runnin' around the way she does, too," Jimmy Randall protested. "It's not a thing for a young girl to be growin' up with."

Doctor Hodgins held up his hand like one who has had enough of a bad tonic.

"Josie Pitman does in public what every man here has done in the privacy of his thoughts and elsewhere. Come, come now, May," he added at her shocked gasp, "there's none of us lily white, and in your business you would know that. Do we take it upon ourselves to judge and punish our neighbours when our own slates are just as smeared?"

"I'm for doin' what's right," May said. "And leavin' a girl to care for her retarded mother don't seem to me to be right."

"And it's right you are to be concerned," Doctor Hodgins agreed. "We all know Josie's limitations, it's her strengths that we don't know. Kit and her mother should be given a chance to take care of each other, providing we, as a community, help from the outside. Drucie might not be the best housekeeper that ever was, but she's the closest thing to family that Kit has. Another year and she won't be needing anybody to see over her. She's strong, is Kit, and more grown up then her size would have you believe."

The reverend took a step closer to Doctor Hodgins and spoke with an angry snort.

"Is the state of her sitting out there an indication of how well she takes care of herself?"

Doctor Hodgins turned on the reverend like a coiled spring ready to snap.

"It's how you would have her, reverend!" he said in a half-whisper.

A silence fell as both men stared at each other, then, "How can we make it better?"

It was Mrs. Haynes that spoke. And what with her hardly ever speaking, it was enough to bring everyone's attention away from the strained air between the doctor and the reverend and focus on her.

"I . . . could bake bread for them," she offered, her eyes shifting from her husband's, and her voice fading fainter with each spoken word.

It was as if the sun rose on Doctor Hodgins's face.

"God bless you," he said deeply, grasping both her hands off her lap and shaking them. "It's in the hearts of people like you where miracles are born, and where would we be without miracles? For Kit and Josie aren't the only two orphans Haire's Hollow has inherited. With Elsie gone, I'm as needy as they are for a pair of worsted socks and a loaf of baked bread."

May Eveleigh gave a quick laugh.

"Blessed Lord, there's many as would be pleased to knit you a pair of socks, Doctor, for all what you've done around here."

"You're right in that, May my dear, there's many a way to pay a bill, for sure," Doctor Hodgins agreed, smiling happily. "Although some things require money and for my part, I'll be willing to pay for any extra food Kit and her mother need, plus clothes. Put it on my bill, May. As for the rest, I'll let you women decide what has to be done. After all, it's the women who carry forth most of God's work in any community. What do you say, Mrs. Ropson?"

"I—it's for the reverend to say," Mrs. Ropson said, coming out of her frozen state and busying herself with putting the tea things back on the tray.

There was a silence as all hands turned to look at the reverend. With a smile weaker than water, he spoke in a low, whispery voice.

"It's not how I would have it, Doctor. You've taken it out of my hands. However, we will do our Christian duty. Sidney will start as of tomorrow going out to the gully and splitting wood for the woman and her girl."

It was hard to tell what come first, the look of surprise on Doctor Hodgins's face or the horrified gasp sounding from Mrs. Ropson.

"Sidney! Heavens, no." She dropped the cover to the teapot as if she had just discovered it to be a dead rat. "Mercy, Reverend, he's much too sick with asthma to be out in the cold. For sure, Doctor, you know that... "

"The boy needs to build up his strength," the reverend said shrilly, raising a hand to silence his wife. Turning cold, squinty eyes onto Doctor Hodgins, he lowered his voice to little more than a thin whisper. "Unless you have problems with the idea, Doctor?"

"No. No problem. If that's what you want," said Doctor Hodgins, shaking his head.

"He'll start this week. I think it fair to warn you, Hodgins, if I learn of anything going on out there that's not acceptable in a Christian home, I'll have both the girl and her mother on a train heading for St. John's before anyone in Haire's Hollow knows the difference. It's God's work."

I pulled back from the window, casting my eyes sideways onto Sid's, but his face was in shadow.

"Better get back," he whispered as some of those inside stirred to leave. Then he was strutting down the hall in front of me, his proud step a bit much for the queasiness that was starting up in my stomach again.

Josie rose as we entered the room, and none too soon as the sitting-room door opened and Doctor Hodgins bustled through. Making fast work of calling out goodbyes to those still inside, he clapped Sid on the shoulder, then quickly ushered me and Josie out the door and into his car.

"Go home! Go home!" barked Josie as she climbed onto the front seat besides Doctor Hodgins, leaving me to crawl into the back. I held my hands to my upset stomach, attempting to squash the memory of Sid Ropson's satisfied face as he had bid us good night, while holding the door open for our departure. All too soon we were at the gully, and I reluctantly climbed out into the cold evening air, the heat inside Doctor Hodgins's car becoming a comforting pillow.

"You go inside," Doctor Hodgins bade, getting out of the car and following behind. "I'm going to split some wood for a fire."

Josie sank into the rocking chair, her hands shoved deeply into the pockets of her new coat, while I changed into a clean nightdress and sweater, and hauled a pair of woollen vamps onto my feet. After Doctor Hodgins had lit a fire and had gone outside to split more wood for the evening, I lit the lamp and made a pot of tea, shooting quick looks at the back of Josie's scarfed head as she rocked in the rocking chair, her woollen-socked feet resting on the oven door for warmth, and her sniffles muffled as she kept wiping at her nose with the sleeve of her coat.

"This'll do you till tomorrow," Doctor Hodgins said, coming in through the door with a last load of wood. "I'll be back out in the morning to check on you and split some more to do you till Josie gets better—or Sid comes."

I stiffened at the sound of Sid's name and poured Doctor Hodgins a cup of tea. Passing a cup to Josie, I lingered by the stove, busying myself with the teapot.

"I can get you a tub of hot water, if you like," I said to her, ignoring the nausea in my stomach and my body's screaming need to crawl into bed. "To wash your hair."

"Don't want to wash my hair," she muttered, blowing on the hot tea to cool it, and slurping it back. Glowering up at me as I continued to stand there, she rose to her feet in a huff and stomped down the hallway to her room, slopping the tea over her cup with each thumping footstep.

"I'll have a word with her," said Doctor Hodgins, laying his cup on the table. "Don't worry about Sid," he said, squeezing my arm reassuringly as he walked past me. "I got a good feeling about that boy."

He tapped on Josie's room door and was inside for but a minute, then was back.

"She'll be wanting her bath, now," he said, tucking up his coat collar and preparing to leave.

"How'd you get her to change her mind?" I asked with some surprise.

"Easy," he replied. "I told her she would feel much better if she were to bathe and wash her hair." He grinned at my puzzled look. "You have to make connections with things she understands," he said. "If she connects cleanliness with feeling good, then she'll clean herself."

Doctor Hodgins left me there, working that one through. Then Josie was coming down the hallway, kicking the washtub in front of her. I shoved another junk of wood in the stove and raised the wick in the lamp to brighten the room.

CHAPTER TEN

PLANTING SEEDS

THE COLD SPELL HAD GIVEN OVER TO a warm southerly wind and Aunt Drucie had just left for home on the afternoon that Sid first started chopping wood. The straight-back walk and hesitating manner that he usually carried around the school was offset by an easy, loping gait that made him look as if he was half-dancing, that first time I seen him walking down over the bank from the road. He was wearing his black wool jacket, like the reverend's, and a pair of pressed trousers—not the sort of clothes to be cleaving wood with. I watched him through the corner of Nan's room window.

He slowed his step and I peered along with him down the gully. Josie was squat behind a rock, watching him with the same intensity as myself. Feeling kind of foolish, I tightened the ribbon around my ponytail and, buttoning up my sweater, went out on the stoop to greet the reverend's spy.

"Did I overstep the bear trap?" he asked with a faint, lopsided grin, rolling his eyes to Nan's bedroom window, then over to where Josie was still hiding.

I nodded towards the axe and the chopping block sitting next to a mountain of birch junks, and stepped back inside.

"Hey, wait . . . " he called out, but the door was already slamming shut. Dumping my school books onto the table, so's he'd have something Christian like to report back to the reverend should he happen to fall up against one of the windows and peek inside, I picked up a catalogue and lay back on the daybed.

An hour must've went by and gradually the fitful thud thudding of the axe and the occasional burst of muffled mutterings gave way to a more regular thud thud thud and a tuneful whistling. Getting up to shove a stick of wood in the stove, I took another quick peek through Nan's room window, this time, standing far enough back so's not to be seen. His jacket was lying stiffly across a junk of wood, and he stood with his white shirt sleeves rolled up, and streaks of sweat trickling down his face. He didn't look as stiff without the jacket and its extra padding puffing up his shoulders. Standing the axe by the side of his leg, he arched his back and rubbed at his neck, looking curiously over at Josie who was still crouched behind the rock, watching him. Slipping back into the kitchen, I poured a jug of water and, taking a glass off the bin, went out onto the stoop. A cup of tea deserved a glass of water.

Ignoring the glass, he reached gratefully for the water jug and, lifting it to his lips, drank till he was red in the face.

"Can I get you anything else?" I asked as he lifted the jug back down.

"Water's fine," he said, wiping at his mouth with the back of his hand. "What's you doing, in there?" he asked, looking curiously over my shoulder inside the house.

"Studyin'," I said primly.

"What're you studying?"

"Oh, English and stuff."

"Hah, stuff! That's what I like studying best. Stuff."

Thinking he was making fun of me, I made to go inside.

"Hey, wait! Here!" he called out. "You forgot this." He took a step closer, handing over the jug. "So, ah, what kind of stuff do you like best?" he asked as I ignored the jug and gave him a haughty look.

"If it's fun-makin' you come here to do, then you can just leave agin," I said, preparing to dart inside.

"Fun-making! About stuff?" he asked incredulously, bringing the jug before his chest and clasping it with both hands. "I don't fun-make about stuff. Leastways, not what I call stuff. Have you ever read about the man who tried to drink the ocean dry?"

I stood quiet.

"Well, he couldn't do it," he said, bending over and pouring what was left of the water over the back of his head.

"Why would he try?" I asked.

"Just to see if he could."

"Sounds stupid."

"Might be," he said, flicking the water off his hair and pushing his glasses back up his nose. "Might be that if it could've been done, he would've done it."

"That's even more stupid," I muttered, stepping back inside.

"Well, that's the kind of stuff I study," he called out before I had a chance to shut the door. "Things that don't have reason until you attach reason to it."

I slammed the door and went back to studying my catalogue. After a while, I managed to shut out the thud thud thud of the axe biting into the birch junks, and was dozing nicely when a loud yelp startled me to my feet. Dashing outside, I stood on the stoop and groaned. Sid was standing there, water dripping off his head and shoulders, and the galvanized water bucket, upside down by his feet. Bounding down over the gully was Josie, barking out her crazy laugh.

"Why'd she do that?" Sid growled, taking off his sloshed glasses and tossing them on top of his coat.

"Might be just to see if she could," I say.

He looked at me with a scowl, then tore after her.

"You mightn't want to do that," I warned, but he was off and running, his gangling arms and legs fighting to plough through the deep snow.

It was a while later that they both trudged back up, him holding onto his ribs and walking with a slight limp, and her with water dripping out of her hair and wearing the dirty grin she use to give Nan any time she carried on inside the house and escaped the sting of Nan's wet dishrag for having done so. For the rest of the afternoon that he stayed there splitting wood, she sat on the stoop watching him, barking out laughing at most anything he said to her, and winging snowballs past his ears whenever he sang out her name teasingly.

She took to sitting on the stoop each time he came, her head following the swinging of the axe as he hoisted it over his shoulder and swung it into a birch junk, and listening to each word he spoke as he kept up a steady stream of chatter.

"Birch is the best for splitting," I'd hear him say from my spot by Nan's room window. "For when the frost sets in, a baby can swing the axe and split the biggest, toughest junk in half with just one swing. Here, let's see your swing," he'd coax and she would snatch the axe out of his hand and start swinging every bit as good as him—and probably faster—while he sat back, rubbing a soothing thumb over his galled palms. "It just keeps you knowing that things aren't always as hard as they might appear, sometimes. Wouldn't you say so,

Josie?" he'd say as he watched her slice the axe down through the biggest, knottiest junks.

She'd bark in agreement and it got so I could hear her laughing the second she spotted him walking down the gully. It seemed she never tired of listening to him talk and watching him swing that axe. And during those times when he'd nip a strip of birch rind taut between his thumbs and forefingers and blow on the edge of the rind, making a loud, shrill whistle, she'd squeal and press her hands to her ears, and chase him around and around the chopping block. Often, he'd whip around and, grabbing hold of her hair, tie it in a knot beneath her chin. Then he'd bolt for the gully with her after him like a surly dog, up and down the gully till she'd finally catch him and wrestle him into a snowbank in a different kind of knot.

"Doesn't it bother you, his comin' out here all the time?" I asked her one evening as we were finishing off supper and Aunt Drucie was taking a nap in Nan's rocker.

"Who comes all the time? He don't come all the time," she said with scorn.

"Nan wouldn't like it," I said, stacking up the dirty plates.

"She would like it," Josie barked, thumping her fist on the table and glaring at me. "She would like it," she shouted again as I ignored her and carried the dirty dishes to the bin.

"What would Nan like about it?" I asked. "What do you like about it?"

She glared at me some more, and then for the first time since I could remember, she burst into giggles.

"Sid's silly," she said, getting up from the table and heading for the daybed.

"Sid's silly," I mimicked, throwing a handful of detergent into the dishpan. "You come help me wash dishes."

"You wash dishes. I don't wanna wash dishes."

"You never wash dishes."

"Heh, Kit, just pour the water and I'll help you with the dishes," Aunt Drucie mumbled from the rocker.

"It's all right, I can do them," I said, pouring the hot water from the kettle into the dishpan. But inside of me, it wasn't all right at all. It picked at me how Josie would do just about anything Sid asked her, and not give me a second look no matter how many times I might ask her to do the one thing. And it also picked at me how Sid came and went as he liked, without ever knocking on the door to say good afternoon, that he was here to start chopping wood now, or goodbye, that he had finished chopping wood and was leaving now. He just came and went as he liked, which was most every second day after school, traipsing around the gully with Josie at his heels like a well-trained dog. And, too, with Sid's coming, Josie was becoming a handful to manage, always wound up and stomping around twice as noisily as she had when Nan was about. Not that I minded the time she spent fooling around with Sid. It was a relief having her outside finally, and not moping around the house. But with Sid's coming, the gully was more noisy than it used to be. And gone, too, was the chance to sit on the stoop, your back resting against the door, feeling the sun on your face, for he would always be watching, any time I come to the door, with his sneaking, sideways looks, and silly questions about *stuff*.

"My, I haven't seen her this lively since Lizzy died," Aunt Drucie half whispered one day, coming up behind me in Nan's room during a particularly noisy wrestling match and peering over my shoulder. Startled, I gave Aunt Drucie a haughty look and, marching out of the room, hauled on my boots and coats. Perhaps Crooked Feeder might be a place to get some quiet and privacy, I muttered. Snapping the door behind me, I headed down the gully, ignoring Sid and Josie in a heap by the chopping block. Within the minute, he was striding besides me.

"I thought you was here to chop wood," I grumbled.

"Let's not forget the spying part," he said.

I sniffed.

"Seen anything unchristian like, yet?"

"Only in your ungrateful attitude towards my act of charity."

"Act of spyin', you mean."

"Well, you've a right to be snotty, it was corn you planted, and you got radishes," he replied, scooping up a handful of snow and letting it drift at Josie who was trailing behind. "It's those that plant corn and then cry when they grow corn and not radishes that got no room to weep."

I just kept on walking down the snow-banked gully and onto the beach.

"Now, there are those who *thought* they were planting radishes," he went on, keeping step besides me, "but planted corn instead. Perhaps someone switched their seeds, or perhaps they thought corn was radishes, or that corn had the same taste as radishes. But they still planted the seeds, and *that*, you see, is what gets noted in the end, the seeds you planted up front."

I came to a stop and looked him full in the face.

"Is you my radish?"

He grinned, his eyes slits of blue behind the lenses of his glasses.

"Lots of good can be done with a radish."

I was spared having to answer by a fury of white charging out of the snowbank and whumping him in the stomach. Turning on my heel, I marched back up the shore. It appeared the days of doing anything alone in the gully were over.

It was a few weeks later that things came to a head. Unpinning the clothes off the line while Aunt Drucie finished off the supper dishes, I shut out the best as I could the sight of Sid taking on the biggest birch junk in the pile and carelessly swinging the axe with one hand, while keeping up a steady stream of yakking to Josie. Slewing his eyes my way to see if I was looking, he went into his speech about nothing being as hard as it seemed, and was just coming to the end of it, when the axe popped off a knot and bounced back, nearly hitting him on the lips. Josie leaped up from her seat, clapping her hands and snorting with laughter.

Taking another swing at the junk, he jumped back again as the axe bounced off the same knot. Then he turned the junk around and took another swing, this time getting the axe stuck. Prying it free, he attacked the junk from a different angle, but ended up getting the axe stuck all over again. I could tell that Josie's ongoing barking and clapping was starting to get to him on account of the red coming and going in his face. But he never said nothing, just kept grinning and prying till he got the axe free. Then, he laid the junk on its side and started chopping. He chopped and chopped, turning the piece of wood this way and that, till the pulp surrounding the knot was a mass of splintered shards. And still he never put a scratch on the knot. And when the junk was splintered so much that it finally come apart, the knot was sticking up from one of the halves, as round and as intact as a steel pipe.

"You might got to work harder on some things, that's all," he said, swinging the axe down in one last triumphant swing across the knot.

Then they were both clasping hands, dancing and screaming. At first I didn't know whose blood it was that was spreading over their hands and dripping crimson onto the snow. Dropping the sheet I was folding, I ran to them the same time as Aunt Drucie come running out of the house.

"Lord above, lemme see, lemme see," Aunt Drucie cried, trying to pull their hands apart, and then I seen the gash on the back of Sid's hand, clear down to the bone, and felt the breath ooze out of me. When I spluttered awake, Aunt Drucie's pointy, wrinkled face was staring down at me as she held the water bucket in her hands, ready to slouze me again. I held up my hand to ward her off and saw that Sid was slumped weakly by her side. Behind them Josie was dancing and singing out like she'd gone mental, "Doctor Hodgins! Doctor Hodgins! Run! Doctor Hodgins! Doctor Hodgins!"

"Sweet Jesus, run," Aunt Drucie chimed in, scooping another handful of water out of the bucket and dousing my face. And then she was hauling Sid to his feet, and me to mine. "Hurry on and get to the doctor, Christ Almighty, get to the doctor!"

Then Sid and I were chasing after Josie, who was half running, half leaping down the road to Haire's Hollow, a trail of blood staining the snow behind us. Taking no time to talk with anyone, we raced past Old Joe on the wharf, and Maisie Parsons and a bunch of youngsters on the road, and got to the clinic where Sid near fainted again when he held out his gashed hand to Doctor Hodgins. I collapsed in a chair, dropping my head between my legs while Josie helped Sid lie back on the examining bed for Doctor Hodgins to better stitch him up.

"There's nothing here that won't heal in a couple of days," Doctor Hodgins said, examining the cut before sinking the needle into it. "Just keep it steady now, it's only blood."

The stitching was mostly done when Mrs. Ropson blowed in through the clinic door.

"What have they done to my Sidney? Oh, Lord, Lord!" she shrieked, turning whiter than Doctor Hodgins's coat as she seen the doctor sticking the needle through Sid's hand.

"It's O.K., Mum," Sid managed weakly, rising his head up off the pillow.

"Ooh, my God, my God!" Mrs. Ropson sank down on a chair, and let her head flop back against the wall.

"Calm yourself," Doctor Hodgins said. "Sid's going to be fine, thanks to Josie for getting him here as fast as she did."

A wail cut forth from Mrs. Ropson's gaping mouth as Josie turned her blood-splattered face towards her. Then she fainted dead away, her body rolling off the chair and thumping to the floor, sprawling at my feet like a beached whale. Sid tried to sit up, but Doctor Hodgins gave him another jab with the needle.

"Leave her where she's the least trouble, son. Kit, get a wet cloth for Mrs. Ropson. We're almost done."

Pouring some water onto a rag, I dropped it onto Mrs. Ropson's face and stood back as she blubbered to. Lumbering to her feet, she fell heavily onto her chair.

"Mercy, what happened? Can somebody tell me what happened?" she asked pitifully.

"I chopped my hand with the axe," Sid said weakly. "It's nothing."

"Nothing!" Mrs. Ropson repeated in astonishment. "You got your hand near chopped off and it's nothing?"

"He still has ten working fingers," Doctor Hodgins said matter-of-factly. "There you are, Sid. All finished. Keep it clean and get in here tomorrow for me to have a look at it. It'll be a week before you can handle an axe, again."

"Handle an axe, again!" Mrs. Ropson charged to her feet, and glared down at Sid's face. "You won't be going back to that hole of a gully on this day—or never no more. And

God forbid if I ever catches you with an axe in your hands again, not even if the good Lord strikes your father dead tomorrow and we freezes to death ourselves, will you ever touch another axe!"

"Mum, now stop it, Mum," Sid begged. He climbed down off the bed and tried to turn her towards the door, but she was as wound up as ever I'd seen anyone, and turning her attention to Doctor Hodgins, let loose with another mouthful that sounded like she'd been saving up for some time.

"You can find somebody else to do your charity work, Doctor. There's enough men going back and forth out there that you don't need Sid to chop wood. Only for looking bad in front of the others that I permitted it, but no more. It's enough that we do, what with the reverend always lending himself out . . . "

"All right, Mum, let's go home," Sid cut in loudly, shoving her towards the door and looking back apologetically at me and Doctor Hodgins.

"And there's where you'll be staying once we gets there," Mrs. Ropson went on as the door shut behind them. "That I'll guarantee you, my son . . . "

Their voices faded away and Doctor Hodgins, looking wearily from me to Josie, pulled out the drawer to his desk and took out three red suckers. Popping one in his mouth, he tossed one each to me and Josie and, leaning back in his chair, lifted his feet to rest on the top of his desk.

"Just when you think you've had every kind of day," he said, his words thick around the candied knob. Josie grunted and we popped our suckers into our mouths and all three sat there for some time, sucking on our suckers and getting our breath back.

CHAPTER ELEVEN

A LIGHT OF WOOD

THE NEXT DAY WE WERE COMING out of school for lunch when I saw Sid leaning against the snow-capped post of the schoolyard, his black wool jacket unbuttoned, and his throat pink against the white of his shirt, as if he had been walking against the wind. He started towards me, then stopped when Margaret Eveleigh caught hold of my arm, and her and her crowd of best friends, all wrapped in matching scarfs and caps and mitts, circled around me, the way they always did since the day of the meeting when Margaret took it on as her Christian duty to watch over me at school.

"Are you all right, Kit?" she asked, her ringlets falling over her shoulders as she looked me up and down. "My gawd, you must've got some fright when your mother near chopped off Sid's finger."

"It's not his finger," I mumbled, standing still while she sized up my blue scarf Nan had knitted and the green mitts that Nan had argued was the same colour.

"Poor Mrs. Ropson, she was in some state leavin' the

clinic," Melanie Saunders said, chewing on the end of her pigtail and peering intently into my eyes. "And she told Mom Sid wouldn't allowed to go choppin' wood for you, no more."

"I knows he wouldn't bawlin'," said Margaret, flicking a dust mote off my collar. "Sure, he was like the baby when he had the mumps that time, and his mother was makin' him take the medicine. Spotty-faced Sid! Did you get the new blue ribbon Mom brought out to you?" she asked, peering around to the back of my head. "You should wear your hair in ponytails more often, Kit."

"Ooh, there's Sid with his finger now," curly-haired Sarah Brett cried out.

"Let's go see it," Margaret breathed. Then they were off, leaving me feeling like a shipwrecked corpse as they skipped on to something a little more stinky further on down the shore—which, in this case, happened to be Sid.

I made it to my rock in the back of the schoolyard without attracting any further attention, and leaned back against the school, looking up over the dense, green woods. The wind sounded a dull rush, kneading through the trees, thickly padded with heavy, wet snow. I snuggled more comfortably inside my coat and was pulling a piece of jam bread out of my lunch bag when Sid popped around the corner, his breath fanning out in front of him, and his ears a bright red.

"Phew, what torment," he said, rolling his eyes and squatting besides me.

I gave a sympathetic smile and, staring straight ahead into the woods, nibbled on my bread crust.

"Doctor Hodgins said it's healing fine," he said, holding up his bandaged hand. "How's Josie?"

"She's fine."

"Heh," he laughed. "I guess she got quite the fright."

"Yeah!"

"How is she?"

"She's fine."

There was silence. Then, without straying my eyes from the woods, I said, "She's tryin' to cleave all the wood so's you won't have to do it."

"Hey, now you tell her to stop that, that's my job. I suppose you think I'm not coming back?" he added after a slight pause. "Don't mind Mum. The worst possible fate is being a lone youngster." He fell silent. Then, "I guess you're a lone youngster, too."

I shrugged.

"That's not how Nan would put it."

"Were you raised as sisters?"

"As daughters."

I felt him staring at the side of my face and wished he would leave now.

"I don't blame Lizzy for hating the reverend," he said, scooping up a handful of snow and moulding it into a snowball. "It's his twisted sense of Christian duty that made him treat her and Josie—the way he did. Hell, there's times I wish the devil'd take them both and spare Christ the bother."

I looked at him, my mouth dropped in shock.

"You heard me," he grinned.

"Were you a crybaby?" I asked, not knowing what else to say.

"More like my mother who's the crybaby. Her arthritis keeps her from getting about the house most days, and with the reverend going off down the shore three to four days out of a week, it's left to me to help her." He shrugged. "What's a lad suppose to do?"

"Who sits with her when you comes out to the gully?"

"I come on the days the reverend's home. So what else do they say about me, aside from my walk, my talk and my being a crybaby?"

"You looks like a ghost."

"Booo hooo," he exclaimed, springing back, a startled look on his face.

I burst out laughing and quickly covered my mouth with my hand.

"That's nice," he said, leaning forward again.

"What?"

"Your laugh. It's the first time I've seen you laugh." Glancing at the school window just above our heads, he stood up and brushed off the seat of his pants. "There's Haynes sneaking a look. I'd better go before he sends another report to the reverend."

"Report?"

"Yeah. He keeps his eye on you. It was him that told the reverend about Josie and you being sick the time of the meeting, remember? Which makes him your spy, and not me, wouldn't you say?" He grinned, then disappeared around the corner of the school.

It was a week to the day that Sid came back to the gully. And on that day he had to fight with Josie to get the axe back. When he threatened to leave again if she didn't give it to him, she threw it down and ran behind the house. She never again sat down and watched Sid chop wood.

It got so that I didn't mind the thumping sound of him wielding the axe into the birch. Lord knows he worked, coming about three to four times a week, splitting wood and chopping splits to start the fire.

"Come on, Josie, help me carry in a load of wood for the night," he'd say when the splitting was done and the wood piled high besides the chopping block. "Fill your arms now, as much as you can carry, that's what we calls a light of wood, not the half-load you got there."

"Too heavy," she'd complain, collapsing against the woodpile as he loaded more junks onto her outstretched arms.

"Nonsense," he'd say, grabbing hold of her shoulder and pulling her forward. "Here, get up now, and in with the load. It's good work, lugging in wood for the fire, for what's a home without warmth."

"Too heavy," she'd bemoan some more, watching him as he squat besides her, stacking his arms full.

"Hah, too heavy," he'd jeer. "How can a light of anything be too heavy when it calls only for that which you can carry. Ain't that right, Kit?" he called out one evening, glancing to where I happened to be standing insides Nan's room, near the window.

When he tired of chopping wood, he worked on a lean-to he started building from the pickets of an old rotting fence half-circling the back of the house. And after it was built, he neatly stacked it full with tiers of split birch. And when he tired of handling wood, he shovelled paths through the snow leading from the door place up to the road, and over to the lip of the gully. "For the Silent One," he used to tease whenever I came out the door on sunny days and went looking for a quiet spot to sit down by Crooked Feeder. Oftentimes he'd follow me, but his ongoing wrestling and snowball fights with Josie slowed him down considerably, and by the time he'd trace my footsteps to whichever nook was sheltering me from the wind, I was usually feeling a bit chilled and starting back home again.

Sid wasn't the only one coming to the gully on a regular basis. True to her word, May Eveleigh come every Saturday morning with a box of groceries and whatever garments of clothes she thought Josie and I might need. Jimmy Randall's wife made the occasional trip, bringing over enough pairs of knitted socks, mitts and scarves to keep a flock of sheep sheared. Others came too from Haire's Hollow, with their cleaning buckets and paint brushes, and in no time the house was cleaner than it ever was with poor Nan, or me and Aunt Drucie, trying to keep up with it. I thought they might've asked what colour I liked best, for they painted my room in a pink so bright that Pirate refused to come in during daylight hours on account of the brightness making him squint. I don't think Josie liked hers either—yellow, the colour of mustard. She hated mustard. And all three of us—me, Josie and Aunt Drucie—screwed up our faces at the green they painted the kitchen. Thankfully they left Nan's room alone, for I don't think Nan could've borne it, as dead as she was, to have the women from Haire's Hollow rooting through her room the way they rooted through mine and Josie's while they worked.

I never minded Mrs. Haynes. Bringing her bags of hot, buttered sweet buns down from the car, she walked so carefully that I always felt as if it were her that was needing help. And she was always jumpy, especially when Pirate pounced out unexpectedly from behind a bush or the daybed. She was the only one of the women who didn't plague me with questions such as—did Drucie drool into her bread dough, and did Josie have a man friend these days, and had I started menstruating yet and, everyone's favourite, did I know who my father was? Nor did she eye the garbage box behind the stove, searching, as the other women were always doing, searching . . . always searching . . .

It was May Eveleigh who found my box of coloured glass. She brought it out on the door stoop one sunny Saturday afternoon, while I was sitting on a rock in the gully,

watching the last of the winter's ice being broken away from
the rocks and carried along by the swollen waters. Josie sat
on a birch junk by the wood pile, watching Sid carve a spin
top out of a sewing-cotton reel.

"Is it safe to have all this glass in your room?" she asked,
lifting off the lid and shaking the pieces of glass around.
I started up in dismay as a feather belonging to the robin
fluttered outside and drifted to the ground. Seeing the box
in May's hand, Josie scrabbled to her feet and dashed inside
the house, knocking May against the door jamb as she did so.

"Landsakes, what's got into her?" May asked.

Before either Sid or I could answer, Josie was ducking
back out, clutching a small cardboard box similar to the one
May was holding, and darted off down the gully.

"What's that she got there?" May asked, staring after her.

I didn't know. I had never seen the box before. Walking
slowly towards May, I held out my hand for mine.

"Not before you tells me what you're doin' with all this
glass," she said, holding it out of my reach.

My nostrils flared. It felt like I was being smothered. But
no words came.

"It's Josie's," Sid said, coming to stand besides me. "Kit's
been hiding it from her. How did you find it?"

May started at Sid's cutting in like that.

"It . . . was on the floor by Kit's bed. I struck it with my
foot when I laid Kit's new stockin's on her dresser." She gave
me a tight smile as she handed back the box. "There's a new
ribbon on your dresser. Mind you comes into the store
tomorrow, and I measures you for your graduation dress."

I took the box and stared at her as she called out her
goodbyes to Aunt Drucie. Smiling at Sid, she walked slowly
up over the bank towards her car.

"Nosey whore!" Sid muttered as she passed out of earshot.

"What's that you say?" Aunt Drucie asked, coming out on the stoop, wiping her hands in her apron.

"I said close the door, Drucie, you're letting the heat out," Sid said, bending over to pick up the feather. "Here you go, Kit. What say we go find Josie?"

Laying the box down besides the stoop, I followed Sid down the gully, taking care not to slip on the muddied sides of the brook.

"It's because they're whores that they snoop around like that," Sid burst out.

"It's because Josie's a tramp," I replied quietly, in no mood for more of Sid's preachings.

"Only difference between a tramp and a whore is a tramp looks like a tramp all the time, and some whores never look like tramps," he said back. "And they're the worst kind because they're hypocrites passing themselves off as something else."

I shrugged irritably.

"Makes no difference."

"Hell it don't. Who are they to call Josie a tramp when they're nothing but hypocrites whoring their souls? The clothes and food that they give you?" He snickered. "Nothing more than salve that they smears over their own sins and thinks they're fooling God into believing they're saints."

"They're not all sinners."

"Everyone's a sinner, Kit. Some know it and some don't. Some eat it for breakfast and pass it off as oats. You heard the almighty reverend. Is it for chopping wood, or spying, that he has me coming out here?"

"Mrs. Haynes isn't a sinner."

"Hah! She's the biggest sinner of all. She lets herself be trampled over, then lends a helping hand to you. Why? She's judged you worse off than herself. Haw! You got more gumption in your little toe. At least you fight for what you want."

I kept quiet and concentrated on picking my steps down the flooded gully.

"So, what do you do with broken glass?" Sid asked as we came out onto the beach and headed for Crooked Feeder.

"Nothin'," I said, then added after a short silence, "I used to pretend they were jewels."

"Did you—ever have occasion to wear them?"

I gave him a sharp look.

"Hey! Just asking," Sid said, holding up his hands in mock fear.

"Over my eyes."

"Your eyes!"

"Yes. It made things look different."

"Different? How different?"

"Different colours."

He thought for a minute.

"That's a right smart thing to do," he said, his brow puckering seriously. "See the world through different colours. It's when everyone starts thinking that theirs is the only colour that things start getting hairy."

"I didn't do it because it was smart," I snapped, suddenly tired of Sid's always trying to make things all right. "I did it because it made things look pretty." Spotting Josie's red head further down the shore, I picked up my step and followed after her. Sid hurried along besides me, blissfully quiet for the first time since he started coming to the gully.

CHAPTER TWELVE

MAY EVELEIGH'S THREAT

IT WAS A WEEK BEFORE GRADUATION and I was rambling through the alder bushes picking pussy willows, when I spotted Mr. Haynes's car parked at the turnaround at the end of the road. His window was down and his head was resting on the door, rolling from side to side, and strange snorting sounds were coming out of him. Thinking he was having a heart attack, I crept closer and peered in. His legs were sprawled across the seat and Josie was scrunched up on the floor with her head in his lap and her hair spread out over his hips like a rusty shawl. He was bucking up and down and her head was bucking up and down, and then I seen his thing go in her mouth and she started snorting again, and turning her head from side to side like she didn't want his thing in her mouth, but he had his hands on the back of her head, and his fingers clutched through her hair and pushed her down as he was bucking up, and his breathing was coming faster and faster, and then, just when I was about to yell out that he let her go, his body stopped bucking and his eyes jerked wide opened and strange strangling sounds started coming from his throat, like he had a swile bone caught in his gullet. And then he stopped strangling and Josie stopped snorting, and he was still except for his hard breathing. And then Josie raised her head up from his lap, wiping at her mouth and laughing that loud barking laugh that told she had just pulled something over on someone and had come out on top.

I never really understood what screwing was, but I could tell from the way the older boys ran off snickering and Margaret Eveleigh and her best friends went off shocked whenever someone yelled at me that first year in school that Josie was screwing all of the men in White Bay that it was something that I didn't want to know about, leastways, not as long as my mother was doing it. That evening, staring through the window of Mr. Haynes's car, with the smell of rotting dogberries whiffing out through, I still wasn't sure what screwing looked like. I only knew that Josie was still doing it.

Backing away from the car, I ran home, and dumping the pussy willows at Aunt Drucie's feet as she came yawning to the door, I ran full tilt down the gully, not really caring which rocks my feet landed on, or whether or not I ever made it to the beach without falling and cracking my skull. I was nestled amongst the boulders at Crooked Feeder, listening hard to the waves rolling upon the beach and trying to imagine worlds of gold, when Sid came.

"Drucie said you looked like you'd seen a ghost," he said, edging down amongst rocks besides me.

I kept my eyes closed.

"What's wrong, Kit?"

"Nothin'."

"You saw Haynes's car, didn't you?"

I didn't answer and he stretched out full besides me, parts of him touching parts of me and giving warmth, and the smell of soap and warm skin feeding my nostrils. I opened my eyes. He was leaning on his elbow, looking down at me, his fair-skinned face tanned from his days of splitting wood, and his eyes the colour of ten skies. A shiver caught fire in my belly and I stared back at him, astonished. That such a feeling could ever be ignited inside of me left me emptied of thought, and that it should come whilst my eyes were still burning with the horrid stenching sight of Josie screwing Mr. Haynes was another profundity of God.

I shut tight my eyes and tried to turn away from Sid, but he gripped my shoulder, holding me besides him.

"Kit," his voice sounded a groan as he dropped his head to my shoulder. "Kit, you shouldn't have had to see that."

"She's a whore," I whispered.

"No! No! *She* isn't the whore," he said harshly, holding his face over mine. "I told you before, *he's* the whore. Don't you see that? She's just a big kid, she don't know how else to play."

His breath fanned over my face, warm, and smelling like sweet pickles. I turned away, struggling to overcome the nearness of him and to absorb the rightness of his words.

"He was puttin' it in her mouth," I blurted.

"Huh?"

"His—thing. He was puttin' it in her mouth."

"Oh, Lord," Sid groaned.

"Is that... how you screw?" I asked, looking up at him at last.

His face was reddening and he sat up with another groan, then started laughing in short snorts.

"What's so damn funny?" I gritted, scrabbling to my feet.

"For Christ's sake," he half yelled, pulling me back besides him. "You're always running off."

I leaned forward and wrapped my arms around my knees

and stared out to sea. Finally, he leaned forward besides me, nudging me with his shoulder.

"It's like this," he murmured. I watched, my face growing hot as he scratched out lines in the grey, rocky sand with a stick, and showed where a man's thing is supposed to go, and where he puts it other times, instead.

"It makes more sense when you're doing it," he said, after he'd done with the scratching and looked up to encounter my blank stare.

Feeling my stomach starting to heave, I got up and started walking along the beach towards the gully.

"Hey, what are you running off for now?" he called out.

"May Eveleigh is bringin' over groceries."

He swore and chased after me.

"Look, Haynes is gone," he said, catching up from behind and taking my arm. "You don't have to worry. Come on, let's go sit down for a while."

I shrugged him off and kept walking.

"Supposin' the reverend finds out she's doin' it again?" I asked.

"Who's going to tell? Haynes?"

"It's not just Haynes she's screwin'."

"Kit, listen to me." He grabbed hold of my arm again, his hand warm against my bare skin. "We don't know that she's screwing any other men right now. This could be a one-time thing. Can you not worry about it? I don't want you to be worried."

He spoke so earnestly, and his eyes were so blue. I looked away and saw the blue of the sky, the sea and the far distant hills. Could there be such a world where everything was blue, as blue as the blue of Sid's eyes? I closed my eyes and held my head down, conscious only of the warmth now, of his hand upon my cool skin, and wondered, why on earth, on this day of all days, when I had just caught my mother screwin' my teacher, that I would become so conscious of Sid Ropson's eyes and his touch upon my skin.

"I want to be there when May Eveleigh comes," I finally said.

He slackened his grip, his hand sliding down the length of my arm, his fingers twirling around my wrist before letting it go, and started walking besides me back up the beach to the gully. Josie was hiding in her room when we got back, with her bed jammed up against the door, as she always did whenever May Eveleigh came to visit—a habit she had taken up ever since the day May had come out on the stoop with my box of coloured glass. Aunt Drucie was sitting at the kitchen table, supping on a cup of tea and chatting as May packed away the groceries.

"I can do this," I said, reaching for the bag of peas in May's hand.

"I can manage," May said, holding the bag of peas out of my reach. "How else can I know what you needs, if I don't check out what got eaten last week. Now then, young lady, you were supposed to come in the store and get measured for your graduation dress. How come you never, and I told Margaret a dozen times to remind you at school?"

She smiled as Sid appeared in the doorway, begging a glass of water from Aunt Drucie.

"For sure you're doin' a fine job of cuttin' down that wood pile and keepin' the door place clean," she said as she pulled a blue polka-dot dress out of the grocery box. "Here you are, Kit. Seein' how you never come in and got measured, you'll have to wear one of Margaret's dresses."

"My, now isn't that pretty," Aunt Drucie said, handing Sid his glass of water, and reaching out to finger the starched cotton.

"It's one of her good ones," May said. "Maisie'll have to make another one for Margaret out of that new material I ordered for Kit's. Here," she looked at me accusingly. "Go try it on."

"I'm not goin' to the graduation," I said, as surprised as May at my decision.

"You're not goin'," May repeated. "Why aren't you goin'?"

I shrugged, wishing upon wishing that Sid was out chopping wood where he was supposed to be, and not standing in the kitchen taking in everything that was being said, like an old fishwife.

"Then for sure you're goin' to the graduation," May Eveleigh said in a no-nonsense voice.

"Aye, won't you be wantin' to wear such a pretty dress, Kit?" Aunt Drucie coaxed, lifting the garment from May's hands and holding it out to me. "Here, go try it on now. Like a good girl."

"I'm not goin'," I said stubbornly.

"Don't be foolish, girl," May said irritably. "Now, hurry up and go put on the dress. And you can look a little more pleased, seein' how Margaret was good enough to lend you one of her good ones."

"My, my, Lizzy'd be proud to see you wearin' such a fine dress." Pressing the garment in my hands, Aunt Drucie give me a coaxing grin. "Go on, now, Kittens, try it on."

Taking the dress, I dashed down the hall to my room and thankfully shut the door. Leaning against it for a minute, I looked at the despicable blue polka dots and kicked the thing under the bed. After a few minutes had passed by and I heard Sid back out chopping wood, I picked the dress up, shook it off, and went back out to the kitchen.

"It don't fit," I said, laying it back on the table.

"Well, blessed Saviour," May sighed. "And how am I

supposed to know that when you took it off before givin' me a chance to see it on you? Now, go put it back on," she ordered, leaning her long, reedy body towards me, and what with her wisps of brown hair framing her face, and the brown widow's spots dotting her face, she minded me of a bulrush in the wind.

"I got a dress," I said.

She exchanged an impatient look with Aunt Drucie.

"Let me see it."

I went into my room and brought out the plain red shift I'd worn to Nan's funeral.

"That's too short," May said.

I shook my head.

"It was too short on you at the funeral, it's too short on you now. Now go put that dress back on."

Sid's face appeared in the window behind May, nodding furiously. Whether he was urging me to put the dress on, or not to put the dress on, I didn't care. I wasn't going to put that damn dress on and I wasn't going to no damn graduation dance.

"Arc you goin' to listen?" May Eveleigh demanded.

I shook my head.

"Well!" She looked sourly at Aunt Drucie, then back to me. "I allows if the reverend finds out you're not going to the graduation dance, he might have a thing or two to say about that. After all, it's fittin' in with the rest of the girls that's part of growin' up, and if you're not fittin' in, then perhaps there should be another meetin', now that you're so high and mighty you're not willin' to take our help. And it's been a while since I've seen you in church, not since Lizzy's funeral, I believe."

I listened, watching a fly crawling up the window in front of Sid's face. When May had finished her talk and I still had nothing to say, she snatched the dress off the table and stalked out the door.

"Go catch her, Kit," Aunt Drucie begged. "It was a pretty dress, heh, why wouldn't you want to wear a pretty dress like that, and to your graduation, too? My, my, Lizzy'd turn over in her grave if you never went to your graduation and you gettin' such high grades."

The door pushed open and Sid stalked to where I was standing.

"I was telling you to put the dress on," he said loudly.

"And I was tellin' her the same," Aunt Drucie cried.

"And I'm tellin' you both that I ain't going to no graduation dance," I shouted and ran down the hall with Sid at my heels.

"You heard what the old bat said, Kit," he pleaded. "She can cause trouble."

A loud scraping sounded from Josie's room as she shoved her bed away from the door.

"Who caused trouble?" she barked at Sid, pushing open her room door the second I slammed mine. "May Eveleigh caused trouble. I don't like May Eveleigh."

"Kit!" Sid rapped on my door. "Kit, come out."

"Go away!" I yelled.

"Who go away? You go away!" Josie yelled back.

"You go away!" Sid yelled to Josie. "Kit, please . . . " His words were cut off by what must've been a whump to his stomach, because I heard the wind whoosh out of him in a soft moan. Loud thumps sounded off the walls as they wrestled their way back down the hall, with Sid pleading with Josie to give over, and she barking at him to give over. Then, Aunt Drucie was fussing irritably with them for carrying on in the house, and ushering them out the door. And then there was blessed silence.

Diving across the bed, I buried my face in the pillow.

"Kit!"

I bolted upright.

"Kit! I'll take you to the dance."

I stared in horror at Sid's face peering in through my bedroom window as I lay sprawled across my bed. Reaching over, I snapped the curtain shut and rolled onto my back, hugging the pillow across my face. The minutes ticked by. I listened. Nothing but ear-ringing silence. Sitting up, I lifted the end of the curtain and peeked out. He was nowhere to be seen.

For the rest of the week I stayed in my room whenever I could, not wanting to see Josie, and not wanting to see Sid. At school I showed up just as the bell rang, and raced off the second we were let out for the day. And lunchtime I snuck down behind Old Joe's brother's stagehead and ate my lunch in peace. I imagine he could've caught up with me if he had wanted to. I figured perhaps he understood better than I did as to why I didn't want to see him, and was content to leave me alone with it, which said a lot for Sid, because damned if I could figure out why I didn't want to see him any more.

As for Josie, I couldn't look at her without thinking of Mr. Haynes and his thing going in and out of her mouth. And try as I might, I could only figure one way that Nan would have chosen to deal with her—had it been her looking through Haynes's car window that day. And even if I had been given the courage and strength of Nan, they had taken her gun the same day they had taken the rest of her things after she had passed on.

CHAPTER THIRTEEN

THE GRADUATION DANCE

THE EVENING OF THE GRADUATION CAME and Aunt Drucie had gone home for the day, muttering as she went about the pretty dress I had turned down, and now here I was sitting home by myself on the night of the dance. A car horn sounded up on the road and I stared out the window, watching in dismay as Josie ran up over the bank and hopped inside a blue pickup truck.

Sitting heavily in the rocking chair, I rocked, May Eveleigh's threat about holding another meeting coming back to haunt me. I rocked for another minute, then rose and marched down the hall to my room. Pulling the red shift off its hanger and snatching a reel of sewing cotton and a needle out of the sewing basket, I flounced back into the kitchen and sat back down in the rocking chair. If I was going to that damn dance, it wasn't going to be in a dress that was too short.

The dress unhemmed and then hemmed again, I fumbled through the bottom of Nan's closet and pulled out her black heels that the women had passed over when they had taken everything else belonging to her after she had passed on, and donated to the church sale. Stogging some brown paper in the toes to make them fit tighter, I wobbled around the house for practice while I waited for the iron to heat up.

I wasn't no more out of the gully when I felt the blisters popping out on my heels. Taking off the shoes, I started walking barefoot along the gravelled road, taking care to keep to the deepest tire ruts where the road was hardest packed and smoothest. Waving at Aunt Drucie propped up in her window, I hurried down over Fox Point and slipped the heels back on just before I come to the first house of Haire's Hollow. I waved to Old Joe as he looked up at me from the wharf. I smiled at Doctor Hodgins as he stepped outside his clinic door. Lifting my head, I marched straight past May Eveleigh's store, and ignored Maisie in her window and Elsie in hers, and whoever else might've been peeking through the curtain from the reverend's house. Holding my breath, I marched up to the church basement door and walked in.

There were dozens of teenagers shrieking and running around, and picking at plates of cakes and salads, and supping back glasses of raspberry syrup. From some of the flushed faces of the older boys, I dare say there was the scatter bottle of brew being passed around. I'd been to church dances with Nan before, and this wasn't much different, excepting for the red and white strips of paper and dozens of balloons dangling down from the ceiling, and Happy Graduation made out of pink tissued roses arcing one of the walls. But Nan wasn't besides me on this evening, with her shadow big enough to blot out the all of Haire's Hollow, and when I started walking across that dance floor to the chairs lining the wall on the far side, it felt like every eye in the place was

staring straight at the spot below my knee where the hemline of my dress hung an inch higher than it ought to have
been. And giving the way Nan's feet splayed out like a duck's
when she walked, it was the most I could do to crook up my
toes inside her shoes and take up that extra bit of slack that
the paper didn't, to keep the things from sliding off my feet
in opposite directions as I walked.

Too, one of my stockings was hooked, but I figured
they'd all be too busy staring at my too-short hemline to
notice a run in my stocking. And seeing's how I didn't plan
on moving from my seat once I got there, until it was time
to go home, which to my figuring would be one hour from
now, just long enough for the women to know that I was
growing up proper and saving them from having to come out
to the gully and pack me off to some God-forsaken orphanage in St. John's, there wouldn't be much of a chance for anyone to notice much of anything else about me. And when I
finally made it to a chair and sat down, and crossed my legs
and draped my arms around the front of my knees to cover
where my hemline ended, I let go of my breath and fixed my
eyes on a spot on the ceiling, while steeling my nerves
against the feel of Margaret's and everyone else's eyes
brailling over me and scrutinizing the blue ribbon I had tied
around my ponytail, even though blue was not a colour to be
wearing with red.

Within minutes, the drone of Old Joe's brother's accordion sounded from a distance, and the shrieking gaiety of
everyone dancing to his jig become a muted haze, like when
you're sitting on a rock sometimes, leaning out over the
water following a wave with your eyes till it slips away, and
you follow another one, and another one, until it feels like
you're slipping away with it, far far away, over the wrinkled
face of the sea.

"Kit!"

I looked up startled. It was Margaret. And her flock of best friends. Fluttering around me in their shiny shoes, coloured ribbons and well-hemmed dresses, they all perched around me, with Margaret sitting the closest, pecking me over from head to toe, twittering as they pecked.

"My, that's a nice dress," Margaret said, even though her upturned nose said it wasn't, and, "Why didn't you bring back that blue ribbon Mom brought you and get one to match your shoes? My gawd, couldn't they have gotten Joey Bennet's record player? I can't stand the accordion."

"Ohh, that record, 'Standin' on the Corner,' I loves it," Melissa Haynes said.

"Oh my Lord, look who else is here," Margaret said with drawled-out wonder. "Sidney Kidney. Looking more like a preacher than the reverend."

I struggled to breathe, the air too warm, and all I could think on as I watched Sid striding towards me, wearing his black pressed pants and black pressed jacket, was Rose Parsons, who was as poor off as me, and how she was always chasing after Margaret and her best friends, and how once, at the church dance with Nan, I rose up to go pee and she must've thought that I was coming over to sit besides her because as soon as she looked up and seen me coming towards her, her face went shocked white, as if someone had aimed a spawny caplin at her, and squeezed the guts till the eggs squirted all over her new dress.

"My gawd, he's comin' over," someone shrieked. "He's fixin' on askin' one of us to dance," another chirped, and "Oh my gawd, he's lookin' at you, Margaret, he's goin' to ask you, Margaret," and a flutter of squeals went up, and Margaret leaped to her feet and ran off, and the rest rose in a flutter and fled after her, leaving me feeling as stripped as a bird feeder in a cat house. I glued my eyes to my shoes and fingered the hemline of my too-short dress as he came to stand before me.

"Begging your pardon, your royal highness, your jewels look lovely tonight."

I felt my face flush.

"I've left my looting pirates outside," he said. "At least, for as long as you'll promise to dance with me."

I heard Margaret's twittering breaking through the noise.

"I—I don't want to dance," I stammered, taking a quick glance up at him.

His eyes shone a brighter blue without the covering of his glasses, and a small smile curved the corner of his fleshy, red lips. Bending over, he placed his mouth near my ear and whispered, "Mum just taught me how. It's easy."

I shook my head vigorously, my hands clenching onto my hemline as someone shouted "Sid the Kid" from amongst the dancers on the floor.

Sid stood back up and the look on his face was the one on Rose Parsons's after I had come back from peeing and saw that Margaret and her friends had just ran off, leaving her standing by herself in the middle of the dance floor, and before I could help myself, I jumped to my feet.

"I'll dance."

Another squeal went up from Margaret and her best friends as I walked onto the dance floor with Sid, and steering him away from where they were standing, I tried to keep my leg with the running stocking hidden behind my good one, which was difficult enough to do when I was standing still and not learning how to dance. And all the while I kept stooping down so's the too-short hemline might look as if maybe it was longer, and maybe, just maybe, I prayed that if

I kept my toes scrunched up real good, then the too-big shoes would keep from slipping off my feet and sliding across the dance floor as I tried to keep rhythm with Sid's feet.

It felt like a thousand waves had slipped by before the dance was over. And finally, finally, Sid was walking me back to my chair.

"The reverend's down the bay this evening, and Mum's feeling sick," Sid said, sitting down next to me. "I told her I'd be back early. Would you like for me to walk you back as far as Fox Point?"

I nodded and we both got up and walked across the dance floor to the door. Everybody always noticed whenever me, Nan or Josie walked into the store, the post office, the church or even just down the road. Nobody ever noticed when we left. But they all noticed on this night. And that's how it was that everyone started saying I was Sid's girl.

CHAPTER FOURTEEN

KIT'S MARK

I T WAS A WEEK AFTER SCHOOL HAD LIT out for summer, and Sid had come down the gully to greet me as I was walking back up from Crooked Feeder. Picking up a flat, sharp-edged rock, he skidded it across the water. Picking up another, I skidded it behind his.

"Do you mind what they says?" he asked.

"No."

"Yeah, you do."

"No, I don't."

"I don't believe you."

"I wish I didn't," I whispered, gazing at the spot where my rock had dropped beneath the sea. "But my heart stops beatin' every single, solitary time someone speaks my name or even just looks my way. Every time Josie walks out the door, I'm scared she's not goin' to come back and they're goin' to come and send me away; even when she just goes to the store, I gets sick to my stomach."

Sid stared at me in surprise. It was the most he had ever heard me say in one breath.

"Hey," he said gently, squeezing my arm. "Nobody's ever going to send you away."

"You can't promise me that."

"Sure, I can," he said easily. "Think it through, Kit. You're fourteen, almost fifteen. Soon, you'll be old enough to quit school. Nobody can make you do anything then. You don't have to worry about being sent away any more. That's done with."

"They sent Rose Parsons away."

"That's different. Her mother was too sick to take care of her, so they sent her away to work. She likes it where she is."

"I wouldn't want to be a servin' girl."

"You won't. Sure, Drucie's like a mother, isn't she?"

"I still worry," I said, skidding another rock across the water.

"Then, stop it," he said almost savagely, catching me by the arm, again. "Nobody's ever going to send you away from here, do you hear me?"

I stared into his eyes, my stomach quivering from the nearness of him, then pulled away and started walking up the beach. He followed behind, skidding more rocks out over the water, and whistling a little tune. I smiled, my mind strangely put to rest. Sometimes it felt like Sid had a way of knowing what others didn't, and I was tired of being scared. And it was comforting having him near. More than comforting. It was like swallowing a mouthful of warmed soft drinks and feeling it fizz into my stomach.

We come to the gully and stepped stones all the way up, the spray from the late-spring run-off dampening our feet. Coming to the top, we peeled off our socks and boots and laid them across the top of a rock to dry.

"You have webbed toes," Sid said, sitting down besides me.

"Nan calls them princess's toes," I defended, wriggling them.

"Let's see." Pulling my foot onto his lap, he examined it more closely. All four toes were perfectly webbed, except for the big one.

"How come she called them princess's toes?"

"On account of some princesses havin' to kiss too many frogs."

"Mmm, looks like you been kissing lots of frogs."

I giggled and tried to wriggle my foot out of his hand, but he held on tighter. Then with a sudden look of seriousness, he let go of my foot and cupping my chin, drew my face closer to his. I stared back helplessly as his eyes grazed over my face and came to rest on my mouth.

Suddenly, the sun was blotted and a shadow fell across us. Looking up, we both shrank back to see the reverend standing on the edge of the gully, his face black against the blue of the sky, his voice shaking with rage as he jabbed his finger at Sid and shrilled, "What are you doing with that girl?"

I pulled away from Sid and scrambled to my feet as the reverend slid down the side of the gully and stood jabbing his finger an inch from the point of my nose.

"You! You keep your whoring blood away from my son!"

"She's not a whore!" Sid yelled, scrabbling to his feet alongside of me.

"She's her mother's blood!" the reverend hissed, still staring at me, the loathing in his voice crawling over me like maggots. I struggled to breathe, my nostrils flaring from the smell of rotting dogberries that suddenly clouded the air around me, seemingly reeking from my own body.

"You can't talk to her like that," Sid said from somewhere

besides me, but his words were lost in another fiery blast spewing forth from the reverend's lips.

"Hell's damnation on you this day," he cursed, still jabbing the finger of shame in my face. "You and your tramp of a mother."

"Shut up!" Sid roared, then lunged after the reverend's arm and, grabbing on to it, twisted him away from me. They stood staring at each other. Then the reverend jabbed the same pointing finger to Sid.

"I'll see her gone if you ever come near this place again," he threatened in a thin crackling voice. "Now go!" he ordered, pointing his finger up over the gully to where his car was parked, waiting.

"Don't you listen to him, Kit," Sid said, his voice choked with indignation. Then, throwing a last vengeful look at the reverend, he clawed up over the side of the gully. I took a step back as the reverend turned his darkened face my way.

"Cover your deformity," he uttered with such repulsion that I immediately stood my good foot over the webbed one. "Isn't it enough that we have to witness your mother's?" Then wrinkling his nose as if he was having difficulty breathing past the stink of me, he lunged up over the gully after Sid. Taking care that he was out of sight, I climbed up behind him and peered over the lip of the gully. Josie had come out on the stoop just as Sid had stormed past and was about to chase after him when she seen the reverend swooping down before her, his black-clad arms flapping like a crow's wings. I couldn't hear all of what he was saying, excepting for "deformed, deformed," which shrilled through the air louder then the rest. And I could tell from the tensing of her shoulders and her cowering backwards that she was frightened of him. Then he was hopping up over the hill to his shiny black car. Sid was waiting for him, and after a shouted exchange over the bonnet of the car, nothing of which I could clearly hear, they climbed inside and flew off down the road.

I walked slowly over to Josie, watching the spurt of dust spewing up behind the reverend's car.

"What did he say?" I asked her, my voice a low murmur, my eyes still following the cloud of the dust.

Slap! I howled in shocked pain as the back of her hand came whopping across my face.

"Sid's gone!" she shouted. "You defarmed! Defarmed! Sid's gone!"

Then she was racing down the gully. Rubbing my hand over my face, I ran blindly inside the house. Stogging the stove full of wood, I filled up the water buckets and lifted them to the top of the crackling stove. Making sure the door was good and shut, I dragged the scrubbing tub out from the back room and sat down in Nan's rocker, waiting for the water to heat up. Stinging far more than any welt Josie could land across my face was the feeling of dirt the reverend's words had evoked within me—dirt and shame, dirt and shame. Could water ever cleanse a soul dirtied by shame?

Josie never came home that evening. It was the first time she had stayed away for the whole night since Doctor Hodgins had brought us home from the meeting. What was curious was, there had been no car or truck blowing its horn upon the road. She had simply disappeared down the gully. The next morning she walked in through the door, smelling like the goat, her clothes wrinkled and her hair a tangled mess.

"Where'd you go?" I demanded, meeting her partways across the kitchen.

"Where'd you go?" she shouted, kicking at Pirate as he scooted for the door between her legs. "You defarmed. You defarmed."

"Don't you go kickin' Pirate," I yelled.

"I will kick Pirate. Pirate's deformed. You's farmed."

"It's not my fault the reverend made Sid leave."

"Farmed! Farmed!"

Aunt Drucie's singing cut through the air as she turned down the gully from the road. Shoving me to one side, Josie stalked down the hall to her room.

"Josie's not feeling well today," I say as Aunt Drucie came in through the door, loosening her bandanna.

"Oh, the dear. Is it the flu?"

"She was up all night with the cramps. Best leave her be. You make a cup of tea, and I'll just be out back, all right?"

"I'll rest a spell before I haves me tea," she said, making for the rocker. "You want one, Kittens?"

"No. I'll just be out back."

Going outside I sat on the grassy spot behind the house, overlooking the bay. It was where I often sat on troubled days, seeking comfort. From here I could look down on treetops and the backs of gulls as they swooped over the face of the wind-clawed sea, and see forever down the open-mouthed bay where the blue of the sky met the blue of the water. All sounds were quietened here, consumed by the stilling wind and rhythmic washing of the sea up over the shore. And as always whenever I sat on this spot, there grew a quiet in me, like that of being nestled amongst the rocks at Crooked Feeder. Only there was no pretending to be living amongst fantasy worlds up here. On sunny days like today, with the sky an endless cloud-beaten blue above me and the sea an endless white-capped blue beneath me and the two sifting together in the far hazy distance, I often-times felt like clutching onto the grass beneath me so's not to be swallowed by the largeness around me. Like living amongst sky.

But, I found no quiet on this day. There was a restlessness around the gully that I hadn't felt since the first days that Nan had passed on, the kind that comes when the tide goes against the wind. Nothing is predictable in that restlessness, and that's how it felt since the reverend drove Sid off, like the tide against the wind. I sat and waited.

It was the next morning, just before Aunt Drucie came over for the day, that Josie left the house and went down the gully again. I was watching from the grassy spot on the back of the house. Funny how you can see something most every day of your life and never pause to think on it, and then one day it's like you see it for the first time and suddenly you can't rest for wanting to know everything about it. That's how I felt, watching her jaunt off down the gully that morning. Without further thought I got up and, waving good morning to Aunt Drucie as she came down over the road, followed after Josie.

Ducking behind rocks and bushes, I followed her up the shore until she disappeared around the tip of Fox Point. Running up to the trees, I gradually worked my way around the point until I saw her. My blood run cold. Sitting on a clump of grass, his punt tied to a rock, was Shine. And he was waiting for Josie.

Shrinking back from the sight, I turned and walked back down the beach, and for the first time since Nan died, I felt tears stinging my eyes. Hopeless! It was all hopeless! Not only was Josie running off again, but it was with Shine, a flesh-eating murderer. What wouldn't the reverend do with that?

I stumbled back up the gully, slipping and scraping both knees, but not looking or caring. Then the wind brought a sound to me. I stopped and listened. *Thud! Thud! Thud!* It was like church bells on a clear Sunday morning, pealing down over the gully to greet me, and I ran the rest of the ways, laughing and singing out like someone truly gone foolish. Seeing me running towards him with the tears streaming down my face and laughing at the same time, Sid tossed the axe to one side and hurried towards me.

"What's wrong?" he asked, grasping me by the arms.

I shook my head, not knowing whether to go with the laughing or the bawling.

"Women!" he exclaimed, leading me around the corner of the house, away from Aunt Drucie's face in the window and sitting me down on the grassy spot. "Always laughing and bawling and not knowing what either is for, like Mum whenever she's having a fight with the reverend, which is most every single time he walks in through the door. I always knows that if she's laughing, it's bawling that she wants to be doing, so I treats her as if she's bawling anyway, and tries to get her laughing instead, which is what I figure she'd rather be doing anyway."

I laughed harder, not picking a lick of sense out of what he was saying.

"Here," he said, taking a grey, pressed handkerchief out of his pocket and wiping at my nose. "Are you all right?"

I nodded.

"W-what do they fight about?" I asked with a snivel.

"Oh, the cut of the tablecloth, the width of my nose, or whether or not it's the sniffles I have, or as the reverend argues, Mum making the consumption out of a drivel of snot."

I laughed a little shakily.

"Who wins?"

"More like who loses. Mum has a drawer full of medicine which she loves to pour down my gullet, sick or no sick."

Sid was grinning as he talked, a soft, curling grin that dimpled the corner of his mouth on one side. I looked down to my feet.

"Does the reverend know you're here?" I asked.

"No." He was silent for a bit, then, "Kit, I'm sorry about what he said. He had no right..."

"It's all right..."

"No, it's not all right. He's a hypocritical bastard and he can cause you trouble. That's why I left when he ordered me to—so's he wouldn't say anything else to hurt you. I would've been back sooner, only he was watching me real close. We have to be careful."

"He'll see you comin' out here."

"I'll come on the days he's gone down the bay."

"But, your mother..."

"She'll say nothing. Christ, she hates it when the reverend's mad at me. Don't worry." He touched my cheek, his finger warm against my skin. "We'll work it out. He's told no one about the other day, he'd rather keep it quiet than have whispers that you're my girl."

I turned away as his finger trailed the curve of my mouth.

"That's why he came out here," Sid said softly. "Haynes told him what they were saying about us in school. Kit, why won't you look at me?"

I closed my eyes, my lips quavering at the nearness of him.

"Shine's back," I blurted out, not trusting to look at him. "Josie's run off with him twice now."

He stared at me disbelievingly.

"She's with him right now," I whispered.

"Shine! But, when did he... Christ! No wonder you're upset. Are you sure?"

"She's mad with me and didn't come home the other night. This morning I followed her. He came for her in his boat, up by Fox Point."

Rising to his feet, Sid smacked his fist in his hand and

swept his eyes down over the gully before squatting besides me again.

"Christ! Shine!" He shook his head in the same hopeless way that I had cried.

"She was drunk the last time she come home."

"Did Drucie see her?"

"No. Not yet. Everyone's goin' to find out, Sid," I burst out, my voice rising hysterically. "They're goin' to make me leave here."

"Shh, we already talked about that, no one's going to send you away, and no one's going to find out about Josie. Shine's been hiding all this time, he won't let anyone see him. If he's moving around in a boat, he's probably camping on Miller's Island, somewhere. Someone will see him, Kit. Then, the Mounties'll be after him in no time."

"Supposin' Josie's with him when they see him?"

"We'll work on keeping her home. What did you fight about?"

"You," I said, hanging my head.

"Me!"

"She thinks it's my fault the reverend drove you away."

"Then she'll be fine once she sees me. I'll tell her I won't ever come back if she goes off with Shine again. That'll keep her home. And you can talk with her, too."

"She don't care about what I say."

"Then make her care."

"How?"

"I don't know. Make her care about you."

I shook my head. "She won't ever care about me."

"Sure she does. Didn't she go for Doctor Hodgins the day the reverend kidnapped you? Didn't she?" He nudged when I didn't answer. "Kit." His voice had fallen to a whisper. "Perhaps it's you who don't care."

"Even if I did, she wouldn't notice," I cried out, making to stand up.

"No, you're wrong," Sid said, pulling me back. "You keep forgetting, she's a kid. She can feel what's in your heart. What's in your heart, Kit?"

"I don't think about it," I said.

"Sure you do."

"No, I don't.

"What did you feel when you saw her with Shine?"

"I don't care about it, I only care about people findin' out. Let go!" I snapped as I tried to get up and he kept pulling me back.

"What did you feel, Kit?"

"I hate her," I said harshly. He was quiet, my words ringing through the stillness.

"You're not alone," he said with a sudden quiet. "There's others that hate her, too . . . the reverend, May Eveleigh, Jimmy Randall, Haynes . . . "

"They have no right," I whispered. "Not them that made her so."

"Then, shouldn't they be the ones you hate?"

"I hate them, too. I hate every damn thing. I even hated Nan."

Then I burst into tears, the shock of having said such a thing terrifying me right down to my toes.

"Sshh, now, you don't mean that."

"No, I don't mean that, I don't mean that," I cried, sobbing all the harder as he rocked me. "I hate that she's not here. I hate never feelin' safe. And it's Jose who always gets us in trouble."

"Shh, that's what we're going to fix—Josie, so's she won't get in trouble with everybody, again."

"How? How can we fix her?"

He pushed me back, and wiped my face with the pads of his thumbs.

"Show her that you care."

"She won't ever listen to me."

"You're not listening, Kit. It's not what you say, it's what you feel. Start changing how you feel towards her."

"I don't know if I can do that."

"Sure you can. Play with her. That's what I do, I play with her. Keep remembering she's a kid. She only wants to play."

Play. The word sounded as foreign as Latin. I gave a short laugh.

"I don't ever remember playin'. Leastways, not with someone. Just Pirate."

"Then don't you think it's time you started having more fun?"

I gave a half-hearted nod, trying to still my snivelling.

"C'mon, then," he cajoled, reaching out and tickling my ribs. "Let's start having fun—me, you and Josie. Before you know it, you'll be wrestling her around the chopping block, and tying her arms and legs in knots, and she'll be chasing after you more than she chases after me and won't ever want to leave home again, she'll be having too much fun."

"God help me," I murmured, brushing away his hands, but I couldn't help smiling. Sid always made things sound right, and suddenly the threat of Shine wasn't so serious.

"Come on. Let's walk." Pulling me to my feet, he held my hand and we started stepping stones down the gully. Soon, we were leaping this way and that, picking up speed the further we went, till we were running and laughing all the ways down to the beach.

"Now then," Sid said breathlessly, as we walked along the shore, "if you were crying because Shine's come back, were you laughing because I've come back?"

"Might be," I replied.

"Might be?"

"Might be that I knew you'd be back."

"Yeah? And how'd you know that?"

"Because the reverend told you not to come back," I said, skipping a little ahead of him.

"Yep, that's the reason, sir, right there." He ran up behind me and, catching hold of my waist, lifted me up and pretended to throw me into the water. I screamed and struggled to get away, but he held me tighter, the dimple besides his mouth deepening as he grinned down at me.

"You oughtn't stare at a man like that," he whispered.

My face grew hot and I felt the hardness of his body pressing against mine. Giving a little laugh, I struggled harder to get away, but his arms tightened around me, his breath caressing my cheek, and it felt as if I were suffocating.

"It ain't no man that bawls and sits home with his mother all the time," I hurtled. It was Margaret's words, spoken without my even knowing they were there, and were meaningless to all but Margaret and her best friends. And on this day, Sid. His smile uncurled itself and he let go of me.

"Is that what you believe?" he asked, coldly. "That I'm a mommy's boy?"

Spinning on his heel, he strolled back up the beach while I stood there, staring after him, willing my tongue to untie itself and call out to him. It was frozen. I followed meekly, not wanting to catch up, but not wanting to lose sight of him, either. Finally, he was at the top of the gully, heading up over the bank for the road.

"I didn't mean it," I called out. But my words, thundering inside my head, sounded no louder than the chirp of a baby chick. He never looked around, just kept on walking with his head down and arms swinging. He kept pace till he disappeared down the road, never looking back. Kicking myself in the leg, I sat down on the chopping block and wrapped my arms miserably around myself.

"Damn!" I yelled. "Damn! Damn!"

"What's that you say, Kit?" asked Aunt Drucie, shuffling onto the door stoop, smoothing down her apron.

"Nothin'," I mumbled.

"You be scowlin' awful hard over nothin'. Is Sid gone, then?" she asked after I never spoke.

I nodded.

She come over to where I was sitting.

"Had a fight, did ye?" she near whispered, leaning her mouth down close to my ear.

"No. Yeah! Boys are stupid."

"Aye. And they gets worse with age. But, don't let it bother you none, 'tis the way of lovers to fight."

"Damn it, Aunt Drucie, I ain't Sid's lover!" I exclaimed, shocked upright on my feet.

"It's just a sayin', Kit, it's just a sayin'," Aunt Drucie said quickly, a touch of merriment in her rheumy old eyes as she took hold of my arm and tried to lead me towards the house. "Heh, you were quick to jump on that one."

"Just don't go sayin' things like that," I said, still tensed with shock. "I don't want people talkin' about me."

"There's no one to speak wrong about you as long as I'm around," said Aunt Drucie, tugging me forward. "'Cuz I thinks of you as me own, I do, you and your poor mother. It's a good turn God give me by havin' me come out here and take care of ye, for it gets lonely livin' by meself, and Lizzy was always one to drop by for a cup of tea. Here, you sit in her rocker," she said, after she had led me inside the house. "I makes you a glass of syrup, like I use to do for her when she come for a visit on hot days. Oh my, I misses her, I do, but it helps me heart to know I'm takin' care of her girls. But I worries about you not goin' to church, Kit."

"It ain't only in church that we finds God, Aunt Drucie."

"They'd be damned in Perpy's Cove if that was the case," said Aunt Drucie. "But Lizzy always liked bringin' you to church."

"I says my prayers."

"Then that'll take care of it. We gets along, hey, Kit?"

I nodded and smiled when she handed me the glass of syrup.

"And Josie?" asked Aunt Drucie. "She don't mind me comin', do she?"

"She likes you comin'," I said. Then, "And I likes you comin', too. We couldn't live here, if it wouldn't for you, Aunt Drucie."

"Aye, that's something about the whole lot of ye," Aunt Drucie said, curling up on the daybed and tucking her legs up in under her. "Ye can't stand being around people any more than I can meself, do you, Kit, you and your poor mother?"

I shook my head, sipping the syrup.

"They thinks I gets lonely, they do," she went on, "livin' on top of Fox Point by meself, but I wouldn't live in Haire's Hollow for a year's grub. Everybody nosin' into your thoughts. I keeps me own counsel, me and Lizzy both, exceptin' with each other. And there we had a right to poke, in case one of us started gettin' addled. For sure nobody else'd know it, for they thinks we were part-addled anyway, for wantin' to live up in the hills amongst the crows."

I nodded as Aunt Drucie went into a yawn, and shifted the rocker so's I could see out the window, down over the gully.

"What do you say, Kit?"

"For sure they thinks we are," I said.

"Aye, for sure they thinks we are. Nothin' wrong with livin' with the crows, what do you say, Kit?"

"Nothin' wrong with crows, Aunt Drucie," I said, rocking and watching, rocking and watching.

CHAPTER FIFTEEN

BROKEN BIRDS

I T WAS LATE EVENING WHEN JOSIE CAME HOME. Thankfully, Aunt Drucie had gone home for the day, and I was still sitting in the rocking chair, watching and waiting. She was drunk, so drunk that she couldn't take two steps without falling down. I met her at the door and, putting my arm round her shoulders, helped her to her room. I was surprised to see that we were about the same height now, and that beneath her clothes, she was all skin and bones, much like how the little robin felt through its feathers and down. I helped her take off her clothes and after she fell across the bed, I pushed open her window to let in some fresh air. She whimpered, snuggling her face into her pillow and reminding me of a baby groping for its mother's tit. Remembering Sid's words that she was just a big kid, I laid a quietening hand on her shoulder before leaving her room.

The next morning drew hot and muggy. Josie was so sick that she just lay across her bed, sticking her head out the window to puke, then resting her cheek tiredly on the windowsill to catch the faint breeze.

The smell of vomit sweltered through the house and, along with it, blue arse fish flies that came in through her window and buzzed around the kitchen like bullets. Scared of what Aunt Drucie would think, and even more scared that May Eveleigh or one of the other women might show up, I lugged the shovel out back to where her room window was and, digging up some black ground from alongside the rotting picket fence, slung it over her vomit. Squatting in the sparse shade of an old spruce, I closed my eyes and waited as she stuck her head out and started retching again. After she had done, I dug the spade deeper and shovelled another layer of dirt over the steaming puke.

It was Doctor Hodgins who showed up, just a few minutes after Aunt Drucie.

"She got stomach upset," I said. "I had the same, but I'm better, now. Want some tea, Doctor? Aunt Drucie?"

"Glass of water will be fine, Kit. I'll go have a look at Josie," Doctor Hodgins said.

"Heh, I'll have a cup of tea, maid, after I checks on Josie," Aunt Drucie said, creeping down the hall behind Doctor Hodgins. They were both back in a minute, Aunt Drucie tutting and shaking her head and Doctor Hodgins with a look akin to pity as his eyes met mine.

"She got it bad," Aunt Drucie said. "The summer flu! Herm Gale was in bed for a week, comin' out of him from both ends, and one as watery as the other."

"Keep giving her water, Drucie," Doctor Hodgins said. "Kit, come with me."

Putting his arm around my shoulder, he walked me up to the road besides where his car was parked.

"She's as hung over as Mope after a two-week binge," he

said abruptly, coming to a stop and leaning back against the car door. "When did she start drinking? Or," he tweaked my chin with a sympathetic sigh, "should I ask, when did she start running off, again?"

"It's her first time," I said.

"First time getting drunk? Or first time running off?"

I thought for a minute.

"She ran off once before. Two months ago. Don't sound like it's much of a problem."

Doctor Hodgins groaned, wiping at the sweat on his brow with the back of his hand.

"It doesn't have to be much for the good reverend to get involved," he said. "What about Sid? Has he seen anything?"

I shook my head.

"Good. He's a good lad. I wouldn't fear him too much."

"Doctor Hodgins, I'm almost fifteen. Soon, I won't be needin' anyone to live with me."

"There's truth to that." He looked at me a little sadly, then gently patted my shoulder. "You know, Kittens, there's more to growing up than crossing off years. Friends, fun. Have you ever had fun, Kit? A best friend?"

Not liking the seriousness in his tone and the troubled look playing over his face, I gave a big smile and started talking like Margaret Eveleigh whenever she was walking and talking with her best friends.

"I talks with Melissa and everybody in school all the time. And I plays with Josie now."

His crinkly grey eyes smiled and he folded his arms.

"Breathe easy, Kit. I'm not hauling you out of your precious gully."

"It's not a gully, it's my home," I said with a startling sharpness.

His eyes sobered.

"You're right, it is your home," he said finally. "And you've a right to it. But there are other things you've a right to—things you ought to be giving more thought to."

"I think about her," I said, glancing towards the house.

His eyes followed my glance and rested there for some time before coming back to me.

"For sure it would seem that she's been left to you. But perhaps she wasn't. Perhaps she's been left to all of us. Think, Kit, is it sacrifice that keeps you here? Or fear?"

The noonday sun was getting hotter.

"It's a tough question, Kittens. What say we leave it for your fifteenth birthday?" His eyes were back to smiling again, and laying both hands on either side of my cheeks, he kissed me on the forehead, then said a little gruffly, "You're a good girl. Keep me in touch with what Josie's up to. That's important, Kit. It's the only way I can help you. Do you understand me? I need to know." A breeze stirred the nearby aspen and I felt the trembling of each solitary leaf right down to the quick. I nodded again, scarcely able to meet his eyes for fear that he would see how much I needed to talk to him right then, about how the reverend had made me smell like rotting dogberries, and how Josie was screwing Shine. But something held me back, something to do with his look of pity, and his sudden concern for what he felt was missing in my life, as well as what God had already provided.

"I'm going down Chouse Brook, fishing with Old Joe for a day," he said, climbing into his car. "I'll be back to check on you tomorrow evening."

"Old Joe turnin' you into a fisherman, is he?" I asked, trying to make light.

"It's his yarns I like more than the fishing," Doctor Hodgins said, giving me a wink before he shut his door. "But, we won't tell him that, will we?"

I grinned and waved as he started up his car and turned it around to head back into Haire's Hollow. I watched him as he drove out of sight, then sauntered down to the grassy spot behind the house, thinking about what he had said about living somewhere else. But, it was an impossible thought. I couldn't think of a day without the gully and its running brook, and the burning red worlds amongst the rocks at Crooked Feeder. Nor could Pirate live anywhere else, I thought, with his need to never be touched, and his want of the meadow and the woods. And what of Nan—and her ongoing sounds? Could she ever find me someplace else? And what of Sid?

Sid. If he ever came back again. And even if he never, there was Josie. Since the minute I had put my arms around her shoulders last evening and helped her stagger to her room, I thought of her as the wounded bird Pirate had brought home as an offering that day. And this time I had to keep it from flying to its death.

The sun moved around, flushing me out of the shade, and I went inside. Aunt Drucie was napping on the daybed, her head propped up close to the window to catch the scattered breeze. Peeking into Josie's room, I saw that she was lying awake on her pillow, her hair damp from the heat and sticking to her face. I made her a cup of ice tea and took it to her, along with a slice of buttered bread. Sitting on the edge of her bed, I watched as she supped back the tea and carefully chewed the bread, dropping crumbs all over the bedclothes and smearing butter on her chin. She watched me as she ate and, when finally she was finished, passed me back the cup. We stared at each other. I tried to think of what to say, and stared absently out the window.

"It's Shine that makes you sick," I said abruptly, thinking back on how Doctor Hodgins had gotten her to wash her hair.

She stared at me, her eyes flat green.

"He's bad," I said fervently. "That's why Nan shot him with the gun, because he's bad. Because he makes you sick."

I laid my hand on her shoulder as she closed her eyes and turned away from me.

"You have to stay away from him. You have to run from him, so's he won't make you sick agin. Will you do that? Will you stay away from Shine?"

She turned to stare at me again and I tried to think of something more to say. My foot hit on something beneath her bed, and looking down, I saw the corner of her box sticking out, the box that she had run with from May Eveleigh.

"I'll be right back," I said quickly. Rising from her bedside, I ran into my room and pulled out the box of coloured glass from beneath my bed. Bringing it back, I laid it on the bed besides her. She watched as I lifted off the cover and, taking out the biggest piece, the yellow, held it over my eyes. I smiled as the sky outside her window turned golden, then passed the piece to her. She stared at it for a second, then mustered up the energy to take it and hold it before her eyes. Turning to see out the window, she gave a satisfied bark. I took out a piece of blue.

"This is my favourite," I said.

She took it and held it to an eye, smiling at the sky outside.

"You can have it if you want."

She nodded, smiling a little more, still squinting through the blue glass. I reached down to lift up her box. It was my thought that she might want to put her piece of glass inside, like I had with my pieces and the little robin's feathers. It was a thought that never got said. The second my fingers touched the box, she brought the broad of her hand slamming across my face, knocking me sideways off the bed, yelping in pain.

I staggered to my feet, partly stunned, and yelled as she grabbed my box of glass and shucked it out the window, scattering the pieces of glass and the little robin's feathers all over the freshly covered puke beneath her window.

"What'd you do that for?" I half cried, clamouring to my feet and glaring down at her. Without waiting for an answer, I slammed out of her room and down the hall, tears of pain and spite flooding both eyes.

"What's the matter, Kit?" asked Aunt Drucie, sputtering awake as I stomped across the kitchen.

"Go back to sleep," I said, wrenching open the door and shoving out through. Marching around the house to where Josie's room window was, I grabbed hold of the shovel and plunged it deep into the thick, dark soil and started pitching it over the glass and feathers, cursing like the sailor as I went. Dig, pitch; dig, pitch; dig, pitch. When the last piece of glass was covered, I marched back to my room, dirtied, hot and sweaty. Flinging myself across the bed, I gritted my teeth and willed back the smothering hot tears that were threatening to pour down my face.

That evening after Aunt Drucie left, I slouched down on the daybed, glaring at Josie as she crept around the kitchen making a cup of tea, her face pale, and her hand shaking a little as she spooned sugar into her cup.

"That's enough sugar," I snapped, thinking of walking into Haire's Hollow to find Sid.

"Not enough sugar," she argued, her voice too weak to sound up a bark.

Footsteps sounded on the stoop. Sid? I bolted upright as the door swung open, my stomach taking flight, then whipped my hand to my mouth in shock. It was Shine, his heavy frame blocking out the evening light and flooding the room with the stench of stilled liquor. The crackie dog scrambled in through the door around his feet and ran sniffing around the kitchen as Shine took a step towards Josie, a bottle of liquor in one hand and a gunny sack in the other.

"You go," said Josie to Shine, shaking her head and taking her cup of tea to the table.

"That your girl?" Shine snarked, looking my way with a rotted-toothed grin.

"That's Kit. That's not your girl," Josie said, sounding a little louder. "You go. Go."

"You like dogs?" Shine asked me as the crackie sniffed at the floor around my feet. Sinking heavily into Nan's rocking chair, he patted his knee and beckoned me over. "Come here, you girl. Come here."

Josie, busy sipping her tea, never looked up.

At that second Pirate sprang out hissing from beneath the daybed, his claws splayed as they swiped at the crackie's nose. Howling in fright, the crackie scampered across the room. Taking advantage of the commotion, I was off the daybed and down the hallway in a second's flash. Something stopped me as I was about to go into my room, and instead I ducked into Nan's closet. I picked the highest shelf up and crawled beneath the blankets. My heart pounded and I shivered to think that the sound of its beating could be heard throughout the house and traced back to where I was hiding.

I strained to listen. Josie was barking at him, like he was bothering her. But it must've been like swatting at flies, because every time I heard her bark, I heard him bark back like a dog, and then laugh—a gargling, stomach-turning laugh that sounded more like snarling than laughing.

Closing my eyes, I turned to the wall and concentrated on breathing and trying to shut out her barks as she fought with him, and his snarls as he fought her back. Then she laughed. Then yelled again. After a while I got tired of trying to figure out whether she was laughing or yelling, and whether or not I should try to sneak into my room and jump out the window and run into Haire's Hollow for Doctor Hodgins. I concentrated instead on the smell of Nan's mothballs still clinging to the blankets and I thought how nice it was to smell the mothballs after all this time, almost like smelling Nan herself, as if she were hiding beneath the blankets with me. And when I finally went to sleep, there was the sound of two hearts beating in the closet that night.

The next morning I woke to the sound of Shine's footstep creaking down the hall, pausing by each room and inching open the doors as he come. I drew a long, deep breath and held it. It was sweltering up near the ceiling, and bundled beneath the blankets and sheets. And the mothballs that had smelled so sweetly of Nan the night before were sharp and sickly by now. The floor creaked near the closet door and I held my breath and prayed to Nan for the strength to be still.

He creaked away. I listened harder as he crept and groaned, figuring that with all the grunting he was doing, he must've been bending over to check for me under the beds. Not finding what he was looking for, he walked heavily back into the kitchen. He rustled around some, then opened the door. The crackie's feet scampered across the floor, then the door shut and there was silence. I strained to listen harder. The springs on the daybed squeaked. Then the sound of Josie's footsteps as she trudged to the bin and dipped a glass into the water bucket. I listened as she came down the hall to her room, shut her door, and then her bedsprings squeaking as she fell across it. Then all was quiet. A bit longer and the blankets began to feel like a weight pressing in on me. Quietly, I climbed down from the shelf and sneaked through the house, looking out the windows. I couldn't see Shine. Satisfied that he was gone, I tore down the hall to Josie's room and barged in through her door.

"You see why you ain't never allowed to go near Shine again?" I yelled. "He's bad. And he makes you bad."

She whipped her head up off her pillow and blinked at me in startled surprise. Then springing to her feet, she lunged at me like a surly cat, scratching at my face and bawling out.

"Get out! You get out! Farmed! Farmed."

I stumbled backwards beneath her weight and fell on my behind. Kicking me savagely in the leg, she slammed her room door and fell heavily across her bed. I scrabbled back onto my feet and whammed my fist repeatedly against her door.

"You don't ever go near him again. You hear me? He's bad! Bad!"

"You's bad! Get away! Get away!" she muffled through her pillow.

"Are you listenin' to me?" I yelled.

Silence. Giving her door one last thump, I went back to the kitchen and, jamming a chair beneath the doorknob, started cleaning Shine's cigarette ashes and spit off the floor, taking time to check out the window every two minutes in case Shine come back. The cleaning done, I unjammed the door and went outside and sat on the grassy spot to keep watch. It was still early, yet a blue haze covered the far-side hills, making for another hot, sultry day. At least she never got drunk last night, I thought, leaning back against the side of the house, using my sweater for a pillow. I closed my eyes tiredly, having hardly slept a wink the night before, and in what felt like minutes, sat up with a start, rubbing at my face. Sid was squat besides me, tickling my nose with a blade of grass.

"I'm giving you another chance, sleepyhead," he said

mockingly.

I hung my head sheepishly, then started speaking in a flurry of blurts.

"Shine was here. Last night, with his dog. I hid in the closet and this mornin' he come lookin' for me."

"Jesus . . . "

"He didn't find me."

"Christ!" He slumped besides me with relief, then was on his knees, his hands on mine. "You're not safe here, Kit. We have to get you out of here."

I shook my head, covering my face with my hands.

"God, I'm sorry, Kit." He wrapped his arms around me, cradling me, his face against mine. "I should never have left you the way I did. I was such an ass."

"No, I shouldn't have said what I said," I whimpered.

He pulled my hands away from my face and whispered softly, his nose a hair's width from mine.

"Next time I'll just trounce you good, instead of running off," he murmured.

I tried to smile, but there was such a feverish look in his eyes that I could only close mine. His hand crept up the back of my neck and he pressed his forehead against mine. As soft as a moth's wings, his lips slowly grazed my brow, my nose, the corners of my mouth. I breathed deeply as his breath fanned out over my face, warm and caramel sweet, and then his lips were pressing against mine, gently at first, then more and more sure. When finally I was bursting my lungs for wanting of air, he pulled back and rested his chin on my forehead.

"It's because I was afraid of kissin' you, that I said what I did," I whispered.

Lifting a finger to my chin, he tilted my face to his.

"Are you still afraid?"

"No."

I closed my eyes as he lowered his mouth and kissed me again. Then he was on his feet, pounding his fist in his hand.

"We've got to do something. We've got to protect you against Shine."

"I'm scared, Sid."

"Of course you're scared. Jesus Christ, half of Haire's Hollow'd be scared if they had Shine coming after them. God, Kit." He dropped down besides me. "What about Doctor Hodgins? We have to tell him. He can help."

"No, he's already worryin' about me."

"He could give you a place to stay till ... "

"No! Once I leave here, he'll never let me come back I know it."

"Kit, you're not safe here."

"There's nothin' we can do," I said with despair.

"There's always something. We just have to think. I've already let the news out that Shine's back. It won't be long before the Mounties are after him."

I shook my head despondently.

"It'll take forever."

Sid grasped my shoulders with a little shake.

"Now you listen to me, Kit, no one has ever been able to get you out of here, not even the reverend, and he could turf Satan out of hell if he tried. We'll find a way to get around this one."

"How?"

"I don't know, I don't know." He slumped down besides me, his head in his hands, and we sat in silence for some time. Then suddenly he was on his feet, pulling me to mine and striding back around the house. Ripping up the rest of the pickets of the old rotten fence, he tossed them in a pile, then started lugging them across the meadow, up to the woods.

"We're going to build you a camp," he said, as I stumbled along behind him, dragging a load of pickets. "Just a makeshift thing that'll do you to sleep on during the nights. Until they catches Shine, which won't be long now, I know it. Everyone's too fed up with Shine to tolerate his bullshit much more, and what with the peace they've been having since he last ran off, they'll be only too eager to go running to the Mounties with whatever information they have about him chewing up and killing people. I'll talk to Mum and get her going after the reverend to encourage the people to come forward. It'll happen, you'll see. The people have to come together, and with the reverend's help they will. Meanwhile, we have to keep you safe, and sleeping out of the house at night is one way of doing that. No one will know. During the days, we can keep watch. I don't expect he'll be doing much visiting during daylight hours. It's evenings that vampires suckle, and that's a good thing, because by then, you'll be safer than any of us in your new bed that I'm going to make for you."

Coming to a large black spruce, its wide, flat branches swooping down like a ready-made tent, Sid dropped the pickets and commenced building a platform off from the base of the tree. Back at the house, he stripped the plastic from inside of the lean-to that he had built for storing the wood, and draped it around the underside of the tree branches to circle around the platform, weatherproofing it. After he was finished building, we went inside the house and brought back an armful of blankets and pillows. Then we carried up some biscuits, water, and even matches and a stub of a candle I found in Nan's room.

"Make sure the front door is always barred and your window is always open," Sid cautioned, back at the house again, standing outside my room window. "The second you hears a sound—run! Take no chances. If it happens to be Pirate, then you can always climb back in. And if it's Shine, make for the woods and stay there until I comes, or until Shine leaves. Here," he passed me a picket with a couple of rusty nails sticking out of one end, "keep this by your bed and if he pokes his head in through the window, whump him in the face. And make sure it's the end with the nails that you slam him with."

I shuddered.

"I don't know if I can do that."

"Decide that when you sees his face coming through your window."

I tried to smile so's Sid wouldn't look so worried, then widened my eyes at the sight of Aunt Drucie dodging down over the bank.

"What about her?"

At that second Josie poked her tangled red head sleepily out the window. Seeing Sid, she broke into a loud grin and hoisted her leg out through.

"You go find some excuse to keep Drucie at home during the next few days, and I'll deal with this one," Sid said, holding out his hand to help Josie as she prepared to jump off the window ledge.

"Do you think it might scare Shine off if Aunt Drucie was around?" I asked.

"Uumph, forget it," Sid snorted as Josie landed on the ground at his feet. "Nothing scares Shine. Then all you'd have is Drucie running around scared to death and sounding the bells about Shine's coming to chew the face off the lot of you. Now there's reason for the Noble ones to haul you out of here."

"You's farmed! Farmed!" Josie barked, landing on both

feet and scowling at me.

"Farmed?" Sid gave me a blank look.

"Later," I sighed, scowling back at Josie and going off to greet Aunt Drucie.

CHAPTER SIXTEEN

THE KILLING

SAFETY WASN'T JUST MY CONCERN. When word got out that Shine was back, a shiver went through Haire's Hollow like that of a near miss. Shine was back. And with him the haunting image of Rube Gale's bloodied corpse, the open-faced grave and the unnamed headstone.

Margaret Eveleigh and her best friends started walking in groups, each keeping their eyes open for the other and walking short distances from the outport, until one of them would start squealing, thinking she had seen Shine's evil eye peering through some bushes, and sending the works of them racing back to the outport as if there was a hoard of devils chasing after them. Their parents chided them for their foolishness, yet the women ceased their dallying in May Eveleigh's store, and the men made fast work of mending their nets and getting off the wharf before evening fell. Even the reverend softened his sermons to say we should all be more accepting and loving of each other, a startling change from the hell-burning damnations he had preached when Shine had first disappeared, leading Old Joe to say that even a man of the cloth couldn't feel safe preaching the word of God with Shine on the loose.

Plus now the outporters had something new to worry about: would Shine come looking for the man that led the Mounties to his still? And it didn't matter there was no such man, that the Mounties just happened upon it. No sir. Not with Shine. What mattered was who was Shine going to look at and *think* led the Mounties to his still? And as Old Joe said, that could hinge on something as far removed from the deed as a scab on a dead dog's arse. Then Shine administered his own law, and the mauled corpse of Rube Gale was fresh testimony to that. And Rube was his drinking buddy who had probably done nothing more than shake his head when he was supposed to be nodding whilst Shine was talking to him. What would he do to someone he believed was trying to put him in jail for life?

The Mounties had been alerted. They came in pairs and was a comforting sight to the people of Haire's Hollow, although they made it clear there was nothing they could do about Shine until someone came forward about the murder or Jimmy Randall's ear. They never come near the gully. Sid kept telling me that was a good thing, because if they were to make a link between Shine and Josie, the reverend would be like a hawk to his prey, using Shine's presence and my safety as a reason to get me out of the gully, and Josie's moral decline as a reason to keep me out of there. One small blessing with Shine's return was that the women, scared of running into Shine, stopped coming to the gully. Aside from Aunt Drucie. And it didn't take much talking to convince her to take a couple of days.

"Just don't say anything to anyone," I cautioned as I walked her home the day Sid built the camp. "And if anyone sees you at home, just tell them you're sick, and me and Josie was just out to visit with you, and everything's fine."

"As long as you're O.K. with it," Aunt Drucie said. "I must say, I'm some tired from this heat, can't keep me eyes open at all. But I'll be worried about you and Josie, Kit. S'pose Shine comes your way."

"He got no reason to. And like I told you, me and Josie's goin' lookin' for raspberries and we won't be home much the next few days, anyway."

"Along the old sawmill road is a good spot for raspberries. Me and Lizzy use to go there, once." She stifled a yawn. "Course, we had stronger legs them days. Heh, for sure Lizzy's were, poor old girl. I misses her, Kit, I misses her a lot."

"I misses her, too, Aunt Drucie. You have a nice long nap, now. Give me a couple of days, and I'll be back with a gallon of raspberries. How's that?"

"Watch out for bears. Your grandfather seen one standin' alongside the old mill, once. That's why me and Lizzy never went back."

"I expect he's gone by now."

"Bloody bears. But we got worse than that to worry about with Shine back. Make sure you bars your door in the evenin'."

"I will. Make sure you bars yours. See you in a few days." Leaving her at her stoop, I ran back to the gully and Sid.

"Now all we've got to do is sit tight and wait for the Mounties to catch Shine, or else run him off again," Sid said, as we sat down on the grassy spot behind the house.

"I still don't know about Josie," I said.

"I think she's going to be O.K. She don't like Shine. She thinks it's him that makes her sick, not the liquor."

I gave something of a smile, sending a silent thank you Doctor Hodgins's way.

"But, is she afraid of him?" I asked worriedly. "She might forget about being sick after a spell."

"I told her I wouldn't come back if she went off with Shine again."

I sighed heavily, then spoke in a half-whisper.

"Suppose she do? Suppose she leads him to the camp?"

"She won't. She wants to please me. Lord, Kit, I know it's not the best of plans, but short of taking you out of the gully ... "

"Let's not get onto that."

"Then we'll have to trust Josie. Come on, Kit. She understands a whole lot more than you think. And she certainly seems willing to go along with everything I say."

"We'll see," I said, and lay back, my hands tucked beneath my head for a pillow, staring up at the hazy sky. Sid lay back besides me, his elbow warm against mine, and if it weren't for the threat of Shine, it would've felt like the most peaceful place on earth, what with the waves washing upon the shore below us, and the gulls crying out above us, and the slight salty breeze fanning off the sea and rustling the air around us.

It was where I spent most of my time the next few days, looking out over the gully for Shine. Sid came as much as he could and helped me make fast work out of a visit from Doctor Hodgins. And I kept paying visits to Aunt Drucie, convincing her everything was fine and no, we hadn't found the raspberry patch yet, but me and Josie were going off again the next morning and spending the day looking. And there was always Josie that had to be watched. At night, after jamming the door shut with a woodchip, I went to my room and barred the door with the bed and lay there listening, waiting, the picket with the nails resting by my pillow.

It was four days past his first visit that Shine came back.

I was in my room, ready to hop in bed for the night, when I heard the crackie yap. Without a second's hesitation, I lunged for the windowsill and jumped. The second my arse touched the ground, Josie's was hitting dirt as well. We stared at each other, then scrambling to our feet, took off for the woods.

It was a night in hell. Swatting flies and ants and whatever other unimaginable creatures that were most likely crawling over us, I curled into a tight ball beneath a blanket and tried to force my way through the night. Aside from a few swats and a square dance of twists and turns, Josie slept like a baby. Once, when the sky was still littered with stars, I bolted upright, terrified to hear a bone-jarring screech coming from the house. It sounded like Pirate. Or was it a screech owl? Then the air was filled with the crackie's yapping and hoarse roars from Shine. Lying back down, I took deep breaths, shutting out everything I'd heard Nan say about the minds of liquor-poisoned men. No runt of a dog would get close enough to hurt Pirate, I soothed myself. Must've been a screech owl. And for sure if it was Pirate, most likely it was the crackie who got the worst of that one.

Morning came early. Climbing the black spruce, I sat on a branch and watched the front door. The last star was still in the sky when Shine finally opened it and lurched out through, the crackie at his heels. I waited till he disappeared down the gully, and then some before shaking Josie. She woke like the baby, eyes and mouth opening at once, and all limbs flailing.

"Careful!" I cautioned as she came grumbling to her feet and leaped off the platform before she had a chance to take in where she was. But she was gone for home, any thoughts of Shine evaporating with the morning dew. Keeping up with her, we both came to the house at the same time, yet despite her rush to get home, her step quietened alongside of mine as we opened the door and peered inside. It was a sight that drew a gut-wrenching shriek out of us both and petrified us in its terrifying cruelty. Pirate was skivvered to the floor with a pig knife, his blood in a thick pool around him and his eyes and mouth shocked open, staring at us—as if he, too, was witnessing the horror of his death alongside of us.

I stumbled backwards and Josie began turning around and around in circles, making little whimpering sounds. I tried to reach out to her, but bent over instead, retching out the cries that were coming from somewhere so deep inside of me that they sounded like someone else's.

"Get Doctor Hodgins! Get Doctor Hodgins!" Josie cried.

"Wait for Sid!" I managed to get out.

"Doctor Hodgins! Doctor Hodgins!" She made to run up over the bank, but I grabbed hold of her arm and pulled her back.

"No!" I said more strongly. "We wait for Sid."

Surprisingly, she dropped down onto the stoop and wrapped her hands around her face. I slumped down besides her and waited, one eye on the gully for fear of Shine coming back, and the other on the path leading down from the road, praying it would be Sid that came and not May Eveleigh or Doctor Hodgins or Aunt Drucie . . .

It was Sid. About an hour later. Seeing him, Josie leaped off the stoop and dashed towards him, shouting and barking. I saw the concern on his face as he put together what she was telling him, and then he was holding out his arms and cradling me.

"We've got to get you out of here," he said, finally. "There's no telling what he'll do next."

"No . . . ohh, I don't know. I can't think, not with . . . "
I choked off, and Sid tightened his arms around me.

"It's O.K.," he soothed. "We'll talk later. First, I'll take care of Pirate."

Not wanting to see, I went down to the gully and splashed some cold water on my face and neck. A few minutes later, Sid was sitting on a rock besides me.

"I've put him in a brin bag," he said. "Josie and I'll bury him out back."

I nodded.

"Kit, perhaps you should stay with Drucie until something's done about Shine."

"What about Josie? She isn't safe, either."

"She'll come with you."

"No. She'll keep comin' home."

"We'll talk with her. She listened before."

"I don't know," I mumbled, rocking back and forth. "I just don't know any more."

"Kit." Sid took me by the arms and made me stop rocking. "I can't let you stay here."

"I know," I said. "I just can't think right now."

Fear, shame, it was hard to tell which was causing the trembling in my voice, but Sid saw them both, and his eyes pained at the little comfort he could offer.

"Bury Pirate," I whispered, rising to my feet. Taking a long shuddering breath, I went back inside the house. Ripping off another scrubbing rag from the tail of Nan's nightdress, I dropped it into the bucket of water and started cleaning the piss, spit and butts off the floor. Tears welled up in my eyes as I started on Pirate's blood, but I gritted them back and kept scrubbing. The door nudged open behind me, and thinking it was Sid, I dropped the cloth and wiped at my running nose.

"Oh God," I cried out in horror as the crackie scampered across the floor and started lapping up Pirate's blood. The doorway darkened and my limbs became like water as Shine lunged in, his eyes filled with pus, and a white froth crusting the corners of his bearded mouth. He stood there, panting, his body shaking like a distempered dog.

I opened my mouth to scream, but it felt like the air had been sucked from the room and all I was gulping in was the stink off his body and the sharp, bitter fear reeking off my own. I managed a yelp before he was on me, smashing me across the face. I fell back onto the floor, my face numbed by the blow, and watched in shocked horror as he straddled a leg on each side of me and looked down, grinning. I opened my mouth to scream, squirming to get away, but he dropped to his knees, imprisoning me with his thighs, and clamped a dirt-grimed hand across my mouth. Smiling a row of rotted teeth, he reached inside his pants and pulled out his dick, as big and ugly a thing as ever I'd seen, with purple veins snaking around its sides, and the smell of rotting dogberries dripping from its head.

He bobbed it in front of my eyes, and I stopped struggling against the hand that was smothering me, prepared to die rather than have that living thing touch me. And just when the light was fading to black, Sid was leaping onto his back, his hands raking across the sneering, whiskered face.

Shine reached back his hand, and grabbing Sid by the scruff of his neck, hauled him over his shoulder and whammed him hard on the floor. Sid groaned, his breath knocked out of him, then shook his head and struggled to sit up. But Shine had let go of me and was now crawling on top of Sid. Stretching a leg across his chest, he straddled Sid the way he had sat astride me and, squealing like a stuck pig, started batting Sid across the face with his purple, swollen dick. Sid screamed, wrenching his head from side to side as Shine continued to playfully bat him in the face, all the time laughing and grunting, laughing and grunting. I managed to get onto my knees and started crawling towards the stove, thinking of finding something that I could beat against the side of Shine's head, but he caught me by the ankle and yanked me back besides him.

"Lemme go, lemme go!" I screamed, clawing at the floor to get away. But my nails scraped uselessly across the smooth surface of the canvas. Sid's cries became muffled, and I knew that Shine had placed his hand over his mouth to silence him—or smother him. "Lemme go!" I screamed, clawing harder at the floor, but his grip was an iron band around my ankle and I collapsed sobbing. Giving one last blood-curdling scream, I swung around to chew at the hand holding me down, and widened my eyes incredulously. Coming through the doorway and swinging the axe up over her shoulder was Josie.

"Oh God!" I cried out as she stomped towards Shine, but my voice, hoarsened by my frantic screams, sounded no more than a piteous moan. I stared hypnotized as the silver arc of the axe, glinting in the morning sun, came full across the back of Shine's head, then fell sideways. A soft groan gushed from Shine and he toppled forward, his hand falling away from Sid's mouth and a growing stream of blood spewing down over Sid's terror-stricken face.

Retching wildly Sid wriggled out from beneath Shine and ran out the door. I lurched to my feet, staggering after him. At the door I stopped and looked back. Josie was still standing there, her body arched forward, her hands held out in front of her as if they still held the axe. Not knowing whom to run to, I sunk down onto the stoop and dropped my head in my hands.

"Kit!"

Sid was standing in front of me, water dripping off him from where he had dunked his head in the gully's brook. His breathing was coming in quick, heavy spurts, and his face, cleaned of blood, was as white as a sun-bleached sheet. Inside the house, Josie had dropped to the floor and was rocking her body to and fro, to and fro, like she had done on the day of Nan's passing. Only she wasn't moaning and crying on this day. She was quiet, as quiet as sin, staring at the blood-soaked face of the man she had just killed.

Then Sid was stepping past me. He grabbed hold of Josie's hand and, grabbing hold of mine, hauled me up from the stoop and led us both down to the gully. We sat there like statues, excepting for Josie's rocking, rocking, rocking.

"We've got to hide him."

I was still, not able to think past the motion of Josie's rocking.

"We've got to hide him."

It was Sid. He fell to his knees before me, his hands grasping mine.

"Do you hear me, Kit? We've got to hide him. Nobody knows but us. And we're not telling." He had taken off his glasses somewhere, and his eyes were bare without them. "We're going to drag him down the gully," he was saying. "Then we're going to put him in his boat and send him adrift. Nobody'll ever know."

"Someone will find him," I whispered.

"It won't matter."

"They'll know it was us."

"No! How can they? No one's seen Shine since he's come back. Why would they connect him with us?"

"I don't know, I don't know. The reverend'll find out. And then he's goin' to send us away."

"No he won't," Sid yelled, shaking me hard. "Do you hear me, Kit? I told you and I told you. Nobody's going to take you away from me. I won't let them." He let go of me and gripped Josie's rocking body. "Stop it! Stop it, Jose, do you hear me? It don't matter that you killed that fuckin' animal. It don't matter. Now listen here, the two of you. We got to get Shine's stinking body down the gully. All right?"

Sid was back to gripping my hands again, but my eyes were closed and all I could think was that Josie had killed Shine and he was bleeding all over our canvas floor and she was never gonna stop rocking, never gonna stop rocking.

"Kit!" Sid's hand smacked across my face.."Kit, it's shock! You're both in shock, but you've got to come out of it. We've got to get rid of Shine. Do you understand me? We've got to get him out of there!"

I nodded.

"Thata girl." He smiled weakly, then taking my mother's hand, squeezed it gently.

"Jose, Kit and me's going to get rid of Shine. Now, you wait here, do you hear me? You just wait right here till Kit and I gets back."

Josie kept staring straight ahead, rocking to and fro, to and fro . . .

"She's going to be fine," Sid said, leaping to his feet. "Come on. She's going to be fine."

We walked back to the house. The smell of blood and fear drenched the air, and the room was alive with black fish flies swarming around Shine's bleeding head. Covering my mouth with my hand, I watched as Sid kicked the axe to one side and turned Shine onto his back.

"Take a leg," he ordered weakly. "I'll take the other one and we'll drag him. Be easier once we gets going down the gully."

We lifted a leg each and started dragging. Josie looked up as we come out through the door, and seeing Shine's body bumping over the stoop behind us, scrambled to her feet and ran up to the woods.

"She's gone to the camp," I said.

Sid nodded and we kept on going, sweating and panting in the heat. Once we came to the gully we dragged him straight down through the brook, the water washing away the bloodied trail as we went. His boat was hauled up on the beach, right in front where the gully ended, and after a spell of tugging and pulling and shoving, we finally got Shine into it. Putting our shoulders against the bow, we shoved it off from shore and watched as it bobbed gently over the growing swells.

There was a bit of a southerly picking up and the boat would be in the middle of the bay soon enough, moving away from Haire's Hollow and drifting further down the shore. And perhaps, I was thinking, if a big enough wind picked up, it might take it straight out to the open seas, and nobody would ever see it or Shine again.

"Let's start cleaning," Sid said quietly.

We retraced our steps, tossing every blood-soaked rock and blade of grass that we come across into the brook. When we got to the house, Sid went to the camp looking for Josie, while I went to the well for water. She wasn't rocking so bad when Sid brought her back. Still, she wasn't talking either, and her eyes were dazed, and as soon as she come inside, she ran to her room and slammed the door.

Ripping up one of Nan's sheets, Sid dropped to his knees and began soaking up the blood. I kept bringing in buckets of water from the well, and after an hour of steady scrubbing, there wasn't a trace left of Shine.

"The crackie!" I burst out.

"What?"

"Shine's dog! Where is it?"

Dropping to my knees, I searched under the daybed and crawled across the floor to search behind the stove.

"Kit, the dog's gone," Sid said, helping me up off the floor.

"No! It was here. It was here," I cried. "Help me."

Pushing Sid away, I ran down the hall and searched under the bed in Nan's room and in her closet while Sid looked through mine and Josie's.

"He must've run off," Sid said, coming back in the kitchen. "Come on, we have to get rid of our clothes."

"Our clothes?"

"They're full of blood," he said quietly.

"Oh." I looked down at my blood-stained shorts and blouse, and at his shirt.

"Are you going to be all right, Kit?"

I nodded.

"I'll find you a T-shirt," I said and went down the hall to my room. After I had changed, I searched through the closet and found an old shirt of my mother's that looked close enough to a man's and brought it back to Sid. "What about Josie?" I asked, stuffing my stained garments into the stove besides his.

"I already checked her. She's clean." He went outside the door and, returning with the kerosene can, poured the flammable liquid over the clothes. Standing back, he lit a match and tossed it in the stove. Flames shot up through the top hole, and Sid pulled the cover back in place.

I looked around the kitchen. The sun poured through the windows, showing dust motes floating through its beams and casting splashes of yellow around my feet and the clean canvas floor. Clean! Everything clean! Except for the pictures burning through our minds. How now were we to clean those? I looked to where Sid was standing by the stove, watching me, and if there were birds living in this house, then the silence that fell between us would've been the storm that they'd still their singing for.

CHAPTER SEVENTEEN

GOD'S LAW

IT WAS LATE EVENING WHEN THE WINDS SHIFTED. Roaring up the bay, they brought with them the lacing rain and fog—and Shine's boat. I watched it from my room window, ploughing through the white caps and heading for the beaches of Haire's Hollow like some ghastly phantom ship, heavily toiling beneath its burden of death, and with the prowling winds at its helm. Fear set my teeth chattering and I pulled back from the window and stared instead at my reflection, and seen how the yellow of my hair blended into the yellow of the lamplight behind me like a great, flickering halo, and I seen what I first thought were raindrops squiggling down the pane were tears streaking down my face. And then I heard what I first thought was the wind howling was the sound of someone screaming.

Pressing my face back against the window, I strained to see through the dark, and there, standing on the edge of the gully, her face whipped by lashing strands of red, was Josie, her rain-drenched clothes clinging to her body, and her fists aimed at Shine's boat. I raced outside and, coming up behind, grabbed her by the arms. She kept screaming and shaking her fists until I got her back inside the house and shut the door.

I scolded her, gentle like, as I skinned off her wet clothes and wrung the water out of her hair. Wrapping one of Nan's knitted shawls around her shoulders, I sat her in the rocker by the stove and poured her a cup of tea. Her lips were blue and she was shivering out of her skin. I stoked up the fire to warm her, and all the while I talked to her, like Sid would've done.

"No need to be scared of Shine no more. He's in God's hands now, and Sid's not goin' to let anything happen to you. No one's goin' to know we did it. And don't go worryin' about what God thinks. He seen what Shine was doing to Sid and me. And if it weren't for you, Shine might've killed me and Sid—or just as well as killed us both. And if all of that don't come across to God, you can be sure Nan's watchin' all what's happenin' and is doin' her part to fix things right. She always said you were given to her on account of her being smart enough for the two of you. So don't think she's not remindin' God now, of how it was him that took her away in the first place, leavin' you behind to fend for yourself.

"Hell, it wouldn't surprise me if she got a flock of angels together right now pointin' the finger at God himself and hoverin' over our roof this very night, makin' sure nothin' more happens to you. No sir, it wouldn't surprise me one bit, no matter how much she hated feathers. It's other things we got to worry about, like keepin' what happened to Shine to ourselves. And this is where you got to listen real good. You can't tell nobody nothin', if they starts comin' out here askin' questions. We never seen Shine. Just keep sayin' that, and anything else that they ask, act like you don't know what they's talkin' about. They'd rather believe that of you, anyway."

After a while the crackling fire and the steady rocking sent her drifting off, and I made her lie down on the daybed. Covering her up, I put more wood in the stove and took her place in the rocker. I rocked through the rest of the night, listening to the wind howling against the tide.

Her forehead grew hotter during the night. The next morning the wind and rain had stopped, and I sat on the door stoop waiting for Sid. Catching a glimpse of him coming down the road, I quickly ran to meet him.

"She has a fever," I babbled. "She was out in the rain last night—we seen Shine's boat."

Putting his arm around my shoulders, Sid talked fast and quiet as he led me back to the house.

"It's the biggest news since the coming of Christ. Old Joe was the first to find him when he went out to check his nets this morning. They've sent a message off to Deer Lake for the Mounties. They should be here by noon. Some of the fishers are going up and down the shore, looking for Shine's camp. Old Joe and his brother is gone over to check out Miller's Island." Sid paused. "Has she said anything?"

"No. They're goin' to find out, Sid."

"Not by us helping them, they won't. We've got to tend to Josie's fever ourselves. Perhaps after the Mounties come, we can get Doctor Hodgins to come look at her."

"I don't think we can keep her quiet about Shine."

"We have to. We'll talk to her good. She listens, Kit, she most always listens. But, we have to wait a day. We don't want anyone looking Josie's way yet, not with Shine just found dead. It don't take much for some people to start making connections, even if there's none."

"Sid, it wouldn't her fault. I mean, she was protectin' us. Perhaps they'd let her go . . . "

"The law might. But, you're forgetting about the reverend. He'd be on to the both of you like gulls to shit, convincing everyone that morally you'd be better off someplace else, that it was Josie's sluttish ways that brought Shine upon you in the first place, and who's to say it wouldn't happen again, this time with you being the victim. He can play it good, Kit. You don't need me reminding you of that."

"Oh God," I cried. "It's gone too far, I'm scared. I don't care about me, no more. I only care about her, and . . . and you." I turned to face him. "They'll find out, Sid, and it's goin' to be bad. They don't have to know about you. It's me that's to blame. It's me that wouldn't leave. I should pay! I should pay!"

He caught me by the shoulders, his eyes hard set against mine.

"There's none of us to blame!" he half yelled. "You hear me? None of us. But, it's her they'll haul off to jail. Her mind couldn't take it, Kit. You know it, and I know it. Even if after the trial they let her go, there'd be nothing left to let go. Josie can't survive without you. Without . . . " he swung his arm around the gully, "Without this. It's all she knows. It's all that keeps her alive." He tightened his grip and whispered harshly, "And me. She has me too, now. She killed Shine to protect me. I won't let them destroy her because of it."

I was quiet, the truth of his words washing over me.

"Do you think it's O.K. to talk with Doctor Hodgins now?" I whispered.

"No. He's a man of the law too, in some ways, and he'd be forced to tell the truth. It wouldn't be right to involve him. Will you trust me, Kit? I'm going to see us through this. I promise you."

I closed my eyes, and felt his lips pressing against my forehead. Taking him by the hand, I led him inside. Josie was sitting up on the daybed, rocking in that strange way of hers, but her eyes fixed right away on Sid as he walked over and sat down besides her.

"How you doing, Josie?"

She never said nothing, just kept rocking.

"Kit says you've got the flu," he went on, laying the palm of his hand across her forehead. "You're hot, for sure. Are you feeling sick?"

She smiled weakly, and watched as Sid reached inside his shirt and brought out a dark red pitcher plant, its heavy belled sides slightly crushed and drooping from the weight of its petals.

"It's for you," he said, pressing it into her hand. "I seen it on the bog on the way over and it reminded me of you. See? It's pretty and red, and it grows alone, and it's got a poison sitting in its centre, and anything that goes in there that don't belong, don't get out. That's God's law, do you hear me, Josie? What don't belong, don't get out! And that's why you hit Shine with the axe, because he didn't belong here. He was going to hurt me and Kit, and you done the only thing you could. It's God's law." Clasping his hands around hers, he leaned over and pressed his check against hers. "God's Law, Josie," he whispered. "No one can judge it but God himself. You done good. Didn't she do good, Kit?"

"Real good," I said, my voice trembling. "I bet Nan's proud of you."

A faint glimmer of yellow appeared in her eyes as she looked up at me.

"Real proud," Sid whispered, brushing back a limp strand of hair. "And you can make us prouder, Josie. You know how you can do that? By not telling anybody what happened with Shine. Not anybody! It's our secret—mine, yours and Kit's. Promise me now, promise me that you won't ever tell anybody anything about the axe and Shine. Do you promise? Do you promise?"

She lay back and nodded tiredly, a small nod, just one dip of her head, and then she closed her eyes. Her cheeks looked more flushed, and her breathing was starting to sound a little raspy. Sid and I looked at each other, then quickly went outside.

"I don't like the looks of her," he said worriedly. "Let me go back and find out what's happening. Perhaps the Mounties are out from Deer Lake by now. If so, and everyone's making a fuss over them, they won't notice Doctor Hodgins making a house call too much. Don't worry," he said, trailing a finger along my cheek. "She's going to be fine."

I smiled the best that I could, but the unease growing within me since the killing was starting to take over.

"Hey," he said, giving me a little shake. "Will you never start trusting me?"

"What about Aunt Drucie?"

"I'll drop in on the way and tell her the two of you's gone berry picking. How's that? What with everything that's after happening, she'll be happy enough to mosey into Haire's Hollow and catch the news. Are you O.K.?"

I pulled away and folded my arms worriedly.

"The reverend says if we kill, we pay," I said, looking out over the gully.

Sid gave a snort.

"You care now what the reverend says?"

"He preaches God's law."

"He uses God's law to fix his own preachings."

"Isn't that what you just did?" I said, turning to face him.

"Isn't that what we all do, sometimes? Take God's law

and make it ours?" he answered almost angrily. "Damn! You think I haven't thought about this, Kit? You think I don't care about God's law? Hell, I'm scared to death of God's law." He kicked at a rock and sent it plinking against the side of the house. "But there are other laws, God's laws too, I suppose," he said, turning to me. "But they aren't so clearly written. And it's those the reverend don't spend much time on, like those of the mind. Well, those are the ones I think about all the time. And my mind can't reason it through that Josie should suffer any more. And that's the one God will judge me on, do you understand me, Kit?"

He cupped my chin and forced me to look at him. "I'm doing what I have to do," he whispered. "I believe that. Now, you have to believe what you're doing is right, too, else the lie becomes your sin. Decide, Kit. Is she deserving of your lie?"

He kept staring at me, but I could find no reassuring answer. It was how the reverend and everyone else was going to be using God's laws that was causing me the most concern. Fear clung to me like a black shroud as I watched him walking away, shadowing my every step and darkening my every thought. I went back inside and spent the rest of the morning tending to Josie and looking out the window, waiting and watching, waiting and watching...

Come noon, Sid hadn't come back and Josie's forehead was burning hot. And she was still, so very, very still. I sat back in the rocking chair and must have dozed, because suddenly I was on my feet, listening to the hard, deep moans coming out of her as she slept.

"Shine! Shine!"

"It's all right," I said, shaking her.

"Shine!"

"Shh ... " I tried to soothe her but her moans sounded

so raw, so deep, they felt as if they were being dredged out of her. "Wake up," I shouted, shaking her harder. "You're havin' a bad dream, that's all, just a dream. Wake up."

Her eyes popped open, dazed and burning. I felt her forehead. The fever showed no signs of breaking and her breathing was starting to sound more and more ragged. Wetting a cloth in the wash pan, I laid it across her forehead and ran out of the house and down the road to Aunt Drucie's. She was just coming out her door, tying her bandanna beneath her chin, on her way to Haire's Hollow.

"Kit!" she called out upon seeing me.

"It's Josie," I gasped, running up to her. "She's burnin' up with fever. Will you sit with her till I gets back with Doctor Hodgins?"

"Aye, you knows I will, but did you hear someone killed Shine?"

"Yes, Sid come by . . . "

"It's shockin', maid, shockin'. . . "

"Aunt Drucie, I got to hurry up."

"Go, go. My my, the poor thing, is it the flu?"

"Yes, no . . . I don't know. She . . . she might sing out Shine's name. We seen his boat last night. She thinks his ghost is goin' to haunt us."

"Poor lamb, go on, go on, run for the doctor. I goes to where she's at."

I raced down over Fox Point and along the road through Haire's Hollow. There was a crowd gathered down by the wharf, everyone swarming around Shine's boat. He must have been in it because there was a piece of canvas covering the top. Old Joe's motor boat putted into sight, coming across the harbour. Just back from Miller's Island, I figured, and everyone crowded onto the wharf to meet him and his brother. There was a third person in the boat, but they were too far off yet to recognize. I saw the reverend's black hat as he walked amongst the people. Then I saw Sid standing on the edge of the wharf. His eyes widened as he looked up and seen me, and I hurried off towards the clinic so's he'd know why I was here.

"They got someone aboard," Gert Combdon was saying as I walked in through the clinic doors. She was kneeling upon the wooden bench that ran along one wall, her nose pressed against the window. Maisie Rice and Darkus Randall were cramming to see around her, a red-eyed youngster with a runny nose sitting on each of their laps.

"My gawd, who is it?" Darkus asked, a touch of scandal already on her tongue.

"Can't see," said Gert.

"He don't look very big, do he?" asked Maisie.

"Looks like someone from Perpy's Cove," said Darkus, edging Gert to one side for a closer look.

"For sure they're down there bad enough to kill," said Maisie.

"The devil takes care of his own, for sure," agreed Gert. "My gawd, sure it's Mope!"

"Mope!" Darkus near pressed her face through the glass. "Well, blessed be, we should a known if there was a still, Mope'd be soaking his head in it."

"Well now, for sure it wasn't Mope that killed Shine," said Maisie. "He got trouble liftin' a spoon outta his cup."

"I got to go see," said Gert, jumping down from her seat. "You take my turn with the doctor, Darkus."

"You can go in next," Darkus said to Maisie, tucking her youngster under her arm and running out the door behind Gert. Maisie was on her feet, fixing to run out too, when the examining-room door opened and Old Joe's brother's Missus was standing there, with Doctor Hodgins.

"What's goin' on? Is he back?" the Missus asked, looking from me to Maisie.

"He's back, maid," said Maisie. "With Mope aboard."

"Mope? Well, I'll be . . . I'll see you next week, Doctor," she said hurriedly, and gussied out the door, leaving Maisie staring after her.

"You can take young Kit over me, Doctor," Maisie said with half a laugh, heading after the Missus. "I'm worse than Gert for wantin' to know what's goin' on." She was out the door before Doctor Hodgins had a chance to agree.

"How about you?" Doctor Hodgins said to me with a grin. "You want to run off, too?"

"It's Josie," I blurted out. "She's got a fever. Bad."

"I'll get my bag," he said, and disappeared inside his office. I ran outside to where his car was parked on the road, and looked out over what was happening on the beach. Old Joe was leading Mope towards Shine's boat. Sid was still standing on the edge of the wharf, and the reverend's hat was shifting through the crowd.

"I keeps tellin' 'em Shine's been kilt, but he won't listen," Old Joe was complaining, hauling the piece of canvas off Shine's boat. "Thinks Shine is goin' to come after him for lettin' the fire go out under the still. Here, how's that." Old Joe pushed Mope up by the side of the boat. "Is that dead enough for you?"

Mope's eyes bulged open and he stepped back in alarm, his head bobbing on his long, spindly neck at the sight of Shine sprawled out in the bottom of his boat, his legs thrown over one of the benches as if he had leaned back too far to fetch something and had lost his balance. Everyone started laughing at Mope's comic-looking face, and seeing how he was the centre of attention, Mope laughed, too. A few of the fishers and Gert crept up to the boat for another look. With

Shine dead, there was nothing for anybody to be worried about. It felt like they were having a party, not standing around a dead man.

"Was it you that killed Shine?" Old Joe's brother-in-law called out to Mope with a chuckle.

Mope shook his head, his good humour giving way to sudden fright.

"N-no sir. I n-never killed 'em." He threw a skittish look towards the boat and took a shaky step backwards. Everyone laughed.

"The only thing Mope killed was a gallon of shine," Old Joe answered.

"Who killed him, then?" Gert asked, shaking her head at the scandalous sight of Shine being dead.

Mope shrugged, his mouth opening and closing several times before any words come out.

"I-I d-don't know," he finally stuttered, looking wild-eyed around at everyone standing looking at him.

"You must know something," Gert kept on. "Was anyone over there with him? Was he goin' to see someone?"

A startled look come across Mope's face as his darting eyes landed on me.

"The gully tramp's girl," he called out triumphantly.

It felt like Josie was suddenly standing besides me, giving me one of her surprise slugs in the guts. Heads turned to where I was standing, and a look of dismay swept over Sid's face. The shroud of fear from this morning tightened itself around me as the reverend looked my way, then coiling his arms up by his sides, he snaked his way through the crowd.

CHAPTER EIGHTEEN

TIDE AGAINST THE WIND

"WHAT ABOUT THE GULLY TRAMP'S GIRL?" the
Reverend Ropson asked, coming to stand before
Mope.

Everyone become quiet and Mope started to quake
faster. I imagined the reverend's paltry eyes creeping in
through his and possessing him to say again the words that
would give him grounds to damn Josie to hell, and me alongside of her. With beads of sweat popping out on his already
sweating forehead, Mope darted his tongue nervously across
his lips.

"I—I—I—"

"With all respect, reverend, sir," Old Joe said, throwing
a look at me that Nan often gave to stray cats shivering in the
snow, "I don't see how you can expect Mope to remember
anything, seein's how he's been sauced for days."

"Try years," Maisie said, catching a laugh from a few
others around her.

"Where was Shine going the last time you seen him?"

the reverend shrilled to Mope, oblivious to those around him.

"T-to get the g-g-gully tramp and her girl."

It was as good as getting a confession. Swinging around, the reverend's eyes lit onto mine like bolts of lightning.

"It's the Devil's milk that made an evil man out of Shine," he rasped. "And it's the Devil's milk that's nursing the soul of Josie Pitman. It's out there," he said, pointing towards the gully, "that you'll find out who committed this foul crime."

At that second the Mounties drove up the road in a dusty black Dodge, and Doctor Hodgins was taking me by the arm and pushing me inside his car.

"Out with it, Kit," he ordered, starting up the motor and stepping on the gas.

I looked out the window, catching sight of Sid furiously shaking his head, his finger to his lips, silencing me.

"She—she was out in the rain last night . . . and got sick."

He was quiet. Then, "It was Shine who got Josie drunk, wasn't it?"

"I don't know."

"Yeah, you know. Kit, this is no time to lie," he said urgently, swerving the car sharply around a turn. "What's after happening out here?"

I fixed my eyes straight ahead, thinking only on Sid and the set look on his face as he warned me to silence.

"Kit!" Doctor Hodgins's tone held out a warning of its own.

"I don't know nothin' about her gettin' drunk," I said stonily.

Doctor Hodgins said nothing more till we were at the gully. Before the car had stopped, I was shoving open the door and running down over the bank. Aunt Drucie met me at the door.

"Oh my oh my, she's gone right off her head," she cried. "She thinks Shine's comin' to get her. Hurry on, Doctor, for God's sake, hurry on."

She was crumpled up in the corner of her room, rocking to and fro, to and fro, her eyes wild in her face.

"Shine's back," she cried out when I rushed in. "Shine's back."

"Shh, Shine's dead, he can't hurt you," I soothed, running over to her. "We seen his boat going up the bay last night," I say to Doctor Hodgins as he dropped to one knee and put his hand across her forehead. "Now that she knows he was dead, she's scared of his ghost."

"And blood! She keeps goin' on and on about blood," Aunt Drucie said.

"It's the time Sid chopped his finger," I said. "She still dreams about the blood."

Ignoring the surly look on Doctor Hodgins's face, I helped him lead her to the bed.

"Blood! Blood!" Josie moaned as we laid her down.

"You didn't do it," I scolded, pulling a blanket up over her. "I keeps sayin' that it wasn't her that chopped Sid, but she won't listen."

"And she never done nothin' the like," Aunt Drucie moaned. "I was watchin' through the window."

"No, she never done nothin'," I said, holding her down as Doctor Hodgins fished a thermometer out of his bag and poked it between her lips.

"How long has she been like this?" he asked.

"She started to get hot this morning."

"This morning?"

I nodded.

"Kit was tanderin' like the easterlies when she come for me," Aunt Drucie said, leaning close as Doctor Hodgins put a stethoscope to Josie's chest. "I was just on me way over too, wouldn't I, Kit. Is it the ague, Doctor?"

Doctor Hodgins pulled the stethoscope away from his ears and the thermometer out of Josie's mouth.

"Are you sure the fever started this morning?" he asked.

"She was fine last night, except for gettin' wet."

He looked from me to Josie, a perplexed frown furrowing his brow.

"Do you have aspirin?"

I shook my head.

"And I don't have any either, Doctor," cried Aunt Drucie.

"Drucie, get me a pan of lukewarm water and a cloth," he commanded.

The second Aunt Drucie was out of the room, he was onto me.

"She's been traumatized. What's happened, Kit?"

"Nothing! I swear!"

"Has she been feeling sick, lately? A cold? Sniffles?" He watched me keenly as I kept shaking my head. "Kit, pneumonia don't set in this fast, there's something else complicating matters."

I looked to Aunt Drucie with relief as she come hurrying back in with the wash pan and laid it on the dresser.

"I'll go get some towels," I said, running gratefully out of the room. Coming back in, I dropped one in the pan of water and stood back as Doctor Hodgins wrung it out and laid it across Josie's forehead. A car sounded up on the road. And then another.

"My, my, who's that now?" Aunt Drucie asked, clicking her tongue against her teeth and sticking her head out the window. "Lord above, it's the reverend! And the Mounties! It's the reverend and the Mounties," she exclaimed, pulling her head back in and looking from me to Doctor Hodgins. Doctor Hodgins stared at me gravely.

"They'll be wanting to speak with you, no doubt," he said, wiping his hands on a towel. "Are you ready for this?"

I swallowed hard, trying to squelch the churning growing in my stomach.

"Wait here," he commanded. Tossing the towel onto the bed, he left the room, closing the door firmly behind him.

"You wait here," I commanded Aunt Drucie, softly opening the door and creeping out behind Doctor Hodgins. There were two of them, each dressed in black, tight-legged pants tucked inside long black boots, brown pressed shirts and black round-topped hats. The reverend come up behind them, and all three nodded politely at Doctor Hodgins, whose solid frame was blocking the doorway, and whose hands on each side of the door jamb, suggested he was about to keep it blocked.

"I suspect you know why we've come," the reverend said, taking off his hat and edging its rim with his fingers. "We'd like to speak to Kit and her mother about Shine's murder."

"Unfortunately, Josie is extremely ill at this time," Doctor Hodgins replied strongly. "I suggest you come back tomorrow, gentlemen."

"What's her sickness, Doctor?" the older of the two Mounties asked.

"She's down with pneumonia."

"I'm sorry to hear it," the reverend half whispered. "Perhaps, if we were to talk with her for just a minute? It's a serious matter, Doctor. I'm sure you're aware."

"I'm aware of nothing except my patient's health," Doctor Hodgins replied.

The older Mountie shifted uncomfortably.

"I'm sorry, Doctor, but if only for a minute."

Doctor Hodgins hesitated, then, "A minute," he said. "And it will be a minute, gentlemen."

"First, the girl," said the older Mountie as Doctor Hodgins turned to lead them down the hallway.

My stomach churned harder and my legs trembled as I stepped into the room before them. The older of the two, with a grey, curling moustache, shifted slowly from foot to foot, as if he was at sea on a restless swell, while the younger one remained steady besides him, keeping the same stern look on his face that I'd often seen on Sid's when he was trying to get Josie to understand something that he believed was important. Unable to hold their stares, I stood as close to Doctor Hodgins as I could without touching him, and kept my eyes to the older Mountie's belt buckle. He bent over to peer into my eyes.

"Are you Kit?" he asked, somewhat kindly.

I nodded.

"And you knew the man called Shine?"

I shook my head. The Mountie faltered, then looked questioningly at those listening.

"But you know who Shine is," he tried again, turning back to me.

I kept staring.

"Does she speak?" asked the Mountie, looking to Doctor Hodgins as the reverend clucked his tongue, impatiently.

Doctor Hodgins arched his brow.

"I expect she's waiting for a question," he replied.

The Mountie sniffed irritably and peered more sharply into my eyes.

"Do you know who Shine is?" he demanded, his tone bereft of his former kindness.

"Yes," I mumbled.

"When was the last time you saw him?" he asked.

"Today," said I.

"Today?" queried the Mountie.

"Alive!" snapped the reverend. "When was the last time you seen Shine alive?"

"Guy Fawkes Night," I murmured, blocking out the memory of Nan shooting at him with the rifle from the partridgeberry patch.

"And that was the last time you saw him?" asked the reverend.

There was a silence, then the reverend was pushing the Mountie to one side and staring into my face.

"Didn't you see him yesterday? Right here?" he spat. I flared my nostrils against the sour smell of his breath wafting into my face, refusing to lift my eyes from the Mountie's buckle.

"What about your mother?" he pushed when I didn't answer. "Didn't she see Shine yesterday?"

"Shouldn't you be asking Josie that?" asked Doctor Hodgins, shifting impatiently.

Tucking his thumbs behind his belt buckle, the Mountie nodded at Doctor Hodgins.

"Perhaps we'll speak with the mother," he said. "After you, Doctor."

"Go alert Drucie, Kit," Doctor Hodgins said, nudging me towards the hall. "We'll give Drucie a minute to cover her," he said to the Mounties and the reverend. "She was sponging her down when I left her."

Relaxing my breath, I darted on weakened legs down the hallway and into Josie's room, pushing Aunt Drucie to one side as she clung onto my arm, crying in alarm, "What can they want, Kit? My God, what can they want with we?"

"Tell them nothin'," I whispered hotly to Josie, grabbing hold of her hand. She was quiet now, with her eyes closed, and the towel Doctor Hodgins had laid across her forehead pulled to one side. "Tell them nothin'!" I whispered again, lowering my mouth to her ear. "Nothin'! God's law! God's law!"

I let go of her hand as the door opened, and sprang back from the side of the bed as the reverend scooted in, the two Mounties behind him.

"Hello, Josie," the reverend said, taking a spot by her bed and leaning over her.

Josie's eyes sprang open at the sound of the reverend's voice, and she shrank back to see him leaning over her bed, staring down at her. Whimpering softly, she flung out her hand towards Doctor Hodgins, her face paling against the white of her pillow, and the red of her hair dulling to that of a dying ember.

Doctor Hodgins wrapped both his hands around her wrist and held her hand against his chest.

"I'm right here," he said quietly. "They just want to ask you some questions."

"You know who the Mounties are, don't you, Josie?" the reverend asked, a quick smile jarring the corners of his mouth. "They're the law. That means you must tell them the truth."

The eldesr Mountie stepped closer to the bed.

"We won't take long, ma'am. You'll pardon us for bothering you while you're sick."

Josie closed her eyes, her breathing coming hard and scratchy.

"We want to ask you about Shine," the Mountie said, and paused as she started whimpering at mention of Shine's name.

"He was killed yesterday," the Mountie started up again. "Were you with Shine yesterday?"

"God above . . . " Aunt Drucie gasped, her hand to her heart.

"Answer the question, Josie," the reverend said forcefully as Josie began to roll her head on her pillow. Then, her eyes shot open and she stared frantically at the faces standing all around her. Opening her mouth, she made to speak, but faltered as she came to the reverend.

"Did you see Shine yesterday?" he repeated almost kindly.

Her mouth started working to say something, and all the time she stared into the reverend's eyes as if hypnotized.

"Shine," he whispered. "Did you see him?"

"Shi-Shine... " she whispered through parched lips, and her eyes started to roll.

"Answer me, Josie," the reverend coaxed. "Did you see Shine yesterday? Answer me, now, and then we'll leave you be."

She steadied her gaze onto the reverend's and worked her mouth to speak again.

"God's law," I said softly, the words leaving my mouth before I had a chance to check them. Her eyes flew to mine, and she screwed up her mouth like a sick baby.

"What's that?" the reverend hissed, looking wildly from Josie to me.

"God's law!" Josie cried, streaks of yellow brimming through hot, pooling tears. "God's law! God's law! God's law!"

"I'm afraid you'll have to leave," Doctor Hodgins said, laying a hand across Josie's forehead as her voice started to rise hysterically.

"What's she saying?" the reverend demanded.

"God's law! God's law!" Josie shouted.

And Aunt Drucie started fluttering around the room, moaning helplessly, "If Lizzy was here now, if Lizzy was here now... "

"Everybody out," Doctor Hodgins commanded. "Kit, see them to the door."

"We'll be back later this evening," the younger Mountie said, backing down the hall and nodding politely to me and Doctor Hodgins.

"Not on this evening you won't, gentlemen," Doctor Hodgins said in the voice of one not used to having his word questioned. "And perhaps not tomorrow."

The Reverend Ropson was the last to go. Leaning towards Doctor Hodgins, he spoke in a hardened whisper.

"Either she bore witness to a murder, or committed murder, Doctor. Will you interfere with the law?"

"I'll do whatever's best for my patient, Reverend."

They stared at each other, their unsung battle raging at its fullest. Then the reverend twisted on his heel and marched down the hall behind the Mounties.

"See them out, Kit," Doctor Hodgins said, turning back to Josie. "Drucie, wet me another towel."

Just as I was turning on my heel to follow after them, Sid's head appeared in the window behind where Aunt Drucie was standing.

"I-I'll be a minute," I said to Doctor Hodgins. "I have to be excused."

I watched from the door till the reverend and the Mounties got into their cars and drove off, and then ran to the grassy spot at the back of the house. Sid's arm snatched out and grabbed me as I came around the corner and I fell against him with a sob.

"Shh, now, you're doing fine," he whispered urgently.

"They know," I cried.

"They don't know nothing. It's the reverend trying to make it look as if they know."

"Doctor Hodgins knows something's wrong."

"Let him think what he wants. We won't say nothing, do you understand? Nothing!"

"Oh God, I don't know! I don't know! I'm so scared!"

"Hey, now, I'm here, I'm right here. You've got to listen to me, Kit. I'm not going to let anything happen to you or Josie. You've got to start believing that. Will you start believing that?"

I tried to hold back my sobs.

"I'm afraid . . . "

"Shh, don't be afraid, nothing's going to happen to you. Just don't say anything."

"I-I've got to get back."

He pulled me tighter.

"I'm always going to take care of you, Kit," he whispered.

"You can't stay here."

"I won't be far, keep remembering that." Letting go of me, he slipped out of sight around the corner of the house.

When I got back inside, Doctor Hodgins was standing by the stove with his back to me.

"Her temperature's dropping," he said. "Drucie's sponging her down. Start getting some warm tea in her as soon as you can, with a bit of lemon. I have to drive by Herm's place, he's not doing so well. Then I'll go and get some aspirin from the clinic, it'll help her rest easier. I'll be back as soon as I can." He give me a long, sombre look.

"There's such a thing as timing, Kit, I'm allowing for it. But when things have ironed themselves out, I expect to be told what happened out here last night."

A silence fell, and in that moment I wished I was able to share with him the burden of the past day, for I believed he would have felt proud had I done so, and I wanted to make him proud. It was as if he heard my thoughts, for his next words held a glimmer of pride.

"You're doing good by Josie, Kit. Lizzy would be pleased." Lifting his bag off the table, he give me a sad little smile. "Why wouldn't she be? You're getting to be every bit as stubborn as the old girl herself." He turned to walk out the door, then paused on the stoop, the sombre look back again.

"You might want to light a fire right about now," he said, nodding towards the stove. "Get the chill out of the house."

I turned a puzzled look towards the stove. Aside from a dry wind picking up, it was warm and stuffy, both inside and out. Pushing back the stove-top, I peered inside. There, halfm burnt, and in full view, was a piece of Sid's blood-covered shirt.

Running around to the side of the house, I grabbed hold of the kerosene can and lugged it back inside. Dousing the damning scrap of cloth, I frantically lit a match and tossed it through the top hole. Flames licked up over the stove and I stood there watching them burn till there was nothing left but ashes.

CHAPTER NINETEEN

SID'S STAND

A DOG YAPPED OUTSIDE, SENDING shivers of added fear down my spine. Shine's crackie! Pulling the stove-top back into place, I ran to the door and cringed to see it standing on the lip of the gully.

"Get!" I shrieked.

"What did you say, Kit?" Aunt Drucie bawled out.

"I'll be right back," I yelled, then ran out the door and, picking up a rock, pitched it at the dog. He scampered backwards a few feet, then just stood there, staring back at me.

"Get, you little bastard," I yelled, picking up another rock and running after him. I chased him, running hard down the gully until I came out on the beach, then turned up towards Fox Point. He had stopped and was sitting near a clump of alders. "You get!" I screamed, letting fire with the rock I still held in my hand. Yelping loudly, the dog started trotting up the beach. I watched for a second, then noted a dark bundle poking out of the bushes where the crackie had been sitting. I took a few steps closer, my heart quickening. It was Shine's gunny sack!

I darted over to where it was sitting and, opening its flap, started filling it with rocks. Dragging it to the water's edge, I lifted it with a loud grunt and heaved it into the sea. It sunk the instant it hit the water. The crackie started yelping again and, casting him a look that warned of a devil's drowning by sea if I ever got close enough, he gave a couple of sharp barks and trotted up the shore. Taking a good look around to ensure there was nothing more of Shine's left behind, I started back up the gully, searching every rock and blade of grass on the way. There was nothing. Last night's rain had washed away any trace of Shine that Sid and I might have overlooked.

A cry sounded as I neared the top of the gully. I ran the rest of the ways, my breathing coming in short, frantic gasps. Scrabbling over the bank, I felt my legs go weak and my stomach curdle with fear. Making off up over the bank to the road was the reverend, and with him, Josie. He had his arms wrapped around her waist like the wings of a jackdaw as he half dragged, half carried her to his car, his black carcass relieved by the red of her hair as it whipped around his head and shoulders like tongues of fire. Chasing after him was Aunt Drucie, shaking her fist and bawling out, "Leave her be! Name a God, leave her be!"

"Stop! Stop!" I shrieked, and started running after them.

"He took her, he did, like the thief," Aunt Drucie cried out as I ran past her. "I'd no more than closed the door to Lizzy's room to relieve meself, when he sneaked in like the cat, he did, and stole her."

"You stop! Stop!" I screamed, racing up to the road, Aunt Drucie behind me. He shoved her into his car, much the same as he had done with me the day he had carried me off, then climbed into the other side. The motor roared to life just as I came onto the road. Tripping on a rock, I fell, my face barely missing the chrome bumper lining the back of the car. I crawled onto my knees but fell down again as the reverend jammed his foot on the gas and sped off, the spurt of heat from his exhaust pipe blasting in my face like a breath of hell. Gasping for breath, I got back onto my feet and started running. The car disappeared in a cloud of dust ahead of me, but still, I kept running. By the time I got to Haire's Hollow, a crowd was already gathering in front of the jailhouse, and Jimmy Randall was standing guard upon the steps before its locked doors. Mercifully, Doctor Hodgins was coming across the path from the clinic, marching resolutely towards the jailhouse steps.

"Doctor Hodgins!"

Everyone turned as I cried out, and Doctor Hodgins grabbed onto my shoulders as I collided against him.

"The reverend got her! He took her out of bed!"

"I know, Kit, and we're going to get her back." He slipped an arm around my shoulders and guided me through the outporters starting to crowd around us.

"I-I only went down the gully to see, to see if… " but my voice became choked and Doctor Hodgins tightened his arm around me, leading me towards the jail.

"Did Josie kill him, Doc?" Old Joe asked worriedly.

"All I know at this point is that Josie is a very sick woman," Doctor Hodgins answered, as much to Old Joe as to the others who were keeping step with us.

"How come it was the reverend that took her, and not the Mounties?" one of the others asked.

"We'll leave that one for the reverend to answer," Doctor Hodgins replied grimly.

"How come she killed him, Doc?" asked Maisie.

"Josie Pitman wouldn't kill a mouse," Doctor Hodgins said, taking the jailhouse steps two a time.

"If he was comin' to take her girl, I'd say she had God-damn good reason to kill the bastard," Gert said, taking the lead in front of Doctor Hodgins. Coming square to Jimmy Randall, she stood arms akimbo. "And if you had any guts, it'd be Shine locked behind them doors, not a sick, retarded woman."

"I'm just doin' what the reverend asked," Jimmy whined, staring nervously from Gert to Doctor Hodgins.

"It's souls the reverend's committed to treating, Jimmy, not bodies," Doctor Hodgins said. "And there's a sick woman in there that needs my help. Perhaps you'd better open that door."

Jimmy was relieved of answering as the jailhouse door swung open and the reverend stepped out, looking pleased as a fox with the feathers still floating around him.

"I was about to send for you, Doctor. I'm afraid Josie's fever is starting to act up."

Still holding onto my arm, Doctor Hodgins brushed past the reverend, and we piled inside. She was laid out on a small cot, trembling uncontrollably as she stared after the reverend.

"Burn in hell," she whimpered. "Burn in hell."

"Sshh, it's not you who's going to burn in hell," Doctor Hodgins muttered, pressing his hand across her forehead. He swore beneath his breath as the reverend's best preach-ing voice sounded back in through the room.

"It grieves me to say, my friends, that Josie Pitman has confessed to killing Shine."

"Son of a bitch!" Doctor Hodgins muttered as a murmur rose up from the people. "Sit with her, Kit," he ordered, and marched outside the jail.

"I wouldn't give a penny for anything Josie Pitman confessed to on this day," he half snarled, standing besides the
reverend. "She's delirious with fever and wouldn't recognize Shine's name from that of her own mother's right
now."

"She had no fever when she offered to speak with me,"
the reverend countered.

"Offered?" snorted Doctor Hodgins.

"That's right, offered," the reverend flashed back. "I'd
forgotten my hat, and when I went back to get it, I found
Josie alone in her room, calling out for help."

"He's the thief!" Aunt Drucie cried out, coming around
the corner of the jailhouse, gasping for breath and holding
up the end of her apron. "The regular thief—come in and
stole her, he did, whilst she was sleepin' like the baby."

"She was weeping like the damned," the reverend countered. "She said she killed him with an axe. Isn't that right,
Doctor?" he hissed, turning on Doctor Hodgins. "Wasn't
Shine killed with an axe? Only you know at this point what
was used to kill him, and perhaps the Mounties. Can you tell
us now?"

By this time half of Haire's Hollow was standing in
silence at the bottom of the jailhouse steps. At the reverend's
question, they all turned their eyes upon Doctor Hodgins.
I peered out around the door jamb and watched as Doctor
Hodgins's hands clenched shut behind his back.

"I said it was an axe," he said dully, "but, I never said it
was Josie Pitman's axe."

"But she said it was!" the reverend cried out. "May God
have mercy."

"Ain't right," Old Joe called out over the growing murmur of the people. "She ain't right in the head and she
shouldn't be called to answer."

"No! She isn't right," the reverend replied. "It's an ill wind upon us, neighbours, and I pray for us all."

"It might be an ill wind, but it's a man we all wished dead that it brung upon our shores," Old Joe shouted back.

"Yes sir, brother, and it's them wishes that helped kill Shine, no different than the hand on the axe handle," Maisie called out. "Is you goin' to arrest all of we?"

Her question fell short as the Mounties pulled up in their dusty black Dodge. Taking courage from their presence, the reverend slipped into his best sermonizing voice and hissed everyone to silence.

"No doubt there's some of us that has judged Shine, perhaps even judged him deserving of death. And come eternity, the sin rests on our own souls for having done so. But when it comes to killing, we can't defer judgment till that day. We judge now! That's why we have our own laws, as well as those of God's."

"Be the Jesus, if the law had done its job, there'd be no sin committed," Gert sang out, as much for the benefit of the two Mounties getting out of their car, as for the reverend.

"That's right, because Shine'd be in jail, not roastin' our youngsters, and chewin' off faces," Darkus shouted.

"That it took a woman to make the place safe to walk in, sir! And a retarded one at that!" Elsie yelled.

The reverend held up his hands for silence as the Mounties made their way through the crowd towards the jailhouse steps.

"There'll be mercy for Josie Pitman," he called out. "That I'll guarantee you, my friends." But his words rang hollow, for there was a fever burning in the hearts of the people for Josie's bravery, a fever as big and as hot as the one eating up her mind as she lay weakly on the jailhouse cot.

"Didn't Mope say he was goin' after young Kit?" Gert sung out.

"Be the Jesus, I'd have killed him too, if he was coming after one of mine," sung out another.

"And she's sick, my oh my, she's sicker than death," cried Aunt Drucie. "Name a God, how could she kill anything?"

"Silence!" The reverend's voice whipped through the crowd. "We cannot—each of us—administer justice as we see fit. I guarantee you there'll be mercy, but it'll be the law that administers it. We can't allow our hearts to stand in the way of justice—no matter who or what the situation calls for."

There was a silence. And in that silence a voice rang out, a strong and bold voice, a voice that sent a quickening through my stomach and a sickness through to my heart as the intent of what it was saying sunk through me.

"It wasn't Josie that killed Shine!"

Heads swivelled and a gasp rung through the people, a gasp as sharp as the air hissing out of the reverend and Doctor Hodgins alike, as Sid stepped out of the crowd, his head gannet proud and his eyes burning into mine.

"It was me," he said loudly.

"He's lying," the reverend rasped, his stunned surprise quickening his words.

"No sir, I'm not," Sid said, still staring at me.

"Lies!" the reverend spat out. "Lies to protect the girl."

"That's what I was doing, all right," Sid said, calm as anything, mounting the jailhouse steps. "Protecting Kit. From being raped by Shine."

A roar went through the crowd as what they'd been thinking all along come to be true: Shine was fixing on raping their girls.

"I was splitting wood when I heard Kit cry out," Sid said, turning to everyone.

"I do, I do know. Besides, I'm only seventeen, and I'm the reverend's son. Listen now." He pulled back and give me a little shake. "I'm the only chance Josie's got, you know that. She wouldn't survive a trial, and if she did, the reverend would see to it that she never goes back to the gully. Or to you. This is her only chance."

"Oh God, but supposin' they put you in jail?"

"They won't! I know they won't!"

"But supposin' they do?"

"Then that's their bloody laws. It still won't make me guilty, Kit. Only God can judge, remember that."

I tried to pull away.

"It'll be my word. I won't put you in jail."

"You won't. You won't be putting me in jail." He stared at me pleadingly as the sound of footsteps came up over the steps. "Please. You have to do this. For me. As I do this for you. And for Josie. Please!" he whispered urgently. Then he dropped his head and kissed me quickly on the lips. I tore away from him as the youngest Mountie stepped back in through the door, looking towards me.

"The doctor's waiting for you," he said.

With one last wretched look at Sid I ran out the door and down over the jailhouse steps to where Doctor Hodgins was waiting with Josie.

CHAPTER TWENTY

DOCTOR HODGINS'S WAVES

WE WERE TWO DAYS WAITING FOR THE TRIAL, and it was over in one. It took place in Deer Lake, a town about an hour's drive from Haire's Hollow. It took the two-day wait for Josie's fever to break, and by that time she never ever got it straight about what happened out at the gully—except that Shine was dead and it was God's law.

Doctor Hodgins ruled Josie unfit to testify and had old Joe's brother-in-law's wife sit with her at his place, while he and I made the trip to the courthouse together. Since the day of Sid's confession, both Josie and I were staying with Doctor Hodgins.

He never said nothing during the drive, his eyes fixed on the road ahead, while I sat nervously besides him. Once, I almost broke down and told him the truth of what happened, but he held up his hand, his eyes still on the road.

"It's the truth I'll tell on that stand. Beware of that before you speak."

I remained silent, though such feelings of fright as ever

I felt with Shine and the reverend mounted with every turn of the road.

"There is one thing, and I want the truth on this one," he said after a spell. He kept looking at the road ahead, yet every sense of him was leaning towards me, listening, feeling for any sound or movement on my part that might tell him a little bit more than what I was willing.

"Are you and Sid ... dating?"

This last word was spoke with such a thickening of his tongue that I cowered from its loathing. Staring out the window at the unfamiliar brooks and meadows sweeping past us, I felt again the wrath of the reverend the day he caught me with my foot in Sid's lap, and the repulsive smell of rotting dogberries as I had stood before him—somehow, shamed.

"I didn't do anything," I muttered bitterly.

Doctor Hodgins stared at me in some surprise.

"I'm not suggesting that you did. I only meant ... " He turned back to the road and sighed heavily. "There's nothing wrong with having a boyfriend, Kit. I'm simply asking if Sid's your boyfriend."

"I don't have boyfriends!"

"That's fine! That's fine! I—it just appeared that way, that's all."

I said nothing more, but my sense of Doctor Hodgins's relief was so sharp that it left me wondering why something that was so fine could affect him so badly.

We spoke no more until we entered the courthouse. Doctor Hodgins and I sat on one side, with the reverend and his wife on the other. I took care to not look their way, but the sobbing that broke forth from Mrs. Ropson every time she looked up and seen her boy with the handcuffs on and the look of pain that flickered across Sid's face each time he

looked her way pricked my heart like a well-whittled stave. Yet
each time his eyes lit onto mine, a light shone from them as
fierce as any that came from the reverend's on a good preach-
ing day. Only Sid's was pure, as pure as the white of an angel's
robe because it shone from his heart, a heart of honour, and
without him even knowing the weight of his offering, or
whether his mind was yet strong enough to carry such a load.

My heart swelled with a proud love. And when Doctor
Hodgins testified to seeing Sid's blood-stained shirt in the
stove out at the house that day, and then swore under oath
that Josie's fever had started up a day before the killing, making it seem as though she would've been much too weak to
do any lifting of axes and implanting them in the crowns of
grown men, I knew he was feeling, too, the rightness of
God's law and Sid's choice to act upon it. And when I moved
to sit on the witness chair, my legs trembling and my voice
quaking with each word spoke, I kept looking to Sid and letting that fierce light of his shine through me and bring forward every damning word that would condemn him for a
murder that my mother had committed. And when the ver-
dict was done, and the judge handed down his sentence of
two years in prison, I sat paralyzed by shock, listening to
Mrs. Ropson's wails cut through the room with the anguish
of a thousand grieving mothers. I fell to my knees, watching
as they led Sid out the door, his face white from the sudden
fright, and his heart breaking into two halves—one for his
mother and one for me.

"They'll reduce it," Doctor Hodgins was saying, pulling
me to my feet. "The reverend won't let it stick. His wife'll
see to that."

"No, no," I whimpered, my knuckles white from gripping the railing in front of me. "It isn't right. I've got to tell
them, it isn't right."

"It's done, Kit," Doctor Hodgins said harshly. "You can't change it, now."

"You! It's you who done this," Mrs. Ropson screamed, coming across the aisle towards me. "You and your tramp of a mother, you'll pay for this, I swear. And you too, Doctor," she cried out, as the reverend held her back. "I curse you this day, I curse you." Her burst of anger spent, she crumpled piteously and began wailing again, "My boy, my boy, they've taken my boy! Mercy, mercy, they've taken my boy."

Stumbling, she allowed the reverend to put his arm around her shoulders and help steady her. He looked at us then, over his wife's weeping head, and in the haggard lines that drew across his face as he led her out through the door, it was clear that his was a look that was thirsting for his own killing instead.

The storm that had been threatening for the past few days broke as we were driving back home. Doctor Hodgins leaned towards the windshield, cursing his slow-sweeping wipers against the heavy rain and his useless headlights against the thickening fog. The trees twisted in fury along the roadside, and the gravelled road turned to grease. I was content to huddle in my corner and watch the dismal greyness outside play out what I was feeling inside. Once, Doctor Hodgins looked at me and growled, as if I was willing the storm through sheer spite. Once, he looked at me as if I was the storm itself.

Back at his house, he asked that we live with him for the coming winter, giving Josie time to get her health back, and me comfort while I attended school. I said no. I was fifteen come September, old enough to quit school and old enough to take care of Josie. Alone.

He argued, but I heard nothing excepting the judge sentencing Sid to two years, and the dragging of his footsteps as the two Mounties led him across the courtroom. Sid was in jail and it was me that helped put him there. I was wanting no comforting on this day.

Nor, did it seem, did Doctor Hodgins. The day after I moved back to the gully, he took his medical certificate off the wall and moved from the house that Haire's Hollow had built for its doctors and took over a fishing shack belonging to one of old Joe's brothers that had died from blood poisoning.

"Why?" I asked, going out to visit him some weeks later. He was sitting on a rickety wooden chair outside the shack, facing the ocean that blew full on his face, and drinking from a tumbler of brew that he rested on the window ledge behind him whilst he puffed on his pipe.

"I'm taking up fishing with Old Joe," he said, his eyes still wandering over the sea.

"You're no fisher."

"Is that right, now?" he said, thoughtfully puffing his pipe. "You think everybody clings to a patch of ground the way you do, Kit?"

"I know you ain't no fisher."

"Sit down," he said, patting a wooden bench besides him. Then, "It's time someone younger took over. I'm getting too old to be borning babies all hours in the night."

"But, they're all still comin' to you. Only difference is, no one's payin' you any more."

"They pay in other ways."

I looked through the door at the jars of stewed berries and rabbit sitting on a plank that served as a cupboard.

"Supposin' me and Josie had stayed with you?"

"Supposing you had?"

"Would you still have moved out here?"

"I still would've closed the clinic doors." He tapped the bench testily. "Sit down, I said, Kit. Sit down and watch. Watch the sea unfurl itself."

He was drunk.

"It's because of the lie, isn't it?" I asked.

The weight was such as he lifted his eyes and looked up at me that I fell to my knees besides him.

"I'm sorry. You shouldn't have had to do that."

"Hush, now," he patted my head. "There's nothing for you to be thinking on here. It's but a short path that we've travelled together."

"Then why'd you do it?"

"Some things won't make sense to you, Kittens. Hah!" he snorted. "They don't make sense to myself, and I've been figuring them for years."

I sat on the bench, turning my collar up against the wind, following his eyes out over the curdling waves sweeping up on the beach.

"It'll be good to sit in a boat and ride those waves," he took up after we had sat in silence for a bit. "They've been doing that for thousands of years. Thousands! Steadily rolling upon these shores. Can man ascribe to such a feat?

"Noo!" he replied drunkenly. "We're weak! Broken! Still answering to the truths of our youth. And you, too, will answer, Kit. There'll always be faces unfurling upon these shores. Any shore. All shores." His face darkened as his thoughts took him to his most recent face.

"I stood a better chance of holding back those waves than talking him out of what he was doing. I seen that in his face, the way he stood there—and took it on himself. It was Josie, wasn't it?"

"Yes," I finally whispered, relieved at last to tell him the truth. "Sid saved me, just as he said. Then, it was him that

Shine ... was straddlin'. That's when she come in. With the axe."

"She saved you both," he said, his voice suddenly low. "Now, he's saving her." He clucked his tongue and raised his glass to the sea. "It's a beauty," he roared over the thundering surf. "God above, can you ever touch him on this one?" He lapsed back into silence, watching the waves roll in. I watched along with him, looking to see some of his faces. I didn't see anything, and after the sun went down and the September chill set in, I went along home.

It worried me with Doctor Hodgins living in old Joe's brother's fishing shack and going off fishing. I wondered if I might not have owed it to him to have stayed with him. But it didn't seem right that I not live in the gully with Josie. After all, it was why Sid went to prison, so's that she and I could live where we most wanted, and where he could think on us, knowing at all times what we were doing, and where we were sitting. I wanted his picture to be real, and for us to be waiting there when he came back. And there were other things I wanted. I wanted to hear his voice on the casterlies as they gunned up the gully, and the thumping of the axe as I dreamt of him splitting wood for our fire, and the rippling of his laughter as he chased Josie around and around the chopping block, tying her hair into knots.

Yet when I thought of Doctor Hodgins sitting on his front stoop, drinking brew and challenging the sea, I wondered that he might be right about those youthful truths he talked about—and might not his face be one to come unfurling upon my shores some day.

All of this I told in a letter to Sid when I got home, knowing how he liked to ponder things like the strength of the ocean and the strength of those who tried to drink it dry. And I laid the letter on the dresser in my room, waiting for word from him, and an address by which to send it. I wasn't sure where the prison was that they kept Sid, somewhere near St. John's, which was a full day's journey by train and might as well have been on the moon itself, it appeared so distant from Haire's Hollow. Each time I made mention to Doctor Hodgins of an address by which to mail Sid's letters, he took on the same intense look that he had the day in the car on the way to the courtroom when he asked if Sid and I were dating. And each time he took on that look, I backed away, thinking back on the smell of rotting dogberries, and preferring a trip to the moon itself, rather than to endure that feeling of shame that always followed it.

Josie waited too for a word from Sid. But just as the fire had dulled in her hair that day as she had lain sick with the fever, so too had a spark died within her. Her skin was pale, and her eyes a flat brown without the yellow specks livening up the green. She moped around the house most days and never bounded down the gully no more, and would never go near the chopping block or the axe. Nor could she be persuaded to bring in a load of wood for the stove. And during those times when I persuaded her to come with me to Crooked Feeder, she'd drag behind, stumbling over rocks and giving to silence. She took to sitting in the rocker, much the same as she had done after Nan died, and was content to just rock and stare out over the gully through the kitchen window. Sometimes she'd spend the whole afternoon there, just rocking and gazing, rocking and gazing.

"Are you dreamin' about Shine?" I asked her one evening when she was dozing in the rocking chair and come awake with a sudden cry.

"Shine's dead, Shine's dead," she mumbled, starting to rock, again.

"Do you remember when Nan died?" I whispered.

She started rocking faster.

"Do you remember what Doctor Hodgins said about Nan being a big, soft spirit who's always watchin' over us? That's what good spirits do, they make bad thoughts go away. Next time you haves a dream about Shine, you just think about Nan. All right? You think about Nan, and she'll make the bad thoughts of Shine and the reverend go away."

She nodded and kept on rocking.

They weren't all bad dreams that she was having. Sometimes she'd give a sudden bark while she dozed off, like the kind she had often given Sid when she'd see him strolling down over the bank from the road, and I was soothed that she was also listening to his footsteps on the door place, and hearing his jesting laughter on the wind.

All of this I told to Sid in letters. And placed them, one after the other, on the growing pile on my dresser.

CHAPTER TWENTY-ONE

WISHING UPON
A STARFISH

OCTOBER CAME, AND STILL NO LETTER FROM SID. Yet news came in other ways.

"He's took up his schoolin' in jail," Old Joe volunteered, dropping off a load of dried, split wood and a salted cod. "His mother had a letter the week. There's a priest that goes to the jail every day and teaches him."

"They says he's doin' right well," Aunt Drucie yawned comfortably from Nan's rocker during one of her visits. "Puttin' on weight, doin' his homework—what you ought to be doin'. My, my, Kit, Lizzy'd be in some way if she knowed you was quit school. Sure you knows I didn't mind comin' over and seein' to a bit a housework and takin' care of poor old Josie. I misses it, I do, gettin' up in the mornin' and comin' over. Is Margaret still bringin' you over homework?"

I dropped my head in my hands with a groan. There were many from Haire's Hollow that came to visit since the killing, but it was Margaret's visits that served me the worst. Claiming me to be her best friend since the day of the trial, and bringing over schoolwork on account of my teaching myself grade ten at home, she came to visit about once a week, and took on an importance in Haire's Hollow as being the one most closest to me, and the one with the most knowing about how Josie and I were doing out here in the gully. She became good at reporting back everything I said about the killing—which was nothing—and real good at reporting back what she figured I wanted to say, but couldn't.

"Must be you got lots on your mind, Kit, and that's why you quit school. What do you think Sid is doin' right now?"

"I've not heard."

"He don't write? Well, he writes his mother most every day. The poor thing near faints every time she gets her mail and there's nothin' there. My gawd, she's in some way, never comes out of her house exceptin' to get her mail. And the reverend either, exceptin' to preach on Sundays. But I don't expect Sid tells her everything. They says the jail is a awful place—murders and everything goes on in there. What say he's not writin' you though, Kit? My gawd, I was sure he was right after you, my dear. And what with everything you both went through ... it was here, was it, at my feet that Shine was straddlin' you? My gawd, what'd you do, Kit?"

"I screamed," I'd say, praying for the kettle to boil. "Have another cookie, Margaret?"

"My yes, they're lovely. They're Mrs. Haynes's, aren't they?" Margaret leaned forward. "They says he hits her. You know, Mr. Haynes. Sure, she always got a bruise or a limp, but she tells Mom it's because she's as clumsy as Mope on a drunk, always fallin' down. Sure he's bad as Shine, hittin' his wife. Did Shine hit you when he was straddlin' you?"

"No. I don't like to think on it."

"Course you don't, my gawd, you must still be dreamin' about it."

"I sleeps pretty good," I'd say, and curse the kettle for not boiling, and heap more cookies on her plate, and pray they'd soak up all the spit in her mouth, leaving her too dry to talk. But it was with the same pending excitement that a prettily wrapped Christmas present held out for a youngster that I held out for Margaret.

"You looks nice with your hair tied back. Next time I'll bring some ribbons and plait your hair with the ribbons pleated in. They'd look real nice on you, and, my dear, when Sid gets out of jail, he won't know you." She leaned forward with a wink and half whispered, "He's after you, I knows he is." Then her eyes widened and she reached for the cloth bag by her feet. "My gawd, I almost forgot," she exclaimed, pulling out a bottle of blueberry jam. "Mom sent this over. She's a bit cross that you won't let her bring out your groceries any more, but she won't see you do without, Kit."

I shoved another junk of birch into the stove and centred the kettle back on the top. It wasn't so much Margaret's lifting the lid of Shine's coffin and keeping the smell of his rotting corpse drifting cross the nostrils of every soul in Haire's Hollow that bothered me the most, but her pointing out to me, every single solitary time that she visited, how poor I was. Others came too, besides old Joe with his truckloads of wood, and Margaret with her bottles of jam. Gert, Elsie, Maisie, Jimmy Randall's wife—they all came, bringing with them bottled moose, rabbit, seal, and salt water trout and salt water ducks. Plus the cellar was filled with turnip, potato, cabbage and carrots.

I could never keep track of who was bringing what— they would just dump brin bags full of vegetables down the hatch each time they came, and I'd never know it was there until I went down the ladder to fill up a bag and bring some inside the house. Except for Mrs. Haynes. I always knew what she brought. It wasn't so much the cookies, but what the giving of them did for her that kept me noticing. Each time she passed over the brown paper bag, still warm and staining up with melting butter from the just-baked cookies inside, it felt as if I were receiving the bounty of her life's work, she passed them over with such reverence. She never come inside. Just held the bag out over the stoop and smiled a sad little smile which always seemed to be more for her than for me. And then she'd walk back up over the hill, pausing every so often to look down over the gully before getting in her car and driving away.

It wasn't that I minded them coming and bringing things. It was the same as what they did for everybody else— never mind the fact that each of their pantries was filled with the same things. It was the sharing that counted, and the knowing that there was always something that set one bottle of jam off from another—a different spice, the size of the jar, how long it was left to boil, to cool and, as Nan had always sworn by, knowing how long to leave the berry on the patch before the killing frost got it.

It was after one of Margaret's visits in early November that it struck me how me and Josie could return the generosity of the people in Haire's Hollow.

"We're goin' berrypickin'," I said, tossing Josie her rubber boots and coat, and thinking also how a jaunt on the barrens might put some colour back in her cheeks.

"Who's goin' berrypickin'? You's goin' berrypickin'."

"I can't do it all by myself. And we got to do our share with payin' people back."

"I don't like berries. You pick berries."

"Yeah you do like them. You're just lazy."

"You just lazy. I'm not lazy."

"You're always lazy when it comes to pickin' berries.

Now, put on them boots," I said, shouting as I'd heard Nan do a hundred times when it come time to get Josie ready to go berrypicking.

"You go berrypickin'. I'm not goin' berrypickin'."

"You're goin'," I shouted in my best Nan imitation. "Or be the Jesus, I'll strap you onto me back and carry you in."

She reared up from the rocker and threw herself on the floor and began hauling on the boots, barking and scowling as she went. Then, snatching up her dipper, she barrelled out the door and in her old-fashioned way bounded across the meadow and up through the woods towards the partridge-berry patch.

It was dark when we got back. Our fingers and mouths were stained with berry juice, and our backs aching from bending over. But our two dippers and pot were full. I spent the better part of the next day picking the berries clean of leaves, sticks and spiders, and two days later we went back to the patch and picked and picked until we had another two gallons. Snow fell, but the ice was not yet ribbed on the glass, and whether or not the worm had crawled out of the berry and planted itself for next year's pickings, I could only guess. By the end of two weeks, we nearly had the patch cleaned.

It was soothing work, picking berries. Although it was much later in the year than Nan would have done the picking, and the sun colder, there were times when I could almost see her, sat down by a moss-covered rock, her legs splayed out in front of her, smiling as the wind brushed her face and the last of the fall leaves drifted around her. It gave me courage to keep picking. At times the wind cut tears out of our eyes and our noses were constantly running, but we kept steady at it—picking, picking, picking, until sometimes we were picking up sticks and throwing away berries, picking up sticks and throwing away berries.

A good way to work the knots out of your stomach, Nan used to say, soaking her feet in a pan of hot water after a day's picking. And now, sitting back with my own two feet in a pan of hot water, and looking over at the two five-gallon buckets of ruby red berries, all cleaned and waiting to be preserved and handed around to the people of Haire's Hollow, I sighed contentedly, wondering how much of Nan's good feeling about picking and preserving partridgeberries was due to the good, honest work, and how much to the pleasure that she received from giving.

Josie showed no such looks of contentment. Coming home from the patch, she'd kick off her boots and storm down the hall to her room, the red in her cheeks as much from her fuming as from the exercise. I sighed, much the same as Nan had done. Berrypicking was never Josie's cup of tea in the best of times. I expect that wasn't about to change.

Aunt Drucie helped with the preserving.

"For sure Lizzy'd be proud to know you're makin' the best of her patch, Kit," she said, tightening the cap on a jar of berries and passing it to me. "And that you're keepin' it secret. More than once I threatened to follow her in, but I allows she would've led me to God's end and left me for the caribou to trek over. By the cripes, she was stingy over that patch."

"Perhaps I'll let you come with me and Josie next fall," I say, taking the jar and placing it in the pot of boiling water with the rest. "How long should they boil?"

"Oh, till you sees the pink bubblin' above the berries. Now, I lets mine boil a bit longer than Lizzy, to sweeten the tarty taste. But Lizzy now, she use to haul hers outta the water at the first sight of a bubble. I'd never say it in front of her, Kit, but I always thought her jam a bit tarty. Better than May Eveleigh's, for sure, 'cuz hers taste worse than pig's slop, as Lizzy always used to say. But I likes mine a bit of sweet, I do. Now, let's have a rest till they's boiled."

It was a stark winter's morning when I handed over the first bottle of partridgeberry preserves.

"Look every bit as good as Lizzy's," Old Joe beamed. "Heh, you wouldn't mind givin' Old Joe a hint as to where to find a patch of his own, now would you, Kit? Lizzy always said she meant to tell me, someday."

"And so I will, Joe," I said solemnly. "So I will. Good day, now, and don't forget to pass your brother over his bottle."

"Aye, you're gettin' to be as hard as Lizzy, God help us," Old Joe muttered, dodging on up over the hill.

"And just as scrooge," Doctor Hodgins glowered as I shooed him away from my stack of jars gleaming on the bin one evening. Slouching down in the rocker, he stared warily at the chimney as the stormy February winds rattled down through, blazing up the fire and spurting smoke up through the cracks around the stove-tops. He'd been coming regularly since the day of the trial, making sure we had enough split wood to last through the nights, and that the roof wasn't going to blow off over our heads.

Or so's he said. I knew it was for different reasons that he came. A man with learning can't lay claim to the youthful truths that he had talked about that evening sitting by the sea. So it was mine that he clung to, and Sid's. And that's why he kept coming out to the gully as often as he did, to see me and Josie, and judge it right that he had lied under oath and helped land a mother's boy in jail. And other things too kept him rooted to Nan's rocking chair that winter; things he brooded over, but seldom spoke of.

"You look like her," he said after we had sat quietly for a spell one evening, and Josie had taken herself off to bed.

"Like who?" I asked, laying my history book to one side and looking up from where I was sprawled on the daybed.

"My wife. When she was your age." He smiled. "With your blonde hair and pretty blue eyes, you could've been her girl."

"Aunt Drucie said she wanted to adopt me."

"She did, and that she did. From the second you were born and she laid eyes on you."

"She was there?"

"Yes, she was, she and ... Mrs. Ropson," he added after a slight pause.

My eyes popped open.

"Mrs. Ropson?"

"She was a good friend of Elsie's back then. She— happened to be visiting when word come that Josie was in labour." He shrugged. "She'd often helped me with birthings back then, so, she came along." He rested his hand on his chin, and went back to brooding again, as if the memory had become distasteful.

"Mrs. Ropson helped born me?"

"That she did," he replied.

"You ... didn't want babies?" I asked, anxious to shut out the picture of Mrs. Ropson handling my squirming, naked body at birth.

"I always figured God would have given us one of our own, if He had meant for us to be parents," Doctor Hodgins said. "Elsie went along with that. Course, I didn't leave her much choice. I thought she'd gotten over it," he paused, "until you were born. Everyone knew Josie couldn't take care of you, and that Lizzy was getting on in years, so she set her mind on adopting you. With Lizzy's blessings, of course."

"And Nan said no?"

Doctor Hodgins's brow shot up.

"And a whole lot more. And right she was to say no. She had love to give you, and love's a better guarantee of happiness than someone else's need to rescue." He rose slowly from the rocker and, striding across to the window, looked down over the gully. His voice was quieter when he began talking again, as if he were speaking to himself.

"It was her needs that I misunderstood—again. Had I but tried, perhaps she might've found in me what she was looking for in a child. And too, there's those that deserve to be rescued—God help them."

Striding back to the rocker, he sat down heavily and started rocking again, the chair creaking beneath his weight. And long after I'd gone to bed I heard him sitting out there, creaking his way through the night, and brooding . . . all the time, brooding . . .

I brooded too, lying there in my bed. What with the wind trying to wrench every board in the house apart, and Doctor Hodgins creaking up his own storm out in the kitchen, there was small chance of blissful sleep on this night, or of hearing Sid's laugh sounding up the gully. It was nights like this that I mostly missed Pirate. And nights like this that I prayed the hardest upon my orange speckled star. Starfish, star bright, starfish, star bright . . .

CHAPTER TWENTY-TWO

THE LETTER

IT WAS COMING INTO SPRING AND STILL no word from Sid. And if it wasn't for Old Joe and Margaret and Aunt Drucie reporting back from his letters to his mother, I wouldn't know even if he was alive.

Josie became my true source of comfort. At least with her I could say his name. Oftentimes while she sat there rocking, and the gulls were calling out as they circled above the house, and the winter's sun sparkled off the snow on the windowsill, I would chat while dicing up potatoes about how one day soon Sid would be walking down that hill again, with his white shirt and padded jacket, and whistling some nonsense song as he pulled a book of ancient proverbs out of his pocket and began prattling, and how he'd be chasing her around the chopping block, tying her hair into knots and wrestling her to the ground.

She'd never say anything, but I could tell by the way the chair would stop rocking that she was listening. Sometimes while she rocked and dozed, her face would redden and her eyes would bulge, and her humming would start coming in short moans, and she would rock harder and faster, harder and faster. I knew then that she wasn't dreaming of Sid whistling and prattling and tying knots in her hair, but that she was standing on the edge of the gully and seeing again Shine's wind-driven boat lunging over the waves and heading for the shores of Haire's Hollow. On those times I'd grip her shoulders and pull her head back against my chest and stroke her forehead, soothing her with more soft-spoken words, thinking all the time that this is what Sid would have me do, this is what Sid would have me do.

"It's fine, it's fine. Shine's gone and he's never comin' back. Shine's gone and he's never comin' back. Sshhh, nothin's goin' to hurt you, now, nothin's goin' to hurt you. Remember what Sid said, God's law. It's God's law."

Most times she'd let me soothe her. Other times, the sudden touch of my hand upon her shoulder, or the sound of my voice if I spoke unexpectedly behind her, would startle her, and she'd rear out of the chair and wallop me across the face. Once, I dropped a plate while washing dishes, and she lunged out of the chair and slugged me so hard in the guts that it took a full minute before I could catch my breath again.

Aside from the stinging of her slap and the bruised ribs, I never minded. It wasn't me that she was hitting, just whatever that sound was that made her jump. I took to doing most everything for her—fixing her meals, putting out her clothes in the morning. And the strangest of all, I took to mauling at her hair—the way she used to do with Nan's. It calmed her when she went into her bad rocking spells. And it gave me something to do besides talking to her. It got so that it became soothing for me to run my fingers through those long, red strands, brushing and plaiting them, and coiling them around her head, always making sure they was neatly combed and prettily braided. She was starting to look like Nan, especially when her hair was coiled back from her face. It was startling to see her look like Nan. I always imagined she had entered the gully the same way as me and Pirate, as an offering that Nan took pity on.

It was pity I expect Nan might've felt for Mrs. Ropson, if she had been walking with me the day I almost ran into her in Haire's Hollow, going into the post office to get her mail. She was all shrunken up inside a black winter's coat, with a black hat and a veil covering her face, no different than one in mourning. I leaped off the road and ducked besides Jimmy Randall's stagehead so's she wouldn't see me. The water lopped up over the edges of my boots and settled coldly around my feet, but I never moved. Rather the freezing Atlantic than the freezing blood between Mrs. Ropson and me.

I never laid eyes on the reverend. I had left off going to church some time before the graduation dance. I knew Nan wasn't pleased, but I felt more at peace with God curled into a nook at Crooked Feeder than I did in the back pew of the church with the reverend pointing his finger of shame in my face. And I got more learning from curling up on the daybed with a book than sitting in Mr. Haynes's classroom and trying to shut out the sight of his purple-webbed nose and chalk-grimed hands. Once, he drove by the gully and stopped. He never blew his horn, and when he seen me come out of the house and silently stare up at him, he drove off. Since the killing no one come by the gully blowing their horns any more.

Spring came. My pile of letters to Sid grew. I couldn't think as to why I never received one from him, but I knew it wasn't because they were never wrote. Each night I turned into my pillow I could see his yellow head bent over a piece of paper and writing as fast as he could to keep up with the words coming to his mind. No matter how many times I looked over his shoulder, all I ever read was "for you and for Josie," "for you and for Josie." And each morning I woke up, I wrote another letter of my own, crying, "It isn't right!, it isn't right!"

One dreary April afternoon after leaving the post office, I walked along the shore to Old Joe's brother's shack. Old Joe's kelp-green motor boat was moored off from shore, and Old Joe was squatting with Doctor Hodgins in the middle of a fishing net they had spread out over the beach, mending the damage from the winter's ice.

"How you doing today, Kit?" Doctor Hodgins sang out.

"Fine," I said, plopping down on a rock and watching along with Doctor Hodgins as Old Joe weaved the wooden, arrow-shaped needle in and around the broken twine squares of the net's mesh.

"You wanna help me with the Doc here?" asked Old Joe with a grin. "Funny thing, sir, he been stitchin' up people for thirty year, but he can't learn how to stitch up a net."

Doctor Hodgins scratched his hair, giving me a baleful look.

"It's like trying to do a fine stitch with double ball mitts on," he said, eyeing the wooden shuttle layered with twine that old Joe was thrusting through a loop, then hauling back taut, forming a knot.

"Tell you what, Joe," said Doctor Hodgins. "I'll do your squid jigging come fall, while you hangs around the shore for a spell, mending the nets."

I giggled.

"What're you gigglin' at?" asked Old Joe, quirking a brow.

"Nan always said you was afraid of squids."

"Hah, Lizzy! I been sittin' on them waters for a good many year, and I ain't run from no squid yet," Old Joe grumbled. "I minds the time when I seen one so big, he was longer than me boat, and just as wide, and his skin shimmerin' so red beneath the water, it looked like he had a lantern in his guts. And he come up outta the water, he did, his tentacles first, as long as them on an octopus and just as strong. Yes sir, you could tell by the way they was curlin' up and splayin' out, how strong they was. And then up come the old humpback whale, sir, as big as the side of a house and black as tar. And his eyes, big as tea plates. And he eyeballed that squid for as long as it took for the squid to puff out his sides like a balloon and then let go with a jet of shit that smattered both his eyeballs. Well, sir, you want to see a whale blow! I dare say she blowed a bloody lake out of her blow-hole that day, and then she was rearin' outta the water. And then I seen the swordfish sneaking out from the shadow of me boat. They teams up, you know—the squid and the swordfish. And before the whale had a chance to dive, the swordfish come up and pierced him through his gullet. And with that, they both went under, the whale on top of the swordfish, and swordfish still with his sword stuck up through the whale. And then the squid let go with another spray of shit, and while the swordfish was gettin' away, the squid wrapped his tentacles around the whale, makin' sure they was good and stuck, and his beak was coverin' the hole the swordfish made, and then he started suckin' the blood outta the whale. Then they sunk down through the shit and I couldn't see 'em. It was another twenty minutes before I seen 'em agin, goin' out the bay, almost down by Chouse Brook, the whale rearin' outta the water, the squid still stuck to him, suckin' his blood, and the swordfish gunnin' for his back to pierce another hole."

Old Joe finished talking, still weaving his needle through the net, whilst me and Doctor Hodgins stared at him in silence.

"That sounds like a yarn I read in a school book," I said,

"And so you might've read it in a school book," said Old Joe. "'Cuz that's where they ended up before the squid got all the blood sucked out of that whale—in St. John's. And that's where they makes up books, ain't it, Doc, in St. John's?"

Doctor Hodgins stirred besides me.

"Yup, that's about right, Joe," he said, clearing his throat and lifting up a section of the net for a closer inspection. "That about right, Kit?"

"Yup! That's about right," I say. "Good day to ye." Shuffling to my feet, I started wandering back along the beach.

"Kit!"

I looked back. Doctor Hodgins was sitting back on his haunches, staring after me.

"There's a letter for you," he said, nodding towards the shack. "Besides the lamp."

I continued to stand there, staring at him, then turned and ran for the shack. Bursting in through the door, I stopped and gaped in wonder at the white envelope sitting on the table, propped up by the lamp, with my name scrawled across its front in Sid's fancy handwriting. Snatching it up, I stuck it inside my coat pocket and figured on running straight home, but sat down weakly on a chair and pulled it out of my pocket, again. Ripping open the envelope, I begin reading.

> *Dear Kit:*
>
> *Doctor Hodgins just told me what I've suspected all along, that none of my letters have been getting to you. I expect the reverend has seen to that. I think of you*

always, waiting for me in the gully, and it gives me strength. I pray you're still there when I return.

I've made a good friend here and my days have become fairly routine, which is a shame in some respects. At first, with everything being so strange, and with all the rules, it kept me always paying attention. I never noticed before how much we miss when we go about our days not paying attention. It seems kind of backwards, somehow, that the only time we're ever really aware is when we're youngsters, and seeing and learning everything for the first time. Maybe that's how it is we can keep moving through later life, because we remember what it felt like to think nothing, and that then becomes our goal — to work our way back there again, and to delight in just being. That's how I feel when I'm with you — I delight in just being. I'll write to you again, Kit. I write to you every day, only I don't mail them any more.

Love, Sid.

I carefully folded the letter and put it back in its envelope. It was just like Sid to be sitting in jail and thinking about the way of things. I laughed. Then cried. Then I laughed again and was reminded of the day in the gully when I had found Josie meeting Shine on the beach and had gone running and crying into Sid's arms and saw for the first time how his smile dimpled the corner of his mouth.

Wiping the tears off my face, I put the envelope in my coat pocket and went outside. Doctor Hodgins was standing a little ways down from where Old Joe was hunched over the net, watching for me.

"When?" I asked after I'd come close enough. "When did you see him?"

"I just got back last night," he said finally.

"Why didn't you tell me you were goin' to see him?"

"I hadn't planned on going to see him." He shrugged, his eyes squinting against the sun and blocking what was unspoken. "But when I found myself in Gander this week, I decided to take a jaunt to St. John's." He shrugged.

I waited for something more, but receiving nothing, left him there, mending his broken nets with Old Joe, and hurried home. Josie wasn't inside. Looking out the window, I saw her cooped down on the grassy spot behind the house, looking down over the gully. Digging a couple of cookies out of one of Mrs. Haynes's butter-stained bags, I went outside and joined her.

"Have one," I said, passing her the cookie.

She took the cookie and idly began eating it.

"What're you thinkin' about?" I asked, hugging the letter from Sid in my pocket.

She shoved the rest of the cookie into her mouth and slewed her eyes warily towards me.

"Do you remember what it was like when Sid was here?" I asked.

"Sid's gone."

"But he'll be comin' back, someday."

"Sid's gone."

"Look." I pulled out the letter and waved it in front of her face. "It's from Sid. He'll be comin' home, someday. Not yet, but . . . "

I got no further. Whipping around, she drove her fist into my ribs and ripped the letter from my hand.

"No," I gasped, grabbing after her as she reared to her feet. "Here, give it back. I'll read it to you."

"That's Sid's letter," she barked, glaring down at me. "Sid's letter." Then she was bounding for the gully.

At least she still knows how to bound, I thought dismally, rising carefully to my feet and limping back inside the house

The next day Doctor Hodgins came to visit. He was looking more sombre than usual, and I expect it had to do with my letter from Sid.

"What's wrong?" he asked, as he noted me flinching from twisting around too quick.

"Nothin'," I said. "Cup of tea?"

"Did she hit you, again?"

I nodded.

"Let me see that," he said gruffly.

"I'm fine."

"I'll judge that, young lady."

I groaned, not for the first time the past twenty-four hours, and let Doctor Hodgins examine my ribs.

"You've got a bruised rib," he announced.

"No kiddin'," said I.

"Kit." He sank down in the rocking chair, looking up at me. "Kit, have you given thought of leaving here? Haire's Hollow, I mean. Now hear me out," he said, holding up his hands at the look of protest that crossed my face. "I'm not talking about shipping you off to God knows where. I have a friend—a wonderful friend—Milly Rice. She has a boarding house in St. John's, it's a decent place, and she ... well, she's getting on in years and the last time we talked, she mentioned getting someone in to help her."

"I'm not leavin'."

"What's here for you?"

"She's here."

"You can take her with you."

"She won't leave here."

"She won't? Or you won't? Kit, my work here is done. I'll move with you."

"I'm not leavin'!" I yelled.

He came to his feet and we stood staring at each other. Then he turned on his heel and marched off up over the bank to his car. I watched after him from the doorway, wondering how much of his wanting me away from the gully might have to do with his wanting a way out of Haire's Hollow himself. A chill crept over me, and I wrapped my arms protectively around myself. There was a power in whatever it was that bound Doctor Hodgins to me and Josie, a power strong enough to make him lie in the face of God, nailing him to a cross of his own making. Whatever that power was, he was helpless to fight it. And however it touched on me and Josie, we were equally as helpless in its quandary.

CHAPTER TWENTY-THREE

GODFATHER'S COVE

IT WAS LATE SEPTEMBER, JUST PAST MY sixteenth birthday, when I sat up in bed one night with a sudden start. Something had woke me. Josie's snores rumbled through the hallway and her bedsprings creaked as she tossed and turned for comfort. I lay back down, but sat up again as a dull thud sounded from outside. Holding my hand to my racing heart, I swung my legs over the side of the bed and crept down the hallway. *Thud!* It sounded louder as I stepped into the kitchen. *Thud! Thud!* Clasping my hands in front of me as if I were in prayer, I walked steadily towards the door. *Thud! Thud! Thud!* Perhaps it was Doctor Hodgins not being able to sleep. *Thud!* Perhaps it was Shine's ghost come back to haunt me. *Thud! Thud! Thud!* I reached my hand to the doorknob. Silence. Perhaps it was the wind gusting up the gully playing tricks on me, thumping a loose plank against the side of the house. But I knew who it was. And when I hauled open the door and seen him standing there in the blue light of the night, with the moon shining silver on his hair, and a burst of fuzz on his chin, my knees buckled, and I would've dropped if he wasn't swooping towards me and lifting me off my feet and holding me tight against him.

"Sid!" I wrapped my arms around his neck, and buried my face into the warmth of his throat.

"Jesus, Kit!" He rocked me with him, his arms squeezing me tighter and tighter, his face burrowing through my hair to rest on the back of my neck. We stayed that way for some time, him rocking and grazing his face against my skin, and me squeezing up against him, smelling, almost tasting, the salty sweetness of his throat.

"Sid...!" My voice choked and hot tears welled up in my eyes.

"Shh, it's all right. I'm home now, I'm home now."

"To stay? Are you here to stay?"

"I'm here to stay."

"Are you sure?"

"I promise."

"Oh, God, Sid, I've hated every day."

"Shh, we'll be fine, now. It's over."

"It's over?" I pulled back and looked up at him, the tears spilling down my face. "Is it really over? It's not been two years..."

"The reverend done his work," he said, wiping my face with the pads of his thumbs. Then, leaning down, he placed his lips on mine and kissed me long and hard. My mouth opened beneath his, and I kissed him back, again and again and again.

"Jesus, Kit." He pulled his mouth to my cheek, kissing it and kissing it, then grazed his cheek against mine as I tried to keep kissing his face, his chin, his brow.

"Hey!" he said with an urgent laugh, taking hold of my

arms and holding me away from him. "You ought not to be kissing a man like that."

"Ohhh!" I was back to burying my face into the tuck of his throat, the sweet scent of his skin flooding my nostrils.

"Kit, listen to me, now," he said, hugging me close and smoothing his hands across my back. "I want you to wake Josie and get dressed. We're leaving here. Tonight, before anyone discovers I'm home."

"Leavin'... " I pulled back and he cradled my face, speaking softly and quickly.

"I'll explain everything on the way. Just get ready. I have a friend waiting for us on the beach with a boat."

"A boat! Sid, did you escape?"

He grinned at my look of alarm.

"Yeah, me and the rest of the boys."

"Sid ... "

"Hush, of course not. The reverend leaves for St. John's tomorrow morning—to meet me. We need to be out of here before he discovers I'm home. Come, let's go get Josie, and I'll explain everything. Quickly now." He steered me inside and down the hall to Josie's room.

"Let me," he whispered, stepping quietly over to her bed.

"Wait... " I cautioned, but too late. The second his hand touched on her shoulder, her fist come up swinging from beneath the blankets.

"Uuggghhh!!!" He clasped his hands to his stomach as she whumped him good.

"I told you," I whispered sharply.

"Kit, if we're trying to wake her, why are we whispering?" he moaned, bending over to catch his breath.

"Who's whisperin'? You's not whisperin'?" Josie barked, coming upright in her bed.

"Josie, it's me! Sid!"

"Who's Sid? You's not Sid."

"It's Sid!" I said, pulling back the curtains and letting the moonlight in. "See? He's back."

She went quiet and, laying back on her pillow, curled away from him.

"Hey, now," Sid said coaxingly, leaning over her. "That's no way to greet an old friend."

"She's feeling shy of you," I said.

"You go get dressed. I'll get her up," he said softly. "Hurry."

I left them there and dashed into my room to get dressed. It was a matter of seconds before I heard Josie's barking laugh. And by the time I got some clothes on, they were both tussling around on the bed, with Sid pleading with her to get dressed, that he was taking us on a boat trip.

What with her excitement over seeing Sid again, it took some doing to keep her calm and get her dressed. But soon we were all bounding down the gully with her in the lead.

"Now, tell us where we're goin'," I said breathlessly, as we came out onto the beach, foolishly thinking we were on our way to Crooked Feeder.

"You oughtn't keep a woman in suspense like that," a deep, male voice boomed loudly. "It's bad for their constitution."

What appeared to be a piece of the night moved. Startled, I jumped back, bumping into Josie, who clung onto my arm.

"This is Fonse, my friend," Sid said quickly, laying a reassuring arm across our shoulders. "I told you I had a friend waiting."

The blackened shape moved to stand before us, engulfing me in shadow as he blocked out the moon and the stars.

"And a friend he'll stay, if be the Saints of all that's patient, ye'll hurry on and get in the boat."

"Where... where are we goin'?" I asked.

"Just an hour's ride," Sid said, nudging us towards the black hull that was half-pulled up on shore. "And never mind Fonse, he's done nothing but complain since we left the jail."

"You did break out!" I whimpered.

"Break out?" Fonse roared. "Now where'd you get a fool idea like that? The Saints be praised, can't a man be in a hurry to get home to a wife he hasn't seen in six months? Or is we goin' to stand yakkin' on this beach all the bloody night?"

With a frightened yelp, Josie turned and ran back towards the gully.

"No, Josie, it's O.K.," Sid called out, running after her. "Dammit, man, will you shut up?" he roared back at Fonse. "Come on, Josie. We're fine. He's my friend. A big-mouthed friend."

Speaking softly all the while, Sid managed to get her back to the boat. With a sudden move, Fonse wrapped both hands around my waist and, lifting me up, planked me down on the wooden seat. A shrieking bark from Josie, and she was lodged down next to me. Then, Sid and Fonse was shoving off the boat, their boots scrunching into the beach rocks as they kicked off from shore. Swinging themselves up over the bow, they clamoured into the boat as we bobbed into the shimmering pathway of the moon. Clumping past us, the boat rocking threateningly beneath his mighty weight, Fonse seated himself in front of the motor, and Sid dipped a paddle down through the water, steering us away from Haire's Hollow. The put-put-put of the engine's pistons rung out through the night, and we headed down the bay. Fonse talked Josie into sitting in the stern alongside of him to help with the steering, leaving me and Sid to ourselves. Pulling a piece of canvas around our shoulders to stave off the chilly night air, Sid snuggled me against him and began firing questions.

"First, tell me where we're goin'," I said, putting my hand over his mouth to silence him.

"We're goin' to Godfather's Cove," Fonse called out over the putting pistons. "Land of the Gods, of which they thinks I'm one, at least Mudder do. Loret, now, she's the wife, and she got other thoughts. And after bearin' five youngsters, she got a right to 'em."

I smiled at the black outline of Fonse's face and turned to the warmth of Sid's breath on my cheek.

"How far is it?" I asked.

"Twenty mile. And that makes for an hour's ride in the chariot," Fonse replied.

Standing up, Sid and I turned our backs to the God and sat on the other side of the seat, pulling the canvas up over our heads for a tent.

"Of course there's those that risk being toppled out and might never get there," Fonse roared, and my mother barked out laughing.

"Why was he in jail?" I whispered.

"He started a brawl at a garden party. Someone's wife went outside for a piss, and when Fonse opened the back door to get some air, there she was, bare arse to the wind."

I broke into giggles and Sid twisted around to see if Fonse was listening. "Anyway," he whispered, "the Mister didn't think kindly of Fonse exposing his wife's arse like that and punched him a good one. Before Fonse was back on his feet, Loret, Fonse's wife, threw a punch at the Mister. And then the wife, still hauling up her pants, come in across and packed a punch to Loret. Then Fonse's mother walloped the wife across the arse and said she shouldn't have been pissing on the doorstep to begin with, and then up she went."

"Did they all get put in jail?"

"Nope, just Fonse. So happened the Mounties was out that night, and they dragged Fonse off and threw him in the back seat of their car." Sid paused. "And that's where the trouble started. According to Fonse, he was trying to tell his side of the story to the Mounties, but the Mounties weren't listening very well, so he leaned over the seat and boxed one of them on the ears and busted his eardrums. He was given six months for hitting a Mountie."

I laughed. Nothing sounded bad on this night as we cut through the water, passing Chouse Brook, heading for a distant point just beyond the black hulk of Big Island. As comforting as the booming of Fonse's voice as he talked to Josie, and her quick barking retorts, was the billion stars still littering the sky, and the warmth of Sid's arm as he slipped it around my waist. I answered his one thousand questions about everything that had happened since he left, from my quitting school and taking up studying at home, right down to the length of Margaret Eveleigh's ringlets the last time she come calling.

Then, Fonse was bellowing out, "Here she be, friends, the cove of all coves."

Throwing back the canvas, we peered straight ahead into the quiet, tree-lined cove before us, its flat calm waters mirroring black the gull-grey dawn. A grey, pebbly beach ringed the water's edge, and a small wharf jutted out from its deepest point. I turned towards Sid and studied him afresh in the morning light. The tufts of yellow covering his chin and top lip banished forever the schoolboy Sid, and in the split second before he looked back at me, grinning his old

familiar grin that used to make me think that he was making
fun of me, it felt like I was looking at a stranger.

He stood up as Fonse abruptly cut the motor, and I saw
that he wasn't as scrawny as he used to be, and what with his
hair inching down over his collar, and jeans and a sweater
replacing his black jacket and white shirt, it felt again like I
was looking at a stranger.

"Aren't we a bit far from shore?" he called back to Fonse.

"Aye! And that we are, my fair fellow," said Fonse, and
I turned to encounter a pair of muddied brown eyes squinting down at me from beneath a thatch of curly brown hair.
"You're as pretty as Sid said you was," he said, passing a
paddle to Sid, whilst picking up the second one for himself.
"See the bobbers?" He pointed to foot-long rectangles of
brown cork floating in widening circles across the greeny
brown reflections of the cove's glassy waters. "That's Fudder's nets. We paddle around them, else we chance gettin'
the propeller tanglin' up in them ropes. And then, you got
yourself a dandy problem."

"What sort of problem does that get you?" asked Sid,
dipping his paddle to the opposite side of Fonse, helping him
steer around a net.

"What happens is the boat gets jutted around," said
Fonse, "so's the stern is pushin' into the wind, and the bow
is in reverse. Now, you see how a bow is shaped like a 'v' to
displace water? Imagine now if it was the broad side of the
stern pushin' into the sea and wind. You see what would
happen?"

"The boat would swamp," I said.

Fonse grinned, his narrow lips peeling back over wide,
white teeth and sending creases rippling back from each corner of his mouth, echoing years of hard laughing, and widening further his square rugged jowls.

"Heh, she's smart as well as pretty," he teased. "Best make friends real quick with Loret, else you might get cat claws across those blooming cheeks."

"Pay no heed to Fonse," Sid said, leaning over the bow as we neared the wharf. "From what he says, Loret's as soft as April snow."

"Who's snow? What snow?" Josie asked contrarily from the stern, blinking herself awake and standing up unsteadily, her hair a tangled maze around her shoulders.

"Here now, it's sleepin' beauty, awake at last," Fonse said, holding out a hand to steady her. "Hold on, we's home!"

The boat bumped to a gentle stop against the wharf and Sid climbed on top, loping the painter around the post. Straddling past where I was sitting, Fonse grabbed hold of the wharf and hauled the boat tight alongside as Sid reached down and helped me and Josie climb out. All hands on shore, we set off on a deeply trenched path through the birch woods, and come out onto a large potato garden, broken with patches of waist-high grass. At the back end of the garden and atop a little rise was a two-storey house, its half-dozen windows looking down upon us, and a thin trickle of smoke coming out of its chimney. A bent-over old woman with iron-grey braids swinging down over her shoulders crept out the door, peering at us through a pair of spectacles perched on her nose.

"The Saints be praised," she sang out in a voice as booming as Fonse's. "If he ain't decidin' to come home. Loret! It's Fonse! He's back!"

A dark head appeared in one of the upstairs windows, and then another, and another, and then the old woman was running down over the steps and throwing herself into Fonse's arms. The door swung open again, and a younger woman, a few years older than me, with her dark hair mostly pinned back and hundreds of curls sprouting all around her face, came running out, shrieking and yelling to the high heavens. Behind her came a youngster, and another, and then a scrawny, white-haired old man, and a younger man, the spit of Fonse, and just as big, with a cowlick twisting a lock of dark hair across his forehead, and behind him, still more youngsters, until they were all shooting out the door and coming towards us like a load of buckshot.

Fonse tried to catch them all in his arms as they come shrieking and yelling and throwing themselves at him. And when the load got too heavy, he buckled to his knees, with them swarming around him, tousling his hair and clapping him on the back, the arms, the neck, the face or whatever part of him was left exposed.

"What a charm, what a charm!" laughed the old woman, breaking away from the pile.

"And who's this he's brought home now?" bawled out the old man, peering at us closely.

"They're my friends," Fonse declared loudly. With one arm around the young woman, and balancing a youngster on his shoulder, he held out a hand towards us. "This is Sid, Kit, and the one peekin' out from behind Kit is her mother, Josie. Don't be fooled by her shy look, she's as fiery as the red in her hair. And this good-lookin' bunch," he said, dropping the youngster off his shoulder and hugging his wife more tightly as he proudly feasted his eyes on his family, who by now were all staring curiously at us, "is my darlin' wife, Loret, and Mudder and Fudder—don't mind Fudder's bawlin' out, he's deaf as a haddock. And this handsome feller is my brother, Bruddy." Letting go of Loret, Fonse started play-boxing with the younger man, the two of them laughing and taking every chance to wrap their arms around the other and hug. "And these," said Fonse, shoving Bruddy to one side and dropping to his knees, gathering the youngsters, shrieking and clamouring all over again, to his chest, "is my youngsters—Emmy, Charlie, Georgie, Jimmy and Timmy."

Loret's, Mudder's and a dozen more muddied brown eyes and wide, white teeth flashed at us, and the brother, Bruddy, stepped forward, his shy smile softening the square of his jaw as he held out his hand in welcome—first to Sid, then to me. Mudder come behind him, holding out her hand, and then Fudder, and Loret, and then the youngsters were swarming around, each trying to gain a spot in front of me or Sid, and staring curiously at Josie, who was still trying to hide behind my back.

"Now listen up, everyone," Fonse ordered, tweaking one of the older ones on the ear and boxing at another. "There's lots to say and do, but the important thing is—today we're goin' to have a weddin', right here in the garden."

"A weddin'!" Loret exclaimed.

"Yup, a weddin'," Fonse repeated, looking towards me and Sid. "Sid and Kit is gettin' married."

A babble of excited shrieks went up and I stared incredulously at Fonse.

"Married!"

The choked sound must've been mine, because suddenly the sea of muddied eyes was swamping over me.

Fonse groaned towards Sid.

"Good Lord, man, haven't you asked her yet?"

A smaller groan from Sid, then he was grabbing at my hand and pulling me towards an old shed, canopied beneath a grove of lilac bushes. Josie started to run after us, but Fonse caught her by the hand and pulled her back.

"Best you stay with us, Josie," he coaxed. "Look, see the

big freckle on Georgie's back? Georgie, haul up your shirt and show Josie your big freckle."

A wail of protest followed after us from Georgie. Then Sid pulled me up short in front of the shed.

"Married! Sid . . . "

"I'm sorry, Kit, I meant to ask you up in the gully. And, well then I thought perhaps it would be better in the boat. But then . . . ahh, I figured I wouldn't tell you . . . "

"Did you think I wouldn't find out?" I asked with some wonder.

He grinned.

"If it could've been done that way."

I threw up my arms, helplessly.

"We can't get married! It's . . . it's . . . "

"It's the only thing left for us," he said urgently, clasping hold of my arms. "Look here." He pulled a white sheet of folded paper out of his pocket. "It's a marriage licence. Fonse helped me get it in St. John's before we came down. It's all set."

"But . . . "

"First, listen, Kit. The reverend leaves for St. John's first thing in the morning to meet me. He plans on setting me up in the university straightaway to keep me away from you. Now," he said as his hands tightened, "do you want me to go away without you, again?"

I closed my eyes and tried to feel what was right, but all I could feel was the warmth of Sid's hands as he squeezed them around mine, and the sweet sour smell of his breath fanning my face.

"No! No, I don't want you to go away again, but . . . "

"But, how else are we going to be together? I can't live at home, again. There's only you, and I can't very well move in, unless . . . " He stared at me expectantly.

"Unless we gets married," I half whispered.

"That's right," he whispered back. "Then we can do what we want. Fonse has a fishing boat. He's asked me to work with him and his brother, Bruddy. We could live here in the cove. Build a life."

"Fishin'?"

"Yeah, fishing. But, we've got to get back this evening. Else, in the morning he'll be leaving to catch the train … "

"You're not a fisher," I cut in.

"I can be anything I want," he said, eagerly. "And for now, that's all I can see."

"No." I turned from him, shaking my head. "I can't see what you're proposin', Sid. I don't want us to be apart either, but you fishin'… and us livin' here … "

He was suddenly quiet.

"Which is it, Kit? The damn house in the gully that's holdin' you back? Or being a fisher's wife?"

"Hah!" I turned to him, snorting. "You think I'd care where I lived with you, or of bein' a fisher's wife?"

"What is it then?"

"It's … it's the runnin' I don't like. The runnin' in the middle of the night and gettin' married, or else you'll end up livin' in St. John's." I stared at him, unsure of everything I was saying. He stared back, looking as perplexed as I felt.

"Well, do you … did you … mean for us to tell the reverend first?"

"No," I said, shaking my head. "No! I just need to know whether or not you'll leave for St. John's if I say no, that's all."

"Jesus! Is that it?"

"No! Yes, that's it."

"I never would have left without you, Kit. Never!" he

swore, dropping to one knee and grabbing hold of my hands. "I swear to God, I will never leave you."

"Then that's good, because I'll tell you one thing, Sid Ropson, it ain't because I'm afraid of any reverend that I'll marry you."

"Are you saying yes then?"

"I don't know what I'm sayin'," I yelled. "Yes! Yes, I'll marry you. I suppose I'm marryin' you. Oh, God . . . "

He let out a shriek and, picking me up by the waist, swung me around till I screamed.

"And it ain't because of the reverend that I'm asking you," he laughed. "I was just chicken-shit, that's all. I didn't know how else to lead up to it. Whooppee!" he screamed, holding back his head and swinging me around again. "It's because I love you, Kit. I'm nuts about you. That's why I'm asking you."

I started to laugh, and he was laughing with me, and then he was hauling me by the hand back to where Fonse, Josie and everyone else was standing around, waiting for us.

"She said yes," Sid roared. And then everyone was shouting and whistling and dancing, and Loret came and took me by the hand.

"Come. We have a weddin' to get ready for."

"We don't expect nothing fancy . . . " Sid began.

"We've got some work to do if we're goin' to make you the prettiest bride around," said Loret, brushing Sid to one side and heading for the house. "A cake, Mudder, we've got to have a cake," she said to the old woman.

"Well, I never!" Mudder exclaimed. "Emmy, go get me as much flour as Aunt Floss can spare. And tell her we're havin' a weddin', and to make a pot of soup if she expects to come dancin' on this day. Jimmy, go get Aunt Lily and tell her we're havin' a weddin' and to bring over her linen tablecloth. Mother of the Saints, Loret," she cried out, running to catch up, "never mind the hair curlin' yet, we got to give the house a cleanin' afore we brings the reverend in."

"Speakin' of the reverend, I'd best go get him afore he goes off to his drinkin' hole for the day," Fonse shouted above the clatter. "Sid, you come with me. Bruddy, you get the brew ready, I expect the cellar's well stocked. Georgie, Jimmy, you boys take Josie down to see the horses, and mind she don't get hurt."

"I got to go get the cloth from Aunt Lily's," Jimmy sang out. "Mudder, can I go with Georgie instead?"

"You go get the cloth like I asked you," Mudder replied. "Timmy, you go with Georgie."

"Emmy, go down to Mam Reid's," Loret called out to the eldest girl, "and bring up me weddin' dress. Mind you don't drop it. Timmy, you go with Georgie and Charlie. Charlie, make sure he don't go near the well."

"And who's goin' to be the best man?" hollered Fudder, striding after the men as they headed for the gate.

"That'll be me, the handsome one," said Bruddy, finger-combing his cowlick back into place.

"Hah!" snorted Fonse, grabbing hold of Bruddy's cowlick and twisting him around.

"And the only one with a new suit," yelped Bruddy, wrapping his arms around his head for protection.

"It's the 'best man' they're lookin' for, little brother," Fonse roared, letting go of Bruddy and clapping an arm around Sid's back. "And I'm the best man here, ain't that right, Sid? And the best man's goin' to be the best man, suit or no suit."

"And who's goin' to play the march if you're the best man?" Loret sung out after them, taking the back steps to the house two at a time, still dragging me by the hand.

"Bruddy, you're the best man, and you'd better get them pants pressed because they been in the bottom of your drawer since the garden party, and we all knows the shape you come home in that night."

A guffaw of laughter went up from the men at the mention of the garden party, and Loret and Mudder crowded me inside the house.

"They'll laugh at it now," said Loret, leading me through the kitchen towards a flight of stairs in the hallway, "but by the love of God, they weren't laughin' the day Fonse got packed off to jail for six months, hey Mudder?"

"That's the way of men, to laugh at what gets the best of 'em," said Mudder, rattling back the stove-top. "And you weren't too sober yourself, when you took a smack at the Missus that started it all in the first place," sung out Mudder as Loret took off up over the stairs with me stumbling along behind her, as helpless as if I'd been picked up and carried along by a squall of wind.

CHAPTER TWENTY FOUR

LIZZY'S BLESSING

"WE'LL GET YOUR HAIR SET IN CLIPS AFORE we does anything else, so's it'll have a chance to curl a bit before the weddin' starts," Loret said, leading me into a bedroom and sitting me down besides a washstand. "By then Mudder'll have the cake in the oven and you can do your bathin', and I can start with the cleanin'. Here," she fixed a mirror in front of me, "you can watch whilst I do's the settin'." Dipping a hairbrush into the wash pan, she wetted down my hair, brushing hard and fast.

"Now then, tell me about yourself," she said.

"I . . . umm, I'm sixteen."

"Mmmm, that's real interestin'," Loret mumbled through a mouthful of hair clips. "Sounds like you're a little bit shy." Bending over, she parted the screen of wet hair in front of my face, and peered in. "So was I when I first met Fonse. Screamin' my way through five birthin's, right there on that bed, with Mudder, Fudder and half of Godfather's Cove lookin' on, cured me of that." She held the comb mid-air and stared at me, wide eyed. "Blessed mercy, is you pregnant!?"

"No! No!" I said, shaking my head and turning red.

She kept staring, then smiled, her face becoming as soft as the morning dew.

"Sure, you're scared half to death." Cupping my face, she examined it carefully. "Sixteen, you say? You don't look no more then twelve. Here, lemme have a look." She bundled my hair into a makeshift bun on the top of my head and peered at me sideways. "We're goin' to make you look twenty and a day, as well as the prettiest bride that ever was, and you'd better be appreciatin' the offer seein's how I'm still the official holder of that grand title. Now then." She let the hair drop around my face. "Perhaps we'll just set the hair around your face in clips, and let the rest hang down straight. Then, I'll let you alone to have your bath."

Twirling a strand of long, wet hair around her finger, she pressed it down into a knob against my scalp and clipped it. Tears sprang into my eyes as the sharp edge of the clip scratched across my scalp, but I never moved, and Loret stood back staring intently at her hairdressing to make sure she hadn't taken too much hair and made the curl too big, and that it was twirled tightly enough to make the kind of curl she was hoping for. I'd never had anyone pay such close attention to me before, and for the first time I was wishing upon wishing that my hair might curl as prettily as Margaret Eveleigh's and make Loret proud of her work, which, in some strange way, would make her feel proud of me. After another half-dozen twirls, knobs and painstaking clipping, she was finished and stood back, admiring her work.

"Mmm, we'll see if it takes. Now, get undressed... what is it, Georgie?" she asked impatiently as the boy with the freckle on his back pushed open the door and poked his head in.

"Jimmy's chasin' after me."

"There'll be more than Jimmy chasin' after you if you don't get that tablecloth from Aunt Lily," Loret cried out, wielding the hairbrush as one might a tomahawk. "Now go on and for the love of Mary, just once, can't you youngsters get along without me comin' after ye. Here, hold on, hold on," she yelled, grabbing after the doorknob. "You go bring up the water for the tub, that's what you can do. And tell Jimmy I said for him to go get the tablecloth, hurry on, hurry on. Now then," she said, coming back to me as Georgie ran down over the stairs, "you get undressed, whilst I goes and helps Mudder clean up a bit. It's not every day she has a weddin' in her backyard, and you can be sure she's goin' to make the most out of this one."

The tub filled, I stood to one side in Loret's dressing gown, hesitantly fingering its rope belt.

"Landsakes, aren't you in that tub yet?" she asked, bustling in through the door with an armful of clothes and dumping it onto the bed. "I allows there's a week's washin' to be done after this day; the youngsters are after slidin' down every mudhole from here down to the Arm. Oh, for God's sake," she bawled out as Bruddy leaned in through the door behind her, fingers tapping overhead on the door jamb.

"Where'd the youngsters put the hammer?" he asked, not seeing me at first.

"Where'd the youngsters put the hammer," Loret mimicked. "Sure, I don't know where the youngsters put the hammer, Bruddy! My God, make no wonder Kit's scared to get undressed. It's like the four winds in here with the draught from the door openin' and closin'."

Twisting his head and seeing me, Bruddy squeezed shut his eyes and hastily ducked back out, hauling the door shut behind him. Loret clawed the door open again.

"Go find the young buggers and make them tell you where they put the hammer," she sung out after him as he stomped down over the stairs. Rolling her eyes, she shut the door, and noting how I was still standing there, fidgeting with the string to my dressing gown, she threw down the shirt she was folding and grinned understandingly. "I'll be cleanin' the boys' room if you needs me," she said, sailing out the door and closing it firmly behind her.

Jamming the edge of the dresser against the door, I threw off the dressing gown and quickly hopped into the tub. Ten minutes later I was back out, tightly wrapped in the dressing gown and sitting on the edge of the bed. Hearing Josie's bark, I went to the window and peered out through the white lace curtains. She was bounding at breakneck speed down through one of the ditches between the potato beds, with Jimmy and Georgie gunning to catch up with her. They disappeared around the back of the shed, and next I seen a flash of red streaking through the woods beyond.

"Are you finished?" Loret called out, tapping lightly on the door.

Edging the dresser back in place, I let her in and took my seat in front of the washstand.

"My, they took easy as anything," she said, pulling out the clips and watching the curled strands of hair bounce down around my face. Running her fingers through them, she stretched them out and fingered them playfully. "Fine hair is best for curlin'. Do you curl it much?" she asked, gathering it in a bunch and holding it to one side of my face.

I shook my head, squirming with discomfort from so much attention. Loret watched me in the mirror, and her face went all tender like, and dropping my hair, she reached both arms around my shoulders and give me a tight hug.

"I swear I've never seen anything as shy as you," she said.

Pulling back, she wiped at her eyes and picked up the brush. "I suppose I should wait till we're at the altar before I starts cryin'," she sniffled, brushing out the curls. "Am I pullin' too hard?"

I shook my head, too surprised to say anything. Even though my hands stayed in my lap whilst she had hugged me, it was a hug I never wanted to let go of. And while it was never something I had ever thought on before, it came to me that this was the first time a woman outside of Nan, Josie and Aunt Drucie had ever touched me.

"Well, the name of the Father!" Loret gasped as the door burst open and Emmy stumbled in through, her arms clutched around a bundle of creamy satin material, whilst the rest of it trailed around her legs and beneath her feet. "Here, lemme have it, oh Mother of Mercy, you're as clumsy as they comes, Emmy, oh my God . . . " Loret's voice trailed off in a pitiful moan as she gingerly lifted the garment from her girl's grasp and held it out so's that it unfolded before me like one of Doctor Hodgins's frothing waves.

"It's beautiful," I whispered.

"Hah, well now you knows the secret," Loret said, holding the dress up against herself. "It's whoever gets to wear this dress makes for the prettiest bride. It was my mother's before me. She bought it off ole Briar Adams. He bought it for his youngest girl, but the weddin' was cancelled on account of the groom gettin' lost in the woods, moose huntin' on his weddin' day. He was found that evenin', but the weddin' never did go ahead because the bride said that any man that can't stay out of the woods long enough to get married oughtn't ever to get married. And she never did marry him, still for all, she ended up havin' eight youngsters for him. Here now," she said as she laid the dress carefully across the bed, "let's see if it fits."

"It fits," I said, as the cool satin slipped down over my bare shoulders and swished against my legs.

"As nice as anything," Loret murmured, doing up the buttons on the back. The door swung open and Josie stood there, her face beet-red from racing and mud up to her knees. "What do you think of Kit?" Loret asked her. "Isn't she pretty?"

Josie looked at me the way one would a fragile Christmas tree bulb. Reaching out, she laid her hand on the sleeve, then pulled it back.

"It's O.K.," I said. "You can touch it. Here." I picked up the tail of the dress and pressed it into her hands. "Sid and I are gettin' married," I said as she fingered the material curiously.

"Who's gettin' married? You's not gettin' married."

"Yes I am gettin' married, to Sid. Sid's goin' to live with us."

"Sid's goin' to live with us? Sid's not goin' to live with us," she barked, turning to Emmy with a grin.

"Why don't you girls go pick me a bunch of black-eyed susans," Loret said. "And some daisies and some buttercups, to make a wreath for Kit's hair. Would you like that, Josie? You and Emmy?"

Then Sid's voice, along with Fonse's and Bruddy's, sounded from outside. And for a split second, before Josie's eyes left mine, a blaze of yellow streamed towards me, and she smiled, a jumbled-toothed smile that stretched boldly across her face.

I stared, never having seen her smile such a smile before, and then tried to smile back. But it was as if my smiling muscles had forgotten how to work, so I reached out my hand and touched her cheek instead.

"Thank you, Josie," I said, wondering what in the name

of the Lord I was thanking her for. But she nodded and kept on smiling, as if that was an easy one to figure, and then tore across the landing with Emmy in tow, leaving me staring after her with a warmth spreading through my heart like that of a mother the first time she sees a smile on the face of her newborn babe.

It was a day of days for sure, what with Sid coming home from jail, and Loret's hug and Josie's smile. And it was just starting as sometime later Loret walked with me down the stairs, the creamy satin dress tucked tightly around my waist, a wreath of black-eyed susans circling my crown, and tendrils of soft yellow curls nuzzling against my cheeks. I didn't know what was choking me up the most—wearing such a pretty dress or having everyone making such a fuss over me. Or perhaps it was the marrying Sid part, because every time I thought of being his wife, I cowered inside, feeling a little frightened of how things must be now, and preferring to think instead of how things were in the past, with us skipping rocks down the gully and soaking our feet in Crooked Feeder, and me listening as he talked about such foolishness as men trying to drink the ocean dry, and crying for radishes when it was corn that we planted. And when I saw him standing there on the porch, wearing Fonse's wedding suit that drooped a little off his shoulders and was a little too long in the legs and sleeves, and him shifting nervously on his feet as he watched me walking towards him all swathed in satin and wreaths of wild flowers, it felt more like we were getting ready for our graduation dance than our wedding.

And after he put a narrow gold band on my finger, and we cut Mudder's cake and toasted each other with Fudder's brew, then waltzed amidst the sea of muddied brown eyes and square white teeth, I felt drunk. Everything was blurred, and nothing felt right—the dress, the tendrils, Loret, my

mother's smile—not even Sid at my side. But I wanted it—
all of it. And as Fonse whipped the accordion into a jig and
Sid grabbed me by the waist and swung me around and
around, with our best man, Bruddy, whooping up a storm
with the youngsters and cheering and dancing all around us,
I held back my head and shrieked with laughter as I heard
Nan lean down from the heavens and bellow, "And so you
should, and so you should."

And later that evening when Sid and I were crouched
beneath the canvas, heading back up the bay, with Josie,
Fonse and Loret hidden beneath a tent of their own in the
rear of the boat, whilst the rain come down so hard it
bounced bubbles two inches off the water, it was kissing him
that I wanted, and the more I kissed him, the more it seemed
fitting that I kiss him again, and again, and again . . .

CHAPTER TWENTY-FIVE

FALL FROM GRACE

"**Y**OU'LL SPEND THE NIGHT," I begged as Fonse helped Josie out of the boat. "What with this rain . . . "

"Heh, it's the nets with Fudder in the mornin', I'm thinkin'," Fonse said. "Perhaps, we can pop up some time after the caplin rolls."

A crack of thunder resounded down the gully, sending Loret jumping to her feet.

"Please yourself with your own doin', Sire," she said, jumping over the side of the boat onto the beach. "But it sounds like the good Lord's orderin' me inside on this night, and that's just where I'm goin', inside."

"Here now, Loret," Fonse called out, but his voice was drowned by another roll of thunder, and grasping hold of Loret's arm, I ran with her up the gully.

Sid came up behind me as I ushered Loret inside the house.

"Kit!"

I stepped back.

"You want to go see your folks?" I asked.

"The reverend'll be leaving early in the morning. I want to catch him before he goes."

"You want me to come, too?"

"You're part of the family now," he said dryly.

Fonse strolled out of the gully.

"I'll get the fire lit," he said. "A cup of tea'll be nice for when ye gets back."

"I'll just be a minute," I said to Sid, and ducked inside.

"Show Loret where to find the sheets and blankets," I said to Josie. "Then take her to Nan's room." I nodded at the sympathetic smile on Loret's face and knew that Fonse must've told her by now about how Sid's parents, and others, saw me as the gully tramp's girl, and how Josie had killed a man, and Sid had taken the blame, damning me forever in his mother's eyes.

"I'll be back as soon as I can," I said to Loret. Drawing on her look of encouragement, I pulled up the hood of my coat and went back out to Sid. Slipping my hand into his, we walked up over the bank to the road, our feet squelching in the mud, and the rain clattering against our oilskin coats.

Strangely enough, it weren't thoughts of the reverend that was creating the uneasiness in my stomach, but Sid himself. Despite the warmth of his hand as he held mine, it wasn't my husband who was walking into Haire's Hollow with me on this night, but a mother's son, just coming home from prison and bringing with him a wife. And not just any wife, but a wife that had helped jail him in the first place, and a wife who his own mother had taken a hand in trying to rid the town of, long before she beheld any thoughts of her son marrying and bringing home a daughter-in-law.

It was raining hard by the time we got to Haire's Hollow,

and aside from Old Joe and Doctor Hodgins, barely recog-
nizable in their oilskins and sou'westers as they stared up at
us from rigging up Old Joe's boat for fishing in the morning,
there was no one to come between us and the dreaded hour.
And when Sid raised his hand to knock on his mother's door,
the fear inside me had grown into a living thing.

The door swung open and she stood there, looking as if
she hadn't strayed from the spot since the last time she
waved him goodbye a year ago—waiting, waiting, for just
such a moment.

"Mercy! Mercy!" she cried out. "He's come back! He's
come home to me!"

And mercifully she didn't see me at first, and was able to
wrap her arms around his neck and drink from him like a
starving mother with nothing left to feed on but her child's
scent. It was the reverend who first saw me. In a dark dressing gown and slippered feet, he came hurrying into the
kitchen, a pensive look on his smooth, pale face. His face
went blank when he saw me staring out at him from behind
Sid and his sobbing mother, and with a soft moan he jerked
forward and grasped hold of the back of the chair that was
closest to him.

It was the first time I had seen him since the day of the
trial, and I was struck by how poor he looked and how white
his skin was. He became whiter as he continued to look at
me, and if it weren't for the chair that he was clinging onto,
I felt he would have fallen. And so did Mrs. Ropson become
white when she untangled her arms from around her son's
neck and saw me standing besides him. And then, just as the
reverend's body began to slacken further and he grasped
more tightly to the chair, Mrs. Ropson's became more rigid.
She began to shake, as if in a rage, first her hands, then her
arms, shoulders, head, as if the strength seeping out of the

reverend's body, leaving him sinking weakly onto the chair, was creeeping into hers, filling her with the same scorning rage that had been sustaining him all these years. And it felt, as I stood there clutching onto Sid's arm, watching the haggard lines appear on her face, then deepen as if they had been there all this time, hidden within her jowls of fat, that it was she who had spawned such rage, and out of some desperate need to keep soft her breast, had nurtured its growth in the reverend instead. And now, seeing me, the bastard child of a retarded tramp standing besides her precious son, she was taking it back, all of it. Only she had no inkling of its growth. And when she turned the full weight of it onto herself, she become like the old harp seal again, floundering for a pan of ice to hold her. And barring that, there was the fathomless sea, that once it took her, would carry her too far down to ever come back.

But it stood no chance of taking her just yet. I could tell by the way her body suddenly stilled and she turned her drowning eyes onto mine that she had something.

"Why did you bring her here?" she raged.

"Mum . . . "

"Why!?"

"Kit's my wife."

Her eyes widened in horror, and a strangling sound came from the reverend. She turned to him, holding out a hand with which to steady herself, but oblivious to his wife's need, and his body now leeched of the spite-driven strength and as emptied as a summer's well, he sunk further into his chair, his face an ashen grey.

"Merciful father," Mrs. Ropson whimpered, turning anguished eyes back to Sid. "When? When did you marry?" Her eyes lit onto mine, and she choked on another, more loathsome thought. "Have you touched *her*?" she whispered with such vile, as if I were the leech itself that she'd just used to sap the life's blood out of the reverend.

Sid took my hand.

"We're leaving, now," he said in a voice sorely twisted with shame and hurt.

"No! You can't leave with her. Tell him!" his mother shrieked at the reverend. "Tell him!" The reverend stared at her, and such a look of contempt filmed his eyes as ever I'd seen him cast towards Josie and me, leaving me knowing with certainty that while it was us that had been the objects of his scorn, it was his wife who had been its creator. With a cry, she turned towards Sid and spat out the poison that had been crucifying her all these years.

"She's your sister!"

A stunned silence laid low the room. Then a low whimpering started deep in my throat, and I whipped my hand to my mouth as Mrs. Ropson turned to me with a look of the damned in their last desperate measure to gain justice.

"It's a lie," Sid whispered.

"No lie!" Mrs. Ropson cried out. "Ask him! Go on, ask him what did it, all this time, living with sin."

The reverend coiled further back in his chair as all eyes weighed down on him.

"Is it true?" Sid rasped.

He shook his head, his hands clasping at the seat beneath him.

"You would lie?" Mrs. Ropson blazed. "Now, with our son married to your—*bastard*?"

"Shut up!" Sid roared, his eyes never leaving the reverend's. "Tell me the truth! Is it true?"

"He would never swear to it," Mrs. Ropson cried, moving slowly towards the reverend. "Never swear that it wasn't true. But I saw it. I know it to be true. And all this time I kept it a secret. For you," she cried, turning towards Sid. "So's you'd never know your father's sin."

The reverend's hands trembled on his lap, and his paltry eyes were colourless as they struggled to hold Sid's.

"I have paid for my sin," he whispered.

Such simple words, and spoken reverently as if a penitence for a long-lasting grievance finally brought to light between the father and son. Yet, there was another presence, equally as connected, but for whom the words sealed a fate even more damning than that of the son, for had not the reverend just introduced himself as my father? I heard nothing else, excepting a soft moan from Sid, and the rain splashing against the window, sounding forever like the house was weeping for the sin committed within it—a sin that was still trying to make itself felt.

"Sid."

Had I spoken? I struggled to breathe, and as hard as I tried to turn to him, my eyes were rooted to Mrs. Ropson, still, now that her venomous secret was out, and my numbed mind churned through the thought that just as lightning is the quietest, yet deadliest, part of a summer's storm, so too had she lain quiet all those years since the reverend fathered me, preparing the grounds for devastation, then struck before battle was properly warned.

Fathered me. The reverend had fathered me. My father—this weak, decrepit thing that had screwed my mother all those years ago, then blasphemed her before God for his having done so. This was my father.

"It's a lie!"

It was Sid's voice, sounding from somewhere besides me, and I recognized that the wooden thing that I was clenching onto was his hand.

"No lie!" Mrs. Ropson cried. "I was there the night she

was born. I saw. Show him!" she demanded, bearing down on the reverend. "Show him." Then she swooped before him and fell to her knees, grabbing for his foot. The reverend shrank back, kicking at her, but I knew what she was going for. And when she finally grasped it and held it betwixt her fleshy underarm and her breast, staring at it triumphantly as if the webbed foot was some sordid sanctimonious medal, a trembling went through me that turned my stomach to water.

Wrenching his foot away, and knocking Mrs. Ropson sideways as he did so, the reverend staggered to his feet.

"I pay for my sin," he shrilled, standing shakily before me and Sid, looking wildly betwixt us. Then he took a step closer to me, his ghastly eyes accusing mine, and his pointing finger weighting down a hand that was making one last attempt to cast blame.

"Each time I see you," he whispered shrilly, "I suffer damnation. Each time I attempt to get rid of you, God brings you back to me. Your mother, the devil, the serpent in my garden," his eyes took on a dull gleam. "She tempted my mortal weakness. And for this, I pay. I pay!"

My legs began to shake as his eyes sought wildly to take root in mine. But Sid was there, wrapping his arms around me and pulling me back from the reverend's hypnotic hold. I sank against him, the weakening in my legs shored up by the weakening in his, when a knock sounded on the door. Having lumbered to her feet, Mrs. Ropson held out a restraining hand to Sid.

"Stay," she ordered, but the door was quietly opening, and Doctor Hodgins stood there as he had the day of the meeting, with the same grave look on his face. The rain dripped off his sou'wester as he pulled it off his head, and his face tensed as he stared sickeningly at the sight of the reverend's bared, web-toed foot and the slipper dangling from Mrs. Ropson's hand.

"You!" Mrs. Ropson sneered, flinging the slipper to one side and limping towards Doctor Hodgins. "It's all your fault. It's you that stopped us from sending her away! Kept her here all these years, for me to see every time she walked by, you and your saint of a wife. Well, God did his part well, didn't he? He took yours away from you, just as he took my boy from me. But, now mine's come back." She turned imploring eyes upon her son and grabbed piteously after him. "Haven't you, Sidney? You've come back to me. You haven't touched her, not as a wife. Tell them . . . "

Sid pulled back from her touch as if it was fire and, holding onto me more tightly, turned savagely to Doctor Hodgins.

"Why didn't you tell me?"

Doctor Hodgins closed his eyes, hard, as if in silent prayer.

"I was going to," he half whispered, then looked at Sid sorrowfully. "But then you went to jail. I thought fate had intervened."

"Fate? You left it to fate? Is it fate that we're man and wife now, as well as brother and sister?" Sid snapped. He turned to me for the first time since we had entered the house, and I closed my eyes against the nakedness of his pain. "Kit!" His voice had dropped to a whisper, and then he was thrusting me at Doctor Hodgins and backing out the door.

"Take her back to the gully. Tell Fonse I'll send money."

A wail went up from his mother as she charged after Sid. Pushing away from Doctor Hodgins, I blocked her path and went chasing after him, myself.

"Sid!"

Rain pelted against my face as I tore into the night.

"Sid!"

He was marching up the road leading out of Haire's Hollow, with his head bent low and the rain pelting at his back.

"*Sid!*"

He turned as I caught up with him and grabbed me tightly by the arms.

"Go back, Kit. There's nothing for us, now!"

"I'm comin' with you."

"No, ooh, my sweet Kit," he moaned, gathering me against him. "It's not fair. It's just not fair."

"I don't care, I don't care, I'm comin' with you."

"Sshh, no." He pulled back and looked at me, his rain-soaked face made all the more wet with his crying. "It's more laws, Kit."

"Damn the laws, Sid Ropson! Since when do you care about laws?"

"I can't touch this one, Kit. It's mine as well as God's. Hell, it's every damn one of them." Then he was kissing my face, my eyes, my lips, and holding me closer and tighter, and I clung to him with a wanting that I felt straight through to my soul, and a wanting that I knew would never stop, not on this rain-filled night, and not on a million rain-filled nights.

"I love you, Sid," I cried out. "There's nothin' that can change that."

"It's damned, Kit!"

"No!"

"Yes! Damned!" He shoved me away savagely. "There's none that can escape this one, not even the Gods. Do you hear me?"

"Gods aren't real, Sid!" I gasped, clinging to him. "They're just stories, bloody stories!"

"We're each of us a story, Kit," he cried, almost gently now. "What of Josie, isn't hers a story, unlike ours, but one of pain despite her innocence. And it's you who's suffered for it. Is that what you'd have for our children, to suffer the pain of our love? They'd be marked, Kit. Just like Josie's marked. It's the way of blood. It's the way of God."

I listened, stunned with knowing that he was already gone. Even as he stood before me, he was already gone. He turned and ran into the night, the rain washing away his footsteps as if he never was, excepting for the growing pain in my chest, and the incestuous burning of the wedding ring upon my finger.

Then Doctor Hodgins was holding onto me, pleading with me to turn back, that there were people watching, and to not say anything as word was out that Sid and I were married, and we wouldn't want it known that we were brother and sister as well.

The trip back to the gully was one in silence. Doctor Hodgins kept up behind me as I marched straight ahead, ignoring the curious faces appearing in the windows, and the cursed boldness of Margaret Eveleigh as she came skipping out of the store to stall me in my headlong flight. Blissfully Doctor Hodgins cut her off before she had a chance to open her mouth, and I kept right on walking. The rain poured with a vengeance of its own, determined to make itself felt through to the marrow on this evening of human misery. There was still light in the sky when I turned down the gully, yet the kitchen lamp glowed softly through its grim greyness, and a bellowing of smoke poured from the chimney.

Shoving open the door, I stomped the water off my boots, Doctor Hodgins behind me, and stared with misgiving at the shocked look on Fonse's and Loret's faces as they beheld whatever look of torment that must've been imprinted on mine.

"Sid's gone," I said, as Josie barrelled from the hallway into the kitchen.

"Who's gone? Sid's not gone," she barked.

"Sid's gone. This time he's never comin' back," I said loudly, as much for my own ears as for everyone else's. Then, feeling the strength leaving my legs, I turned and walked towards my room.

She was on my back like a scalded cat.

"Sid's back. Sid's back," she hollered. "You's farmed. Farmed!" she yelled, as Doctor Hodgins pried her arms from around my neck. Then, Fonse and Loret were helping Doctor Hodgins hold her back, and Doctor Hodgins was telling them who he was, and I slammed my room door shut and pounded my fist against the door. I yelped as the side of my fist scratched across the nail holding Old Joe's starfish in place, and in a frenzied cry, I pried the dead fish from my door and flung it into an opened dresser drawer. Falling across the bed, I plunged my face into the pillow and chewed back the spiteful cries wailing up in my throat.

CHAPTER TWENTY-SIX

LORET'S BARGAIN

THE NEXT MORNING I STOOD STUBBORNLY on the beach and shook my head for the hundredth time at Fonse's and Loret's plea that I pack mine and Josie's things and move with them to Godfather's Cove.

"It's what Sid wants," Loret cried. "Doc Hodgins said. Please, Kit, come with us."

"No," I said quietly. "I thank ye for everythin'."

"Dammit, you're as stubborn as they comes," Fonse said. "I'll be leavin' you this mornin', but I'll be back. I promise you, we won't rest with ye here alone."

"We'll be fine," I said. I stood on shore, waving until they were a dark blot on the sea. Turning, I caught sight of Josie looking down on me from a little ways up the gully. A scowl darkened her face, and she raced back to the house.

Summer came. It felt like I was being lifted up and carried along by a mindless wind, my feet never touching the ground, rocks, grass beneath them. The leaves turned to red, gold, brown, and Old Joe come by with the winter's wood.

The caribou trekked across the barrens, and I trekked with
them, filling the pantry with buckets of partridgeberries, and
watching the clouds drift overhead. Everyone came as
before, but I ignored all their questions about Sid. Word had
spread quickly about the wedding in Godfather's Cove, and
what exactly Doctor Hodgins had told everyone, I didn't ask.
But from the well-intended comments made in passing, I
expect it must've been that the reverend and his wife weren't
willing to accept me as their daughter-in-law. So, choosing
neither, Sid had ran.

"Lord, it's hard to think of you as a married woman, Kit,"
Margaret said during one of her visits as I stogged the stove
full of birch. "Yet, you looks different, somehow. Not like
the same Kit at all."

"Have a piece of cake, Margaret."

"Mmm, looks good. Who made it?"

"Aunt Drucie."

"Aunt Drucie!" Margaret shuddered. "Don't take it to
heart, Kit, but the way she drools in her bread dough, brrr,
turns my stomach. It was the reverend, wasn't it, that couldn't
hold the thought of havin' you in the family? I must say, Kit,
you looks awful calm about everything, what with Sid runnin' off and leavin' you like that."

Strangely enough, I was feeling the same calm inside. It
was as if I had stepped into somebody else's shoes and were
allowing them to walk my path with no inkling of touching,
tasting or feeling. With Sid's leaving I could no longer imagine a world where such things as love, desire or joy could
exist; better to sense nothing at all, to move through the
world and glimpse it from a distance, than to split God's gift
in half and live in its underside with no rays of light dispers-
ing the darkness.

Not so what Doctor Hodgins thought.

"It's Godfather's Cove you should be thinking on," he advised repeatedly from his seat in the rocker, a seat that was most always taken up by him the past six months since Sid left. "Fonse, Loret—they're wonderful people, Kit. And they care for you and Josie."

"This is my home."

"It's become your coffin."

"I won't leave here."

"He's not coming back this time."

I fell silent. I always fell silent whenever Doctor Hodgins tossed that one in.

"You've got to give yourself a chance. Living here in the gully, waiting, every day, waiting, you'll waste away. And that's not what he wants for you."

"I'm tired," I said, rising and heading for my room.

"Name of God, Kit," he yelled, coming out of the rocker and grabbing me by the arm. "You can't wait forever. And even if he did come back, he'd still be your brother. Time won't change that."

"No one can be sure."

"The reverend admits to the timing of it. And with the marked foot . . . it's pretty certain."

"But you can't be sure."

"You know it. Sid knows it. That's why he left. Now you've got to be strong, too. Go with Fonse. Take Josie and make a life. A new life. That's why he left you, Kit, so's you could be free."

"We're married."

"It can be annulled."

"Not in my heart it can't."

I stared helplessly into Doctor Hodgins's eyes and, seeing pity in them, shook off his hands and flew down the hallway to my room. He took a couple of steps after me, then paused for a second before turning back and taking his seat in the rocker. I lay across my bed, staring up at the night sky and listening to him creak, creak, creak his way through the night. Come morning I swore I would take that damn rocker and drag it out to his shack, and see, perhaps, if it might serve to keep him home a bit more.

Come morning he was gone and Josie was in his place, creaking her way through the morning. She hardly spoke to me since the night I told her that Sid wasn't coming back, and spent most of her time as she had during his time in jail, sitting in the rocker and creak, creak, creaking. Except this time there was an anger in her towards me, a hard anger that wouldn't let me touch her the way that I used to, or even talk to her. And a couple of times she had hit me square across the face and ran off before I had a chance to catch my breath.

"I didn't make him leave!" I yelled at her one day when she snatched a slice of bread out of my hands and threw it on the floor.

"You's farmed!" she yelled back. "You's farmed!"

"It's deformed," I argued weakly. "Now you pick up that bread. Pick it up!"

"You pick it up!" she yelled, picking up the slice of bread and firing it across the room at me. "You pick it up!"

"I told you and I told you, it's not my fault. I didn't make Sid leave," I cried out. "Can't you hear me? I didn't make Sid leave."

"You's farmed!"

"Who's farmed?" a voice called through the kitchen window. It was Fonse.

A smile lit up Josie's face, the same as if it had been Sid, and she boisterously hauled open the door and bounded outside, barking out her crazy laugh.

"I swear, it's only him that she'll listen to any more," I said as Loret came in the door.

"That's because she's the only one around here with sense," Loret replied, giving me a hug, a smile covering the look of concern on her fine features. Fonse poked his head in behind her.

"I'll do up some splits and keep Josie entertained while you girls prattle," he said.

"You won't get her near an axe," I said. "Not since . . . "

Fonse nodded. "Then, we'll go for walk down the brook."

"There's a good lad," Loret said. She closed the door behind him and took a seat in the rocker. "Tell the truth, Kit. Is she gettin' too hard for you to handle?"

"No," I said reassuringly. "She gets mad over every little thing, but nothin' I can't help."

"Sounded like you were about to come to blows just now."

"She won't get it out of her head that I didn't send Sid away."

"Perhaps whatever's wrong with her to begin with might get harder to handle as she grows older. Now, now, don't go arguin' with me till you hears what I got to say," Loret commanded as I opened my mouth to protest. "Poor old Effie Stride's boy got worse over time. They had to strap him down sometimes, he got so hard to handle. I'm just worried about you here, all by yourself."

"I'm not all by myself."

"You got Doctor Hodgins, who's just as worried as me and Fonse. Aside from that, you got no one, Kit." Loret's muddy brown eyes rounded like a cow's.

"Oh God, Loret, are you going to start that agin?"

"Start what agin?"

"Start talkin' me into leavin' here."

"Would you? If I was to say I needed you for a little while?"

"Don't try to trick me, Loret."

"Trick you? Well, if that's what you thinks, maybe I won't tell you anything else then."

"All right. What is it?"

A tender look took a hold of her face, and she smiled.

"I'm havin' another baby, and ... "

"Oh, Loret ... "

"That's not what I'm on about," she cut in, waving my fawning to one side. "Lord knows, there's nothin' wonderful about havin' a baby, leastways, not till it starts breathin' on its own." She nestled deeper into the rocker, beaming me a smile that could guide drowning ships to shore. "It's just that I've been spottin' this past while, and the doc said it might be good for me to stay off my feet as much as possible. So Fonse and Mudder thought, perhaps, we could hire you to come live with us, just till the baby's born," she added quickly. "And perhaps for a few months after." She leaned forward. "What'll you say, Kit? You could be her god-mother."

A silence fell between us.

"It ain't exactly a life's sentence," she said, laughing at my troubled look.

"I'm sorry, Loret. I'll come, of course I'll come. You need me."

"Well don't sound too excited now, Kittens, Lord Almighty!"

"No, I mean it, I want to help you, Loret."

Loret got up and, tightly folding her arms, strolled over to the window.

"Oh, it's me who should be sorry," she said. "Puttin'

pressure on you this way, it's not fair. You love your home, why should you leave it? For sure it's pretty enough, lookin' down over the water."

"It's pretty in Godfather's Cove, I won't mind."

"No! No, you stay here," she said, turning to me a determined air. "I only wanted it if it was what you wanted."

"But the spottin'. . . "

"Hah, the spottin' was nothin'," she said, looking a little sheepish. "I just thought I'd throw it in there, give you a good reason for comin' should you feel you were being a burden, or some such foolishness. Hey now," she said, as I kept looking at her worriedly, "I'm here to make sure you're all right, not to add to your troubles. Come on." She grasped me firmly by the shoulders. "Let's make some tea. The savages are coming."

She shot Fonse a warning look as he stepped inside, and no more was said about me and my mother moving down to Godfather's Cove. I quietened Doctor Hodgins with the same troubled look when he came to visit the next day, and I was preparing a speech to deliver in case any of them ever tried to convince me of moving again, when Margaret come for a visit.

"My God, Kit, how can you stand livin' out here all by yourself? I'd be mental." She leaned closer, her ringlets falling over her shoulders. "They're sayin' there's a strange footprint in the bog, same size as Shine's, and it's pointin' to here. Have you heard any strange noises, lately?"

I shook my head.

"Oohh my God, gives me the shivers." She looked at me quite shrewdly. "Someone's been writin' letters from all over the place to Fonse Ford, down in Godfather's Cove. They says it's Sid." Margaret leaned closer. "I'm only tellin' you in case it's important that you know. Aunt Dottie Gilliam—

that's Mom's cousin, she lives in Godfather's Cove—well, she was up the other day and happened to see Sid's handwritin' on one of Mom's store books. Well, she recognized it as the same as was on Fonse's letter that she happened to see sittin' on the counter in the post office, one day."

"Thank you, Margaret. The kettle's boiled."

"Kit, you wouldn't be hidin' somethin' from me, would you?"

"No. I never hear from Sid. And I never will. Please, don't ask me to talk about it, Margaret."

Margaret shook her head solemnly.

"Although I can't say I'm not curious. But I'll wait till you're ready to talk." Laying her cup on the arm of the rocking chair, she leaned forward. "Kit, there's something that I wants to ask you. Me and Melissa—well, you knows Melissa goes out with Teddy Randall. And well, you knows I been datin' Josh Jenkins. We was talkin' the other night about there being no place to go. You know, have a beer without a dozen youngsters crawlin' up your hole. So, we thought about comin' out here some evenin's. And young Arch Gale, well, he was saying how pretty you are, and we was thinkin'—perhaps now with Sid gone, might be time for you to start seein' somebody else. You can't go wastin' away out here, Kit. What do you say?"

"I got to go find Josie," I said. "You finish off your tea now, and don't mind me leavin' for a minute."

I was out the door and down the gully in half the time Josie ever made it. Later that evening when I was sure Margaret was gone, I came back to the house and started hauling clothes out of the drawers and shoving it into a broken-strapped suitcase and Nan's cotton flour bags she had put aside to make aprons and pudding bags. The next morning I had tea with Aunt Drucie, then walked into

Haire's Hollow and down to Old Joe's brother's shack and
rapped on Doctor Hodgins's door. That afternoon Josie and
I were sitting on the beach with the suitcase and three
stuffed flour bags as Old Joe's kelp-green boat putted to
shore with Old Joe bent over the bow and Doctor Hodgins
steering from the stern. The suitcase come apart as Old Joe,
standing on the beach in his hip rubbers, lifted it over the
bow to Doctor Hodgins, and a clump of slips and stockings
fell into the water, and along with it, the starfish, with the
nail still protruding through its centre.

"What have we here," said Old Joe as he snatched at
the garments before they scarcely had a chance to get wet,
and plunged his hand through the water to rescue the
starfish.

"You might as well keep it," I grunted, hoisting myself
over the bow of the boat. "'Cuz its wishes must've been
meant for you."

Old Joe tossed me the undergarments and studied the
fish with a quirked brow.

"Did you say the verse before you wished?" he asked.

"Yup," I said, helping Doctor Hodgins stuff the clothes
back into the suitcase.

"Hmm," said Old Joe, shifting back his cap and smoothing back his hair. Then, "Did you know that if a starfish
tears off its leg, it wishes upon wishes till it grows back a
new one?"

"Nope."

"And that the old leg wishes upon wishes till it grows its
self into a new fish?"

"Nope."

"Perhaps you give up wishin' too quickly."

"Perhaps," I said. "Or perhaps its wishes ran out after
you scraped it from the sea."

Old Joe scowled, and lifting up a rock, he nailed the fish to the bow of his boat.

"Might be it was meant for me," he said, standing back and examining it with a grin. "Might be the first voice it hears is the only one it'll answer to."

"Might be," said I as he pushed off the boat and leaped up, swinging his legs in over the side. Fixing myself comfortably on the seat, I faced the wind as Doctor Hodgins stood arms akimbo at the stern, and Old Joe squatted with Josie before the engine, putting our way to Godfather's Cove.

CHAPTER TWENTY-SEVEN

DOCTOR HODGINS'S PROMISE

BRUDDY WAS THE FIRST TO SEE US trucking up over the garden.

"Kit!" he exclaimed, setting down the water buckets as he come outside the wellhouse and seen us. "Emmy, go get your mother," he sung out as Loret's girl followed out behind him, the water dipper in her hands. "Tell her it's Kit, she's come back."

He come to meet us, his strides lengthy, his smile white against the brown of his skin.

"It's good that you've come, Kit," he said, taking the suitcase from Doctor Hodgins and warmly shaking Old Joe's hand as I introduced them. "Loret's worried sick about you."

"Kit!"

It was Loret, coming out the door and down over the steps towards me. Behind her come Mudder, then Fudder and two or three of the youngsters, reminding me of the other time when it was Sid who was walking by my side up over the yard and not Doctor Hodgins and Old Joe. Tears sprung to my eyes, and thinking they were for her, Loret swooped her arms around me, hugging me tightly, while Mudder and Fudder nodded in welcome, shaking Old Joe's and Doctor Hodgins's hands. And then everyone was laughing at the sight of Josie, bounding across the yard with the boys in tow, barking out her crazy laugh, red hair flying on the wind.

"What was it that made her change her mind, Doctor?" Mudder asked, as we all trekked into the kitchen and Bruddy carried my bags up over the stairs.

"For sure it wouldn't her own senses," Loret chided.

"I haven't got it figured out yet," Doctor Hodgins replied, giving me a wink. "Have you, Joe?"

Old Joe shook his head.

"She's not as open-mouthed as Lizzy, for sure," he said, tousling young Jimmy's head as he scooted by.

"Here, all you youngsters, outside till we calls ye," Mudder sung out, bustling to the stove and pulling a dish of baked beans from the oven. "Now then, everybody sit down, we haves a bite."

"I'm afraid we can't stay . . . " Doctor Hodgins began, but was interrupted by Mudder buckling a chair behind his knees and planking a plate of beans before him. "You knows you ain't goin' anywhere till you haves a bite," she argued. "Haul in that chair besides you, Joe."

"A bite, indeed," Fonse said, rolling back the rug by the stove and hoisting up the cellar door. "This calls for a celebration, what'd you say, Bruddy?" he asked as his brother thumped down over the stairs and into the kitchen.

"And that it does," agreed Bruddy with a grin. "It's not every day we gets a chance to celebrate, what'd you say, Loret?"

"I say the both of you haul your arses to the table," said

Loret, wagging the bread knife at Bruddy as she finished slicing a loaf. "There'll be time for celebratin' after dinner. This is what you don't miss in a man, Kit," she said with a sigh. "They're like a youngster for the tit when they gets a reason to drink."

"Never mind it's the middle of the day," said Mudder, pouring up the tea. "How'd you like it, Joe?"

"To the top," said Old Joe, eagerly eyeing the five-gallon jug of brew Fonse was hoisting up to Bruddy through the cellar door.

"How long you been around here, Doctor?" roared Fudder, wrinkling his weary old brow, and easing himself into a chair next to Doctor Hodgins.

"Oh, a good many years," roared back Doctor Hodgins. "Since before Kit was born." He give me a smile, then seriously studied the plate of bread Loret laid in the centre of the table. "Looks like we're in for a scoff, old buddy," he said with a grin as Old Joe pried his eyes from the jug of brew and lifted them to the plate of beans Mudder was placing before him.

"Aye, sir, it's a scoff she be," said Old Joe, his grin widening as I took a seat besides him. "Be a shame to miss it, heh, Kitty Kat?"

It was a wobbly Doctor Hodgins that strolled down over the garden later that evening.

"You're keeping her pretty steady, Joe," he said as Old Joe marched straight ahead towards his boat.

"Aye, 'tis a clear set of eyes you need to steer a boat," said Old Joe.

"That's right," said Doctor Hodgins. "We could run her into a whale."

"Aye. Or Big Island," added Old Joe. "Wouldn't be the first time a rudder got splintered on her shoals."

"You're fools to be leavin' this late," I chided, all the time wishing I was going back with them, to where the sound of Sid's chopping wood still rose upon the wind, and his laugh carried up the gully, and there was the hope of waking some night and there he would be, his hair silver in the blue of the night, as he'd toss down the axe and come running towards me.

"Find happiness here, Kit," Doctor Hodgins was saying, slowing his step as he spoke. "They're a good people, salt of the earth, and they'll treat you and Josie like their own. That's all I ever wanted for you, Kit, a family of your own. Now that you have that, it can give me some rest. I can answer to her up above that I seen you through the best that I could, and that in the end you fared well."

Come the moment we were standing on the beach, and Doctor Hodgins clasped his hands around my face as Old Joe stood quietly besides him.

"You're not too unhappy, are you, Kit?" Doctor Hodgins asked.

"Will you come visit?"

"Sure I will! Plenty of times."

"And you, too?" I asked Old Joe.

"You knows I will, Kit. I'll miss seein' you runnin' past the wharf every day," Old Joe's voice cracked. "Always had a smile for Old Joe, you did, you and Lizzy. It won't be the same without havin' one of ye to visit in the gully."

My mouth screwed up, and before I could stop myself, I burst out crying. Doctor Hodgins's arms went around me and he pulled me tight, crushing my face into the sweet-smelling wool of his jacket as I cried. And cried.

"It's a deep pruning you've taken, Kitty," he hushed, rocking me. "A deep pruning. But, it's those that are well pruned that bring forward the strongest rose. Hush now, hush." After I'd cried myself out, he wiped the wet off my face with his hands and cupped my face gently. "You know where to find me. I'm never leaving that shack till the good Lord takes me. No matter what it is, I'll be there for you."

"I'm here, too, Kitty Kat," said Old Joe, wiping at his eyes. "Just like I was always there for Lizzy. You just come for me. Any time."

Then they were shoving off the boat and climbing aboard. I watched as they dipped their paddles into the water and began steering clear of Fudder's nets.

"Bye, Kit," Doctor Hodgins sang out as they faded into the dark.

I stood listening to their banter, their paddles splashing into the water and scraping against the boat. Their voices became more muffled, then the pistons popped into life as they cleared the nets, and the put-put of the engine sounded their course as they motored their way out through the mouth of the cove.

I stood there for a minute, listening as they faded away, and saw in the full light of the moon a face unfurling in one of the cursed waves as it lopped upon shore. A prickling of goosebumps swept over my arms. I made to call out to Doctor Hodgins, but chiding myself for my foolishness, I wiped away my tears instead, and walked back up over the garden to where the Fords were waiting to show me my room.

Opening their home as well as their hearts, they unpacked me and Josie in a small attic room that looked down over the garden and the gill-netted waters of the cove. I stayed there as much as I could during those first few days, listening to the house rock with laughter, yelling and tears. And when I did venture down, I said nothing, satisfied to watch the others coming and going like a herd of caribou during hunting season, yet moving around each other with

the grace of a roomful of square dancers. It seemed like day
or night, there was always someone stoking the fire or stirring sugar into a cup of tea; and during the day, there was
always someone sitting at the table, scoffing back a lunch,
and Mudder running to and fro, serving and baking and
cooking.

Despite her being half the size and with half the words of
Nan, Mudder had a rock-iron will and spite enough to see
her orders carried through. Like the captain of a ship, she
bellowed out orders from the helm—which, in her case, was
the kitchen—and gave out lashings to any who dared lip
back.

"Loret said you're not goin' to church," she said, marching into the sitting room where I was tidying the daybed my
first Sunday in the cove.

I held a cushion before me, a feeling of discomfort stirring inside. No doubt Fonse and Loret had full knowledge
of the circumstances surrounding my birth and upbringing
and of Sid's leaving, yet thus far, no word had been spoken
and I felt grateful for not having to relive the knotted journey that had brought me before them. Now, with Mudder
standing accusingly before me, her Sunday coat buttoned to
her throat and her green feathered hat clamped tightly
across her coiled braids, I stood with a sinking feeling, wondering how I was to bring forward bits of the past to explain
why I never wanted to go to church no more.

"Now, Mudder!" said Loret, coming through the doorway behind her. "You knows why . . . "

"Leave us be, Loret," warned Mudder, her eyes not
budging from my face. "Now, I'm not a hard woman, Kit,"
she said, her voice lowering. "I knows what chased you out
of church, and I knows what chased you to our door. And I
welcome you, you knows that. But there's certain things we

abides by in this house, and Sundays with the Lord is one of 'em. And from what I've heard about your grandmother, I expect church is where she'd be marchin' you this day 'cuz, after all, we got our own reverend here."

"Aye, a bleedin' drunk," cut in Bruddy, popping his head in behind Loret. "For gawd's sake, Mudder . . . "

"A bleedin' drunk or not, it matters little to me," snapped Mudder. "I holds me own counsel with God when I sits in that pew, and the reverend can tend to his. Now, are you comin', Kit?"

"It ain't only in church that you find God," I said, my voice little more than a whimper.

"Aye, but it's in church that He'll find the Fords on a Sunday," she replied. "We can't always expect Him to come lookin' for us. And it's a message we sends to our neighbours when we dresses up outta respect to Him."

My feelings of discomfort grew with each second of silence that greeted Mudder's words, then Loret was bustling across the room and taking hold of my arm.

"Landsakes, Mudder, you got the poor thing near frightened to death. Why don't you go on, and me and Kit'll catch up with you. Is that all right, Kit?" she murmured.

I swallowed, my throat dry. Mudder had turned and was leaving the room as Loret spoke. She stopped as she come abreast to Bruddy, who was leaning against the door jamb, reminding me of Sid, the time he had stayed in the house like an old fishwife whilst I stood arguing with May Eveleigh about my not wanting to wear Margaret's polka-dotted dress to the graduation.

"Go get your brother," Mudder said sharply as she bustled past him. "He's been fixin' the toggle to bar the wellhouse door for near on an hour, now. Must be some toggle that takes more than a dozen minutes to fix."

Bruddy slewed his eyes towards me and Loret as Mudder sailed past him, and giving her the grand salute, as would any well-trained sailor to his captain, he sauntered out behind her.

"I'll get my hat," I said, and despite my resentment at being ordered around like a youngster by Mudder, I gave Loret a reassuring smile and ran up over the stairs and into the attic. Scrounging around inside one of the flour sacks, I pulled out my hat. It was crumpled, but I smoothed it out the best as I could and perched it on my head. No doubt Mudder was right about Nan wanting me in church on Sundays. And what was to stop me now? There was no Reverend Ropson brazening down at me from the pulpit, and, as was with Mudder, I'd always kept a clear counsel with God.

The house was quiet when I ran back downstairs. Bruddy was waiting outside, his hands deep in his pockets, a concerned look quietening his muddied, brown eyes.

"Mudder hurried everyone on before the youngsters got too dirty," he said. "So Loret asked me wait for you."

I smiled and started down the rutted dirt path towards the church, still feeling awkward over Mudder's talking-to.

"Don't mind Mudder," said Bruddy, as if knowing my thoughts. "She comes between all of us like a sabre whenever heads butt, whether it be Fudder and Fonse, Loret and me, or Emmy and Georgie." He chuckled. "And she don't let no one outta her sight either, till the matter's settled."

"I guess she's had lots of practisin'," I said. "What with so many runnin' around."

"Aye, she's had her fill all right. And God help us when it's her who gets mad. I tell you, brother, the house becomes quieter than a mouse in a pan of bread flour."

"Does she stay mad for long?"

"Nay. Only for as long as it takes to hear her out. Then

we chides with whoever it was that made her mad in the first place, and teases and tickles her till she gives over." He chuckled again. "It ain't always a pretty sight watchin' Mudder and Fonse goin' at it, but you'll get used to it."

I grinned, my awkwardness disappearing at the thoughts of Fonse shrinking back from Mudder's small, wiry frame. No doubt he was the bull-strength in the family, rigging up the boat for fishing in summer, and cutting and hauling eight-foot logs for selling to the logging company in the winter. In between times, he tarred roofs and mended fences and collapsing cellar walls, while haranguing with Bruddy, who was always alongside of him, and whipping his boys into helping hands whenever they happened in sight.

Fudder peddled along, his wiry body bent over with arthritic cramps that kept his fingers too scrammy for doing close work, and his hearing too far gone to hear Fonse's cries of warning over a recklessly tossed hammer or junk of wood, and his step too slow to step aside from a falling chopped tree—all of which sent Fonse into a round of cursing whenever he near missed Fudder, which he immediately blamed on the boys so's as to not make Fudder feel that he was in the way.

The boys never felt their father's cursing, and most times continued on with whatever it was they was talking about before he started his ranting, and more often than not, they wouldn't have been able to repeat in a month of Sundays whatever it was that had started the telling-off to begin with. And with Josie along, barking and bounding, and teasing and tripping the boys, or flicking at their caps with a stick, there was an added distraction for Fonse to be careful over, giving way to an increase in his rounds of swearing and ranting, and an increase in his list of daily prayers to the Saints.

All this flowed past Loret like an irksome summer's rain that drenched you to the skin, while bathing you in its softness. Coaxing Fudder inside the house for another cup of tea, whilst lecturing Fonse over her shoulder for his fickle-mindedness, and fixing the boys' caps straight on their heads as she walked past them, she appeared to be in all places at once—kneading down the bread for Mudder, sewing up doll's clothes with Emmy, sweeping, mopping, washing, and when she seen her way through the housework, was out ripping the rind off the birch as Fonse sawed up the firewood, tacking down haystacks with the boys, and making fast work out of any notion I might have about her not feeling well. The air was sharp with her bawling out orders, yet Mudder argued her laugh could sweeten a pantry full of crabapple tarts and nourish the most sullen of scowls into the sweetest, most savoury of smiles.

It was an argument that tested well with Josie. From the moment she leaped out of Old Joe's boat in the cove and bounded across the garden with Loret and Fonse's youngsters, her scowls over Sid's leaving disappeared. There were times during those first few weeks when I would sometimes catch her looking at me, the old sullenness souring her face. And each time I attempted to question her why, or explain how Sid's leaving was hurting me, too, she would bound out the door with a loud bark to silence me. But with helping Fonse split wood and mend fences, and tormenting the boys into a quarrelling, wrestling frenzy, her scowls appeared less and less as time went by, till she was giving me as many smiles as she was Loret's crabapple pies.

I smiled too. I smiled till my face ached, to show them how grateful I was to have been taken into their family. Still, my head pounded from all of their talking, and when everyone was talking at once, I closed my eyes to follow the thoughts of one, before getting carried away on the words of another. Sensing my confusion, Loret put me in charge of making the beds, and weeding the potatoes and turnips, all of which kept me out of the crossroads in the kitchen, and gave me moments of quiet. And when the baby was born, it became my special job to keep her little garments washed outside of the family's, and a stack of diapers, cleaned and softened, by the side of Loret's bed.

She was a special little thing, they all claimed, and what with her brown curly hair and eyes like cocoa, she was more of a Ford than ever was. And from the way she took to following Fudder's finger as he moved it from side to side in front of her eyes, it was clear that she was the quickest yet to learn, and probably the smartest little girl ever to have been born in the cove, perhaps even in the whole of White Bay. At least, that's what Fonse was often heard to say over his tumbler of brew. And sometimes when I picked the little thing up in my arms, and she held onto my finger whilst staring straight through to my heart, I was forced to agree that this truly was a case where Fonse was right, and Little Kitty was a gift straight from the Gods.

"Do you like her?" I asked Josie one early summer's morning. She had strayed along the beach from the rest of the youngsters to where I was perched on a rock in the sun, rocking Little Kitty and watching as Loret and Fonse, leaning over the side of a punt a couple of hundred yards away from shore, lowered the last of the gill nets into the calm, flat waters of the cove.

"I like her," Josie replied. Bending over, she shoved her face near Kitty's and bellowed, "Boo! Boo!" as she had seen Fudder do a hundred times or more.

"Sshh, not so loud," I said as Little Kitty's eyes startled awake. Loret looked over Fonse's shoulder and waved as Josie leaned over Little Kitty again, this time sounding her boos a little softer.

"I wanna rock," she demanded, plopping herself down on a rock next to me.

"Just for a minute, then," I said. Wrapping the bunting blanket more snugly around Little Kitty, I laid her in Josie's lap. "Don't hold her too tight. Make sure the blanket stays around her feet, it's still a bit cold."

It must have been how it looked to Nan, watching Josie rocking me, her hair, flaming red in the noonday sun, falling around me like a blanket, her hand awkwardly patting my side, unable to gain a proper rhythm. I squat down on my haunches, staring up at her with a sudden curiosity.

"Do you remember when I was a baby?" I asked.

"You not a baby. Kitty's a baby," said Josie.

"But I used to be a baby. Do you remember?"

She studied my face, a frown puckering her brow.

"You not a baby," she said, wrinkling her nose and tweaking one of Little Kitty's fingers. Then her eyes caught mine, the yellow flicks growing brighter.

"Nan rocked the baby. I rocked the baby."

"Whose baby did Nan rock?" I asked, grabbing hold of her arm as she rocked, and holding her still. "Whose baby?"

She stared at me, her brow knitting the way it used to whenever she was trying to pin Nan's hair back into her hairnets.

"I rocked the baby," she barked. "Nan rocked the baby. You never rocked the baby."

"Do you remember havin' a baby, Josie? Do you remember Doctor Hodgins and Mrs. Ropson holdin' a baby?"

She stopped rocking, her arms suddenly slack around Little Kitty, as her eyes, flooding with lights, darted from one of mine to the other. I held my breath, alarmed at the foolhardiness of my probing. Of what use would such memories serve us, now?

"Baby cries," she said, tightening her hold around Little Kitty and resuming her rocking. "Baby cries. Boo! Boo!" She ducked her face into Little Kitty's belly, rubbing it from side to side, making Little Kitty smile widely and flail at the red hair encasing her face. Sensing Loret watching us, I looked out over the water and gave her a wave, then tightened the blanket around the baby's legs. At that second Georgie thundered along the beach bellowing, "Jimmy caught a flatfish, Jimmy caught a flatfish!" Rearing up from the rock, Josie planked Little Kitty into my arms, and tore up along the grey, rocky beach to where Jimmy and Emmy and the two younger ones were wildly examining a quivering sole they had just hooked out of the water. I strolled onto the wharf, holding Little Kitty's squirming body upon my shoulder, as Fonse started paddling to shore.

"How's my Queen?" boomed Fonse, steadying the boat against the side of the wharf for Loret to climb out.

"Beggin' for her nap, no doubt," said Loret, taking Kitty and holding her off so's she could best see her face. "My, my, she's the doll," she crooned, her eyes caressing the small round face and puckered, petal mouth. "The little doll."

"You can pass the doll right here, now, sir," Fonse said, climbing onto the wharf and loping the painter around a post. "'Cuz it's time I had a waltz with me little sweetheart. Here, give her to me. Oopsy, baby," he said, lifting Little Kitty out of Loret's arm and tossing her over his shoulder.

"Don't toss her so hard, Fonse, for the love of the Lord," Loret cried out, running after him as he danced across the wharf.

"Let's get away from your mother, me little darlin'," Fonse said, tucking Kitty's face into the curve of his chin and lengthening his stride up the beach. "She's a jealous woman, she is."

"For the love of God, jealous!" Loret exclaimed, slowing her step as I caught up. "You'd think be the God she was a sack of spuds, the way he tosses her around." She smiled as a charm went up from the rest of the youngsters as Josie wrestled the flatfish away from Jimmy and tore off along shore.

"They gets along well, don't they?" she said, watching Jimmy and Georgie tear off after her, threatening her with a rock to the head if she didn't give back the fish. "I heard somethin' of what you were askin' Josie, Kit. Words travel well over water, you know."

I glanced at her sideways to check how she was meaning her words. Her dark hair was pinned back, with dozens of tiny, windblown curls dancing free around her warm brown eyes. She smiled. "You can tell me to mind my own business, you know."

"You must think I'm silly," I said.

"It ain't silly to be curious about your mother. Do you think she understood any of it, I mean, havin' a baby and all?"

"Nan said she believes she was havin' bad cramps," I laughed. "I bet she watched what she ate after that day."

Loret draped her arm around my shoulders.

"Does it bother you much that she's your mother?"

"I can't think of her as my mother." I gave a small laugh. "I only remember Nan, and this big, gallopin' person who Nan had to protect me from, else she'd have trampled me to death."

Loret laughed and we both turned up into the yard after Fonse, who had started singing to the high heavens with Little Kitty fidgeting on his shoulder.

There was only one thing missing in this full life in Godfather's Cove with the Fords, and that was Sid. His cheques came regularly every month. There was never a return address, and they were never stamped from a fixed place. Halifax, Toronto, Boston, New York; I followed him on Fonse's globe. It seemed he was no longer settled in a place than he was moving on again.

I cursed him his freedom to just keep running like that. Moving easily through my chores, and helping with the baby, I managed to keep a contented look. And so I was content. At least, with all those around me. But Sid felt like a shadow that grew longer as the year wore on, and beneath my quietness was a clatter of emotions more severe than ever the Fords could make over a Sunday morning breakfast. That the reverend had bedded my mother filled me with a revulsion that could never be outmatched, not even by Shine. That I was born out of such sin was as far removed from my order of things as was the idea to others that I appeared in the gully one day, with an offering in my mouth, the same as Pirate. And that Sid was my half-brother was as impossible to grasp as was the fact that the woman-child who thundered across the meadows, barking out laughter and jumping with glee, was my mother.

Yet, no matter how twisted with shame, disgust, despair my stomach became, I felt an emptiness that no amount of Mudder's pudding or Loret's hugs could fill. Sometimes I caught Loret watching me, and I knew that she wasn't without understanding. Nor was she without hoping that, in time, I would get over Sid. And I wasn't without knowing that she was hoping for a courtship between me and Bruddy.

From the first, I could tell he was taken with me, always passing me more bread at the supper table, and offering to help me with the weeding, or the stacking of Little Kitty's diapers. Mudder, Fudder and Fonse noted it also, and many was the time during that year Bruddy got more than his fair share of attention as everyone praised his good looks, his

manners around the women, his way with youngsters, his
laugh, his cowlick and whatever he happened to be doing,
saying or thinking whenever I walked into the room. It got
so he became more hesitant to set foot inside the door, from
all of the blushing that he was doing from the constant prais-
ing. And while I loved the warmth of his chuckle and the
softness of his eyes, it was Sid's eyes that I saw every single
morning that I opened mine, and Sid's laugh that I heard
every single night before I fell asleep. And while I wished
upon wishing that the terrible aching in my heart would
stop, I simply missed him more and more with each passing day.

Another year was almost gone by, and Little Kitty was
just after taking her first step, when Loret first made mention of her thoughts. We were in Loret's room, with me folding up a stack of diapers on the bed, and Loret sitting in the
rocking chair that Fonse had made for her out of a kitchen
chair, trying to get Little Kitty down for her afternoon nap.

"Bruddy's thinkin' about clearin' off a piece of land and
buildin' a house of his own this spring," she said easy
enough, pulling up her sweater and poking a nipple into
Kitty's groping mouth. "Might be he's thinkin' on gettin'
married someday," she added when I never spoke.

I stacked another diaper onto the growing pile, and
smiled down into Kitty's drooping eyes as she suckled noisily on her mother's tit.

"Might be that he got his eye on somebody," Loret
mused. "Lord, Kit, ain't you even curious?"

"About what?" I asked. "She's drooling a lot. I think she's
cuttin' another tooth."

"About who he might be interested in," Loret nailed out.
"Unless, of course, you knows who the lucky girl is."

I shook my head.

"Bruddy's one of the best catches around," she went on. "All the girls are linin' up around him."

"Um humm."

"Kit, don't you think he's handsome?"

"Yes."

"Well then . . . "

"Well then what?"

"Well then," Loret sighed. "Well then, you might want to stand in line yourself," she all but snapped. "For Pete's sake, maid, have you never noticed the way he looks at you?"

"I don't think on Bruddy that way."

She plucked her nipple out of Kitty's mouth.

"You keep thinkin' he's comin' back, don't you?"

I pressed down hard on the stack of diapers.

"You've got to get past him, Kit. And if there's one sure way of doin' that, it's findin' someone else. You can trust me on that one. Lord, I thought I'd die when Joe Reid dropped me, and took up with the Widow Burton. But then, along come Fonse, and it felt like I'd seen the sun for the first time in my life. It'll be like that for you, too, if you'll let it."

"I could never love another man," I said quietly.

"Yes, you can and you will," Loret argued. "Just give Bruddy a chance."

"No! Sid is the only man I could ever love. Know that, Loret."

I cringed at her pitying look.

"I think I do know it," she whispered sadly. "God bless you, but I think I do know it."

We were both quiet for a while, her feeding the baby, and me slowly folding the last diaper.

"It's such a joy to hold your own child," she murmured, tracing Kitty's button of a nose with her finger. "I want that for you, Kit. You never had a mother. Perhaps I'm thinkin' if you were one, you might get back some of the love what's owed you."

"You've already given me more than what my heart could hold. I feel blessed."

Loret smiled sadly.

"It's a frightened little heart you have, Kit. No more than a bird's. Do you know that when a bird gets hurt, it mostly dies of a heart attack, and not from what hurt it in the first place? That's what you remind me of, a little bird that's been badly hurt and threatens to run off the second anyone tries to make it fly agin. Well, you ain't no brittle-boned bird, Kit. You're a full-blooded woman who deserves more than what you've gotten. And I won't watch you die!" This last was spoken with a note of such fierceness that Little Kitty startled awake. "Hey now, go to sleep," her mother soothed, stroking her cheek. "It's your Aunt Kit who ought to be quakin' in fear, not you, little sweet."

I left her there, rocking and cooing the baby to sleep. Pulling on a sweater, I walked down to the beach and around the cove, the aching in my heart more fierce than ever before. Not because I was wanting a baby to hold, for every time Kitty opened her mouth and started bawling, I gratefully passed her back to her mother, thanking the good Lord babies weren't something that jumped out of the grass and stuck to your breeches like burrs and came home with you. Nor was I caught up on likening myself to a bird, holding that uninteresting thought for Josie. It was the "brittle-boned" part that caught me by surprise. And the "full-blooded woman."

I couldn't ever remember feeling like a girl, most certainly not brittle. Running up and down the gully every day, and back and forth to Haire's Hollow, and always keeping everything inside when Margaret Eveleigh, or Mr. Haynes, or even Josie or Nan was hollering things at me, I always felt like I could stand straight-faced through any kind of ill wind. And a woman was May Eveleigh, Mrs. Haynes, even Loret herself. Not even when I started menstruating had I felt much difference in how I saw things, and according to what Nan had said once, when a girl starts menstruating, that's when she becomes a woman. I guessed somewhere I had crossed a line without knowing it. Till Sid came along. And that's what was making my heart ache all the more, the knowing that I had become a woman somewhere, since the day he first strolled down the gully. And he was the reason for it. And now that I was growing into the best of me, he was gone.

CHAPTER TWENTY-EIGHT

MRS. ROPSON'S PLEA

SENSING THAT SHE HAD CAUSED me some unrest, Loret was especially kind that evening. Warming up some milk and climbing up to the attic, she sat besides my bed, and we supped, quietly. When we had done, she kissed me on the forehead and went to her room. I lay there for long after, thinking on nothing special. I must've fallen asleep, for the sky was much darker when something woke me.

"Kit!"

It was Bruddy, whispering my name from half-ways up the ladder to the attic. I held my breath, thinking Loret must've said something to him. The ladder creaked. He was coming up.

"What is it?" I whispered back loudly, hoping not to wake Josie.

"There's someone come to see you."

I sprang upwards.

"Who is it?"

"A woman."

A woman. Throwing back the covers, I pulled on my housecoat and crept down the ladder. A low murmur sounded from Fonse's and Loret's room as I passed by, and then Mudder's and Fudder's, and I sensed the entire household awake, listening to hear who was visiting me in the middle of the night—and why. Perhaps it was Aunt Drucie. Perhaps something had happened to Doctor Hodgins . . . Hurrying into the kitchen, I stopped and placed my hand to my heart. It was Mrs. Ropson.

My mouth dropped and I felt the blood leave my soul. Something had happened to Sid. And it was his dying wish that she come and tell me. I must've gone faint, for Bruddy quickly led me to a chair besides the table, where Mrs. Ropson was sitting. She was wearing a black cape, with the hood barely resting on the back of her head, and her black gloved hands clutched around each other in a claw-like grasp. Her eyes were sunken black holes in the gaunt light of the oil lamp, and the wrinkles on her face heavily shadowed. And if it weren't for the quivering of her mouth and the glistening of what could very well have been a tear trickling down her cheek, she would've far more resembled the jackdaw than the reverend had that time he made off with Josie.

Clutching my arms around myself, I gave a small nod and waited for her to speak. She tilted her head to look at Bruddy, and I saw the oldness around her eyes as the light from the lamp shone into them.

"Leave us, Bruddy," I said, and grasped my hands in my lap to keep them from shaking. Bruddy reluctantly walked out of the room. Her lips quivered as she watched him go, and it felt as if she was still wrestling with herself as to the wisdom of making such a journey, yet here she was suddenly in front of me, still not having come to a decision.

"Has something happened to Sid?" I finally asked.

"No." She lifted her eyes to mine and I was struck again by their oldness—weak, rheumy oldness. And as a hint of her old scorn towards me come creeping back, she hid them in shadow, not willing to gut this moment of forced humility. "Bring him home," she whispered, her sunken eyes reaching out to mine.

"I can't do that," I whispered.

"You're the only one who can."

"How?"

"I don't care how."

The silence was pregnant with sin, the reverend's, hers. Now mine?

"Go away," I said, rising from the table.

"No!"

"I can't do what you ask me."

"Why can't you?" she rasped. "Here." Clutching inside her cape, she hauled out a brown envelope and slid it across the table towards me. "Take it. And bring me back my boy."

I stared at the envelope.

"It's a sin he won't let me commit," I said.

"You're a woman! Make him!"

"What makes you think I'd bring him home to you?"

There was a silence as the withered old woman hiding beneath the hood came to realize that the prize wasn't there for collecting, simply because she had made the journey. She raised her head and stared at me.

"The reverend's dead. Yesterday. I sent Sidney a telegram, but there's been no word that he got it." Reaching out to me, she took hold of my hands. "I don't want to die without my son knowing it. Please! Bring him home."

"Go now," I said, pulling away from her grasp. And turning from her, I flew down the hallway and tapped on Bruddy's room door.

"See to her," I said, and ran back up over the stairs and up the ladder to the attic. I watched her through the window, a bent-over old figure, all wrapped in black, leaning on Bruddy's arm as she made her way down to the beach where a boat was tied up waiting for her.

The next morning Bruddy met me in the hallway on my way into the kitchen and handed me the brown envelope, taking care that no one saw the exchange between us.

"Thank you, Bruddy," I said, putting the envelope in my pocket.

"Are you all right?" he asked, a finger lightly touching my wrist. That he had been a part of last night's events had lent itself to an air around us, hinting to those subtly watching from the kitchen as they went about their morning chores of some sort of alliance between us.

"I'm fine," I said and, brushing past him, started helping Loret set the table for breakfast.

There was an unnatural hush over the meal, and everyone took longer than usual to feed themselves, listening for a dropped word or a significant look about the late-night visitor. Taking extra care not to look straight at me, they directed most of their concerns about the pending rain and the gate needing fixing to Bruddy, knowing that he'd be the one most likely to drop something if they kept him talking long enough. Bruddy spoke easily, tending to their concerns, yet the veiled glances he kept sending my way served to heighten Loret's and the others' speculating looks, and, no doubt, the new camaraderie that had sprung up between us was serving to fulfil a fancy of his as well, that of his silent calling for something more from me than what I was willing to give.

It was towards noon when Loret finally got on with it. Marching into the boys' room with Little Kitty clinging to her shoulder, she stood, one arm akimbo, and glared as I tucked in the sheets. "For God's sake, Kit, are you goin' to tell me what the old bat wanted?"

I frowned whilst plumping up the feather pillow.

"Old bat?"

"Yes, old bat! It didn't take much pryin' to crank open Bruddy's mouth, God bless him, and even less to figure out it was Sid's mother that come here in the middle of the night, bangin' on our door." Loret spat out the word "mother."

I pulled up the quilt and tucked it neatly around the pillows.

"Oohh!" Patting Kitty's back at a fired-up pace, she plopped down on the bed. "Damn it, Kit, you got the most frustratin' ways. It's only helpin' you that I'm thinkin' of. I don't trust why she come here, and I sure as hell don't trust you to put what she wanted straight."

I raised my brow and give the pillow one last good smack.

"Don't go huffin' on me now," she warned. "My words don't always sound right, but you knows what I'm sayin'."

"The reverend's dead. She thought I should know."

The hand stopped patting, and she fixed the fretting Kitty impatiently on her lap.

"So? Why would she bother comin' and tellin' you, when it's you she was most likely wishin' dead? And in the middle of the night like that!"

I shrugged again, and held out my arms to Kitty.

"Here, lemme rock her. Is it time for her nap?"

"You're not leavin' this room till my mind's clear."

"There's nothin' else to tell," I said, lifting the baby out of her arms.

"What about the envelope?"

"Money," I said, pacing up and down the room, soothing

Kitty's soft cries. "I'm givin' it to Doctor Hodgins to take back the next time he comes."

"Money!" Loret scorned, following close on my heels. "You'll be givin' Doctor Hodgins more than her sin money to take back. You tell her from Loret Ford that God stopped tallyin' up her good deeds the day she tried to run a starvin' youngster out of her home and into a devil-run orphanage."

Kitty started to bawl.

"Sshh, it's O.K., it's O.K.," I murmured, jiggling her harder as I walked.

"It's not bloody O.K. then," Loret yelped. "She thinks she can come rappin' on our door any hour the day or night . . . "

"Please, Loret. She won't come back, agin."

Loret threw up her hands and plopped back down on the bed.

"Lord, I'm sorry, Kit," she half whispered. "It's just that I can't stand seein' you get hurt any more." She looked up at me, tears filming her eyes.

"What is it, Loret?"

She didn't answer and I tucked Kitty's head beneath my chin and sat besides her. "You're carrying on too much over this," I said. "There's something else, isn't it?"

"Oh, I hates to tell you this . . . "

"Tell me!"

"He's got a girl."

I shake my head.

"Who?"

"Sid."

"Sid . . . ?"

"Yeah, Sid. He's got a girl."

A girl. Sid.

"How do you know?"

"He wrote Fonse a letter last month. I was goin' to tell you, but first I was waitin' to see if something might start up betwixt you and Bruddy. I thought it mightn't hurt so bad if it did."

I laid my face on Kitty's curls and rocked her gently.

"You want me to take the baby?" Loret asked softly.

I rocked harder.

"Why don't we go in my room," she coaxed. "You can sit and rock her in my rockin' chair."

I just kept rocking and finally Loret left, leaving me sitting on the bed and rocking Little Kitty with all the seriousness of the most devout mother as she garnered the most precious thing of all in her lap, and in the solemnity of that moment, everything else ceased to exist, making it possible to just keep sitting there and not feel nothing, nothing at all about the knowing that Sid had taken another girl.

CHAPTER TWENTY-NINE

OLD JOE'S WISH

IT WAS A COUPLE OF WEEKS LATER THAT another cheque came from Sid. It was stamped St. John's. It was near on a year now that he was in the one fixed place. I expected it was because that's where he met his girl. Loret paused in her powdering Kitty's bare bottom, noting me examining the stamp mark. Putting the envelope in my apron pocket, I went out to hoe the potato garden.

It was early May and the pale yellow sun was slow in readying the ground for planting. Forking over the potato beds, I bawled out to Josie as I caught sight of her swinging on the wellhouse door. Fonse had just fixed it last week, and already he had sounded her out for such a thing. Sticking out her tongue at me, she went running off to where Jimmy was scrabbling over the fence with Emmy in hot pursuit. Throwing down the hoe, I went over and twisted the toggle to bar the door, brushing my knee against a stinging nettle as I went.

I swore beneath my breath and, scratching my knee,

went back to the hoeing. It felt like the mindless breeze that
had been carrying me along ever since Sid took off into that
rain-blasted night had stopped the second I heard about his
girl, leaving me to take note of where I was placing my foot,
and where I should be placing it next, and what I was to wear
on this day, or tomorrow, and what I was doing, saying or
thinking, until I'd become jumpier than a cornered frog,
leaping at the slightest sound, and snapping back at the
youngsters as if I was one myself.

The days wore long, and at night I lay awake as if it were
the summer's sun shining through my window, and not the
inky light of the moon. It was during one of these long
evenings that a telegram come from Doctor Hodgins. A stiff
gale had blown up from the east, bringing with it a freak
snowfall and whirling it into a blinding whiteness. I had gone
to bed early with the rest of the household, listening to the
wind rattling the snow off the window and trying to shut out
Josie's snoring as she slept the sleep of the dead in her bunk
next to mine. I sat up when I heard the muffled pounding on
the door, thinking for a second that it was Mrs. Ropson come
back. Bruddy's footsteps sounded across the kitchen floor,
and pulling on a pair of socks and a housecoat, I knelt down
by the attic door and listened.

"Fonse!" Bruddy called up over the stairs in an urgent
whisper. "Fonse!"

I lit down over the ladder the same instant as Fonse come
out of his room, buckling up his belt, with Loret behind him.

Bruddy was talking low to a young man who stood
solemnly by the door, bundled inside a winter's coat, its fur-
lined hood caked with melting snow.

"Charlie just brung a message from Doctor Hodgins,"
Bruddy said, passing a folded piece of paper to Fonse as we
crowded into the kitchen. "It's Old Joe. He never come back

from fishin' down in Chouse Brook this evenin'. The weather's too bad for them from Haire's Hollow to go lookin', but Doctor Hodgins figured me and you might try it—if the sea's a bit calmer our way."

"Blessed Lord," said Mudder, coming into the kitchen, wrapping her nightgown around herself.

"Perhaps he camped over when the wind come on," said Loret, peering over Fonse's shoulder as he leaned nearer the lamp, scrutinizing the message.

"He never took no gear," said Fonse, passing the message to Loret. "What's the cloud like?" he asked Charlie, crossing to the window and cupping his hands to see out through.

"Startin' to blow off," said Charlie. "Might be lighter on the water the once, if the moon shines through."

"Go," Fonse said, beckoning the young fellow to the door. "Send back a telegram that me and Bruddy's on our way to Chouse."

"Think we should wait for light?" asked Bruddy as Fonse leaned out the door behind Charlie, squinting up through the gusting snow at the cloud covering.

"We'll be fine," said Fonse, closing the door and striding to the row of coats and oilskins lining the wall by the back of the stove. "Mudder, make up a Thermos."

"We don't want all hands washin' upon shore by mornin'," said Mudder worriedly.

"We'll see what's it like outside the cove," said Bruddy, pulling on a sweater. "If it's not clear, we'll be back."

"Then crawl in bed with the baby, Kit," said Loret, marching over by Fonse and hauling an oilskin coat off the hook. "'Cuz I'm goin' too."

"You're not goin' out in this!" said Fonse.

"It's Old Joe you needs to be worryin' about, not me,"

she replied, dragging a pair of rubber boots out from the pile in the corner.

"You knows you're not goin' out in this," said Mudder.

"Yes I am, Mudder, and don't try to stop me."

"Loret, for gawd's sake . . . " began Bruddy.

"Shut up, Bruddy." Loret dropped the boots and, nudging Mudder to one side, faced Fonse. "You got plans on not comin' back?"

"Noo!"

"Then I'd rather the fright of sittin' alongside of you in the boat than sittin' here without you. Now hold on, I goes and gets dressed."

So saying, she swept down the hall and up over the stairs.

"Fonse, you're not goin' to let her go?" Bruddy cried out.

"Damn hell's tarnation, the woman's got a mind like a bull!" Fonse said angrily, hauling a pair of oilskins up over his pants and jamming his feet into a pair of rubber boots. Bruddy turned to Mudder, pleadingly.

"She'll pay no more heed to me than she does Fonse," said Mudder, searching through the cupboards for the Thermos. "Kit, pass me the teapot."

At the mention of my name, Fonse and Bruddy looked my way with something akin to surprise.

"Good Lord, Kit," said Fonse, lowering the sweater he was about to pull over his head. "We're forgettin' Old Joe's your friend."

"He's afraid of drownin'," I burst out, then bit down hard on my lip.

"Hey, now," said Bruddy. Coming up behind me, he laid his hands on my shoulders and gave me a gentle shake. "Old Joe's not drowned. We'll find him."

"Course we will," said Mudder. "He's a man of the sea. Most likely, he's holed up in Chouse Brook."

"He'll be all right, Kit," said Loret, sweeping back into the kitchen. "We'll find him, won't we, Fonse?"

"Yes, and that we will," said Fonse. "Loret, is that the baby?"

"Oh, I thought she'd gone back to sleep," said Loret, hurriedly pulling on a pair of boots. "Will you lie with her, Kit, so's she don't wake up Fudder? Landsakes, he might be half-deaf but he's not dead, and the last thing we needs is him comin' along."

My eyes lingered around the kitchen at them all pulling on sweaters and caps and mitts, and Mudder, halfways through packing the Thermos into a lunch sack, handed it to me with a knowing nod.

"I'll go lie with Kitty," she said. "You keep the fire goin'."

I accepted the Thermos gratefully and packed it inside the lunch sack, along with a flask of brandy she had waiting on the bin. Finally, they were all bundled.

"Let's go then," said Bruddy, tightening his sou'wester and opening the door. A gust of wind-driven snow blasted across the kitchen, and I grabbed hold of Loret's arm in sudden fear.

"Please don't go," I cried.

"Now, now, Kit, don't you start," said Loret, hauling Fudder's wool cap down over her head. She wrapped her arms around me and hugged tightly. "Won't be so bad on the water, there'll be no driftin' snow. Keep the fire goin', and don't fret too much."

Then Fonse was shooing her outside, giving me a sympathetic look before shutting the door behind them. I ran to the window and watched as they hurried down over the back steps, black hulks struggling against the blacker night. The wind parted the snowclouds every scattered second, allowing pale, moon-lit glimpses as they vanished into the snow-whipped haze. Old Joe was out there, somewhere. Alone. And cold. And no doubt Doctor Hodgins was sitting alone right now, watching his waves pitching up over the black-ened shoreline, thinking, praying, that Old Joe's wouldn't be a face to come rolling upon his shores by morning. Mercy on this night, I prayed. Mercy on this night.

I dragged the rocker over to the window and sat down. Josie got up and emptied her chamber pot into the slop pail at the end of the hall. I thought to call out, to tell her of what was going on, but I felt stronger reaching out to Old Joe with my thoughts, sitting alone in the half-light of the lamp. And for sure if I prayed hard enough, and all those others missing him as well, Old Joe would feel us helping him through this night.

The wind drifted the clouds further and further apart, allowing more light. Once, in between the gusts of wind, the drifting snow settled long enough for me to glimpse some-thing dark moving up over the yard. I kept watching, then I saw it again, a dark shape crawling clumsily towards me I rose from the rocker and pressed my face against the win-dow, my hand covering my beating heart. The snow lifted again, and all was wiped out. I pressed harder, my hands cupped to block the reflection of the lamp. Then I saw them—Loret, Fonse and Bruddy—all holding onto each other, and all walking and stumbling and falling as if they were one. I rose from the rocker and stood with my back to the heat of the stove. They were a fright to look at as they stumbled through the door, their sou'westers dripping water and snow, their faces fixed in shocked horror. Loret cried out as she seen me, and Fonse tightened the arm he held around her shoulders to steady her. His other hand, he held onto the door jamb to steady himself. No one moved for the moment, as if we were turned to stone. Then Mudder come running down over the stairs, her hands held out in prayer as she come into the kitchen.

"What's happened?" she cried out, then reached out as Loret fell towards her.

"Kit! Oh, gawd, it's bad," said Fonse, staggering towards me and laying a cold, wet hand onto my arm.

"He got his boat caught in the nets," said Bruddy, wild-eyed with fright. "He was swamped. He—he's dead." His words ended in a choked whisper.

"He know'd about the nets," said Fonse. "But one of 'em had floated farther out, what with the wind. He never cut his engine in time."

"Praise be the Lord," moaned Mudder.

"I guess he must've figured on comin' here for the night," whispered Bruddy. "Too far to go home in this wind, and no gear to hold over in Chouse Brook for the night. He could've done it, too ... "

Some of Loret's cries and Mudder's prayers sounded through the dim noise that was rising in my ears.

"Did you find him?" I cried out.

"We found him," said Fonse, drawing me closer. "He—he didn't drown. He was—he was ... " Another silence fell in the room, then Loret turned to me with an anguished cry.

"He had himself tied to the bow of his boat. Why'd he do that?"

I closed my eyes and allowed Fonse to rock me, his hands ice cold through the cotton of my nightdress, his rubber coat wet against my cheek.

"Why?" Loret cried out again, then broke down sobbing. "I'll never forget it, seein' him tied to his bow like that, his head just floatin' above the water, all chilled with ice."

"Stop it, Loret," Bruddy moaned.

"No, don't hold it back, my child, cry it out," soothed Mudder. "You, too, Bruddy. 'Tis a hard thing to see a body dead, but it's only a body, emptied now, its soul in heaven no doubt, 'cuz he was a good man, else he wouldn't have helped Kit and her poor mother the way he did."

"We would've missed him," whispered Fonse. "Thought it was a piece of driftwood, till Bruddy's torch caught hold of something orange. It was a starfish. Nailed to his bow."

A shivering sob swept through me. A starfish. Old Joe's starfish. Was he praying hard, I silently anguished, and Fonse held me tighter as I broke down sobbing harder than Loret, thinking on Old Joe strapping himself to the bow of his boat, praying Starfish, Star bright, Starfish, Star bright...

After I had spent my tears and was gulping back shivering sobs, Fonse held me away, looking gently into my face.

"Here now, I've made you all wet. Loret, help her get dry. Bruddy and me'll go wire a message to Haire's Hollow. I expect his family's all sittin' up, waitin' for word. We got him fixed away in our boat. Perhaps, if they don't mind the wait, we'll take him home ourselves, in the mornin', soon as the wind dies down."

Old Joe's brother and one of his brothers-in-law was down before sunrise. I hid in my room, not wanting to see Old Joe anywhere but squatting on the wharf, calling out my name, and grinning his gummy grin as I hurried by on my way to school.

They stopped, just long enough to hear what Fonse had to say about the drowning, and finding Old Joe. Then they put him in their boat and took him home. Fonse and Bruddy slipped a tow rope around the bow of Old Joe's boat, which was still floating above the water, and towed it to shore. We waited a couple of days, then, leaving the youngsters and

Josie with Mudder and Fudder, Fonse, Loret, Bruddy and I climbed into Fonse's boat and headed up the bay to Old Joe's funeral.

The wind had died itself out finally, but the swells rolled us around frighteningly so, grey and bloated beneath the sunless sky. I fought from becoming seasick, and judging from the ashen colour of Loret's face, mine wasn't the only weak stomach making this journey. My eyes lingered on the gully as we boated past, and a pang of loneliness swept over me as I saw the old grey house leaning back against the side of the hill, its door and windows boarded up, and its chimney bereft of smoke. But a larger pang took hold of me as we rounded Fox Point and Haire's Hollow sprung into view, with its wharf jutting out from the side of the road and the one boat missing from the dozen that bobbed colourfully on the harbour.

The service was started by the time we got to the church. All of Haire's Hollow was crowded inside, heads bowed, silently weeping alongside of the family. Loret, Fonse and I stood with those standing behind the back pews. I searched amongst the bowed heads, half expecting to see Sid's. He wasn't there. Neither was Doctor Hodgins. I bowed my head and listened to the new minister, a little younger than the Reverend Ropson, lead the congregation in prayer over Old Joe's coffin.

"I'll be back," I whispered to Loret when the last hymn was sung and the pallbearers were fixing to take Old Joe to the cemetery. Backing out the church door, I looked once more to where a kelp-green boat used to be moored off from the wharf, and ran along the beach to Old Joe's brother's shack. Doctor Hodgins was sitting outside puffing on his pipe, a blanket draped across his legs against the damp air, and a tumbler of brew resting on the wooden bench besides him.

He lifted the tumbler off the bench as I come up to him, and nodded for me to sit.

"Broodin' with the waves, agin?" I asked.

He was silent, and I noted the dried pathway down his cheek from where a tear had travelled some time before, and I was minded of the last time a tear had travelled down Doctor Hodgins's cheek, the day Nan had passed on, and he had been walking with me along the beach, listening to a seagull wail. Taking hold of his hand, I held it against my cheek.

"It ain't fair," I said, and began to sob.

Doctor Hodgins laid his arm around my shoulder and brought his forehead to rest on mine. "No, it isn't," he answered, his voice breaking as he spoke. "And the fault is ours for expecting it to be so."

"I d-don't understand," I cried.

"No. Nor I. That's the mystery of life, Kit, we enter it, we leave it. We just got to learn to allow for it."

"He t-tied himself to the cleats. So's the f-fish wouldn't get him."

"He had the last say in that, didn't he?" Doctor Hodgins whispered, turning his head to look out to sea. The swells were foaming hard upon the beach, brazen, relentless.

"I just thinks of him, sittin' there," I cried, "watchin' the water comin' into his boat. He must've been c-cold." I began to sob harder.

"Sshh now, water numbs the skin. God got ways of making death bearable. Shh now."

I sobbed some more, then pulled back from Doctor Hodgins, wiping my nose with the back of my coat sleeve.

"It was the starfish that told them where he was," I quavered. "Fonse said the rope wouldn't have held him till mornin'."

"He must've been wishing really hard."

"For sure he must've. What will you do now—without your fishin' partner?"

"I guess I'm going to have to find another one," he said, balancing his brew between his knees and relighting his pipe. "Old Joe wouldn't want his nets rotting on the shore."

"You could come live with us. Down in Godfather's Cove."

"I expect it's getting rather crowded around Mudder's table."

"There's other shacks. I mean . . . "

He gave a small grin.

"I know what you mean, Kit. And perhaps I will some-day. Perhaps I will."

I tightened my scarf.

"Fonse and Loret are waitin' for me, I'd better go."

I stayed sitting for a minute, then, "Do you think I never wished hard enough for Sid?"

He puffed his pipe, then took a swallow of brew.

"You're right, Kit, it ain't always fair," he said, looking at me sadly. "It can be damn bloody wearying. But some things can never be changed, no matter how hard we wish."

"Starfish can re-grow themselves."

"That's the way of starfish."

"Sid has another girl."

He took another swallow, then turned back to the sea.

"You were talking to him?" he asked.

"No. Loret told me."

"It's time to move on, Kit."

Sensing the same stubbornness rising in his tone that always come whenever I talked about Sid, I rose to leave. He laid his tumbler and pipe on the bench and rose along-side of me.

"You've got spirit, Kit," he said, laying a hand on my

shoulder. "A strong spirit. It'll go a long, ways to colour things right for you. I promise you that."

I kept my eyes down and, despite his mindset against me and Sid, crushed my face against the comforting, tobacco smell of his coat. Then pushing away, I hurried along the shore, looking worriedly over my shoulder at him sitting there in the cold, thinking the same tormenting thoughts I was thinking myself—about Old Joe wishing upon wishing to a starfish as the water swamped him, and of Sid taking another girl.

"I swear, it would take a thousand suns to brighten up the faces around here," Loret said some days later as I moped around the house, idly picking up after the youngsters and missing something else that she had said.

"I'm sorry, Loret," I mumbled, and wandered into the sitting room, looking out the window. Indeed, things just kept looking greyer and greyer since Old Joe's funeral, and the restlessness I had been feeling the days leading up to his death had become a consuming fire. Always, I kept seeing Loret standing up to Fonse the night in the kitchen, and taking her place besides him as they went into the ill night to search for Old Joe. Always, I kept thinking of Old Joe wishing upon wishing on his starfish and having his wish come to be. And always, I kept thinking about Doctor Hodgins, sitting alone in front of his shack, brooding with the waves.

That's where I should be, I mumbled angrily, tossing and turning in my bunk: sitting besides Doctor Hodgins, watching and brooding, watching and brooding. That's what I'd been doing since the day Sid left, watching and brooding for him to come back. And now he was never coming back. Not if he married another girl.

I tore out of bed and, pulling on my housecoat, crept down over the ladder, the stairs, and made my way outside.

It was a quiet night, fit for the torment inside of me. Bruddy found me walking through the potato garden, kicking at the ground foundering over from the beds.

"Not a night for sleepin'," he said, appearing from behind me, his cowlick carefully combed into place.

"Goodness!" I exclaimed, jumping back and clasping my hands to my heart.

"I didn't mean to scare you," he said softly. "You're gettin' dirt on your nightdress."

"It's a housecoat," I said, for want of better words.

"It's a woman's garment, for sure," he said with a grin. "I don't know too much about them, except for what I sees on clotheslines."

His teeth shone whitely through the night, and I imagined the warmth melting his brown eyes.

"There's lots of girls in Godfather's Cove that would like to teach you about women's garments, Bruddy."

The night hid from him the blush that followed my bold words. But there was a driving recklessness stirring inside me as the sudden truth of what Sid was about came crashing in on me. His was not a love that could fade like the coloured roses on an often-washed dress. Like mine, it had rooted in a parched soul, and each shuddering sob that had passed between us had worked to bring together two hearts as one, like the single trunk of a tree, and was now too grown to ever take apart without destroying the whole of what was flowering above it. And I wasn't about to let him do that.

Bruddy was chuckling.

"How do you know about what other girls might be wantin' to teach me?"

"Loret."

"Loret!" Bruddy laughed. "If she said it, then it must be. There's not much she don't see."

I glanced anxiously towards her room window. It was dark.

"Take me to Haire's Hollow," I gasped to Bruddy, the words coming out of my mouth before I even knew they were in my head. "Please take me, Bruddy. Now! While Loret's still sleepin'.'"

"Tonight?" he asked in surprise.

"Yes! Please." I grabbed onto his shirt. "I need to see Doctor Hodgins."

"Doctor . . . Kit, are you sick?"

"No—Yes! It's not serious, but I need to see him—before it becomes serious. Please, take me," I begged. "I-I don't want to worry Loret."

"Loret! Cripes, you'd have them all out wringin' their hands if they woke up and found us gone in the middle of the night."

"Then let's leave now. We'll be back before anyone's awake."

He looked at me quietly, contemplatingly.

"Why can't we leave in the mornin'?"

"Because Loret will want to know everything. And I just don't want to have to explain. Not yet. I'll tell her when we gets back."

"Is it to do with Sid?" he asked quietly.

"Yes!" I say deeply. Then, "Yes it does, Bruddy. I need to give his mother back something, to be rid of her once and for all. Do you understand? And I need to do it now, right now before Loret talks me out of it or . . . or . . . something else happens and makes me change my mind."

He stood hesitating, and I knew he was thinking on his feelings for me, and how my ending things with Sid's mother might be a way of ending things with Sid as well.

"Don't ask me anything more about it, Bruddy. Just take

me. Now!" I stood back staring at him so hard I was trembling. "Please, Bruddy."

"You can't go in your housecoat," he mumbled, looking down over the cove with a sigh.

"You'll take me, then?"

"Be quick. It'll be black as tar if we loses the bit of moon."

"Thank you, Bruddy, thank you," I breathed, clutching at his hands.

"Thank me after I get us there," he said, brushing me off and heading down over the garden towards the cove.

It was as if my ankles had sprouted wings. I flew in through the house and up over the stairs and climbed the ladder to the attic without making the barest of creaking sounds. Taking the money out of the envelope Mrs. Ropson had give me, I put it into my cloth bag along with the money Sid had been sending over the past two years. Tossing a dress and some other garments into the bag, I hurriedly crept back down the stairs and prayed that everyone would stay sleeping for a minute longer. God answered my prayer, and I took it as a sign that this was a journey he was wanting me to make and ran faster down over the garden to the cove where Bruddy was waiting with the boat.

There was a small lop on, nothing to be worried about. The thin crescent moon glimpsed through the clouds, casting light on Bruddy's worried face and highlighting for him the determined look on mine. We spoke little. It was as if he knew that once we set off from shore, my only need of him was to steer the boat.

It was close to three in the morning when we finally put ashore by the wharf in Haire's Hollow. Climbing onto the wharf, I knelt down as Bruddy was about to toss up the painter for me to loop around the post.

"No, wait," I stopped him. "I'm not going back, Bruddy."

He stared at me for a second, then, "Now, listen, Kit, I just can't let you run off... "

"And you can't stop me, neither," I cut in. "Just tell Loret I'm with Doctor Hodgins and he'll be down the morrow or the next day to explain everything." I scrabbled to my feet and started backing away. "I-I'm sorry, Bruddy. Take care of Josie; I'll be back."

Then he was leaping up over the side of the wharf, and I turned and ran. His hands came down heavy on my shoulders, and as if I were no more than Little Kitty, he spun me around to face him.

"You're goin' after him, aren't you?" he asked.

Closing my eyes, I held my head down and said nothing. His grip slackened, feeling more like a squeezing embrace.

"You've got courage, to go after him, Kit," he half whispered. "More than him. If you were mine, I would never have left you. Never!"

I stared at him and, with a twist of my shoulders, escaped his hold and ran off.

"Go on," he shouted after me. "Go get him that don't want you."

Ducking off the wharf onto the beach, I turned, checking the windows of Haire's Hollow. There were no lights about. Running past Jimmy Randall's stage, I threw one last look behind me to make sure Bruddy wasn't following. He wasn't. He wasn't leaving, either, just standing there in the middle of the wharf, his arms folded as he watched after me. I would've liked to have gone back, to explain things better to him, to make him understand why Sid had left me, why he had never come back. Had I been *able* to explain why. Bruddy had hit upon the one thing that no amount of restless thinking had been able to defend—why Sid had never come back, if only to see that things were all right with me, and all right with Josie. But there was no time now to think about such things. The sense of urgency that had been growing within me since I first heard the news about Sid's girl was driving me towards some distant point that I could not even perceive. Taking off up the shore, I kept to the shadows of the bank, straining to see through the dark and keep myself from tripping over pieces of driftwood and rusted tin cans. Ten minutes later, I was coming around the turn to Old Joe's brother's shack and Doctor Hodgins. I rapped as easy as I could, not wanting to startle him, but his eyes fair bulged out of his head when he opened the door and seen me standing there.

"Nothin's happened," I said quickly, stepping past him. "Loret and everyone says hello. They just dropped me off on the wharf and is fixin' to go on back."

He stared after me in silence, then closed the door. Moving quietly, he struck a match and lit the lamp sitting on the table. Raising the wick, he turned to look at me as a dim light shadowed the room.

"Now then, young lady, what brings you here in the middle of the night?"

"I'm goin' to St. John's. To get Sid."

He groaned, partly from dread, partly from expectancy, like Loret whenever she come upon the youngsters doing something that they were warned off from, yet, with the knowing it was what they were apt to do, no matter how many warnings were offered.

"You've heard from him?" he asked.

I shook my head.

"Kit, if he had wanted you, he would've gone down to Godfather's Cove after the reverend's funeral."

"Sid was here?"

Doctor Hodgins looked at me in surprise.

"I thought you would've heard by now. I'm sorry. With Old Joe . . . I forgot to mention it."

I turned to the window, thinking on Mrs. Ropson.

"He got here just as the funeral was starting," Doctor Hodgins said. "His mother was near hysterical with relief, but he left right after."

I nodded. Sid was here. And he never come to see me.

"Did he go to the gully?"

"I'm sorry, Kit."

"Did he go to the gully?"

"I don't know."

"Will you take me to the train in the mornin'?"

"Why are you doing this?"

"Will you?"

"You oughtn't to be doing this."

"You said you'd be here for me, no matter what."

"I'm not going to help you make a mistake."

"It's not yours to judge."

"It's mine if I help you make it."

I stared at him steadily.

"Very well then, I'll do it without you," I said, walking to the door.

"Just a minute," he ordered, holding up his hand. "Where do you think you're going?"

"St. John's."

He snorted.

"You'd get to the end of the road and wouldn't know which way to turn. Listen to me, Kit . . . "

"No! I'm done listenin'," I say. "I've been listenin' to others all my life. And fightin'! Fightin' to hold onto what's mine. And thankin' everybody for lettin' me do so. Well, I'm tired of smilin' for your blessin's, all the time smilin', feelin' grateful but never proud. I want to live my own life, as I see fit. And I want Sid. You can help me if you wants. But I'm goin' after him."

Running his hands through his thinning tufts of hair, he yanked open the door and strolled outside to where the water was lapping at the shore.

"I'm not one of your faces," I snapped, the wind taking my words as I|chased after him. "And whether Sid comes back or not, I won't ever be. I'm makin' my own decisions now, and you're not responsible for them."

"It's wrong."

"Not in my mind. And I won't be spendin' my days broodin' on a stoop, either," I said, "no matter how I come to think on things. There's other ways to pay penance, ways more deservin' of time."

The wind ruffled the shirt against his back. I stood still watching him. He shivered, his hands deep in his pockets. Finally, when I was shivering too, he turned.

"Might as well get some sleep," he said tiredly, brushing past me. "We can't go anywhere till morning."

I stepped inside the shack behind him and shut the door.

"What now?" he asked, as I stayed where I was, staring after him expectantly.

"I want you to fix it so's I can never have babies."

His brow rose in utter astonishment.

"Christ almighty," he swore, coming towards me and seizing me by the shoulders. "How the hell do you know about such things?"

"It's the only way I can be with Sid."

"I can't do that."

"You did it to Josie." His mouth dropped, and I hurried on. "Nan told me, but she never meant to. I swear she never said it to a livin' soul, except to mutter it out loud once, when she got mad at Josie for runnin' off." I paused. "I always remembered it, although I never knew what she meant. Till now. Till I started thinkin' on the same thing, myself."

He sat down heavily. And for the first time that I'd known him, he looked sorely shaken. "It don't seem fair that I'm askin' somethin' more from you," I whispered. "But it all seems to be sproutin' from the same seed, somehow. Well it weren't me that planted those seeds. And I'm not settlin' no more for what someone else thought up for me. God must've meant for you to help me, else he wouldn't have took Nan and put you in her place." I gave a small laugh. "He must've known she wouldn't been able to keep up with everything that's after happened—wouldn't been able to keep protectin'... my mother."

I stared off and Doctor Hodgins raised his hand and held onto mine. We looked at each other with a quiet that spoke beyond the secrets that we shared, and told of a long-lasting trust. And of an understanding and an acceptance of the way things were with me. And in a strange way, with him.

"I didn't do anything to Josie," he said finally. "Perhaps I could have intervened, but I felt it was God's wish that you be her only child. There's a pill he probably intended for you, a new method to control pregnancy. I'll get it for you."

"Is it for sure?"

"If you take it right."

"Sid won't trust that. I want what God did to my mother."

"You'll do as I say on this one," he almost roared, hauling a blanket off the bunk. "Now get some sleep; you'll need rest. I swear to God the old girl's come back," he muttered, snapping open the door and shutting it firmly behind him. I watched through the window as he settled himself heavily into his chair and, tossing the blanket up over his shoulders, pulled a box of matches and his pipe out of his pocket. Hauling another blanket off the bunk, I sat down in a chair besides the window, looking out over his shoulder at the sea rolling up over the shore. Wrapping the blanket around me, I settled more comfortably in the chair. This was one night when I was going to sit, watching and brooding, alongside of him.

CHAPTER THIRTY

KIT'S LAW

THE NEXT DAY I WAS ON MY WAY TO ST. JOHN'S. It was hard to tell if it was the journey itself or its destination that was filling me with the most fear. Clinging to my rattling seat in the Newfie Bullet, we thundered across meadows and plains at forty miles an hour, and entered deep forests, and crossed over bridges and rivers, outrunning herds of caribou and moose around each winding turn. Doctor Hodgins had assured me as I was climbing on board that there was nothing to be scared of, and had pressed a piece of paper with the name and address of his friend's boarding house into my hand. He was bawling out instructions on how to get a taxi, and warning me about the Portuguese sailors down on the docks, even as the train was pulling out of the station and hurriedly leaving him behind. And if it weren't for Maisie Rice about to give birth to a breeched baby, I've no doubts that he would've been climbing aboard the train himself, and going to St. John's alongside of me.

Despite my fears about heading into the city alone—and

it so far away—it felt right that I do so. Like Loret, going out
into the storm-driven night with Fonse. No fear had she for
what might come. Such was her strength, and her trust in
his. And such was their love, built upon strength. Neither
had I felt fear with Sid, no matter how frightening a decision. Like our marriage. It was because I loved him that I
married him. And it was because I still loved him that I was
going to fight for him. No more watching and brooding,
watching and brooding. And if he was unwilling to move
back to Haire's Hollow now that he had a taste of living
somewhere else, then I was willing to take up living right
alongside of him no matter where it was. And Josie would
just have to make do. I was willing to do most anything, as
long as it would put me next to Sid for the rest of my life, and
the closer we got to St. John's, the more unsettled I became
over another fear—that of Sid himself. Supposing it wasn't
because we were half-brother and -sister that he no longer
wanted me? My stomach lurched sickly. Supposing he
wanted the other woman more?

I squeezed my eyes shut every time the thought shot
through my mind, which was every second that brought me
closer and closer to knowing. And when the train finally
trudged its way through the rusted meadow of steel tracks
that lay at the feet of the grey, windswept city, with its hundreds of rain-soaked windows staring down at me, I became
more and more determined to cling to my seat and wait for
the train to move off again, taking me back to the gully and
Josie and Loret and Fonse, and everything else that was loving and warm and comfortable in its commonness.

But I never. Making my way down the rickety train steps
with my bag in my hand, I sucked in my breath and held it,
recoiling from the sharp, fousty smell of the city, and
remembering what Nan had said once about people dying

from the plagues. "It's in the cities that germs gets bred," she had said. "All them people living on top of each other—sure, no sooner is the breath out of your mouth, than it's into the gob of another, without gettin' a chance to circulate and clean itself of whatever germs it's carryin'."

"Taxi, Miss?"

I started at the gravelly voice sounding from behind me, and give a slight nod to the scrawny, red-cheeked man who tipped his hat as I turned to face him. Giving him the piece of paper with the name and address of Milly's boarding house on it, I mutely followed and climbed into the back seat of his car, just as Doctor Hodgins had instructed me to do.

Clutching my bag, I stared mesmerized out the window at the hundreds of houses and the squalor that we drove by, and more people than all of a hundred outports brought together as one. As frightened as I was at the thought of seeing Sid again, his was a comforting face to think on in this whirling clutter of roads, cars and buildings. Once, we came in view of the harbour and I shrank back from the sight of the fishing boats and ships, minding Doctor Hodgins's warnings about drunken Portuguese sailors.

After it felt like we were going in circles for an hour and my stomach was getting queasy from my head being giddy, we pulled up in front of a peeling, two-storey house with "Milly's" painted over its front door. Paying the taxi man, I took my bag and walked slowly inside.

Everything was just as Doctor Hodgins had described it to be—a small room with a white-railed, steep stairwell leading up one side, and a cluttered counter in its centre, piled high with papers and dirtied mugs, beyond which sat a grizzly haired old woman, knitting the back to a sweater.

"A room?" she said, not taking her eyes off her knitting.

"Yes. Please."

"Where you from?"

"Haire's Hollow."

Her mouth dropped, and coming to her feet, she peered harder through her specs.

"You're here, already? Sure, I just got Johnny's message!"

"W-Who?"

"Johnny!" She gave a hard laugh. "That'd be Doctor Hodgins to you, I suppose. Hah! What with two baywops for parents, he'll always be Johnny around here."

I fixed a smile on my face and nodded politely. She sobered and peered at me more closely.

"Heh, do you know what a baywop is?"

I shook my head.

"It's you! One who was born and bred in the bay!" She gave a hard, rattled laugh and I nodded, politer still. Sobering again, she shuffled out around the counter and started up the stairs.

"Heh, come on then," she said, rubbing the small of her back. "You can carry your bag, I suppose? I'd help you but I got a bad hip. Good old Johnny gives me pain pills every time he comes. How's he doing?"

"He's fine. You've... known him long?" I asked, becoming a little less tongue-tied with the effort of lugging my bag up over the stairs.

"We started school together. Smart as anything, Johnny was. Course, I only made it through to grade six, had to go to work," she puffed, coming to a stop at the top of the landing to catch her breath. "But Johnny kept on with it. Brother, you couldn't stick him on a sum. Heh, poor Elsie. She was a good soul, though pinched as it was."

"Pinched?" I rested my bag on the edge of the step, looking up at her.

"Yeah, pinched. She come from the Gut. That's over by

the harbour. Her mother liked the drink," Milly snickered, "like everyone else in the Gut. And sickly! Well, she was always sickly. I said back then Johnny married her to guarantee he'd always have a patient." Another hard, rattling laugh and Milly hobbled down the hall. I followed, wondering if it wasn't for something that Doctor Hodgins had me stay with Milly. For certain he knew she was the one to talk.

"You looks like her," Milly went on, opening up a door and stepping inside a small room. She held the door wider and I stepped past her, laying my bag on the narrow bed, and taking a peek through the paint-stained window onto the street below.

"I'll get you some water," Milly said, taking the wash pan off the stand. She glanced at me in the mirror on the wall before her. "What brings you here, a young girl like you, all by yourself?"

"I'm—here to meet my husband."

"Husband!" She looked around, squinting me up and down, shaking her head. "Lord, you don't look old enough to be married."

I grinned nervously.

"I'm not so young."

"Heh, there's something about you that speaks of time. Though, if Johnny sent you to me, it's because he's wanting me to keep an eye on you. When's your husband coming?"

"I'm—goin' to meet him. Doctor Hodgins said you could help me find my way around?"

"Hah, like I figured, gathering the lost sheep. Where's your husband staying?"

"The university."

"What's he learning?"

"Uh, to be a teacher."

"A teacher? That's nice." She shuffled to the door. "I'll get your water."

An hour later I was freshly washed and neatly dressed, and sitting on the edge of the bed, feeling slightly irritated as I listened to the roar of cars and trucks shuttling by, blowing their horns and squealing tires from every which way. How could a body stand such noise? I lay back on the pillow and closed my eyes. Perhaps if I was to sleep a little, I might feel more like myself. As it was, I was a bundle of nerves, and half-sick from the fousty-smelling air.

Squeezing my eyes shut, I tried to pretend that the roar of the cars was the roar of the surf pounding upon the shore, and the blowing horns were seagulls, circling the sky and calling out. But it felt like there were springs on the back of my eyelids and the second I stopped squeezing them shut, they popped wide open again.

After a while I gave up trying to sleep and sat up on the edge of the bed. It was about an hour before four. I had planned to see Sid later in the evening, when he had finished his schooling for the day. It felt easier somehow, to meet with him in the evening. Evening time was when sweethearts walked, when each other's faces would soon be covered in darkness. I wanted it to be dark when I met with him. Dark, but not too late, not so late as he'd be off with his other girl before I got there. And I was wanting it dark, dark as pitch, so's he couldn't see how nervous I was—especially if we were to do something. Not that I was scared of making love with Sid. Just that I knew I'd be so damn shy of doing it that my face burned like fire every single time my mind went to it. That's why I wanted it to be dark soon after I met up with him, so's he couldn't see my face burning like fire when he touched me. If he touched me.

The thought that he wouldn't touch me wasn't one

I dwelled on for long. The fact that I had come all this way
to find him, and alone, would surely convince him of my loving him, and how nothing would ever make it stop. Surely,
he would see how futile it was to be away from me, that it
was just as well to be living as husband and wife than to be
living in a dream, thinking on it every day.

It was about a half-hour before five, and I couldn't con-
tain myself no longer. Throwing on a sweater, I stood in
front of the mirror and looked at myself. Loret had cut my
hair a few days ago, and it hung straight and wispy fine to
just below the collar of my blouse, and it was darker. Its yellow dulled by the winter's sun. I leaned closer to the mirror
and smiled, then grimaced, not liking how it rounded the
curve of my cheeks when I smiled. Pulling back a safer distance from the mirror, I tucked my hair behind my ears.
I leaned closer to the mirror. My eyes were grey, clear grey,
like the down on a goose, Loret once said, and just as soft.
I bit my lips to make them red, as Loret showed me the day
of the wedding, and pulled back from the mirror, practising
a smile, a small smile that Loret said was sure to hook the
heart of the most hardened man. I smiled. Sid wasn't a hardened man. He was sweet and soft. And kind.

"Oohh!" I threw myself impatiently on the bed, then
come back up and walked determinedly to the door. I was
going, light or dark. I'd find some other way of hiding my
face. Besides, we wouldn't be doing anything in the daylight.
Perhaps we would just walk and talk, like we always done,
and by the time night come, I wouldn't care.

If he comes with you, a small voice kept nagging. And
let's not forget the other girl . . .

Yanking open the door, I ran down over the steps to
where Milly was still sitting behind the cluttered counter,
knitting.

"Can you show me how to get to the university?" I asked.

"Your husband knows you're coming?" she asked.

"Yes," I said, opening the door and stepping outside. There were roads and cars going everywhere. How did a body find his way back home? Milly came to the door behind me, holding onto the small of her back.

"See that smokestack? That's the hospital. Walk past that, and up over the hill, and then look down, and you'll see it, three buildings in the middle of a field. That's the campus."

"Thank you."

"Got plans, do you?"

"No," I said quickly, my face flaming.

She rattled out a laugh and punched me lightly on the arm.

"It's your supper I was thinking on."

Blushing furiously, I started walking.

"Not scared, are you?" she sung out. "It's just five minutes from here."

"No, I'm not scared." I paused, my step faltering mid-air. "Is it that close?"

"That close."

My knees went weak. Sid was just over the hill. Five minutes from where I was standing. I swallowed hard and tried to get my breathing regular. Suppose he wouldn't come back with me? Why ever would he? Nothing had changed! Nothing . . .

"What's wrong?" Milly asked as I'd stopped walking altogether.

I turned back and ducked past her inside the boarding house.

"Do you have any clips?" I asked breathlessly.

"Clips?"

"Hair clips."

She blinked.

"In me hair, I do."

"C-can I have two?"

"Two?"

"Just two."

"I suppose." Reaching up, she ruffled through her nest of grizzled hair and, pulling out two clips, passed them to me.

"Thank you," I said, and ran back up over the stairs, leaving her staring after me, a quizzical look marring her face. Closing the room door, I quickly wetted down the two straight strands of hair on each side of my head and, twirling my fingers through them, clipped them against the side of my face. Turning my head from side to side, I checked to make sure they were the same size. They were. Satisfied, I sat back down on the bed, and careful not to muss up the two curls, laid my head back on the pillow. I lay there for an hour, waiting for the curls to dry, pretending the cars were waves and their horns were seagulls. I must've dozed because, suddenly, I was lying on my back at Crooked Feeder, soaking my feet in the water, and watching Sid a little further up the shore, drifting shale across the sea. He turned to look at me, and my stomach quickened to see his teeth, as white as the lace edging the waves, and his eyes the colour of ten skies.

I woke with a start as a set of tires squealed outside, and angry voices competed with blowing horns. Pulling the clips out of my curls, I jumped off the bed and stood before the mirror, smiling to see two yellow coils bounce alongside of my face. Taking up my hairbrush, I gently combed them out, and smiled again to see them float softly, just like they had done on my wedding day. Loret would be proud. Opening the door, I walked down the stairs and, smiling grandly at

Milly, laid her clips on the counter and walked out the door.

"You remembers how I told you to get there?" she called out, shuffling out on the doorstep behind me.

"I do," I said, crossing the street.

"I can come with you, if you wants."

"No, I can do it."

"Mind you don't get lost."

I waved without turning.

"Just keep looking for the smokestack," she hollered. "That'll always set you right."

I nodded and kept on walking.

"Watch out for the God-damned sailors," she hollered again. "You got your purse?"

I held my bag off from my side, and took the corner. For sure there must be more than one youngster lost all the time, I thought, what with all them roads. Passing the smokestack, I came out on a bit of a hill and looked down upon a large green field with three big buildings sitting in the middle of it. Ignoring the churning in my stomach, I picked up my step and tried to breathe more easily. The air was damp, but the sun was starting to shine and the second I started walking across the field, I heard songbirds singing, no different than those in the gully, and right away I felt a little comforted. It must make for a common ground amongst people from different places when they can hear the same birds singing, I was thinking, for who hasn't lain an extra minute upon a pillow early in the morning, smiling at just such a thing?

Taking the envelope with Sid's address on it out of my pocket, I checked and seen the name "Reyer's Residence." To the left of the centre building, and smaller than the other two, was a red-brick building with the words "Reyer's Residence." Soon enough I was walking up the steps, half expecting Sid to have seen me coming for him by now, through one of the many windows, and come bolting out the door any second. He didn't, and I kept walking. Up the last two steps and in through the large wooden door, feeling smaller than Little Kitty as I stood beneath the high ceiling in the vastness of that tiled room.

A young, dark-haired man, not much older than Sid, skipped through the door behind me.

"Please, I'm looking for Sid Ropson," I said, as he slowed his step and stood before me.

"Yep, you've got him," he said cheerily. "Only, he's not here right now."

"Can you tell me where he is?"

Saucy brown eyes looked me over good.

"I suppose I could. Do you think he'd want me to do that?"

"I-I'm from Haire's Hollow."

"Oh! Well, that does it then." He grinned, then seeing as how I wasn't grinning back, he cleared his throat and managed to look more serious. "He's at the orphanage."

"The orphanage?"

"The orphanage."

"Could you—please tell me how to get to the orphanage?"

A studied silence. Then, "See that smokestack over there? That's the hospital. Follow the road in front of it to your right, till you comes to Buffy's Chip House. The orphanage is on the other side. Can't miss it, dozens of orphans running around in front of it."

I nodded, and headed back towards the smokestack.

Seemed like no time before I was walking past Buffy's Chip House and coming in front of a huge white house, the size of a dozen houses all built into one, and looking as pretty as anything with its fields of grass around it and low-hanging poplars, not at all what I thought Loret's devil-run orphanage would look like.

Walking up a wide cobblestone pathway, I knocked timidly on a thick oak door, and then again when no one answered. Standing back, I screwed up my nerve and, lifting the handle, stepped inside a front room dressed as a porch, a large, fancy porch with a towering ceiling and a closed door directly in front of me and another leading off to the right. Sid's voice sounded through the one on the right. I walked quickly towards it, and bent my head, listening. He was teaching. Arithmetic.

The door burst open and I pulled to one side, startled, as a couple of youngsters darted past me. Sid kept on teaching. Knees shaking, I peered around the corner of the door jamb. He was standing near a window, by a tall wooden cabinet that was slightly taller than he, reaching for a stack of papers that were resting there, and joking as he talked.

I caught my breath as I looked at him, mindful of another place—of me—just a few short hours ago, standing in front of Milly's mirror, watching myself as I stood, now, watching him, his hair hanging straight and wispy fine to just below his shirt collar. And it was darker, its yellow dulled by the winter's sun. There were other things. He wasn't as tall as I remembered him, nor his shoulders as wide. But my eyes remained rooted to his hair, hanging straight and wispy fine, straight and wispy fine. A churning started low in my stomach. Then Sid, having found what he was looking for, held back his head and smiled, and the churning became a heaving state as I watched his smile rounding the curve of his cheek as he talked.

My vision became hazy, and with all the new places I had been in the past day, I forgot for a moment where I was, seeing only the curve of Sid's cheek, and his wispy fine hair, the curve of Sid's cheek and his wispy fine hair. He moved, and I jolted back behind the shelter of the door jamb, my breathing faint. The haze filming my eyes became more and more speckled with black, and I stumbled across the darkening porch towards where I remembered the door to be. Lifting the handle, I ran outside and breathed deeply of the sun-blessed air. Birds were singing and I walked woodenly forward, not knowing from whence I came, or where I was going. My ears must have picked up a sound, for suddenly I was turning back and there, staring at me through one of the windows, was Sid. Even through the window, I could see his face paling. The baby-down fuzz on his chin had thickened and deepened a darker brown, adding a strangeness to his face. Yet his eyes, though rooted in uncertainness as they stared into mine, were as sharp a blue as they always had been, and piercing a path straight through to my soul. He pressed his forehead against the window, as if to get closer to me, and for one taut second I felt a flicker of hope, a softening through my numbness to what my heart was seeking. But just as quickly, another thought killed it. Could I ever again see anything but the curve of his cheek and his wispy fine hair?

Shame swamped me. Sid's face disappeared and one of his cursed Gods was glaring instead, through gouged-out sockets that betold of his having loved that which was denied him, a law that not even legends could do away with. Wicked! It was a wicked thing I desired, that I lusted, that I wanted above all else. And the smell of rotting dogberries was suddenly drowning the air around me, no different than the day in the gully when the reverend, my father, stood pointing his finger of shame and ordering his boy away from the gully tramp's girl. Me, his daughter, the gully tramp's girl, and his son, my brother. The air was suddenly

too rancid to breathe, and turning away from the orphanage, and Sid, and the reverend's pointing finger, I started
running, past Buffy's Chip House, the smokestack, and still
I kept running. Once I thought I heard Sid singing out my
name, but I ducked down a different road and kept on running, down this way and that, past the train tracks, till I
came to the docks.

I sat breathlessly on a quay, too numb to separate the
gulls' screeching from that of tires, or to feel the wind that
swept off the harbour's water and dusted my face. Voices
sounded all around me and I rose, needing to move on, but
not wanting to go anywhere, excepting to find a spot with no
people so's I could take out in quiet the cold, sickening lump
in my stomach and feel it through, like holding onto something precious that no one else ought ever to see, despite its
quickening rawness cutting me clear through to the bone.
Sid could never be my husband. Never! And more than that,
there was shame in my loving him.

Shame! I drew a long, sobering breath and stepped hurriedly over a coil of rope as two dark-skinned men, who
could've been sailors or fishers, stopped with their smoking
and yarning to watch me. I cringed beneath their oily stares,
yet oddly enough, it felt fitting that they see me so, for it
was a wrap of filth that I wore, no different than the dirt
shrouding their lusting eyes. And it had swaddled me all this
time from the day I was born, the reverend's sin, seeded in
a darkened, unnurtured womb, its godless mark growing
slowly over time, till it sprouted into life, announcing the
reverend's fall from grace with each kick of my tiny webbed
foot.

I cringed and glared at the two swarthy sailors as I
would've at Mrs. Ropson, had I been able to shrink back to
the day of my birth and watch her look of horror as Doctor

Hodgins held me naked in his hands, naked excepting for her husband's adulterant mark.

Dare you touch me! I screamed silently at the two sailors and Mrs. Ropson, dare you touch me whilst my flesh lies caked with the reverend's sin. I turned and fled off the wharf for fear of wanting to plunge myself into the cold, dark waters surrounding it, and cleanse myself forever of its dirt and shame. Screeching brakes and honking horns sounded all around me as I foolishly raced down the centre of a road. A woman shrieked as I leaped out of the way of an oncoming truck, and stumbled in her path, and still others sung out. I kept running. Then a shaft of sunlight struck me full in the face, blinding me. Clean! I heard Nan's voice bawling at me no different than if she had been standing on a cloud in front of me, and her hand reaming down from the heavens, shoving a sogging wet washrag in my face. Clean! she bawled out, again. Be Jesus, it's a God-given right to be clean, but He left it for us to do some of the work!

I raised my hand before my face as one might a shield to protect it from a foe, excepting there was the added pain of another foe striking from within. Clean! Tears brimmed my eyes, and I sprang between two half-rotted buildings to escape the staring people and honking cars. Clean! I was on the docks again, and running. A grove of trees stood in the near distance and I raced towards it, wishing for the jolting disorder of the rocks in the gully, and the squalling easterlies that would pummel me amongst the rocks at Crooked Feeder, and where I could finally lie still and allow the blazing shaft of light to burn red on my eyes and force even this merciless day to turn quiet. A small wooden bench poked out of a bunch of shrubs amidst the trees, and I gratefully collapsed, sinking low so's to hide myself from anyone walking by. It felt like sitting on the stoop again, on the day that Nan had died. Time felt like nothing. The wind blew. Seagulls cried. And coal smoots from some giant burning chimney drifted around me like black snow. And I felt nothing, nothing at all, excepting the sound of my heart beating against my breasts, and tears wetting my face.

The tears were dried when Sid found me.

"Kit!" His voice sounded with relief when he peered around the shrubs and seen me. "Kit!" Then, he was sitting besides me, his hand reaching for mine, his breathing coming hard and shallow. "How did you find me?" he asked. "Who brought you here?"

I kept from looking at him just yet, and allowed him to wrap his hands around mine, warming them.

"Why'd you never come back?" I asked finally, when my heart had quietened from the nearness of him and my lips had ceased their trembling.

"Kit! I've tried," he whispered. "A thousand nights I've begged for courage to go back. But I was afraid, afraid of weakening—of becoming your husband. And you would've hated me if I had, you would, yes, you would have," he said, holding up his hand to quieten my protest. "I saw what it did to Mother, living with the reverend's sin." He held my hands tightly. "You've always fought for what was just," he half whispered. "Fonse, Loret, it would've worn at you, all the time thinking, wondering what they were thinking, how they were feeling. And I would've known it. Every time I looked at you, I would've known it. That's why I was afraid to come back, afraid you'd stop loving me. I'm weak, Kit; I can't risk you not loving me."

He brought my hand to his cheek, his face twisting with the fear of having said that which till now had only been spoken in his heart. And now, having shown himself, was at risk of losing the one thing he still desired more than the rightness of laws.

I caressed his cheek, my finger circling the spot near his mouth that dimpled when he smiled.

"No, not weak," I whispered. "It's me who's weak, still wanting you after all this time—knowin' that some things can never be changed, no matter how hard we wish—like the wind, it can never be stopped."

"Shh, we don't choose who we love," he murmured, rubbing his cheek against my palm. "I still love you. I've dreamt of this day, when you would come and say something—any-thing—to change how things are with us, so's none of it won't matter any more, that I'll be free to go home to you and Josie. Then, when I'm not dreaming, I try to forget you—I try and try, but you're always there, you and Josie, calling, calling out to me—and that damn gully, the brook, all the time I hear it, babbling, babbling. And I can never quite hear it, just feel it, pounding through my veins as if it were a part of me, and all the time sounding me back to you. God help me."

"You can come," I cried, not able to bear his anguish. "Not yet, perhaps, but someday. It's not fair that you should be here, living in an orphanage that was meant for me. We're still crippled—still apart—still living in his sin."

"I don't know if I can, Kit."

I swallowed hard.

"Is it because of your girl?"

"God, no, there's no girl!" He laughed bitterly. "Fonse told me about how Bruddy was keen on you. So I made her up—so's you'd forget about me."

"You fool," I cried, hugging my arms around his neck, the choking lump in my throat giving way to little sobs. "But I'm glad you done so, for it brought me to you. You must come back, Sid. It's not just the pitcher plant that's the thing of beauty. It's other laws that made it so—the rain, the bog and the sun. It couldn't have grown without those."

"Lord, what're you saying?" he mumbled through my hair, rocking me.

"I'm sayin' you're part of my law—the law that governs me. And Josie. We're a different thing without you."

"Oh, Kit," he half laughed, half cried. "What kind of stuff have you been studying on?" And then he was holding on to me so tight that I never thought it possible that he could ever let me go again. And I held on just as hard. When at last he let me go, he led me back along the docks and through the roads, towards the smokestack that rose above the city like a chimney from hell, belching out a smoke as grey as the film smothering my eyes.

Sid let go of me on the stoop of Milly's boarding house, and I squeezed my eyes hard to hold back the tears burning to make themselves seen.

"Kit!" He lifted my chin and I looked into his eyes, the colour of ten skies, and my mouth quivered to smile.

"I'll always love you," he whispered.

I nodded, my throat too choked to speak.

"Perhaps I will come. Someday."

"I'll tell Josie."

"Tell her I thinks of her."

His face became squiggled through the cursed tears.

"I miss you," he whispered. "I think of you every day, sitting out back, looking down over the sea. Don't forget me, Kit."

"Forget you?!" I laughed crazily, the tears flowing freely now. "How can I? How can I when everything brings you to me, each draught of wind, each thud of an axe. You're every-where, Sid, just like Nan." Then I was pushing him away from me and bursting in through the door to Milly's. She come to her feet as I went running up over the stairs, but Sid's voice sounded from the doorway and it was to him that she went.

The shaft of light flickered through the room window as I burst in across, and became stronger as it found me, but I wasn't wanting its comfort yet. Dumping my clothes and things onto the bed, I started folding and packing them into my bag. Dusting off the dresser and the washstand, I made sure there wasn't a fleck of dried skin or strand of hair left behind for Milly to clean. And when I had everything packed and cleaned, I dumped my garments out on the bed again and refolded them better, smaller than before, so's they wouldn't bulge out the bag as much. I swear I must've packed that bag a dozen times before I finally got it right. Then finally, I threw myself across the bed and lay flat on my back, allowing the light to wash over me.

"I love him," I whispered harshly, opening my eyes to its warm, yellow heat. "I'd drink the oceans dry if it could change things between us. Every damn one of them." Then the light became too bright, forcing me to close my eyes as it burned red on my eyelids. And with the cars sounding like waves, and their horns honking like seagulls, I waited to feel the quiet.

CHAPTER THIRTY-ONE

REDEMPTION

THE NEXT MORNING, I MADE FAST work in getting out of Milly's boarding house. She trailed behind me as I lugged my bag down over the stairs, and despite my reassurances that I was all right and just needed to be alone, she kept steady with her rantings till I finally agreed to a cup of tea. After, she helped me get a taxi from her doorstep, arguing all the time that Johnny ought never to have allowed me to come to the city by myself, and now here I was, in some kind of state, and having to take the train back home all by myself.

Thanking her warmly, I finally escaped into the taxi and sped off to the train station. There was still a hope that Sid might be there, that something might have happened after all during the night, and it would no longer matter that he was my brother, and he would be packed and coming home alongside of me. But in every face I searched, I kept seeing his bluest eyes as they caressed me goodbye. I boarded the train, back to riding on the mindless wind again, and feeling nothing, nothing at all, just a sense of the train jolting and shaking all around me, and trees blurring by my window. And it wasn't till I got off the train late that afternoon in Deer Lake did I take note that I hadn't sent a telegram to Doctor Hodgins telling him to meet me.

Even that didn't matter. And when the conductor helped me aboard a wood truck that was heading down to White Bay, I was glad to be sitting with a stranger who didn't mind my not talking. He drove me straight through Haire's Hollow, past Old Joe's brother puttering around the wharf, and blew his horn at one of Maisie's youngsters that ran across the road, and at Maisie herself, holding onto her new baby as she darted across after it. I said goodbye to the truck driver as he dropped me off by the gully, then started down the path to the house.

It was the first week in June and the meadow was still flat, the new shoots straining beneath last summer's dead. The door was stuck from being unused all these months. Putting my shoulder against it, I shoved it open and stepped inside. The air was musky, dank. I wandered listlessly through the rooms. They echoed silence and looked shabby, poor and smaller than before. Laying my hand on the cold stove, I sat down in the rocking chair and creaked slowly back and forth, back and forth. The tears came softly at first, and then with such an uncontrollable force, the huge, gulping sobs sucking out my breath, that I ran frightened to the door and leaned against it. The wind blew hollowly in my face. No more would it bring promises of his laughter. No more would the nights hold pregnant dreams. A cold stove and an empty wind. Is this it then, a cold stove and an empty wind?

A yap, like that of a hurt dog, sounded from the woods where Sid had built the makeshift camp to protect me and

Josie from Shine. I looked towards the road. I figured Old Joe's brother would have had time to let Doctor Hodgins know I was back by now, and was expecting to hear his car any second. The yap sounded again. Letting go of the door jamb, I walked across the meadow and up through the woods.

The picket platform had collapsed on one end, brought down by the weight of the winter's snow. Seeing something sticking out from beneath one corner, I bent over for a closer look. It was Josie's box, the one she had like mine that I used to keep my coloured glass in. I reached out to pick it up and jolted backwards as Shine's crackie came snarling from beneath. He yapped at me, eyes glazed and mouth foaming. Distemper!

"Get away!" I yelled, stumbling backwards. "Get away."

Snarling, it took a step towards me, then started walking around in a dazed circle. I took another step back. It appeared to be watching me, then, whimpering sickly, walked confusedly through the woods. I darted forward and grabbed the box, but having lain under the snow all winter, it came apart in my hands, its contents—a handful of black hairnets—tumbling to my feet like mangled webs. Nan's hairnets. The torn ones that she had been throwing out for years, some with the clips still in them. Entangled in one of them was the piece of blue glass I had given Josie the day she slapped me in her room, and one of the little robin's feathers. And sticking wetly onto the cardboard cover I still held in my hand was the letter from Sid that she had ripped from my hands and ran with down the gully.

A low snarl sounded from behind the bushes, and snatching up the clump of hairnets, I ran back through the woods and out on the meadow. The put-put of a motor boat echoed through the air. I ran to the back of the house and, looking down over the gully, saw Old Joe's brother as he cut his motor and drifted towards shore. Stuffing the hairnets and piece of glass into my pocket, I shut the house door and ran down the gully to the beach. The letter from Sid I held in my hand against my heart.

"Hello!" I said, waving, as Old Joe's brother lowered a paddle into the water and shoved himself ashore.

"It's Josie," he said by way of greeting. "She's havin' some kind of fit. Fonse Ford come up for Doctor Hodgins last evenin'. He's not back yet."

"A fit?"

"That's what I overheard him sayin' to the doctor. Said she throw'd herself down the well."

"The well! Take me there. Please?"

"For sure, for sure. I knew you'd be wantin' to go, when I seen it was you in the truck. Figured you was away and never heard yet."

I lunged through the water, getting both feet wet and, heaving myself up over the side of the boat, climbed inside. There was a bit of a wind on, and the bow of the boat rocked hard against the swells, sending a steady spray of water over my face and a salty taste in my mouth. Old Joe's brother tossed me a bit of canvas, and I wrapped myself good, staring straight ahead to Big Island, and beyond that, Godfather's Cove.

The sound of Fonse's hammer as he nailed a lock onto the wellhouse door was the first thing that greeted me as I come up from the cove and started up over the garden with Old Joe's brother in tow.

"Loret!" he roared, tossing the hammer to one side, barely missing Fudder's head, as he seen me coming. "She's back. Kit's back."

The door flew open and Loret and Doctor Hodgins and

Mudder came scrabbling onto the bridge, then Emmy and Jimmy and Bruddy, and lastly, Josie.

"You's farmed!" she barked, leaping down over the steps, hair flying, and barging headlong towards me. "You's farmed! You's farmed!"

I held out my hands to stop her, but she ploughed headlong into my stomach, knocking me flat on my back. But not before I saw the frightened, wretched look on her face.

"Here, Josie!" Fonse shouted, coming up behind and taking her by the shoulders. "Leave off, girl! Leave off," he ordered gently. But she was spitting mad as well as frightened, and flailed her fists angrily at my face, all the while screeching out "Farmed! Farmed!"

"Lord have mercy," Loret sang out, helping me to my feet as Fonse pinned Josie's arms behind her. "Thank God you're back, Kit. She's been throwin' fits ever since she woke up and found you gone. I swear, if it wouldn't for Doctor Hodgins, I don't know what we would have done with her, hey Fonse?"

"She's been a handful, all right," Fonse said, trying to hold her still as she kept struggling to get free.

"Go home," she yelled at me. "I'm goin' home."

"Hush now, we'll have no more talk of that," Loret scolded. "Kit's back, everything will be fine."

"Go home," she yelled at Loret.

"We're goin' home," I said, grasping her hands. "I just come from home, look, see what I found?" I pulled the clump of hairnets out of my pocket. "The box was soaked to pieces," I said. "We'll find you another one."

She went still as I pressed the hairnets and the piece of glass into her hand. Then, lifting her eyes, she stared at me through the curtain of hair, blinking rapidly, as if holding back tears. Only once had I seen her cry. The night in the rocker after Nan had passed on. Not even during her darkest hour with Shine had she cried. What turbulence was this, then, moving her so? A tightening of my heart as she continued to stand there, sullenly blinking back tears, told me what Sid had tried to tell me all along, that it was never her. It was always me. Despite my feeling timid by everyone's watching, I took a step closer to her and tucked a strand of hair behind her ears. And without knowing I was going to, as if the movement towards her was too great to halt, I leaned even closer and kissed the bared cheek.

"I'm never leavin', agin," I said shyly. "Tomorrow, I'm takin' you home."

A grin tugged the corners of her lips and the yellow flickered in her eyes. Pressing the hairnets back in my hand, she fished out the piece of glass and gave a loud, barking laugh. Then she went running across the garden, holding the piece of glass over one eye.

"Go chase her, Emmy," Doctor Hodgins said, prodding the younger girl on the shoulder as she dallied besides him.

"You too, Jimmy," said Loret, nudging her son. "Run on now. Josie's fine."

The two chased after Josie, and Doctor Hodgins turned to me, along with Mudder, Fudder and Loret. Bruddy stood a little to the side, his hands jammed in his pockets as he silently appraised me, his eyes shorn of the merriment that usually accompanied them. I looked guiltily at my feet.

"Did she—did she jump in the well?" I asked.

"I guess she thought you'd gone the path of Lizzy," Doctor Hodgins said. "And—Sid." At the mention of Sid's name, everyone's eyes fell away from mine, and then Mudder and Fudder was inviting Old Joe's brother back to the house for tea. Bruddy turned to follow them.

"Wait, Bruddy!"

He halted his step, but kept looking after the others.

"I—I'm sorry. I shouldn't have taken off like that."

"I've been rused by pretty girls, before," he said with a curt nod, and then with a trace of his old grin touching his face, "but hear me well, Kit Pitman, you only get one shot at a shell bird." The others laughed, and Bruddy, his grin becoming more bashful, raised his hand in parting and followed after Mudder and the rest.

Loret, Fonse and Doctor Hodgins stood silently. The breeze ruffled their hair, yet their eyes were steady on mine, waiting, studying. Loving. My heart, which I'd thought dead, fluttered a little.

"He'll be back someday," I said. And then, after a small pause, my voice deepened with feeling. "But, it'll be my brother who's come home."

Loret broke down with a sob.

"My heart's breakin' for you, Kit," she cried, flinging her arms around me.

"Lord, Loret, it ain't more tears that I'm needin'," I muffled into her neck. "I swear I could float my own boat if I saved them up this past day."

She laughed, pulling me tighter.

"I vow, if you ever run off agin, I'll come after you like I would one of the youngsters."

"Now you'd best hear me," I said, pushing her back. "I mean it when I say I'm goin' home tomorrow."

"Hush now, there's no reason for you to be sayin' that..." But Fonse took hold of her arms, pulling her away from me.

"We'll talk about it, later, Loret," he said. "Right now Kit needs a bite to eat, she looks like she's goin' to faint." Taking hold of my shoulders, he leaned over and kissed my brow. "I'm proud of you, Kit. I know you could've persuaded him, but you done what the Gods feared to do—you cast down your pride, and you found peace. I can see it in your face." And then Loret was sobbing into her hands and running for the house.

"Loret!" shouted Fonse. "Lord, Loret . . . " And then he was chasing after her, leaving me alone with Doctor Hodgins.

"You were right," he said, watching after Josie as she climbed a fence, Jimmy and Emmy scrabbling after her. "She wouldn't survive without you."

"Are you goin' to try and keep me from goin' back home?" I asked with a sigh.

"Not likely," said he, ruffling his hands through his tufts. Then, "I'm sorry, Kittens. You know I would've stood behind you, no matter how it had turned out."

"I know. Come." I tucked my hand into his and we walked up over the yard to where the Fords were waiting for us.

It was a good six months later, just before dawn, when I woke to hear a *thud thud thud* coming from the front of the house. My heart leaped. I lay there for a minute, foolishly telling myself it was Doctor Hodgins having another broody night and taking it out on the wood. *Thud! Thud! Thud!* Rising, I pulled on a dress and sweater and crept slowly through the half-darkened house. *Thud! Thud! Thud!* I came into the kitchen. *Th-thud! Th-thud!* It was mixed up now with the sound of my heart beating. The rocking chair creaked as I stepped past it, and the wind rustled at the window. How full the morning felt now, with its offering of something more . . .

I opened the door. The thudding stopped. I stepped outside. It was Josie. She was standing by the chopping block, her hair streaming over her forehead as she rested on the axe. She grinned as I came onto the stoop, then hooking the axe into another junk of birch, flicked it onto the chopping block and started chopping.

I sat down shakily on the door stoop.

"Fool!" I whispered to myself.

She tore a strip of birch rind off the junk and, holding it taut between her thumbs and forefingers, held it to her lips and blew on it, startling the air with a sharp whistle. She barked out laughing as I cringed, and giving her a bit of a smile, I rose from the stoop and idly walked up over the bank onto the road. Once there, I turned towards Haire's Hollow and kept walking. There was nothing I wanted to do, and no one I wanted to see. Yet I kept walking. The sun popped a ray over the south-side hills, brightening the sky and chasing the morning shadows from around my feet. A thin dribble of smoke spurted from Aunt Drucie's chimney, and I hurried past, not wanting her to see me walking by and not dropping in for tea. I kept walking, keeping to the smooth, rutted tire tracks. Down the last part of the hill, then along the road through Haire's Hollow, past May Eveleigh's store, the reverend's house—empty, now, with Mrs. Ropson visiting Sid in St. John's—the wharf, the spot on the water where Old Joe's boat used to float. I paused for a moment. Doctor Hodgins was squat on the beach nearby, putting the finishing touches to a fresh coat of kelp-green paint on Old Joe's boat, hauled up and flipped over, its keel to the sun. Past the clinic, the schoolhouse, the jailhouse, Shine's makeshift grave on the hill just outside the graveyard, long since filled in and with a piece of clapboard nailed to the tree above it, like a tombstone, with the words "Guy Fawkes" stroked on it in white paint. And finally, the church.

My step slowed. Then, without further thought, I walked up to the door and pulled it open. It was dark, shadowed inside, and silent. My breathing became shallow.

Reaching out my hand, I trailed it across the back of the pew where Nan, me and Josie use to sit, as far away from the Reverend Ropson and his pointing finger as we could get. Slowly, I started walking up the aisle, my breathing of a sudden coming so fast I could scarcely keep up with it, past the pew where Margaret Eveleigh and her best friends sat, and then, where the upper-ups sat, and the very front pew where I sat with Doctor Hodgins the day of Nan's funeral. I stopped there, looking up at the pulpit. I half expected to see the reverend standing there, his eyes raking over the congregation as he preached hell and damnation, and his tongue flicking over dry, bloodless lips. Surprisingly, I neither saw nor heard anything, only silence, muted, heavy silence. The door creaked open behind me, but I didn't turn, knowing who it would be.

"Is it God you've come to visit?" he asked.

I took a deep sigh, then sank down on the altar steps.

"I don't think so," I said.

Doctor Hodgins came the rest of the way down the aisle and sank down on the step besides me. We sat in silence for some time.

"Might just as well have begged him to come back," I said, finally, "for all the good I'm doin'. I swear to God, the way I keep listenin' to the wind, I'm as bad as you for watchin' the waves." My voice caught and I laid my cheek on Doctor Hodgins's shoulder, breathing deeply of his warm, familiar smell, allowing the few tears I had left to seep down my face. "I don't know where all the water comes from," I sobbed, "I've cried so much."

"It'll get better."

"I know. It already has—sometimes. It's just that . . . sometimes . . . " I faltered and took a deep breath. "This mornin' I heard Josie up choppin' wood. It's the first time she's chopped wood since Shine . . . and I thought . . . "

"Shh, it's all right. These things will happen."

"Sometimes I think back on how happy we were, just running up and down the gully—it don't seem real that I ever felt that happy."

"You'll feel it again, life's like that, patched with moments. Damned if I know why we expect to be happy all the time," he went on, still rocking me. "Even when we were youngsters with everything being handed to us, we were never happy, always wanting more and bigger. But, there's more than happy, Kit. There's peace. And pride. And those things measure good. You must feel proud, knowing you walked away from what you wanted most in the world, all for a greater thing. There's not lots who've shown your courage, Kittens, and you're hardly more than a girl yet." He rocked some more, then, kissing the top of my head, held me away from him.

"You've done Lizzy proud," he whispered, smiling into my eyes. "Real proud. And it'll be a blessed day when I'm called out to the gully again, in the middle of the night, to bring another Pitman into the world."

I laid my face upon his shoulder, allowing him to rock me some more. The shaft of sunlight struck through one of the windows, and I managed a bit of a smile as I watched it broaden, catching zillions of dust motes in its ray as it crept up over the aisle and shrouded me in its warmth.

If you were to perch atop a tree on Fox Point and look down, you would see a thin sliver of ice glazing the gully's brook as it suckles its way down to the seashore. Flanking the gully's sides are withered mats of timothy grass, struck down by a sudden frost and scented with a brew of wet ground, burning birch and fresh-cut sawdust. To the side of the weather-beaten shack squat on the hill-

side besides the gully is a towering woodpile of fresh-sawed logs. And standing next to the woodpile is Josie, grunting loudly, her long red hair streaming around her face as she swings an axe into a birch junk resting sideways on the chopping block.

And if you were to hop onto a windowsill and look inside the house, you would see me, Kit, my fine yellow hair tucked back into a hairnet, humming softly as I check the lids on a row of preserving jars, still wet with steam and with a pink froth bubbling a quarter of an inch above the red berries inside. A sharp whistle cuts through the air and I run to the window, shielding my eyes from the sun as I look up over the bank to the road. A man with a thick, woolly beard gracing his chin treads slowly down over the bank. Josie drops the axe and stares. The man watches her, then lifts a piece of birch rind, taut between his forefingers and thumbs, to his lips and pierces the air with another ear-splitting whistle. Josie barks out a crazy laugh and charges towards him. Lifting back her fist, she reams it into his belly, and bounds down over the gully laughing wildly. He staggers after her, half-bent over, clutching his stomach, a grimace distorting his face.

He straightens up as I step off the stoop and start walking towards him, my arms held out before me. Tears wet his eyes and his hands tremble as he reaches for me. Choking back sobs, I embrace my brother who has come home.